Lady Rogue

"This is a love story created by the sure, deft strokes of a master!" —*Romantic Times*

Star of India

"Amanda McCabe's story [is] a thoroughly enjoyable read." —*Romantic Times*

Spirited Brides

"These stories are exceptionally sweet . . . one winner of a book." —The Romance Studio

"Fun, witty, romantic . . . a capital read!" —Huntress Book Reviews

"Brimming with romance, passion, humor, well-drawn characters, interesting plots, and plenty of ghosts, these stories are unforgettable." —Romance Junkies

"These books are a delight to read!" —Reader to Reader Reviews

"You'd do well to add *Spirited Brides* to your collection of traditional Regency and Regency-set historical romances." —Romance Reviews Today

continued . . .

ROGUE GROOMS

Lady Rogue
and
The Star of India

Amanda McCabe

A SIGNET ECLIPSE BOOK

SIGNET ECLIPSE
Published by New American Library, a division of
Penguin Group (USA) Inc., 375 Hudson Street,
New York, New York 10014, USA
Penguin Group (Canada), 90 Eglinton Avenue East, Suite 700, Toronto,
Ontario M4P 2Y3, Canada (a division of Pearson Penguin Canada Inc.)
Penguin Books Ltd., 80 Strand, London WC2R 0RL, England
Penguin Ireland, 25 St. Stephen's Green, Dublin 2,
Ireland (a division of Penguin Books Ltd.)
Penguin Group (Australia), 250 Camberwell Road, Camberwell, Victoria 3124,
Australia (a division of Pearson Australia Group Pty. Ltd.)
Penguin Books India Pvt. Ltd., 11 Community Centre, Panchsheel Park,
New Delhi - 110 017, India
Penguin Books (NZ), 67 Apollo Drive, Rosedale, North Shore 0632,
New Zealand (a division of Pearson New Zealand Ltd.)
Penguin Books (South Africa) (Pty.) Ltd., 24 Sturdee Avenue,
Rosebank, Johannesburg 2196, South Africa

Penguin Books Ltd., Registered Offices:
80 Strand, London WC2R 0RL, England

Published by Signet Eclipse, an imprint of New American Library, a division of
Penguin Group (USA) Inc. *Lady Rogue* and *The Star of India* were previously
published in Signet editions.

First Signet Eclipse Printing, June 2010
10 9 8 7 6 5 4 3 2 1

PUBLISHER'S NOTE
This is a work of fiction. Names, characters, places, and incidents either are the
product of the author's imagination or are used fictitiously, and any resemblance
to actual persons, living or dead, business establishments, events, or locales is
entirely coincidental.
  The publisher does not have any control over and does not assume any responsibility for author or third-party Web sites or their content.

Lady Rogue

*To Katie Fish, the "real" Lady Kate,
and to her parents, Hugh and Anita Fish,
for being three such wonderful friends.*

Chapter One

"So that is it, then? That is all that is left?" Alexander Kenton, late of His Majesty's army and now the new Duke of Wayland, stared out of the library window at the bedraggled garden beyond. Yet he did not see the overgrown, rain-soaked bushes and trampled flower beds. He saw only the great tangle his life had suddenly become.

The solicitor, seated at the desk behind him, rattled papers and coughed uncomfortably. "I fear so, my lord."

Alex laughed bitterly. "Well. You have to admire a brother who can manage to leave such a thorough mess in such a brief time."

"Indeed, my lord," the solicitor answered, in a small, uncertain voice.

Alex pushed back from the window and returned to his seat before the fire, stretching his booted feet to its meager warmth. "Tell me, then, Mr. Reed, what we have to live on, Mother and Emily and me, once all of Damian's debts are settled."

Mr. Reed consulted his papers again. "Fair Oak, the house and the farm, of course. And the Kenton

Grange. Those are entailed. Aside from your personal belongings, and the few family jewels now in the possession of the dowager duchess, I fear there is little else."

"Emily's dowry?"

"Gone, my lord. Long gambled away."

"Damn," Alex cursed softly. "The farm has not been worked in years! Not since my father's time."

"I do believe that Lady Emily has managed to keep some of the fields under cultivation. Much of the land, though, has lain fallow since your late father's time. Your brother was not—not much interested in farming."

"Damian was not much interested in anything but gambling and whoring."

The solicitor blushed.

"Forgive my bluntness, Mr. Reed," Alex said. "Years in the army will do that to a man."

"Quite understandable, my lord."

"So, in effect, all we have to restore this old pile and give Emily a proper come-out is my army pension."

"There is a small income from the tenants still left, my lord, and Lady Dorothy has an annuity of her own. But, in essence, yes, you are right. I fear so." Mr. Reed gathered his papers together and stood. "If you have no further questions of me at this time, my lord, I will leave you to your supper."

"Yes, of course. Thank you, Mr. Reed."

Alex turned his gaze back to the flames as the library door clicked shut, leaving him alone with his thoughts.

They were not happy, tranquil thoughts.

"I should have stayed in the army," he muttered. "Spain and Belgium were simpler than this."

But then, with the war ended, there had been no point

in staying with the army. He had longed for home, for the green coolness of Fair Oak, for the company of his family. His excellent father had died almost five years ago, when Alex had been in the heat of the fighting. His older brother had died last year of a fall from a horse, during a race. Alex had not wanted to be the duke, but he had come home prepared to do his duty.

He had not known until just now how badly Damian had bungled things.

In less than five years, Damian had managed to gamble away a very comfortable fortune. He had spent so recklessly on mistresses, parties, horse races, and cards that everything that was not entailed had had to be sold to pay for them.

What was Alex to do now? He himself could live comfortably, if frugally, on his pension. His mother, though, was aging, and not in good health. His sister, who had held the household together for so long, deserved a fine Season, a good match. His ancestral home was collapsing about his ears. Even now, he could see plaster loosening from the ceiling, damp seeping down into the carpet and the draperies.

Yes, he should have stayed in Spain.

The library door opened, and Emily's golden-curled head popped inside. "Alex? Has Mr. Reed gone?"

Alex looked around at her, and smiled. Even in such dire circumstances, his sister could not fail to cheer him. She was a bouncing, elfin little thing, seemingly always laughing. Even in a faded, mended blue muslin frock, she shimmered.

"Yes, angel-puss, he has gone."

She came and sat in the chair next to his, stretching her own feet to the fire. "It is very bad, is it not?"

Alex could not lie to her. Not when she turned her wide, guileless blue gaze onto him. "Yes."

Emily sighed. "I knew it. I had hoped, though, that there would be something. Even Farmer Ellis, who sells us our butter and eggs, won't want to give us credit any longer!"

"What do you know about butter and eggs, angel?" Alex laughed.

Emily's lips pursed. "A great deal as it happens, brother. Our housekeeper left above six months ago, and someone had to deal with such things. Mother is not able."

Alex grew somber again. "I am sorry, Em. You should not have had to take on such tasks."

"I do not mind. But now I shall not have to, as you are here, and will no doubt conceive a great plan for our salvation!"

"I do not have a plan as yet, Em," he warned. "Damian left us in a very great mess, and it will take time to sort it out."

"Hm, yes. He was very naughty. Not at all like you, Alex."

"You do not think me naughty?" he teased.

"Of course not, how could you be? You have all those medals for bravery, and valor, and good deeds, and who knows what else. Earning all those would not have left you much time for anything else."

He laughed. "Quite right!"

A companionable silence fell between them. They sat and listened to the crackle of the fire, to the soft patter of the rain hitting the windows.

Then Alex said, "You may have to wait until next year for your Season, Em."

She shrugged. "I like it here at Fair Oak. Much more than I would in London, I'm sure. Who needs balls and routs?" Her face was wistful, despite her lighthearted words.

"You must have a proper Season!"

"So I shall. When things are better for us." A bell rang out from the direction of the drawing room, and Emily rose and smoothed her skirt. "That will be Mother, summoning us to supper. Thank goodness Cook is still with us! I fear I would be quite hopeless in the kitchen."

Alex caught her hand in his, and kissed it gently. "Things *will* be better for us soon, Em. I promise."

She smiled down at him. "I know. *You* are with us now; how bad could things be?" The bell rang again. "But come. Mother will be becoming impatient."

As Alex took her arm and led her from the library, she said, "What will you do now?"

"I think, sister dear, that I will go to London. Perhaps the solution to our troubles is there!"

Chapter Two

"Does it always rain in London?" Mrs. Georgina Beaumont leaned her forehead against the cool glass of the morning room window, watching the endless silvery sheets falling down on the small, beautifully manicured garden.

Lady Elizabeth Hollingsworth, seated before the fire with her feet up and a blanket tucked about her cozily, laughed.

Georgina's new dog, Lady Kate, a small white terrier Georgina had saved from being drowned by a farmer in Scotland, looked up at the sound of laughter. Then she yawned, stretched out on her satin cushion beside the fire, and went back to sleep. For once she was not barking and running about like a tiny bedlamite.

"Georgie," Elizabeth said. "It rains just as much in Venice as it does here."

"Hm. But it seems a much *warmer* rain there. Romantic. Here it is merely dreary."

"Then come away from the window, and sit here by the fire. What do you think we should do this evening? The Beaton ball? The Carstairs musicale?"

Georgina left the window and sat down on a settee next to the fire. She eyed Elizabeth worriedly. "Should you not stay home tonight, Lizzie? We were out so very late last night."

"I am *enceinte*, not ill!" Elizabeth protested. "I am barely showing as yet. I must have fun while I can, before I grow as big as a house." She tugged the blanket aside to peer down at her belly, only a bit rounded beneath her pale green morning dress.

Georgina laughed at the vision of her petite friend as round as a full moon, waddling about Bond Street. "I shall have to paint your portrait when that happens!"

"Don't you dare!" Elizabeth protested. "But I promise that if I grow fatigued I will say so. And no doubt you, under Nicholas's orders, will drag me home immediately."

"What a proud papa Nicholas is becoming! I vow one would think he had done it all himself, the way he has been preening about."

Elizabeth smiled softly at the mention of her husband. "Yes, he will be an excellent father. It seems we have waited an age for this, and now it is upon us!"

"I am so happy for you, Lizzie."

"Well, you, I am sure, will be the most excellent of godmothers."

"Oh, yes! I shall teach him or her to paint pictures and run wild."

"You will teach them to be true to themselves, to enjoy life. Those are the most valuable lessons of all, you know."

Georgina's laughter sounded a bit sad, even to her own ears. After three marriages, she remained childless. She had thought it all for the best; her life as an artist, racketing about the Continent, was not a very stable one. But now, seeing her friend's radiance, she could not help but be a bit regretful.

"Well, it was very good of you to come stay with me now, Georgie," Elizabeth continued. "I know how you miss Italy."

"I would not miss this time with you for the world! Besides, we are having a marvelous time, are we not?"

"We are! I am only vexed that Nicholas will not let me ride with you in that curricle race next week."

"*I* would not have let you in any case! You can watch safely from the side of the road as I trounce that arrogant Lord Pynchon."

"And I will make a great deal of money from wagering on you!" Elizabeth turned her head as a single ray of yellow-white light fell from the window across the carpet. "I do believe it has stopped raining! Shall we go out? I need to visit the lending library."

Lady Kate sat straight up, her ears perking at the mention of the word "out." She leaped off of her cushion and trotted over to the cabinet where her leads were kept, barking her sharp "go for a walk" bark.

"I think Lady Kate is in agreement," said Georgina. "We should take her for a run in the park, as well."

"What a good idea! And let us call at my brother's house and see if my niece Isabella would like to accompany us. We could take her to Gunter's for ices after. She is rather lonely, with Peter and Carmen still on their wedding trip."

"Oh, yes, let's! We shall make a day of it."

The first thing Alex saw was the hat.

It was wide-brimmed, fine-milled straw, with fluttering streamers of pale green and white satin. Perhaps not precisely appropriate for London in early spring, but certainly fetching.

Then his gaze lowered to the lady beneath the hat, and he very nearly fell from his saddle in startled admiration. She was—well, she was very *vivid*. Quite a contrast to the giggling young misses his friends had taken to hurling in his direction since his return to London.

She was not very tall, but her posture, her manner of walking, made her seem almost Amazonian. She wore a pelisse of a green that matched the streamers of her hat, and the hair that fell from beneath that hat could only be described as red. Not a fashionable auburn, or a demure dark blonde, but the very red and gold of flames. Or—or a sunset.

Good gad, man, he berated himself. *You're beginning to sound like some deuced poet!*

Yet if he were to turn to poetry, surely a woman like this one would be all that was needed to inspire him.

She was strolling alongside the river with a petite female companion and a little girl. Looped about her gloved wrist was the braided lead of a small white dog, who was darting about in a most unpredictable manner and barking at every unsuspecting passerby. The woman laughed merrily at the dog's antics. Not a ladylike simper or giggle, but a full, deep, rich, laugh.

Alex could not help but smile at the infectious sound of it.

"Why, Freddie! I do believe Wayland is ogling La Beaumont."

Alex's two companions, his old Etonian friends Mr. Freddie Marlow and Hildebrand Rutherford, Viscount Garrick, pulled up their horses on either side of Alex's, and followed his gaze to its object.

"I say, I do believe you are right, Hildebrand! What excellent taste you show, Wayland. Mrs. Beaumont is extraordinary. Though, I must say I rather prefer her friend, Lady Elizabeth Hollingsworth, myself. I always had a weakness for pocket Venuses!"

Alex scarcely glanced at his friends. The dog and the little girl were walking down to the edge of the river, and the two women followed. A breeze threatened to carry away that fanciful hat, and she clutched at it with one gloved hand.

"The woman with the red hair is a Mrs. Beaumont?" he asked.

"Mrs. Georgina Beaumont, the artist. Surely you have heard of her?" said Freddie.

Alex feared he knew little about art. Or artists. "Is she married?"

"A widow!" Hildebrand said with a certain glee. "Three times over. That is even better, eh? Good sport, what?"

Alex turned a glare onto him, and Hildebrand stifled his chortles behind a gloved hand.

"As I said, she is an artist," offered Freddie. "A deuced successful one, from what I hear, though I'm a complete bacon-brain about painting and music and such."

"She's come from her home in Italy to stay for the Season with Lady Elizabeth," said Hildebrand, now recovered from his giggling fit. "It's quite the fashion to be in love with one or the other of them. Though Lady Elizabeth *is* married, more is the pity."

A thrice-married artist. Alex almost laughed at the thought of the looks on his family's faces if he brought such a woman home to the Grange! Not, of course, that Mother and Em were such high sticklers as all *that*.

They just maintained certain standards, despite their straitened circumstances.

But then, Alex had always had a great weakness for red hair.

He looked from one of his friends to the other speculatively. "I take it, then, that one of you has been introduced to the lady?"

"I haven't," Freddie said, his wide brown eyes looking positively downcast at this fact. "Hildebrand has."

"At Lady Russell's card party a fortnight ago," Hildebrand preened. "Should you like me to do the honors, Wayland?"

Alex gave him a long look, and Hildebrand coughed uncomfortably. "Er, yes," he said. "Just so. Most happy to perform the introductions, I'm sure."

They had only just turned their horses in the direction of the ladies, when disaster struck.

The small white dog, who had been regularly menacing any and all unwary pedestrians, now broke free from the lead the little girl held, and bounded away down the riverbank after an errant duck. In a swift white blur, it became airborne, and landed with a great splash in the murky river. Only its pale head was visible as it drifted off, carried inexorably away by the current.

"Lady Kate!" Mrs. Beaumont cried. She lifted her skirts indecently high above her ankles, revealing green kid half boots and an inch of white stocking, and dashed off after her dog. Her hat fell from her head to dangle down her back by its ribbons.

The little girl followed, shouting, "Be careful, Georgie! You'll fall in the river!"

The petite woman, Lady Elizabeth, ran after the girl, crying out, "Help! Help!" to no one in particular.

Mrs. Beaumont nearly slid down in the mud at the edge of the river, tottering precariously on those half boots. "Lady Kate! Come back, darling!"

Alex was already sliding from his saddle, and striding away across a busy thoroughfare and a wide greensward that separated him from the rather bizarre party of ladies.

He had faced many a dire situation in Spain, when he had had to think and act quickly, decisively, and calmly. To be sure, he had never seen a situation quite like this one in Spain, but he knew at a glance what had to be done to save the dog.

He stripped off his coat and boots, pushed them into the arms of the beauteous Mrs. Beaumont, and jumped in after the dog.

Georgina watched in astonishment as the man—a man she had never seen before in her life!—dove into the murky waters after the escaping Lady Kate.

It had all happened so very quickly that she felt all in a daze. One moment she had been strolling along with Elizabeth and little Isabella, laughing and enjoying the day. Lady Kate had been frisking about, as usual; she was quite the most curious and excitable dog Georgina had ever seen. Then, all at once, Lady Kate had twisted out of her lead, scampered down to the river, and splashed right in!

And the man, whose coat and boots Georgina now held, had appeared seemingly out of nowhere and gone in after Lady Kate. Like some sun-bronzed guardian angel.

Georgina bit her lip in anxiety as she watched the man seize Lady Kate about her torso and pull her along toward the bank. The dog struggled mightily in his grasp, howling and frightened that her adventure had ended so badly, but the man hung grimly on. Finally, they both stood before Georgina, dripping with great quantities of dirty water but safely on *terra firma*.

"I believe, madam," the man said, his voice brandy-rich, rough with laughter, "that this belongs to you."

Georgina laughed, hiccuped really, with embarrassment and consternation and a dawning realization of the utter absurdity of their situation. "Yes, indeed, it does! Thank you so much, sir. You have gone quite above and beyond the call of gallantry! I do not believe I can thank you enough."

"He is a *hero*, Georgie," little Isabella Everdean piped up. She gazed up at their rescuer with adoring chocolate-brown eyes.

Georgina very much feared she was doing the same. Gaping at him like the veriest moonstruck half-wit! It was just that he was so very *beautiful*, even dripping with mud and odd plant life, his light brown, curling hair plastered to his head. Her artist's eye skimmed over his high cheekbones and firm jaw, lightly shadowed with afternoon whiskers. His nose was straight as a knife blade; his lips firm but strangely sensual. And his eyes, alight with laughter, were a clear, sweet, heavenly blue.

And they were looking directly into hers as she gaped at him.

She looked down, startled. Which was not at all like her! She was never startled by any man; she had met too many, had married three, and been propositioned by a numberless horde. She had thought herself rather *blasé* about men.

This one, though, had her *blushing*. She could feel the heat creeping up her throat into her cheeks, no doubt clashing horribly with her hair.

Elizabeth was looking at her rather peculiarly, so

Georgina knew that her odd behavior was not going unnoticed.

She forced her gaze back up to meet his, and she smiled. "How very rag-mannered you must think us, not even introducing ourselves after your heroic actions! I am Mrs. Georgina Beaumont."

He bowed, rather awkwardly with his arms full of wriggling terrier. "Alexander Kenton, at your service."

"And this is Lady Elizabeth Hollingsworth and Lady Isabella Everdean, her niece," Georgina continued.

"Lady Elizabeth, Lady Isabella." He bowed again in their direction. "How do you do."

Isabella giggled.

"Bella," Elizabeth chided. "Say how do you do."

"How d'ye do," said Isabella.

"It was so good of you to rescue Lady Kate," Elizabeth said. "I have told Georgina that she needs a stronger lead."

"You may be assured she will now have one!" Georgina snorted.

"May I carry Lady Kate now?" beseeched Isabella, going up on tiptoe to pat the muddy dog.

"You will get your frock all dirty!" cried Elizabeth.

"Why don't we wrap her in my coat?" Alexander suggested. "Then perhaps I could escort you to your carriage, and make certain she is safely stowed aboard?"

"Oh!" Only then did Georgina notice the interested crowd they had gathered. Many a quizzing glass was turned in her direction, and two gentlemen in particular, a Viscount Garrick she had already met and a man she had not, had edged their horses in closer to their little scene.

Ah, well. Georgina shrugged philosophically; she was quite used to people gawking at her escapades.

"You *have* gotten yourself into a scrape, Wayland!" said Viscount Garrick.

Alexander frowned at him, and shifted Lady Kate in his arms.

Elizabeth looked over at the two horsemen. "Are they with you, sir?"

"Unfortunately, yes," Alex murmured.

"Well, then, you must all come to my house for tea! We will have you dry and warm in a trice, sir. I am certain my husband will have some garments you could borrow."

"That is very kind of you, Lady Elizabeth, but . . ." Alex began.

Elizabeth lifted her hand, forestalling all protests. "No, I do insist! We want to thank you properly. Is that not so, Georgina?"

Elizabeth smiled at Alexander, and, slowly, like sun coming from behind the clouds, he smiled back. "Quite so, Elizabeth." Georgina said. "Quite so."

Chapter Three

Georgina had been wrong about Alexander Kenton. He was not beautiful.

He was otherworldly.

Dry and clean, his hair was a light brown, tinged gold by the sun. Tiny lines radiated out from the corners of his eyes, which were vividly blue against the bronze of his skin, every time he laughed. His shoulders were very broad beneath his borrowed coat, and his bearing was quite poised and straight and correct. He must have been in the army, like her first husband, Jack.

Georgina thought he looked like a Caravaggio painting.

He was also a duke.

A frown pulled at her brow at the thought. *That* was a bit problematic. Peers, especially dukes, seemed the very worst of lechers, always cornering her in dim corridors or dark garden bowers, always thinking she would be full of gratitude for their ham-handed attentions. Her trusty sharp-tipped hair ornaments had quickly disabused them all of such notions.

She would have so hated to use one on this particular duke!

But thus far there seemed no danger of that. Alexander Kenton was a very charming duke. He had taken the entire Lady Kate situation with such good humor, as no other man of her acquaintance would have done. He even fed the dog, now dry and clean and not a bit sorry for all the trouble she had caused, bits of his tea cakes and sandwiches. He conversed with Isabella quite as if she were grown-up. He laughed and joked, and did not once try to flirt with Georgina in any but the lightest and most respectful way.

His two friends, Viscount Garrick and Mr. Marlow, were a bit sillier. They told horrifyingly bad jokes, and obviously thought themselves quite the wits for it. Occasionally, one or the other would cast her provocative glances. Or rather, they would simply roll their eyes and wiggle their eyebrows in what they obviously fancied passed as provocative ways.

But Alexander; ah, now, he could easily prove far too attractive for her own good.

". . . Is that not so, Georgina?"

Georgina's attention snapped back to Elizabeth, from whence it had wandered into the clouds. "I beg your pardon?"

Elizabeth's gray eyes were slate dark with concern. "Are you quite all right, dear? You look flushed. Did you catch a chill by the river?"

"Indeed not! I am quite well. It should be Lord Wayland we are concerned about catching chills."

Alexander laughed. "Not I, Mrs. Beaumont! I am healthy as a horse."

"Perhaps I should give you both a dose of castor oil," Elizabeth mused.

"No!" Georgina and Alexander both shouted.

Lady Kate barked riotously, quite as if she also had been offered a dose.

"You must forgive Elizabeth," Georgina said. "She feels it her bounden duty to nurse and cosset everyone who comes into her sphere."

"Indeed I do not!" Elizabeth protested.

"You must remain healthy for this evening, Wayland," Freddie Marlow said. "You would not want to miss Lady Beaton's ball."

"We are also attending the Beaton ball!" said Elizabeth.

"It is predicted to be a dreadful crush," Freddie answered, obviously delighted at the prospect.

"It always is. It is simply a great pity that my husband is in the country this week and will have to miss it!"

Georgina glanced at Alexander over the rim of her teacup. "Perhaps we shall see you there, then, Lord Wayland. That is, if you have not caught a chill."

He grinned at her. His smile was very wide and white against his tanned skin. "I could wish the same for you, Mrs. Beaumont. But perhaps you would allow me to escort you and Lady Elizabeth to the ball? In the absence of your husband, Lady Elizabeth."

Yes, yes, yes! Georgina's mind shouted. Aloud she said, "How very kind of you! Have we not imposed on you quite enough for one day?"

"Nonsense! I have not had so much fun since I returned to England. Please, do allow me to escort you."

Georgina exchanged a look with Elizabeth, and nodded. "Then, we would be honored. And I promise you, we will leave Lady Kate at home!"

Alexander laughed. "I thank you for that! I should

so hate to have to fish Lady Kate out of Lady Beaton's Italian fountain."

"Why, Wayland! You sly rogue," Hildebrand exclaimed as they rode away from Lady Elizabeth's house. "You have solved all your difficulties most neatly, all in one afternoon."

Alex frowned. He would never have told anyone of his family's troubles, if he could help it; crying of misfortunes was not at all his style. But Hildebrand and Freddie had been his friends since they were boys, and when they had come upon him completely foxed one day after dealing with five of Damian's creditors, he had told them everything.

Yet Alex could not see that anything much had been solved by their afternoon. They had had a very nice tea with three very lovely ladies—one lovely, red-headed lady in particular. He had also ruined a quite fine coat by wrapping it about a muddy dog; a coat he could ill-afford to replace at present.

He expressed this to his friends, and added, "How tea and a ruined coat can solve my troubles, I fear I could not say, Hildebrand. Perhaps you would enlighten me?"

"You nodcock! Don't try and cozen me. I saw how bent you were on charming Mrs. Beaumont."

Alex shrugged. "She is a very beautiful woman."

"And a very *rich* one! She has widow's portions from three husbands, as well as a rather handsome income from her dabbling in painting."

"She is perhaps not entirely *respectable*—not with the highest sticklers, anyway," Freddie chimed in. "Racketing all over the Continent by herself."

"All the better!" said Hildebrand. "She wouldn't

expect you to live in her pocket. You could do worse, Wayland."

Alex was so startled he pulled up his horse right in the middle of the road, causing quite a muddle of the traffic behind them. He stared at his friends, his jaw tight with displeasure. "Are you suggesting," he said very quietly, "that I pursue Mrs. Beaumont for her money?"

Hildebrand sputtered. "Why . . . is that not what you were thinking of?"

"It could not be Lady Elizabeth," Freddie said. " 'Old Nick' Hollingsworth is an absolute jealous fiend when it comes to his beloved wife."

"I was not thinking of either of those ladies in such a way," Alex answered, still quiet.

"Oh, well, I just thought . . . when you offered to escort them to the Beaton ball . . . but I . . ." Hildebrand broke off in a state of utter confusion.

"Oh, look!" cried Freddie in relief. "Here is Wayland's lodgings."

"Indeed it is!" Hildebrand replied, in equal relief. "Well, we shall leave you, then, Wayland. See you at the ball, what?"

Then the two of them dashed off, leaving Alex alone in front of the narrow town house, where he rented the second floor while he was in London. Clifton House in Grosvenor Square had been lost long ago by Damian.

He left his horse at the mews at the foot of the garden, and went up to his small sitting room to pour himself a brandy and settle in for a good brood.

He, marry that lovely Mrs. Beaumont for her money? Distasteful in the extreme.

Not that he had not thought at all of marrying for money. Really, in the eyes of many, it would be an eminently suitable solution. A wife of means could not only restore Fair Oak, buy a new proper London house, and finance Emily's launch; she could also guide that launch and help Emily make a good match.

The wife, of course, in turn, would get to be the Duchess of Wayland. Not a shabby return on investment, some would say. He had even noticed many women eyeing him speculatively at balls and routs.

Alex had made and discarded many other, less feasible plans to recoup his family's losses. Some, made in the midst of sleepless nights, had been positively bizarre. He had half made up his mind to look about this Season for someone suitable. Not a young miss, but perhaps someone older, a spinster or a widow. Someone kind and practical, who understood what was expected of her in the marriage and what she could expect in return. Someone he could be friends with; perhaps even admire.

Someone like—Georgina Beaumont.

Alex tossed back his brandy, and reached out to pour himself another.

He truly had not thought of such a thing when he met her that afternoon. He had heard of her, of course; every lady of fashion clamored to have her portrait painted by Mrs. Beaumont. No doubt they paid handsomely for the privilege.

But all he had thought when he saw her was how lovely she was, how vibrant, how confident, how *alive*.

After years of the dust, death, and boredom of war, followed by the strain of his family's situation, that vivid life had been intoxicating. He had been drawn to her, as to a roaring fire on a bitterly cold winter night. He had wanted to stay longer in her presence, to throw aside the polite platitudes they were actually voicing and ask her how she came to be an artist. Did she enjoy living in Italy; did she love her husbands? What did she like to eat for breakfast?

Would she let him sit near her and kiss her, just once?

Alex laughed bitterly at himself. She, no doubt, would find him a very dull fellow. A military man, crusty and cynical, with no deep knowledge of art, could not possibly interest a woman such as her.

If he were to make her such an offer, the use of her money for the use of his title, she would no doubt treat it with the contempt it deserved, and laugh him from the room.

But . . .

But if she *were* his wife, he could make love to her. Maybe even more than once.

"Alex, you old idiot," he remonstrated aloud. "You have spent far too many years in the Spanish sun. Your brain is baked for even thinking such thoughts of a woman you met only two hours ago!"

And he had gone his own way for too long. He could not rely on a woman to solve his difficulties now.

A soft knock sounded at his door. Alex, so caught up in visions of Georgina Beaumont, thought for one insane instant that perhaps it was she at the door. Then reality returned, and he sank back into his chair.

No doubt it was some other creditor of Damian's, come to collect his due.

"Enter," he called out, suddenly weary beyond belief.

Yet it was not creditors. It was Hildebrand and Freddie, looking equal parts wary and shamefaced.

"I thought you two were going home to change for the ball," he told them. "What brings you back to my humble abode?"

At his easy tone, they broke into smiles, coming into the room to seat themselves and help themselves to the brandy.

"We came to apologize," said Freddie.

"Apologize?"

"For our—misconceptions of your intentions toward Mrs. Beaumont," Hildebrand said. "We truly didn't mean to offend, Wayland. Just want to be of assistance, looking about for suitable heiresses and such."

"What we really want," Freddie added, "is to find *three* heiresses, one for each of us."

"But a man is lucky to find one such in a Season," sighed Hildebrand. "So when we find her, we shall concede her to you."

"Very kind of you." Alex laughed. *Now* he remembered why he was still friends with these two after all these years, despite their silliness—they could always make him laugh.

"Yes. But we can see now that you are absolutely right about Mrs. Beaumont."

"Am I? How so?" Alex said, still laughing.

"She would be most unsuitable. Despite all her money, she is so dashed independent," answered Freddie. "Living alone in Italy and all. They say she even works with *male* models there!"

"Does she indeed?" said Alex, growing more interested by the moment.

"She is going to race her curricle against Lord Pynchon next week," Freddie said. "The betting book at White's is full of nothing else."

"What are the odds now?" asked Hildebrand.

"Three to one, in her favor."

"Hmm. There, you see, Wayland?" Hildebrand said. "She would not be a good duchess at all."

"She probably would not have him at all," commented Freddie. "She has often said she intends never to marry again. If he *did* make her an offer, she would no doubt turn him down flat."

Hildebrand nodded sagely. "No doubt you are right, Freddie."

Alex looked at them in astonishment. "Are you suggesting that if I made an offer to Mrs. Beaumont—which I have no intention of doing!—she would not see the advantages of it? That she would turn me down flat?"

Hildebrand and Freddie looked at each other. "Yes," they chorused.

"Hmph," said Alex.

Hildebrand shook his head. "But then, you are a handsome fellow. The ladies giggle over you wherever we go. Even Miss Pym has dropped poor Freddie quite flat since you appeared and danced with her at the Merritt rout."

"Here, now . . ." Freddie began, only to fall back silent at a glance from Hildebrand.

"Mrs. Beaumont seemed rather taken by you," Hildebrand continued. "She did not even laugh at my jokes! Perhaps she would be tempted by your own self, even if she has no desire to be a duchess. What do you think, Freddie?"

Freddie, still stung by the reminder of the defection of Miss Pym, said, "I still say she would have none of him."

"Well, I say she would!" cried Hildebrand. "I wager you fifty pounds they will be betrothed by the end of the Season."

"Done!" answered Freddie.

They looked expectantly to Alex, who raised his hands in mock surrender. "Do not look at me! I want nothing to do with any of your ridiculous wagers. Besides, I have only just met Mrs. Beaumont; the two of you are being extremely presumptuous."

Hildebrand smiled smugly. "We shall see, Wayland."

Chapter Four

"Lord Wayland is very handsome, is he not?"

Georgina looked up from brushing her hair at her dressing table over to where Elizabeth was sprawled across Georgina's chaise. Elizabeth was already dressed for the evening, in a lovely pale blue silk, but she was eating a box of sweets, and the sugary, sticky smears threatened her lace-trimmed bodice.

Lady Kate was fast asleep on the bed, utterly exhausted after all her adventures.

"Lizzie," said Georgina, "were those four cakes at tea not enough for you?"

"I know, I know! I could scarce lace myself into this gown as it is, but I cannot quite forgo eating sweets. The babe must be a girl. My old nanny always said women bearing sons craved salty foods, daughters sweets. But you are quite avoiding my question."

"Oh? Which question is that?"

"The question of whether you prefer lobster patties or goose liver paté, of course," Elizabeth scoffed. "It is the question of whether or not you consider Lord Wayland the handsomest man we have come across so far this Season! Excepting my darling Nick, of course."

Georgina drew the mass of her curly hair up off her neck and turned her head this way and that, studying the effect in the mirror. She was hesitating, and that was not at all like her. Usually she and Elizabeth chattered endlessly about anything and everything, from difficulties with their art and their careers to their romances (until Elizabeth married, that is!). Now, though, she did not want to *talk* about Lord Wayland; she only wanted to *think* about him for a while.

Why should that be?

She dropped her hair, and smiled at Elizabeth's reflection in the mirror. "I did not notice," she said indifferently.

"You! Not notice a gentleman's handsomeness, or lack thereof?" Elizabeth cried around a mouthful of sweet. "Ha! You are an artist, Georgie. It would be positively unprofessional of you not to notice."

Georgina smiled wryly. "You know me too well, Lizzie. Yes, Lord Wayland is quite handsome. By far the handsomest man we have met this year. Much more handsome than that Lord Percy, who every young miss has been sighing over."

"Hm, quite. Lord Percy is a young puppy, who lacks distinction. Unlike Lord Wayland. And those blue eyes . . ." Elizabeth sighed.

"Lizzie! You are a married woman."

"So I am," Elizabeth said unrepentantly. "And a very happy and faithful one, too, as unfashionable as that is. But you are not married, Georgie."

"No, and I intend to remain in that blissful state."

"Hm. Suit yourself." Elizabeth shrugged. "No one ever said you had to *marry* Lord Wayland. Just—be friends with him."

Georgina laughed. "Lizzie! You utter rogue!"

"I? A rogue? Oh, no, dear. I fear you claimed that title long ago. Lady Rogue!"

"Lady Rogue?" Georgina rather liked that. She preened a bit in the mirror, pursing her lips and batting her lashes. She and Elizabeth giggled. "Well, this rogue would like to be alone now, so she can bathe and change for the evening."

"Of course." Elizabeth stood up, and crossed the room to kiss Georgina's cheek before leaving, still in firm possession of the box of sweets. "You will want to look beautiful for Lord Wayland!"

Georgina shook her head at her friend's retreating figure, then turned her attention back to the mirror, reaching for her enameled powder pot. She had never considered herself beautiful, or even pretty. Her slanting green eyes were too widely spaced; there was a sprinkle of freckles across her too-small nose. And her hair, the despair of her youth, had never been any color but *red*. So unfashionable.

Yet she knew, without vanity, that many considered her beautiful. She had a hard-won air of confidence in herself, a fearless carriage that gave off such false impressions of height and loveliness. She liked that; it increased her fame and furthered her career. Yet *she* did not think herself beautiful at all.

She wondered if Lord Wayland thought her so.

For she certainly thought *him* beautiful. Those suntouched brown curls and brilliant blue eyes would be such a joy to paint.

He was kind, as well. No other man, with the exception of Elizabeth's Nicholas, would have jumped into a muddy river after Lady Kate like that. And afterward, when other men would have railed about ruined pantaloons and the undoing of neck cloths, he had laughed. He had treated it all as a lark, as one of those silly, strange adventures that could beset one in the course of life.

"What a very unusual man," Georgina murmured. She fiddled with a scent bottle, lifting and dropping the jeweled stopper aimlessly as she thought about this man and their most strange meeting.

She wondered if he would like to have his portrait painted. In thanks for saving Lady Kate, of course.

Her musings were interrupted by the arrival of Daisy, Elizabeth's lady's maid, and two footmen bearing the bath.

"Oh! Now, just look at you, Mrs. B.," Daisy cried. "You've not even begun to get ready, and the carriage is ordered for nine."

"I am sorry, Daisy. I was woolgathering."

"I see that. Well, you just get in your bath, and I'll see about getting your gown pressed and ready." Daisy threw open the vast wardrobe and rifled through the myriad of colorful silks, satins, and muslins hanging there. "Which gown would you like to wear?"

"Oh, I don't know, Daisy. Something very dashing, I think!"

"Well, I think we won't have any problem finding something like *that*, Mrs. B.!"

It was a much-sobered Alex that presented himself on the Hollingsworth doorstep at half-past eight, immaculately attired for the evening. He bore a bouquet of roses for Lady Elizabeth, and a very large mass of very expensive orchids for Mrs. Beaumont.

He looked down now at the large purple blooms guiltily. They could be nothing but an apology, albeit a feeble one, for even thinking of—whatever it was he had been thinking of.

He almost turned and left, sure his guilt must show on his face for all to see, when he was forestalled by the butler answering his knock.

Lady Elizabeth was waiting for him in the drawing room, seated beside the fire. Alex had the fleeting, distracting thought that those flames were the exact color of Mrs. Beaumont's hair.

Elizabeth coughed delicately to catch his attention, and said, "Good evening, Lord Wayland."

Alex bowed quickly. "Good evening, Lady Elizabeth."

"Are those lovely flowers for us?"

"Indeed they are." He handed her the pink roses. "I know it is more the usual thing to send posies *after* a ball, but I wanted to thank you and Mrs. Beaumont for your kind hospitality this afternoon."

"You wish to thank *us*?" a voice cried behind him. "We should be the ones thanking you, Lord Wayland!"

Alex turned, and saw Georgina just entering the drawing room, fastening an emerald bracelet over one gloved wrist. He had read about one's breath "catching" in one's throat, but he had never experienced it before. Now he found that it was exactly as described; his breath lodged halfway up his throat and refused to pass any farther.

His impressions of that afternoon had been entirely correct, and not his imagination at all. Georgina Beaumont was a stunning woman. She wore a gown of brilliant green satin, draped low across her shoulders and, he couldn't help but notice, across her magnificent bosom. The gown was embroidered with gold thread on the bodice and along the hem; tiny emeralds winked amid the embroidery.

More emeralds swung at her ears, and her hair was drawn up and crowned with an emerald and topaz tiara of an unusual, spiked design—Russian, no doubt.

That tiara would probably keep Fair Oak going for a year.

Yet Alex did not see the splendor of her jewels. He saw only that she was lovely, that her smile was warm and wide and sincere as she greeted him. Unlike the silly simpers and smirks that had greeted him since he arrived in Town.

Her smile did not say, "Oh, grand, here is a *duke*." It said only that she was happy to see him.

He hoped.

"We should be thanking you," she continued as she advanced into the room and paused at his side. "Not one man in a hundred would have done as you did. You saved Lady Kate's life."

Alex's breath released then, and he was able to reply. "It was entirely my pleasure, ma'am. I have been quite a useless fribble since I returned to England; I was glad to have a mission again. I trust that, er, Lady Kate has suffered no ill effects from her swim?"

"Indeed not. I am happy to say that she is quite recovered."

As if summoned by the sound of her name, Lady Kate came bounding through the drawing room door. She took one glance at Alex, and dashed to his side, dancing up on her hind legs in order to plant her front paws on his immaculate breeches. She grinned in doggie delight.

"Oh, no!" Georgina cried. "Lady Kate, do get down from there!"

"I thought you had shut her in your room for the night, Georgie," said Elizabeth.

"I did, but she must have escaped. She does so hate to be excluded from any excitement. Come away, Lady Kate!"

"It's quite all right, Mrs. Beaumont." Alex leaned down to pat Lady Kate on the head and rub her silky ears. "I like animals very much. When I was a lad, I had a dog much like this one, but it was black."

Georgina watched as Lady Kate's stubby tail quivered in ecstasy. Such an effect this man had on females, both of the human and the canine persuasion! "Most of her type of terrier are black, I believe," she answered distractedly.

"However did you come across a white one, then, Mrs. Beaumont?"

"She saved Lady Kate from certain doom!" Elizabeth cried.

"Indeed?" Alex looked up at Georgina. "I should love to hear the tale of the rescue—the *first* rescue— of this admirable lady."

Georgina laughed. "It is not a very engrossing tale! Elizabeth, Nicholas, and I were on holiday in Scotland last autumn, when we came across a farmer about to drown a poor pup, because she was white."

"A horrid man!" said Elizabeth. "He said the 'wee beastie' was of no use, because she was too bright to be hidden from the game she was meant to be hunting."

"Yes," said Georgina. "She looked at me so imploringly. I could not leave her to her fate, so I bought her from the farmer for a shilling."

"A well-spent shilling, I would say," said Alex.

"I think so. Though you might not think her quite

so 'admirable,' if you were to look down now and see
her eating your flowers!"

Alex looked, and saw that Lady Kate was indeed
munching on an orchid. He laughed, and held the bedraggled bouquet out to Georgina. "Actually, they are
your flowers! In thanks for such a grand tea this
afternoon."

She accepted the flowers with a smile, and buried
her nose in their exotic perfume. "They are beautiful.
Thank you, Lord Wayland."

Elizabeth watched them, a suspiciously smug smile
on her face. "Well, then," she said. "Shall we have
some sherry before we depart? Or perhaps some tea?
We do want to hear of your time in Spain, Lord Wayland. Both my husband and my brother were there,
you know . . ."

Chapter Five

Lady Beaton's ball was indeed a "dreadful crush," just as predicted. The line of carriages went around Grosvenor Square, and the receiving line of those guests that had already arrived went through the front doors and down the marble steps.

Georgina did not mind the delay, though. It only meant that she had more time to sit in the warm darkness of the carriage with Lord Wayland, without the distractions of a crowded ballroom.

As Elizabeth had whispered in her ear while they gathered their cloaks, he even liked small dogs and brought flowers *before* a ball.

Lud, was the man *perfect*?

So Georgina set herself now to find a fault with him, as she studied him where he sat across from her. His nose *was* a tad crooked, as if it had once been broken. His cheekbones were rather sharp, and the lines about his eyes were too deep for his youngish age, as if he had been squinting into the Spanish sun too long. He did not possess the smooth olive beauty of so many of her Italian friends. Or the golden perfection of her first husband, Jack.

No, Alex possessed something much more interesting than mere bland beauty. His features spoke of intelligence and experience, of pride.

And there was certainly nothing wrong at all with his figure. His shoulders required absolutely no padding, and his breeches fit his long legs like . . .

Georgina turned away, fanning herself. Very well, then, so there were no faults there. She looked back to him, turning her study to his attire. His cravat was simply tied, with a stickpin of a tiny, insignificant diamond in its snowy folds. His waistcoat was of plain ivory satin. Not very stylish, compared with the pinks of the *ton*. But Georgina, who loved flamboyant fashions for herself, rather disliked it in men. And, having a wide friendship with artistic sorts of people, she had seen some flamboyance!

She much preferred Lord Wayland's quiet elegance.

So, he was handsome, he dressed with good taste, he liked her dog, he had a nice laugh, performed great deeds in the park, was a war hero, *and* a duke.

Georgina conceded with a sigh. He *was* perfect. Probably too perfect for her own flawed self. However, that did not mean she could not enjoy his company while she had the chance.

"I do believe we have arrived at last!" said Elizabeth.

Georgina shifted her attention to the carriage window to see that their wait was indeed over. *Thank the gods,* she thought. She could certainly use a glass of champagne. And had it suddenly become overly warm in the carriage?

A footman opened the carriage door, and Alex stepped out first to assist Georgina and Elizabeth. Georgina was quite touched to see the care he took with Elizabeth; Lizzie thought her condition was still hidden, but it was really becoming quite apparent beneath her lacy sash. It was clear that Alex had apprehended this, and he held her arm tightly to help her ascend the steep front steps.

Georgina left her cloak with the Beatons' footman and joined Alex and Elizabeth at the end of the receiving line, at the foot of the grand staircase. This was always one of her favorite moments of a ball; the chance to look ahead and behind her, and see who was in attendance. To see if there was anyone who might need to have their portrait painted, or if there were any friends to greet.

Tonight, though, there could be no one more fascinating than the person she was with.

Alex detested balls.

They were always overly warm, overly scented with the perfumes of the guests and the masses of flowers, and full of uninteresting conversation. He was also a rather poor dancer, which could often prove quite embarrassing.

He could see, as he and Georgina and Elizabeth at last greeted their hostess and entered the ballroom, that this particular rout would be scarce any different from those he attended since his return to London.

The dancing had not yet begun; the musicians were tuning up behind a bank of potted palms, and the crowd was milling about waiting for the opening pavane. It all seemed very aimless, with ladies exclaiming over one another's gowns, gentlemen inquiring after one another's latest acquisitions at Tattersall's, couples claiming one another for the dances, and footmen moving about with full trays of champagne glasses.

Yet he knew it was not at all aimless. Reputations were made and broken on the whispers behind fans,

the gentleman-to-gentleman asides. It was a precari-
ous, expensive world, one that some people, such as
Alex's brother, would pay anything, do anything, to
stay in. In the end, the gambling and the spending had
broken Damian, and all their family.

And Alex had been far away, unable to stop any of
the madness and unhappiness.

In the midst of these renewed pangs of guilt, he felt
the light pressure of Georgina's fingers on his arm. He
turned to look down at her.

She smiled at him, and went up on tiptoe to murmur
in his ear, "Absolutely horrid, is it not? Like a gathering of clucking chickens."

He laughed. "Horrid."

"Ah, the things we go through for our art, Georgie," Elizabeth sighed. Then she drifted off to greet a
group of friends.

"Indeed," Georgina said. She tugged at his arm.
"Shall we join the fray, Lord Wayland? I do believe
people are beginning to stare."

Alex looked down at her, at her inquisitive green
eyes, and he knew then that he could never be the
cause of another person's unhappiness, as he had been
with his family, being far away and unable to curb
Damian's excesses. He had only known Georgina
Beaumont for a very brief while, but he knew that
she would be very angry, and very hurt, if she found
out about his friends' silly wager, and his own secret
temptations toward her.

He had no wish to see those eyes full of anger. He
wanted them to laugh at him, to sparkle and smile—
to fill with admiration, as he was certain his did now
as they looked at her.

He turned back to the ballroom, and saw that they
were indeed attracting attention. As a new duke, with

a scandal for a brother, he had become accustomed to the attention, even though it still made him most uncomfortable. Yet now he found that a new duke with a beautiful, famous woman on his arm was an even greater object of interest than a duke alone.

Mamas glared at Georgina, even as they urged their daughters to stand up straighter and smooth their hair. Some of the gentlemen, obviously admirers of "La Beaumont," looked crestfallen; others took out their quizzing glasses and eyed the two of them speculatively. Sophisticated young matrons and widows studied Georgina's gown, then looked down at their own lesser creations in chagrined comparison.

The elderly Lady Collins, a notorious eccentric, said, loud enough to be heard even over the large crowd, "Is that that artist chit with young Wayland? I would wager that hair of hers is *dyed!* Never saw that red in nature."

Georgina giggled.

Alex frowned. "What an old harridan that Lady Collins is."

"Nonsense!" Georgina replied. "I plan to be just like her when I am seventy; I will say what I please, and care for none. Is that champagne I see over there? Shall we force our way through the masses and get a glass?"

"What a grand idea, Mrs. Beaumont. I was just thinking the exact same thing myself."

As they ventured into the crowd, Alex looked about for Hildebrand and Freddie. He intended to ask them to call off that silly wager as soon as possible; he did not care two straws if it was "ungentlemanly" to cancel a wager once it was made. He wanted to become friends with Georgina, and he did *not* want such nonsense hanging over them like a dark cloud.

Yet they were nowhere to be found, and he soon found himself in the midst of a large circle of Georgina's acquaintances, all of them eager to be introduced to him. In the middle of their conversation and laughter, he quite forgot about Hildebrand and Freddie and any wagers at all.

"What a handsome fellow your duke is, Georgina!" whispered Lady Lonsdale, a very stylish lady whose portrait Georgina had once painted, and who had become a friend. "I am quite envious."

Georgina laughed, and looked to the dance floor, where Alex was engaged in a country-dance with Elizabeth. "There is no need to be envious, Harriet! He is not 'my' duke. Lord Wayland and I only met this afternoon, and he kindly offered to escort Elizabeth and myself this evening, since Nicholas is from Town."

"Hm. Only out of the kindness of his heart, I am sure." Lady Lonsdale fluttered her feathered fan. "Tell me, how did you and the duke meet?"

"He jumped into the river after my dog."

"Ha!" Lady Lonsdale laughed most heartily. "Are you telling me a corker, Georgina?"

"I assure you I am not! Lady Kate escaped from her lead and went for a swim. Lord Wayland very gallantly rescued her from being carried off, and Elizabeth invited him to take tea with us at her house in thanks."

"Oh, my dear! Such an *on dit*. One of the great heroes of the Peninsula ruining his attire rescuing the dog of a famous artist! It will be in all the papers tomorrow, you know."

"I only hope that the scandalmongers do not imply that I am on the hunt for a new husband."

"Your appearing here with him tonight *will* be sure to cause talk."

"There is always talk. I am quite accustomed to it."

"And you do nothing to discourage it!" Lady Lonsdale's tone was gleeful.

Georgina shrugged blithely. "It is good for my career to be noticed! As long as there is no true scandal. That would be quite disastrous."

The dance had ended, and Alex was leading Elizabeth toward them, the two of them happily laughing and chatting.

"He *is* very handsome," said Lady Lonsdale. "And he does seem to like you a great deal."

"His lordship has been very kind . . ."

"No doubt." Lady Lonsdale lowered her fan, and smiled as Elizabeth and Alex reached them. "Lady Elizabeth! How very radiant you are this evening. Marriage must certainly agree with you."

"It does indeed!" Elizabeth replied merrily.

"When shall we have the pleasure of seeing your scamp of a husband again?"

"Very soon, I am sure, Lady Lonsdale. There was a bit of an emergency at our country estate, which he went to look in on. But may I present his worthy substitute this evening, His Grace the Duke of Wayland? Lord Wayland, this is our friend, the Countess of Lonsdale. Georgina painted her portrait last year, and she is a great patron of art!"

"So you must be certain to be nice to her!" Georgina laughed.

Alex grinned, and bowed to Lady Lonsdale. "I shall endeavor to do my best, Mrs. Beaumont. How do you do, Lady Lonsdale."

"You must not listen to their fustian, Lord Way-

land! They will have you believing I am an ogre who
does naught but sit for portraits all day, and lord it
over poor, groveling artists," said Lady Lonsdale. "I
am very glad to meet you, though, Lord Wayland. I
have heard that you performed quite a dashing feat
in the park today. I am sorry I missed it."

"Yes, well, rescuing fair damsels in distress is a spe-
cialty of mine."

"So I understand." Lady Lonsdale smiled at him
over her fan.

The orchestra struck up the lilting strains of a waltz,
and Alex turned to Georgina. "Mrs. Beaumont, would
you do me the great honor of dancing with me?"

"Thank you, yes." As Georgina accepted his arm
and went with him to the dance floor he had only just
vacated, she said, "I feel I should warn you, though,
that I bring more enthusiasm to the dance than grace."

"I will confess in turn—my feet are of the two left
variety." One of his hands slid into hers, and the other
landed warmly at her waist. "But I daresay we shall
rub along well enough together."

"I daresay we shall."

Indeed they did. Their steps seemed well matched,
and soon they were swaying and swooping amid the
other couples, taking the corners in dashingly executed
spins that sent Georgina's emerald green skirts
swirling.

She laughed merrily after one especially energetic
turn, bringing the gazes of the other dancers in their
direction. "I cannot recall when I had such fun
waltzing!"

"Nor I! Dancing is usually a bit of a chore, something I had to do with my sister at country assemblies
when I was a lad. But this is quite nice. Quite—
different."

"So the evening has not proved to be so tedious as you had feared?"

"How did you know I feared it would be tedious?"

Georgina smiled slyly. "I have my ways!"

"Well, I never expected that *your* company would be tedious. And this ball has not been at all, thanks to you and Lady Elizabeth."

Georgina hummed a bit to the music as they turned and swayed. "I do believe this is an Italian song. I could almost think myself home again!" She closed her eyes, and smiled at the blissful moment of music and Alex's warm arms about her.

All too soon, the music ended.

Georgina found herself quite unaccountably disappointed.

"Shall we take a stroll on the terrace?" Alex asked. "It is sure to be cooler outside."

"Oh, yes, what a lovely idea!"

There were several couples gathered on the Beatons' terrace, walking, talking quietly, or watching the brightly lit ballroom through the open doors. A few bolder guests could be glimpsed slipping about the garden beyond.

It was quite an extension of the ball, but much cooler, and lovely beneath the stars.

Georgina leaned against the marble balustrade, and sipped at the glass of champagne she had caught from a footman's tray on the way out of the ballroom. It was truly a beautiful night. The London sky was uncharacteristically clear, lit by an almost full, pale silver moon. The scent of early roses from the garden hung sweet in the air. The champagne was cool and delicious as it slid down her throat.

And Alex's arm was warm and delicious when he leaned on the balustrade beside her.

"Do you miss your home in Italy very much, Mrs. Beaumont?" he asked quietly.

Georgina smiled at him. "Dreadfully."

"Will you tell me about it? I have been to Spain, and France, and Belgium, but never to Italy."

"Are you certain you wish me to speak of it? Once begun, I often cannot stop!"

"I am certain. Tell me, please."

"Well, I have two homes in Italy. One is a small villa at Lake Como, which I purchased after my second husband passed away. It is quite old, sixteenth century, and something is always falling to bits. The plasterer has to be called in almost every year!" Yet even as she complained, her face lit with a small smile.

"Were there no more modern houses available in the area?"

"Oh, yes, certainly. But this particular one boasts a very fine fresco in the room I use as a dining room, a lovely work of a classical party group eating grapes and dancing. There is also a very good view from the terrace, where I often have luncheon parties when the weather is especially fine. And there are endless vistas for sketching!"

She paused to sip at her champagne, and Alex did the same. He turned her words over in his mind; they had conjured for him a vision of not only a beautiful place, but of a life lived beautifully, with friends and parties and endless vistas of loveliness.

He so envied her in that moment.

He drained his glass, and said, "What is your second home?"

"That is my city home, in Venice. A very small place, also very old and crumbling, but not without its own charms! Elizabeth and her husband have purchased a house just across the canal, and they visit me there in the winter."

"I am truly jealous, Mrs. Beaumont."

She laughed brightly. "Jealous, Lord Wayland? Of me? Why, you are a duke! Surely you possess far finer properties than my small homes."

Alex thought wryly of the large town house, and the hunting box in Scotland, both lost to his brother's profligacy. "I think what I am jealous of is your freedom. It is obvious that you love your life, that you love what you do."

Georgina tilted her head, gazing up at him quizzically. "I do. I think there is nothing more wonderful in life than to have a blank canvas before me and a paintbrush in hand, with an Italian scene to paint. And I have the best of friends, who share that passion. But what is there in your own life, Lord Wayland, that you would wish different? What would you wish to put in its stead?"

He looked down at her, standing there beside him in the moonlight. A tiny frown of concern pleated her ivory brow. He wanted, more than anything he had ever wanted before, to kiss her. He wanted to kiss away that frown, to hold her against him, and lose all his troubles in her warmth and happiness.

He even lifted his hand a tiny bit toward her, but he was saved from his own folly by Elizabeth's voice calling to them from the open terrace doors.

"There you two are!" she said. "The last dance is about to begin, and then of course there shall be a mad dash for supper. You would not wish to miss Lady Beaton's lobster patties."

Alex's hand fell back to his side.

Georgina laughed, and placed her empty glass on

the balustrade. "Certainly not! I have heard such glorious things about those lobster patties."

"As have I." Alex held out his arm to her. "Shall we?"

Her hand was as light as a bird on his sleeve. "Thank you, Lord Wayland!"

As they reentered the ballroom, Alex at last caught a glimpse of Hildebrand and Freddie, just as they were departing. They saw him, and sent him laughing little waves before they left, their heads together as they whispered gleefully.

"Was that not your friends? Mr. Marlow and Viscount Garrick?" said Georgina. "Do you not wish to go after them and bid them good evening? I could save you a seat in the dining room."

Alex took one last glance at Hildebrand and Freddie's departing figures, then shook his head. "Anything I have to say to them can certainly wait until tomorrow. The lobster patties, however, cannot wait."

Chapter Six

"Was the ball last night not a crush? I vow all the *ton* must have been there," Elizabeth sighed.

It was very nearly noon, but they were only just beginning their morning toast and chocolate in the breakfast room. All the morning papers were spread across the table, as they perused them for mention of their names and descriptions of various gowns and *on dits*.

"Hm, quite," Georgina replied as she spread marmalade on her toast, almost dragging the ribbons of her morning gown through the stickiness. She was not yet entirely *awake*, though she did notice, with much gratification, that they were mentioned several times in papers. "Even that funny old Lady Collins was there."

"And everyone seemed quite interested in your handsome escort!"

"*Our* escort, Lizzie!" Georgina protested. "Did Lord Wayland not escort both of us to the ball?"

"Well, yes, of course. Most proper. But anyone could see it was *you* he was there for, you he was interested in. How could he not be? Every young buck in Town is at your feet."

"Lord Wayland is hardly a young buck. He is quite the most distinguished gentleman I have met this Season."

"Oh, yes. Quite." Elizabeth grinned mischievously. "Perhaps even the most distinguished gentleman you have seen in—years? I know I have not seen anyone so distinguished."

"Are your husband and brother not so, Lizzie?"

"I love Nick with all my heart, and in my eyes he is the finest man in the world. Yet *distinguished* is not the first word that springs to mind when one thinks of him. Peter, of course, is quite distinguished in his own fashion, and is much less formidable since Carmen and Isabella came into his life." Elizabeth frowned in thought. "But Lord Wayland has an openness and amiability that I fear my dear brother often lacks. His manners were very charming, as I'm sure you must agree, Georgie."

"Yes," Georgina murmured. She stared down into her half-empty cup of chocolate. "Very charming. You are right in saying that it has been a long time since I have met such an amiable man."

"Not since—Jack?" Elizabeth suggested gently.

"Lizzie!" Georgina protested. "Jack has been gone for almost ten years. I have met many men since then. I even married two of them."

"Old men you married out of desperation and pity," Elizabeth argued. "Have you never thought of marrying again for affection or even love?"

Georgina laughed. "My dear friend, it is good of you to try to matchmake for me! But I only met Lord Wayland yesterday, and here you have us wildly in love and off to Gretna Green."

"Not Gretna Green! St. George's, Hanover Square."

"Lizzie . . ."

"Oh, all right! I won't say another word. But, Georgina, I do only want your happiness."

"I *am* happy! I have everything I have ever wanted. I have my work, independence, wonderful friends, and a lovely home. I am quite content."

"All those things are delightful, Georgie, as I well know. My own work is so vital to me. Yet a good marriage can make all those things even more splendid; it can make life complete!"

Georgina shook her head. "*Good* marriages are few and far between. I have ample proof from the horrid things my clients have told me of their husbands, as they sit for portraits."

"I, too, hear dreadful things. Not every marriage, though, is like that. Nick and I are very happy, as are Peter and Carmen. You and Jack . . ."

"Marriages like those are rare. I had my one love. And I will never give up any portion of my delicious freedom for anything less!"

"No," Elizabeth said quietly. "Of course you will not. You *should* not."

"Excellent. Then, may we cease to discuss my matrimonial prospects, and decide what we want to do this afternoon?"

"We must plan my *salon*, of course! It is to be *next* Friday, and I have not begun a thing. But first, will you tell me one thing, Georgie?"

"What is that?" Georgina asked warily.

"Will you at least *see* Lord Wayland again?"

"Oh, yes. In fact, he is calling at four to take me driving in the park."

Elizabeth caught up the folded copy of the *Gazette* and tossed it at Georgina's laughing head. "Horrid

girl! Not to tell me, *me*, your bosom bow, and let me
rattle along like that!"

"Oh, Lizzie!" Georgina giggled. "I am sorry to keep
it to myself. You just looked so very earnest and dear,
arguing for matrimonial bliss."

"Hmph." Elizabeth looked over at Lady Kate, who
was perched in the window seat, waiting for the day's
excitement to begin. "Do you see how shabbily we are
treated, Lady Kate? After all our good attempts to assist!"

"Lizzie! I will cry peace. I will keep you informed
of all my social engagements from now on. Now, I
have something very important I should like your advice on."

"Oh, yes? What is that?"

"What should I wear on this drive?"

Georgina studied the array of garments laid out
across her bed, all of them neat and fashionable muslins and silks in every color of the rainbow. She held
up first one then another in front of her, twisting about
before the mirror.

"What I really need is something new," she mused
as she tossed another rejected gown onto the pile.
"Something stunningly original!"

Except that a *modiste* would take at least a week
to fashion something "stunningly original," and Lord
Wayland would be calling for her in an hour. And
Georgina was already possessed of a wardrobe that
was original, and overly vast to boot.

She flopped down before her dressing table. "Why
am I being as fidgety as a schoolgirl?" she asked Lady
Kate, who was peering out from beneath the hillock
of frocks.

The dog's ears perked up, and she tilted her head
as if considering.

"I am thirty years old," Georgina continued. "This is hardly the first time I have gone driving in the park with a handsome gentleman. And I have never thought twice about what to wear before!"

Lady Kate whined.

"Yes, quite! I suppose Lizzie has a point. There must be something unusual about this Wayland. Something—special."

Lady Kate barked.

"Exactly! Therefore, I must spend more time with him. Either he shall prove himself to be no different from any other charming man of my acquaintance, or he will show what it is that makes him so special."

Lady Kate's tail wagged vigorously.

Georgina knelt down beside the bed to receive a doggie kiss on the nose. "You are the best conversationalist I have ever met, Lady Kate. Most understanding. Best of all, I know you will never tell anyone of my cabbage-headed behavior today! Will you?"

Lady Kate sighed.

"You are not going to wear *that* coat, are you?" Hildebrand said, around a mouthful of Alex's leftover luncheon beefsteak.

Alex look down at his completely respectable, as he had thought, green coat. "What is wrong with it?"

"My dear fellow, what is *not* wrong with it?"

"The color is bilious," offered Freddie.

"The cut all wrong through the shoulders," said Hildebrand.

"And the length . . . !" sighed Freddie.

"Oh, very well!" Alex tore off the offending coat and tossed it onto a chair. "What do you suggest I wear in its place?"

"Where are you going?" asked Hildebrand.

"Not that it is any of your business, pup, but I am going driving in the park."

"Alone?"

"With a lady," Alex growled.

Hildebrand and Freddie glanced at each other speculatively. "Mrs. Beaumont!" they cried.

"My dear fellow," clucked Hildebrand. "You cannot escort such a dashing lady dressed like a country curate. Where are your other coats?"

"There." Alex pointed at an abandoned pile on the carpet.

Hildebrand left his steak and went to poke at the pile with the toe of his boot. "Do you mean to say that you tried on every coat you own, and that that green *thing* was the best you could find?"

Alex's jaw was taut. "Yes," he answered shortly.

Hildebrand clucked in dismay. "Wayland! You must hie to Weston immediately, at once!"

"Hildebrand. Even if I could fly out the door and land at Weston's doorstep, it would not help me this afternoon. I am due to call on Mrs. Beaumont in less than an hour."

"If only he could still wear his regimentals!" Freddie lamented. "Ladies find them demmed attractive."

"If only. It looks as if you've had these shabby bits since before you bought your commission, Wayland!"

"I have. Most of them," Alex said.

Hildebrand shook his head. Then he plucked up the blue coat from the top of the pile. "Wear this one, then. The color at least is good, and it looked fine the other day. Then tomorrow, Freddie and I will take you to the tailors ourselves."

"Yes," said Freddie. "Can't be shabby if you're going to dangle after an heiress."

Alex froze in the act of shrugging into the blue coat, and turned a glare onto the hapless Freddie. "I am not *dangling* after anyone. I am merely going for a drive in the park with a lady."

"Of course, of course," Freddie stammered. "N-no insult meant, Wayland. None at all."

Hildebrand turned Alex toward the door, away from the hapless Freddie. "Well, Wayland, you should be going! You will be late, and ladies do not like us to be late. Do they, Freddie?"

Freddie took a gulp from his wineglass. "Not at all!"

Alex glanced at his watch, and saw that he was indeed about to be late. He gathered up his hat and gloves, and turned one more stern glance onto his friends. "Very well. Just try not to drink *all* my wine while I am gone."

"No! Of course we would not do that."

"Of course." Alex paused at the door. "And one other thing—I want to have a talk with the two of you about that ridiculous wager you concocted."

"Wager? What wager?" Hildebrand cried, all innocence. "You *really* should be going now, Wayland."

"Very well. I will speak with you later, then." Then Alex left, closing the door softly behind him.

Hildebrand and Freddie ran to the window, to grin and wave as Alex's curricle drove away.

"D'ye think he fell for it all?" Freddie asked anxiously.

"Of a certes," said Hildebrand in great satisfaction. "We will be toasting our friend's health at his wedding breakfast before the Season is out!"

*   *   *

Alex glanced up once to his window before he guided his curricle into the traffic, and saw his friends waving and smiling like a pair of bedlamites.

They were up to something, he could tell. Ever since the three of them had first met at Eton, Freddie and Hildebrand had always behaved like the silliest clunches when they were concocting a scheme. Sometimes it had been smuggling a toad into a don's bed, or coaxing a larger allowance from their fathers, or trying to catch a pretty opera dancer's attention.

Now, it obviously had something to do with him.

But right now, Alex had weightier matters to consider than what those loobies were about. Matters such as Georgina Beaumont. And why he was so very anxious to see her again.

Perhaps it was only that he had been gone from England for so long, and then immured at Fair Oak when he did return. He had been in company with his fellow officers' wives in Spain, of course; and in Seville there had been a lovely innkeeper, Concetta. Yet it had been a long time since he had spent any amount of time with a pretty, unmarried *Englishwoman*.

Yes! he thought in relief. That would account for it. He had simply formed an infatuation for the first lovely woman to smile at him. In the clear light of a respectable afternoon drive, without the excitement of a swim in the river or the glitter of a ball to distract, he would see that really she was quite ordinary. Then there would be no more hours of anxiously thinking about her, of waiting until he could respectably see her again.

And he could get on with more businesslike and unpleasant matters—such as trying to raise some blunt.

Alex drew up his curricle outside Lady Elizabeth's town house and leaped down, much relieved by his thoughts. Now he and Georgina could enjoy their afternoon, without any silly romantical thoughts interfering!

Then he saw her again.

She emerged from the house before he could even ascend the front steps. She was wearing an afternoon dress of sunshine-yellow muslin, with sheer, gauzy white sleeves and a gauze Vandyke collar. It seemed she was *made* of light today; the late afternoon sun reflected on her brilliant hair and the yellow of her gown, and Alex's eyes dazzled as he looked at her.

She put on the bonnet she held, a white straw confection tied with wide yellow ribbons, and then came toward him, her hand outstretched. Her merry smile could have eclipsed even that sun.

Alex knew then, with a desperate, sinking sensation, that the feelings that had struck him when first he saw Georgina had not been mere gratitude for her attention, or his long deprivation of female company.

Those feelings had come from *her*, and her alone. From the sheer force of her beauty and her vibrant personality. She was unique, she was—special.

"Oh, Lord Wayland!" she said, taking his hand in her own gloved one. "How very good of you to rescue me from madness."

Still much struck by these new and strange emotions, Alex assisted Georgina into his curricle and climbed up beside her. He had never been so glad of anything than he was to have the reins and the driving to distract his thoughts. "Madness?" he asked.

"Yes. You see, Lizzie has decided to launch her own *salon*. Every Friday evening she will invite painters, writers, singers, what have you to her drawing room."

"It sounds delightful."

"Oh, yes! No doubt it will be. But she intends to hold the first one next Friday, and this afternoon she is in an uproar trying to decide exactly *who* to invite, and what food to serve." Georgina sighed. "Right now, the butler, the cook, little Isabella, and Lady Kate are all gathered together, offering their opinions, and Elizabeth is nay-saying them all. I tell you, I escaped only just in time. Perhaps, if we are gone a *very* long time, all will be settled by the time I return."

Alex laughed, his heart lightened, his doubts forgotten. As he had the day before, he quite forgot all his worries the moment he was in her company. Money, marriage, his family—there would be more than enough time to worry over those when he was deprived of her presence.

"Then, Mrs. Beaumont, I shall endeavor to take the long way about the park," he answered with a grin. "If there *is* a long way."

"If there is, I am certain we can find it."

"And, when the *salon* does come off, I am sure Lady Elizabeth will have a mad crush on her hands, and invitations will thereafter be highly sought for her Friday evenings."

"Of that I have no doubt. Certain high sticklers do not entirely approve of Lizzie, but she is the very center of a younger, more dashing set here in London. The *salon* will be a great success, and fun as well." She smiled at him. "You will be invited, of course. As will your friends, Mr. Marlow and Viscount Garrick."

"Now, that invitation I happily accept! I cannot speak for my friends, though. They are good enough fellows once you get to know them, but not precisely what one might call artistically minded."

"So I have gathered, from our very brief acquaintance!" Georgina laughed. "But I'm sure they would add an interesting element to the guest list."

"Then I will pass the invitation on to them."

Alex watched Georgina from the corner of his eye as she laughed and turned her face up to the warmth of the sun.

"You really are very lovely," he blurted, before he could even think.

Then he felt his face burn.

Chapter Seven

Georgina looked at Lord Wayland in shock, wondering if perhaps her ears had deceived her. A *compliment*, from the so-perfect duke? And a blush from him besides!

She found herself hopelessly, absurdly delighted. She even had the most unaccountable urge to giggle. Several swains in Italy had composed poems to her "emerald" eyes; some had even written songs and then sung them beneath her window. No flowery tribute had ever moved her so much as the fact that Lord Wayland thought she looked lovely today.

How very curious.

She waited until the need to giggle and simper had passed, then said, "Thank you very much, Lord Wayland! What a very kind thing to say."

He smiled at her, a wide white flash against his sunbronzed skin, and Georgina once again felt the giggles coming upon her.

She covered her mouth with her gloved hand.

"I speak only the truth, Mrs. Beaumont," he answered. "But I am sure that you must hear how lovely you are every day."

"Oh, not *every* day," Georgina answered lightly. "Every other day only, Lord Wayland."

"Then, I shall have to make it every day," he said. "If you will but do one thing for me."

"What might that be?" said Georgina, hoping against hope that it might be a kiss.

"Will you call me Alexander? Or Alex. Lord Wayland makes me feel too fusty! It makes me look about for my father."

Georgina smiled. Well, it was not a kiss, but it was a very nice thing nonetheless. "Very well. Alex suits you so much better than Lord Wayland. And you must call me Georgina."

He smiled in return. "Done."

As they turned into Hyde Park and joined the parade of worthies, Georgina thought that Alex seemed more at ease than he had when he first arrived at Elizabeth's house. When she had emerged to greet him, she had had the very odd sensation that he had not quite been expecting *her* to be there; as if he had arrived to escort someone else and had gotten her by mistake. He had looked quite surprised.

In the midst of all her excited anticipation, she had felt a small prick of uneasiness. She liked him so very much, had so carefully prepared for their drive. What if *he* did not like *her* so much? What if all the easy accord she had sensed the night before had been all in her imagination? What if she was making a wigeon of herself over a man who could have no regard for her?

The confident, sophisticated artist existed only in front of the scared, lonely, awkward orphan she had once been. At the thought of looking foolish in front of this man, little Georgie Cheswood completely took over Mrs. Georgina Beaumont.

But not now. Now Alex seemed more the man who had fished Lady Kate out of the river, who had waltzed so *vigorously* with Georgina. He was smiling, at ease, seemingly happy as he nodded to the people they drove past.

So Georgina, too, relaxed, and set herself to enjoying the sunny afternoon and the lovely man beside her.

"Your horses are very grand," she said.

"Scylla and Charybdis. They are not perfectly matched, I fear," Alex answered ruefully. They were, in fact, a pair that had once belonged to his brother, and were now almost all that remained of the Kenton stable. "Not at all fashionable."

Georgina examined them, one perfectly chestnut and one with a white star on its brow and white socks. They *were* prime goers, even if not perfectly matched. "Perhaps not. But they are strong and healthy, and very graceful. Good-looking, too." Much like their master, she reflected. "I should love to have some like them for my own curricle."

Alex looked at her, one brow raised in surprise. "You own a curricle, Mrs. Be—Georgina?"

"Oh, yes. It is not here, of course. It is at my villa. When I want to drive here, Elizabeth's husband gives me the loan of his."

"Yes," he said slowly. "I did hear that you and Lord Pynchon were to have a race."

Georgina laughed. "So you have heard of that! Yes. That silly popinjay was spouting off about how women should never drive, because we are so slow and such menaces on the road. So I asked if he cared to make a small wager on that point."

"Did you?" Alex's voice was quiet. "Do you often gamble, Georgina?"

Georgina remembered then, much to her mortification, that Alex's brother, the late Duke of Wayland, had caused a great scandal with his huge gambling losses. Even in the *ton*, who often routinely lost hundreds of pounds on the turn of a card, he had been notorious.

"Oh, no," she hastened to assure him. "A bit at silver loo now and then, but never high stakes. And I hardly ever wager. Only to bring ridiculous loobies like Pynchon down a peg. I have much better things to do with my money."

"Such as that charming bonnet," Alex murmured. "Well, if you ever need to go driving, my horses are at your disposal."

"Why, thank you, Alex!" Georgina cried. "They *are* darlings. And you must be sure to come and watch me trounce Pynchon. It will be an easy victory over one so ham-handed! Everyone will be there."

"When is the race to be?"

"A fortnight from Saturday, at the White Hart Inn, just outside of Town."

"I shall be sure to be there."

"Excellent! Oh, look, there is Lady Lonsdale waving to us. Shall we go speak to her?"

"By all means." But as Alex turned toward where Lady Lonsdale waited, perched on her gray mare, he looked at Georgina with a rather serious gleam in his eyes. "You will be very careful in this race, will you not, Georgina? And you will have a physician in attendance?"

"How very solemn you are!" Georgina laughed lightly, but she was secretly pleased that he was so very concerned. No man had been careful of her or her well-being for such a very long time. "Of course I will be careful. And you will be there to watch out for me, will you not?"

"Oh, yes," he said. "I will certainly be there."

*   *   *

"I had a very nice time," Georgina said, accepting Alex's hand as he assisted her from the curricle. "I never would have thought I could say that about a sedate drive through the park at the crowded hour, but so it was!"

Alex's hand lingered on her own for one long, warm, sweet moment. Then he stepped away. "I, too, enjoyed the afternoon."

"Will you not come inside to say hello to Elizabeth?" Georgina stepped around to pat Scylla's and Charybdis's noses in farewell.

"I fear I have kept you quite late, and you will be wanting to prepare for your evening."

"Oh, we are having a quiet evening at home. Elizabeth was rather tired from her exertions at the ball last night, and I insisted she rest."

"Yes." Alex hesitated, then said, "Forgive my boldness, Georgina, but is your friend quite well?"

"Well? She is, er, in a delicate way."

Alex blushed just a bit, which Georgina again found so charming. "I *had* perceived that! But I mean, is she having a difficult time of it? She seemed pale last night, and a trifle short of breath."

Georgina frowned. "I confess I have been rather concerned. She tries to pretend that everything is the same as ever it was, but it is not. She is so tired, where before she never was."

"My old nursemaid, who is now retired to a cottage on my family's estate, saw my mother very ably through four difficult confinements, and only one of the babes was lost. She has a great knowledge of herbs and cures. If you like, I could give you her direction and you could write to her. I am certain she would love to share her knowledge with you."

Georgina felt the prickle of incipient tears. She blinked very hard, and turned to bend her head over Scylla's neck. Never had she been so touched by a man's thoughtfulness. How many men of her acquaintance would be so concerned over the health of a strange woman and that of her unborn child? Concerned enough even to speak of the indelicate.

None would be. None but this man.

"That is so kind of you, Alex," she said softly. "So *very* kind! Elizabeth is my dearest friend, really almost my sister. I will do everything I can to help her."

"Yes. Of course. Well." Alex coughed, and shifted his feet uncomfortably.

Georgina almost smiled at that adorable discomfiture.

"Perhaps," he continued, "if Lady Elizabeth is feeling well tomorrow, you and she, and Lady Kate and Lady Isabella, would care to take a picnic to the country? I am sure my friends Marlow and Garrick would accompany us. Fresh air and sunshine would probably be beneficial to Lady Elizabeth."

"I am sure it would!" Georgina cried. "That would be most pleasant. I will speak with Elizabeth, but I know we have no fixed engagements tomorrow."

"Then, we shall call for you at noon." Alex took her hand, and raised it to his lips. "Until then, Georgina."

"Yes. Good day, Alex."

Georgina watched him until his curricle turned a corner, out of her sight. Only then did she go inside the house, her hand curled carefully around that kiss.

"Georgie!" Elizabeth called through the open drawing room door. "Is that you?"

"Yes, it is me." Georgina left her gloves and bonnet on a table in the foyer, and went into the drawing room.

Elizabeth was ensconced on a chaise before the fire, a blanket tucked about her and a book open on her lap. Dark purple smudges still shadowed her gray eyes, but she seemed a trifle less pale.

"How are you feeling, dear?" Georgina sat down next to Lady Kate in a deep armchair across from Elizabeth.

"Oh, much more the thing! I had some tea and biscuits earlier, after I settled some points about my *salon*, and Lady Kate and I have been having a coze. I even think I might enjoy a bit of trout for supper!"

"Lizzie. I know I have said it before, but I must say it again. You should go to the country, to Evanstone Park, and rest."

"Georgina!" Elizabeth laughed. "Don't fuss so, dear. If I do feel worse, I will go to Evanstone and wait for the baby to make its appearance. For now, though, I am quite well. I want to stay here in Town, and enjoy myself with you and our friends, just for a bit longer."

"If you are quite sure . . ." Georgina said uncertainly.

"I am sure! Now, enough about me. I want to hear all about your afternoon with the handsome Lord Wayland."

Georgina settled back in her chair with a blissful sigh, the golden afternoon still warm around her. "It was delightful! Lord Wayland is such a fine man, so very kind. He was all that is amiable. He even offered to let me drive his cattle, which are quite fine." Georgina paused, stroking Lady Kate's soft fur thoughtfully. "I do think, Lizzie, that perhaps Lord Wayland—or Alex, as he asked me to call him—is not *all* that he shows to the world."

Elizabeth looked up, surprised. "Whatever do you mean, Georgie? Not all that he shows?"

"Oh, I do not mean that he hides dire vices behind a pretty facade! Far from it. I suppose I should have said he is *more*," Georgina mused.

"Well, I would not wonder at it!" said Elizabeth. "His family must be quite in a stew still."

"How do you mean? What do you know about the Kentons, Lizzie?"

"Only gossip, really. If I knew anything ill of Lord Wayland, I would have told you straight away. But Nick knew Damian Kenton, Alex's brother, slightly, during his old raking days before our marriage."

"The late duke? I have heard so many rumors about him. What was he really like?"

Georgina and Elizabeth leaned their heads together in avid interest.

"A bad 'un," whispered Elizabeth. "Always gambling, whoring; he lost huge amounts, without a thought for his family."

"Hm, yes. Alex said something about his brother's gambling."

"Yes. But this present duke, I think, is not much like his brother," Elizabeth suggested. "Would you not say so, Georgie?"

Georgina smiled. "Oh, yes. I would definitely say so."

"Then, you will see him again?"

"He has asked us all—you, me, Lady Kate, and Isabella—on a picnic tomorrow. Do you think you feel well enough?"

"Of course! The fresh air will do wonders for me, and the baby. I quite look forward to it!"

"Good. So do I."

* * *

Georgina lay awake long into the night, turning Elizabeth's words about Alex's family over in her mind.

So Damian Kenton had been a wastrel, just as she suspected. Racketing about Town, losing money, while his mother and sister sat in the country, and his younger brother fought for his country in Spain and at Waterloo.

Perhaps that, then, was a part of the secret solemnity in Alex's so-blue eyes. Perhaps he felt guilt that his family had been in such straits when he was too far away to help them. Helpless to shield them from his brother's excesses.

How well Georgina knew that feeling! Helpless guilt had been her companion throughout her childhood.

She rolled onto her side, to watch the bar of moonlight that fell from her window across the carpet. There was also one other, small thought that bothered her.

If Damian Kenton had been such a terrible spendthrift, what was the condition of the Kenton fortunes now?

Not that she cared a great deal for such things. She had lived in genteel poverty for much of her early life, and she knew very well that honesty and humor were to be valued above gold. Money was merely something that—facilitated life.

But now she was wealthy. She could sense that Alex was a proud man, and if he was in dire straits, he could find the idea of a friendship with her to be made awkward by vulgar lucre. Or, even worse, he could find friendship with her sweetened by her money.

And Georgina would not care for that at all!

Chapter Eight

"Georgie, do you think these flowers look better here, or over on that table?"

Georgina tilted her head, examining the large vase of pink and white roses. "They look lovely in either place."

Elizabeth sighed in exasperation. "That is not very much help! The guests will be arriving in an hour, or less, and I cannot even situate the decorations. At least the refreshments are prepared and laid out." She glanced toward the open doors of the dining room, where a sumptuous repast was spread. "Perhaps the crab cakes would have been better than the mushroom tarts?"

"The mushroom tarts are delicious!" Georgina paused before a mirror, and straightened the amber combs in her hair. She smoothed the bodice of her saffron-gold gown. Was it just a trifle *too* low-cut? Would Alex like it?

She giggled, and tugged the satin bodice just a bit lower.

"Georgina, you are not attending!" Elizabeth cried.

"Of course I am," Georgina answered. "Why are

you so very worried? You have given many routs before, Lizzie."

"This is my first *salon*, and I want it to be a great success. I want people clamoring for invitations to my Friday evenings!" Elizabeth picked up the vase and moved it to the other table. "Here, I think."

"It was so very charming over there, though," a masculine voice drawled.

Elizabeth whirled around in a flurry of sapphire silk skirts. "Nicholas!" she cried, and ran across the room to fling herself into her husband's arms. "You are here at last! I thought surely you would never arrive in time."

Nicholas kissed her, and held her close against him. "I'm sorry, my love. We had a broken wheel on the road. But I swore to you I would not miss your *salon*, and here I am." He smiled at Georgina. "Hullo, Georgie! You are stunning, as always."

"Thank you, Nick. I am very glad you are here; you can persuade your wife to cease rushing about and sit down, before her ankles swell."

"My ankles are *not* swollen!" Elizabeth protested. But she did sit down, and propped her slippered feet up on an embroidered footstool. "How did you find Evanstone Park, my love? Not too much damaged, I hope."

"Nothing that couldn't be repaired. The storm did a nasty job on the roof over the east wing, though." Nicholas poured himself a measure of brandy from the array laid out for the party, and sat down next to his wife. "What have you two been up to while I've been away?"

"Nothing out of the ordinary way," said Elizabeth. "We went on a delightful picnic yesterday, and attended the Beaton ball last week. A terrible crush, as always."

"I hope that you have been resting enough, Lizzie," Nicholas said sternly.

"Of course I have!" Then Elizabeth grinned mischievously. "And Georgina has a new admirer."

"Another one?" Nicholas laughed. "Georgie, you really ought to leave *someone* for the other ladies."

"I hardly have *every* man in London at my feet!" Georgina protested.

"Oh. Only half, then?" asked Nicholas.

"No! And he is not my *admirer*, Lizzie."

"Of course not. He is just here every day, escorting you to balls, and on picnics and drives. Sending flowers . . ."

"He is being kind. He has been away from England for so long; he doesn't know anyone else yet."

"That is not it at all, and you know it!" said Elizabeth. "He obviously likes you. He probably wants to marry you."

"No!" said Georgina firmly. "I am hardly suitable."

"You are the most suitable! He could do no better. I think that he . . ."

"Ladies, please!" Nicholas interrupted. "Who is this new admirer that has the two most unflappable women I know in such an uproar?"

"Alexander Kenton," said Georgina. "The new Duke of Wayland."

Nicholas's dark brows shot up. "Hotspur Kenton?"

"You know him?" Georgina asked hopefully.

"I knew *of* him, in Spain. Everyone knew of Colonel Kenton of the Sixteenth. He was absolutely fearless, but an excellent leader; never asked his men to do anything he wouldn't do himself. I had heard that

Damian had finally stuck his spoon in the wall." He grinned at Georgina. "So he is your new suitor, Georgie? Should I have a talk with him, find out his intentions?"

Before Georgina could respond to this bit of nonsense, the knocker at the front door sounded, and Elizabeth jumped out of her chair.

"The guests are arriving!" she cried. "Does everything look quite all right?"

"Perfect, darling," said Nicholas. "Now, I will go upstairs and change my clothes before I disgrace you." He paused to kiss Georgina's cheek. "See you later, Duchess."

Georgina smacked him on the shoulder.

The *salon* was proving to be a rousing success.

Painters, poets, musicians, patrons of the arts, and even politicians stood in groups large and small across the drawing room. They spilled out onto the small terrace, and flowed into the dining room where the refreshments beckoned. The mushroom tarts were consumed; the champagne was drunk; the harp and the pianoforte were played. Elizabeth was glowing with pleasure at her success, and the two paintings of Georgina's that were displayed were greatly admired.

In short, it was looking to be a rather perfect evening, aside from one small flaw.

Well, a rather large flaw, actually. Alex had not yet appeared.

Every time the drawing room opened to admit a new flood of guests, Georgina would turn eagerly, searching their faces, only to be disappointed.

What was wrong with her, behaving like a silly schoolgirl when she was all of thirty years of age? Men handsomer than Alex Kenton had taken her driv-

ing before, had escorted her to balls and routs. They
had been charming, pleasant company, enjoyable to
flirt and dance with. And she had forgotten them almost as soon as they were out of her sight.

Why should this man be any different?

Because, she admitted to herself with a rueful sigh,
he *was* different! She had so wanted him to see her
paintings, to see how admired they were, that she had
a talent. That she was not a mere empty-headed Society matron, dabbling in watercolors.

Because she wanted him to admire her, blast it! To
be intrigued by her.

As she admired him. And was intrigued by him.

But how could she win his admiration if he was not
even here!

". . . do so love this one, Mrs. Beaumont!"

Georgina turned her attention from the door to smile
at the woman beside her, a small, blonde viscountess
who had been examining her paintings. Georgina
could not, unfortunately, remember which viscountess
she was.

"Oh, yes?" she said helpfully.

"Yes!" The viscountess gestured with her glass of
champagne at an informal study Georgina had done
of Elizabeth, Nicholas, Lady Kate, Isabella, and Elizabeth's brother and sister-in-law, Peter and Carmen,
the Earl and Countess of Clifton. They were gathered
around a tea table on a country house terrace, a scene
of domestic harmony and great friendship, much
laughter and love.

Georgina smiled to recall that particular golden afternoon at Evanstone Park, when she had been
sketching away to capture the scene.

"I would vow I was there!" the viscountess—was it
Lady Dalrymple?—continued. "You have captured

the scene so beautifully. Is it perhaps available for purchase, Mrs. Beaumont?"

Georgina shook her head. "I fear not. That was done only for my own pleasure. As was that one." She indicated her other work on display. It had the setting of the same terrace, but it was a solitary portrait of Carmen. A tall, raven-haired, striking Spanish woman, she was posed dramatically against the white marble of the terrace in a mantilla and gown of black lace.

Georgina had resisted all the efforts of Carmen's husband to buy it from her. There was something about it that reminded Georgina so poignantly of her days following the drum on the Peninsula with Jack.

"An excellent likeness of Lady Clifton," Lady Dalrymple said. "Such a pity neither of these works are available! Perhaps, however, you will be in London long enough to begin a new work? I had been thinking of a new portrait of myself, to present to Lord Dalrymple on our anniversary."

Georgina smiled, sensing a new commission. "Perhaps, Lady Dalrymple, you would permit me to call on you some time next week, so we may discuss it further?"

"I would be ever so delighted, Mrs. Beaumont! Now, I must go and speak with Lady Elizabeth. Her *salon* has been such a quiz!"

Georgina watched her leave, then turned back to her own painting. It truly was a scene of great marital harmony; Nicholas standing behind Elizabeth, his hand on her shoulder as he looked down at her open sketchbook. Little Isabella cuddled on her father's lap, while her mother leaned forward to tie her little slipper ribbon. Lady Kate dozed contentedly in a patch of sunlight.

A perfect instant, captured forever.

Georgina loved it, this scene of her dearest friends. It cheered her immensely; yet it also made her feel rather wistful. Lonely, even.

"It is truly exquisite," a man said from behind her.

Georgina looked over her shoulder, and gave a small cry of delight. "Alex! You have come."

"Yes. I do apologize for my lateness." He moved up beside her, peering closely at the painting with his quizzing glass. "I am just an old army man, of course, and know little about art. But I can truly say that that is one of the loveliest paintings I have ever seen."

Georgina had received many compliments on her work over the years, many of them from more knowledgeable critics than this one. None, though, had ever made her feel like crying with utter joy.

Just as his compliments on her beauty had made her feel like giggling and blushing.

"I thank you," she said. "This is my favorite painting I have ever done; it brings me great happiness."

He nodded. "A scene of great beauty. I can see why it would make you happy just to look at it." He looked down at her, and smiled. "Though I do wonder, Georgina, why you looked so sad as you examined it a moment ago. Was there a flaw that you just detected?"

Georgina's gaze flew up to his. "I did not—how did you . . . ?"

"Oh, I have a rather embarrassing confession to make," he said with a rueful little laugh. "When I first came in, I stood over there and watched you in secret for a moment."

Georgina looked away, flustered. And very pleased. "Alex, how silly! Why would you do that?"

"Because you looked so very pretty," he said softly.

Then his jaw tightened. "That was a very clumsy compliment. Forgive me."

"What is there to forgive? First you admire my painting, then you say I look pretty. Such calumny!" she teased.

He smiled, and turned rather awkwardly to the portrait of Carmen. "Is this your only other work displayed?"

Georgina nodded, letting him change the subject. "Yes. Do you know the Countess of Clifton?"

"I have met her once or twice. She was of invaluable service to us during the war."

"She is a very fascinating person, and a joy to paint. I think she has passed on her beauty to Isabella!"

"So she has. But I am rather surprised, and disappointed, not to see more of your work."

"Oh, Elizabeth would have covered the walls with my paintings if I had let her. I did not want to appear *ostentatious*, though."

Alex threw back his head and laughed extravagantly, a deep, warm sound that caused heads to turn in their direction. "Georgina," he said, "I fear you cannot help but be a bit ostentatious! Your beauty will always make you conspicuous."

"A-ha!" she cried. "Another compliment. That is three in one evening."

"I seem to be quite the poet tonight."

"So you are. Well, Lord Byron, if you would truly like to see more of my work, and are not just being polite, I would be happy to show it to you. I am sharing Elizabeth's studio while I am here, and I have several pieces in there."

Alex glanced around uncertainly.

"You needn't worry about my reputation," she said. "I am no young miss you will be forced to wed if you're found alone with me! I am only going to show you my paintings; it's all quite respectable, and we will not be gone long."

He grinned. "You will think me quite old and fusty."

"Not at all! But maybe *you* should be wary of your reputation, being seen with a lady rogue like me." She caught up some glasses of champagne from a footman's tray. "We will just take these with us."

The studio, faced on two sides with windows and with a skylight overhead, was flooded with moonlight. Silvery shadows were cast around props and easels; satin drapes seemed to undulate from the corners. It all seemed terribly romantic, a perfect spot for secret trysts and whispered, passionate words.

Georgina forced such fanciful thoughts from her head, since it was obvious that Alex had no such intentions on this night. She lit a lamp that sat on a small table, and set about taking holland covers down from her finished paintings.

"These are mine," she said.

Alex stepped closer to examine them. They were mostly portraits, of course; two of a duchess and a baroness that were waiting to be sent to their subjects, and one of Isabella. There was a wedding portrait of Elizabeth and Nicholas, and several small studies of Lady Kate.

He spent the longest time on the last three works. He even drew out his quizzing glass to look at them, turning his head this way and that.

Georgina could hardly stand it. She hated it so when people looked at her work and did not say anything; she always imagined the worst, that they disliked it.

"What do you think?" she asked at last.

"Beautiful," he breathed. "You are truly gifted, Georgina. Even I can see that."

She laughed in profound relief. "Did you think I was just some fluffy-headed female, dabbling about with watercolors?"

"Certainly not! No one ever *buys* fluffy watercolors. But to see them—thank you, Georgina, for giving me this privilege."

"I am the one who is privileged, to share what I love so much with someone who appreciates it. Which do you like the best?"

"Well, your portraits are certainly fine. You have quite captured your subjects, both their outward appearance and their personalities. Why, I can almost *see* the mischief in Isabella's eyes!"

"Yes! It was quite a struggle to make her sit still for longer than two minutes."

"They are lovely. These, though—I feel I am *there*, in all three of them."

Georgina examined the paintings under discussion. "Landscape is rather new to me. I have always sketched the places I have been, but I never tried it on a larger scale until recently."

He gently touched the painting hanging in the middle. "This is your villa in Italy?"

It was a sun-drenched scene of a white stucco villa, crowned with red tiles and iced with wrought-iron balconies. In the distance could be seen the azure expanse of Lake Como.

"Yes," said Georgina, "that is Santa Cecilia."

"And the others?"

"This one was painted in Scotland when we were there on holiday last year." She indicated the vision of a ruined castle, set atop a hill covered with purple heather. Then she turned to the last, a small, cramped, dark-stained house, set back in a tangled garden, with a storm breaking over it. "This is the house I grew up in."

Alex looked from the painting to Georgina, his blue eyes serious. "Not a very cheerful aspect."

"No. Never go to gloomy Sussex, if you can help it!" Georgina forced a light laugh, and turned away from the painting. She went to sit down on the chaise she used for her models, and poured herself a glass of champagne.

"Is Sussex so gloomy?" Alex leaned back against the wall, watching her.

"Perhaps not so very, all of the time. Perhaps just the home of the Reverend and Mrs. Smythe."

"Your parents?"

She shook her head fiercely. "Never! My aunt and her husband. I painted that when I went back there a few years ago, for my aunt's funeral." She held up the glass. "Care for some champagne?"

"Yes, thank you." He came and sat beside her, taking the glass she handed him. "Would you tell me about them? About your childhood?"

"It is very dull."

"I don't care," he answered, surprisingly intent. "I find I want to know everything about you, Georgina Beaumont."

Georgina studied him carefully, longing to see the truth of those words in his eyes. Longing to trust this man, this perfect man, with the truth of her less than exalted past.

Then she nodded.

"My parents, Gerald and Maria Cheswood, were carried off by a fever when I was just ten years old," she began. "My father was the youngest son of a baronet. His family disowned him when he married my mother, the daughter of a merchant from Bristol. They refused to take me in when my parents died, so I had to go to my mother's sister, my Aunt Hortense, and her husband, the Reverend Smythe."

"They of the gloomy house."

"Yes. It was not very much like living in my parents' home! My mother was a very *joyful* woman, and so affectionate. She was always devising games and parties, so we were very merry, even though there was not much money. And she and my father were very much in love." Georgina paused to take a deep sip of the champagne. "In the vicarage there was no joy, no affection. Only sermons and housework. Endless housework. They deeply disapproved of me, you see; disapproved of my red hair, and the fact that I laugh at things that are funny."

"It sounds dismal," Alex said quietly.

"So it was! It certainly showed me what I did *not* want my life to be like. But then, when I was fourteen, a miracle happened."

"What was it?"

"My aunt decided it would be best if I was sent away to school."

"School was a miracle?"

"To me it was. You see, three things happened to me there. Mrs. Bennett, who taught art, was the first. I had always scribbled, you see, but she taught me technique, color. She made me see what a wonder art could be, what a salvation."

"The art world owes a great thanks to Mrs. Bennett, then!" he exclaimed. "What were the other things?"

"When I was sixteen, Elizabeth came to the school. She also loved art, and we became bosom bows. As we remain to this day."

"And the other?"

Georgina looked down into her glass, deep into the golden bubbles. "When I was almost eighteen, the brother of a schoolfriend came to visit her before his regiment went to the Peninsula. His family did not approve of me, just as my father's did not approve of my mother, but Captain Jack Reid and I went to Gretna Green a month after we met, and then I followed him to Portugal." She looked up at Alex. "He was killed almost two years later."

"I am sorry, Georgina. So many good men were lost there."

"Yes."

They were quiet for several minutes, wrapped in moonlight and champagne and thoughts of times past.

"I have bored you quite enough, I think!" Georgina said at last, with a laugh. "I want to hear about *your* childhood now."

"Oh, no!" Alex shook his head. "That *is* a dull tale."

"I want to know everything about you," she said, echoing his earlier words to her.

"Then you shall. Another time."

"Yes," Georgina sighed. "We have been gone rather a long time, and I did promise you there would be no scandal."

Alex took her hand and raised it to his lips. "Thank you for sharing your paintings with me, Georgina. And for talking with me."

Georgina stared at their joined hands, expecting to see sparks shooting from them, or perhaps even moonbeams, so delicious were the feelings that emanated from his skin on hers. Alas, that heat was all in her mind; there was only her pale fingers in his sunbronzed ones.

She wished, with all her being, that they could just sit that way, together, forever.

"Thank you for listening to me," she whispered. "Alex."

Now kiss me, she added silently.

But he did not. He only drew her to her feet, and smiled down at her.

"We should rejoin the others," he said.

"Oh, yes," she murmured. "Yes, we really should."

Chapter Nine

By Jove, but he had wanted to kiss her!

Alone in his quiet lodgings, Alex ruminated on the evening, on missed opportunities.

She had been so very lovely, the lamplight turning her hair to pure flame, her green eyes wide as she looked up at him. Her hand had been soft in his, and she had smelled so very tempting with her rose perfume. He had never been so tempted by anything in all his life. Had never wanted to do anything more than he had wanted to kiss Georgina Beaumont.

She had wanted to kiss him, as well. She had leaned gently toward him as they talked; had watched him carefully, quizzically. She was no green girl; surely she had sensed his own desire.

Probably she was wondering now what had made him run away so cravenly.

Just as he was wondering himself.

Alex threw himself back into his armchair with a deep groan. The truth had to be acknowledged now, if only to himself.

He did want Georgina Beaumont, in the physical sense. He found her beautiful, and desirable beyond belief. But he also wanted much more from her than her body. Her confidences in the quiet studio had proven that beyond a doubt.

He was so proud, and pleased, and moved that she would tell him of herself, of the woman behind her glittering Society self. He wanted to know more, to know *everything*. To know about her marriages, her friendships, her home, her favorite food, her favorite color.

More than that, *he* wanted to confide in *her*. To tell her of his troubles, ask for her advice. Relate all his happy childhood memories, his life in the army, his hopes for the future. He had always been a great one for keeping his own counsel, for there had never been anyone he felt he *could* talk to. Now he found himself wanting to tell all to this woman.

This woman he had known only a few days, but who it felt as if he had known forever.

Alex sighed, and closed his eyes. Yes, the veriest truth was that he was no hardened rake like his brother had been. He could not take Georgina as his mistress, no matter how great his desire for her was. He wanted her for his wife, his duchess, his love.

So, a small voice said at the back of his mind. *You ask her to marry you, you have a wife you adore, and plenty of money besides. Where is the rub?*

Ah, he answered that voice, as a wise man once wrote, therein lies the rub. Money.

If he asked Georgina to marry him, he would have to tell her all. That his brother had squandered his family's fortune, and they were left with little more than Alex's army pension. That they would need some of her money to rebuild.

She would surely laugh him out of her life, being

the independent spirit that she was! She thought well enough of him now, when she thought him a distinguished, self-possessed, self-made man. What would she think of him then?

Truly, he had never had a luckier, or more disastrous, moment than when Lady Kate decided to take a swim in the river.

He would just have to take things slowly with Georgina, and bide his time until he could see his way clear to what he should do.

"It was a lovely *salon*, was it not?" Elizabeth said happily, wriggling her stockinged toes where they lay on her husband's lap, being rubbed.

Georgina lolled on the chaise, warm with champagne and happy memories of those moments in the studio. "Umm, lovely. A great success."

"Yes. So many people came there was scarce room to move. And even more will come to the next Friday evening, I am certain."

"Is a *salon* not a chance for great conversation, my love?" Nicholas asked with a teasing grin. "One can hardly have a fascinating conversation if one cannot even breathe."

"There was a great deal of conversation!" Elizabeth protested. "Was there not, Georgie?"

"Hm? Oh, yes. Certainly."

"But I noticed that *you* quite vanished, for nearly an hour," said Elizabeth. "You minx."

"Yes!" Georgina cried merrily. "I do freely admit to minxdom. I was showing Alex my paintings in the studio."

"Oh-ho!" said Nicholas, waggling his eyebrows comically. "Alex is it now?"

"He *asked* me to call him Alex."

"What happened in the studio, Georgie?" Elizabeth asked in desperately curious tones.

"Nothing happened," answered Georgina. "At least not in *that* way. We talked."

"Talked? For all that time? What about?"

"Lizzie!" Georgina protested, laughing. "Such curiosity. We only talked of this and that. Nothing of consequence. I find him very pleasant company."

"Pleasant company, eh?" said Nicholas. "Well. Nothing wrong with that, is there, Lizzie my love?"

"Of course not," Elizabeth answered slowly. "I find him to be quite a pleasant gentleman myself. Does that mean that nothing of a more—serious nature is happening, Georgie?"

Georgina took the last sip from her champagne, then looked down into the empty glass, puzzled by Elizabeth's question. How could she answer something that she herself did not know? "I—well, honestly, my dears, I am not sure. Perhaps there is. He is not the sort of man one can just flirt lightly with, is he? I do like him, very much. I am not sure, however, what his feelings are toward me."

Elizabeth and Nicholas stared at her in obvious shock.

"Oh, my," Elizabeth said finally in a small voice. "Well, of course he must be in love with you. Almost every man you meet is in love with you! He is very fortunate to have your affection in return."

"People would say *I* am the fortunate one," Georgina answered. "To have the interest of a duke. If indeed I do have his interest, which I am not at all sure of."

"Are you saying you are feeling—uncertain, Georgie?" Elizabeth said, her eyes growing even wider. "You?"

"Yes, me! I am—oh, I just don't know. I do not know what my feelings are for him, or his for me, or what is happening at all." Georgina placed her empty glass carefully on a small side table and stood. "I do, however, know one thing. I am tired, and I am going to retire now."

"Would you like to drive my curricle tomorrow? Get in form for your race with Pynchon?" said Nicholas. "We could all go into the countryside for the morning, and have luncheon at the White Hart Inn."

"That sounds delightful." Georgina kissed his cheek, and Elizabeth's. "Good night, my dears. It was a lovely evening."

"Good night, Georgina," they echoed.

"And please do not talk about me as soon as I leave the room."

"Would we do that?" cried Elizabeth, all wounded innocence.

"I am only warning you."

Georgina left the drawing room and closed the door behind her. But she left it open a tiny crack, and leaned her ear against it.

"Do you think she is in love with him?" Elizabeth asked.

"Oh, yes," Nicholas answered. "Undoubtedly. Have you ever seen Georgie *flustered* about a man before?"

Elizabeth sighed happily. "Hm. Yes, I do believe that you are right. It must be love."

Georgina smiled, closed the door all the way, and went up to find her bed.

Chapter Ten

"Pardon me, my lady, but there is a gentleman caller," announced Greene, Elizabeth's butler.

Elizabeth, left alone for the morning while Nicholas and Georgina went driving, looked up from her sketchbook in surprise. "A gentleman caller? Why, here I had thought my days of attracting suitors were long over!" She pressed her hand to the small bulge of her stomach with a laugh.

Greene sniffed in disapproval. "It is Lord Wayland, my lady. I told him it was not your at-home hour, but he insisted."

"Lord Wayland?" Elizabeth interrupted. "Surely he has asked for Mrs. Beaumont, not me!"

"He did first inquire after Mrs. Beaumont, but when I informed him she was on an outing, he asked if you were at home."

"Oh, yes, Greene! Do show him in."

As the butler departed, Elizabeth struggled to her feet, and glanced around the morning room in great consternation. Things were in such disarray, with her own sketches and some of Georgina's piled about everywhere. Shawls and hats were tossed around, Nicholas's newspapers were trampled on the floor, and Lady Kate sat before the fire busily gnawing on a bone she had unearthed in the garden.

Elizabeth took it away from her, much to Lady Kate's consternation, and shoved it under a shawl.

"Hush, Lady Kate!" she admonished. "It would never do for a duke to think we are slovenly."

Lady Kate sat back on her haunches with a loud huff, but she quickly cheered up when Alex came in the room. She bounded up to him, barking in joy.

Alex bent to pat her head. "Good morning, Lady Kate." Then he straightened, with a smart bow for Elizabeth. "And good morning to you, Lady Elizabeth. I trust I find you well?"

"Quite well. I fear, though, that Georgina is not at home."

"Yes, your butler said she was on an outing."

"She and Nicholas and my maid Daisy have gone to the countryside, so Georgina may practice her driving before the race next week. I was meant to go with them, but mornings are not—er, not my best time." She laughed nervously.

"No," he answered kindly. "I should imagine not."

"I am joining them for luncheon. Perhaps you would care to come with us?"

"I would, very much. Thank you."

Elizabeth beamed at him. "Well. Would you like to sit?"

Alex looked about at the piles of paper that covered every seat. "I would, but . . ."

"Oh! I do apologize." Elizabeth pushed some sketches off of a chair and waved him to be seated, then returned to her chaise. "I fear we are rather informal in our family rooms."

"Please, don't apologize. I think this is a charming

room." He picked up one of the sketches, a scene of a country pond. "Is this one of G—Mrs. Beaumont's?"

"Oh, yes. Lovely, is it not? And you needn't call her anything but Georgina in front of me. I won't tell."

Alex laughed ruefully. "You will think me foolish, Lady Elizabeth! Mooning over sketches and such."

"Never! A man who has the good sense to admire Georgina could never be a fool. Except for this man named Ottavio, whom we knew in Venice. He took to serenading her every night beneath her window. Quite gave the neighbors fits, as he sounded rather like a dying cow . . ." Elizabeth broke off. "But I don't wish to bore you with my ramblings!"

"On the contrary. I am all fascination." He placed the sketch carefully on a table, then sat back in his chair. "You have known Georgina a long time, I understand, Lady Elizabeth."

"Oh, yes. Since we were at school. Georgina was a bit older than me, but we quickly bonded over our mutual love of art. She is my dearest friend."

"Then, I should very much like your counsel. If I may?"

"Please do!" Elizabeth leaned toward him in interest. "There is nothing I love more than to give advice."

"I would like to know if—that is . . ." Alex looked away, a faint, warm blush spreading across his cheekbones. "Do you think Georgina would ever want to marry again?"

"Well," Elizabeth breathed. "Are you planning to make her an offer?"

"I—might be." He shook his head. "Lady Elizabeth, I must be completely honest with you. I think your friend is the most fascinating person I have ever met. I want more than I have ever wanted anything to make her my wife, to do anything in my power to make her happy. Only you can tell me if I have any hope."

"Only Georgina can answer that for certain," Elizabeth said carefully. "I do know that she admires you. I also know that her marital history has not been—entirely satisfactory."

"She told me of her first husband. Captain Reid."

"Yes. Jack was very dashing, and Georgina was devastated when he died. She did not tell you of her other two husbands, though?"

"No. There was not time."

"They were no Jack Reid!" Elizabeth's voice dropped confidingly. "In their seventies, the both of them. She married Sir Everett out of desperation. She had only enough money to return to England when Jack died, and only his meager widow's pension to live on. Her family, and his, refused to take her in. So when Sir Everett met her and made her an offer, she could see no choice. He wanted a housekeeper, you see, but was too much a nip-farthing to pay for one. He was a terrible bully; Georgina's letters to me then were quite despairing. Fortunately, he died after only a year, and left her a tidy portion."

"Dreadful," said Alex. "Was the next one as bad?"

"No. Mr. Beaumont was quite an old dear, and so besieged by his grasping children. Perhaps you are acquainted with Mr. Theodore Beaumont, who is so fond of pink waistcoats?"

Alex grimaced.

"Exactly so. Well, Mr. Beaumont had been a friend of Sir Everett's, and he and Georgina had become friends as well. By the time old Sir Everett died, Mr. Beaumont was quite ill. So he asked Georgina to marry him, and help keep his children at bay. So she did, and hired herself an art teacher. She had always been so talented, you see, and in the year she lived on Mr. Beaumont's estate, she developed that talent into what you see now."

"How did it end?"

"Mr. Beaumont died, of course. Peacefully, thanks to Georgina. He left all that was not entailed to her, which so infuriated his children. Georgina's portion amounted to over fifty thousand pounds, you see."

"Good gad," Alex gasped. "Fifty thousand?"

"Yes."

"I—never would have thought it so much." Alex's healthy color drained away, leaving him pale as the white damask of his chair. "She would never have me."

"Why not?"

"A woman of such fortune?" He laughed, a humorless bark. "Of course she would not."

"Most people would say that a woman of her background, despite her fortune *and* a flourishing career, would never be equal to a duke."

"I am not most people."

"No. You are not," said Elizabeth. "You have been honest with me, Lord Wayland, so now I will be honest with you. I know that your family's fortunes are not what they once were, due to the regrettable actions of your late brother."

Alex nodded gravely. "I fear that is too true, Lady Elizabeth."

"I also know that Georgina cares nothing for such things. For her, money is only a convenience, and if she lost it all tomorrow she would not care one whit. She would simply find a way to make some more. If she loves you, money, or lack of it, will never stand in her way." She smiled at him. "And I know that you do not care for her because of her fortune."

"I would love her if she were an orange seller," Alex declared.

"Of course! So marry her, if you can get her. I will dance at your wedding with greater joy than I have ever danced before."

"Thank you, Lady Elizabeth. I promise you that I will do my very best to, er, get her."

"I am sure you shall. I give you a warning, though."

"A warning?"

"Yes. Georgina is the dearest, most generous soul. But she has the pride, and the temper, of a lioness. Never cross her, and your courtship is sure to go smoothly."

She almost laughed aloud at the worried look on his face. "A—temper."

"It's the red hair, you know." Elizabeth rose, drawing her shawl about her shoulders. "Now, I have enjoyed our coze, but we should be going, or we shall never be in time for luncheon! I am quite famished."

"There's Elizabeth now!" Georgina drew up the curricle in the yard of the White Hart, and waved as Elizabeth leaned from one of the inn's windows. "Are we very late, Lizzie?"

"Not at all! We were early."

"We?" called Nicholas, alighting from the curricle and reaching up to assist Georgina.

"Lord Wayland came with me, isn't that grand? We shall be such a merry party!" Elizabeth waved again, then withdrew, pulling the casement closed.

"Why, Georgie!" Nicholas teased. "Are you blushing?"

"Certainly not!" Georgina protested. She did, however, feel just a trifle warm.

"You *are* blushing! Looks terrible with your hair."

"How insufferable you are, Nick!" she laughed. "However can Elizabeth tolerate being married to you?"

"It's because I'm so handsome, of course." He held out his arm. "Shall we go in? Your wild driving has given me quite an appetite."

"That 'wild driving' is going to win me fifty pounds of that dreadful Lord Pynchon's money, come Thursday. I will confess to being a bit peckish myself, though." Her steps quickened a bit as they entered the inn.

"And eager to see Lord Wayland, too, what?"

"Of course not! Ah, here we are."

A substantial luncheon was already laid out in the White Hart's best private parlor, cold meats and cheeses, vegetables, and a lemon trifle.

Elizabeth was busily dipping pickled onions into heavy cream and plopping them into her mouth, while Alex watched her in appalled fascination.

"Hello, my dears!" she cried, wiping cream from her chin. "How was your drive?"

"Marvelous! Nick's new curricle is a wonder; I must order one for myself." Georgina kissed Elizabeth's cheek, then sat down next to Alex, drawing off her gloves. "You are feeling better, I see, Lizzie."

"Yes! Quite well again. And Lord Wayland here has been quite an amusing escort on the drive out."

Georgina smiled at Alex. "It was good of you to come, Alex. Such a grand addition to our luncheon party!"

"How could I resist the company of two such charming ladies?" said Alex, pouring Georgina a glass of wine. "And you, too, Hollingsworth. We did not have much chance for conversation Friday evening, and I had heard that you, too, were an army man."

Nicholas grinned. "Who has been spreading rumors about me? Yes, I was in the army, in Spain. Before I met Lizzie and settled to being a responsible family man."

"Ha!" said his wife, popping another onion into her mouth.

"I was told you were wounded at Alvaro," said Alex.

Nicholas's expression grew quite somber, and he reached for the wine. "Yes, I was. So were Lizzie's brother and his wife. A sad day for our family."

"A sad day for many," Alex agreed quietly. "I did hear that General Morecambe . . ."

"Gentlemen, please!" Georgina interrupted. "It is too lovely a day to spend in gloomy reminiscences. You will have Elizabeth and me in tears soon, and that will never do. I become quite red and blotchy when I cry. Save it for your club, please."

Alex laughed apologetically, and lifted Georgina's hand to his lips in a quick salute. "You are quite right, of course! We shall discuss whatever you and Lady Elizabeth choose."

Georgina beamed at him.

Nicholas scowled in mock despair. "We all know what *that* discussion will be—art."

"There is nothing wrong with art," said Elizabeth.

"Nothing at all," agreed Georgina. "Are you going to eat *all* those onions, Lizzie dear?"

Elizabeth prodded at the empty bowl with her fork. "I fear I already have. Do you think the innkeeper will bring some more?"

"I daresay he will," Georgina answered. "*I* shall not

be riding in the carriage back to London with you, though!" She reached over to spear a piece of roast chicken. "Speaking of art, did you see that egregious landscape Mrs. Sayers had displayed at her Venetian breakfast?"

"No, I didn't!" Elizabeth replied avidly. "She has been telling everyone that she has a Canaletto."

"Lizzie, if this was a Canaletto, I will eat my new pastel crayons! The light was not at all right . . ."

Nicholas and Alex exchanged subtle, despairing glances over their wineglasses.

Nicholas leaned closer and murmured to Alex under his breath as the ladies grew louder and more excited. "You see what I put up with every day, Wayland?"

"I do see," answered Alex.

"And you may wish to take this on for yourself?"

Alex studied Georgina's animated face, her glowing green eyes, the graceful flutter of her gesturing hands. "I think I very well might. How do you find it, being married to an artist?"

Nicholas grinned. "My dear chap," he said, "it is bloody *marvelous*."

"Your friends are very—animated," Alex said as they strolled along a country path after luncheon.

Georgina smiled. "Yes, they are. Quite out of the common way."

"That must be why you are such great friends."

"Hm?"

"You are rather out of the common way yourself."

Georgina studied him carefully, searching his expression for any kind of censure. She did not see any there, only open, honest humor. "Is that a compliment?"

"A very great one, I assure you."

"Then thank you. *You* are rather out of the common way yourself." She sat down on a fallen log, tucking the skirts of her Pomona-green carriage dress about her. "Elizabeth and Nicholas are the only people I feel I can truly be myself around. And now you, of course."

He sat down next to her, at a proper distance but close enough that she could feel the warmth from his shoulder and thigh.

She longed to rest her head against that shoulder. But she feared he would think her fast, even more so than he might already, so she simply folded her hands in her lap instead.

"Do you mean that, Georgina?" he said quietly, almost eagerly. "That you feel able to be yourself with me?"

"Yes. You are not at all what I always suppose dukes to be like."

"Oh? What do you suppose?"

"That dukes are stuffy, toplofty creatures with too much starch in their cravats. Or that they are arrogant lechers!"

Alex laughed. "I am not like that, then?"

"Not at all. You are one of the least toplofty people I have ever met. And not at all arrogant or a lecher!"

"Well, I was not brought up to be a duke. I was brought up for the army, just as if had I had a younger brother, he would have been brought up for the Church."

Georgina picked up a leaf that had fallen onto her skirt, and twirled it around idly. "Tell me, Alex, did you like being in the army?"

"Very much. I was never terribly comfortable in Society, and my parents were very social people, always trotting my brother and me, and later my baby sister, out for their suppers and card parties. It was a relief to escape that, to be among men who valued discipline and camaraderie above witticisms and a fine leg for dancing."

Georgina grinned at him. "And no ladies expecting you to do the pretty?"

Alex laughed. "There *were* ladies about, to be sure, but they were soldiers' wives, and accustomed to a less exacting society." He paused for a moment, then went on thoughtfully, "I did not like it all, of course. Battle is such a hellish thing, and the times between could be deadly dull. But in many ways it was a life that suited me, like trying to uphold a peerage could not. I do miss it."

Georgina feared she knew of what he spoke. She would hate it if she were forced to give up the art she loved for a more narrow, constricted existence.

Such as that of being a duchess, for example.

She shrugged off these misgivings, and said, "Well, I think you will make a superb duke. From all accounts, a far better one than your brother!" Then she startled guiltily. "Oh! How very rude of me, to say things like that about your family. Sometimes I do speak without thinking."

Alex laughed. "Georgina, what you said is far milder than what I have said myself about Damian! And what I have heard my mother say." He shook his head. "I daresay I may be a better duke than poor Damian was. As much as I dislike it."

"Alex, I . . ." Georgina broke off, not certain what it was she had wanted to say.

"There is one thing that I appreciate about being a duke, and giving up my commission."

"Oh? What is that?"

"Coming back to England and meeting you, of course."

She smiled at him, and gave in at last to the temptation to rest her head on his strong shoulder. He smelled wonderful, of wool and starch and soap, and of Alex. "That is something I, too, appreciate."

They sat together quietly for a while, warm in the sun, listening to the birds and the distant voices from the inn yard.

And Georgina knew that there was one other thing she greatly appreciated, a gift that Alex had given her that she had so lacked in life. Had so craved.

Stillness.

But finally the sun slipped below the tops of the trees, and Georgina bestirred herself to rise. "We should be going, I suppose. We are meant to attend Lady Carteret's musicale this evening."

Alex rose beside her, and took her hand in his as they turned their steps back toward the inn. "I suppose your friends will be looking for us."

Georgina, thrilled to her very soul at the feel of her hand in his, said in a daze, "I doubt it. Lizzie is probably napping, which she does every afternoon now. She and Nick can go home in the barouche, if you will ride with me in the curricle."

"I should be delighted."

"Good! I do need to practice my driving a bit more."

"Georgina." Alex tugged on her hand, halting their steps. "Are you certain you wish to drive in this race?"

"Of course! I made the wager. I can hardly decamp now."

"Will it not be very dangerous?"

Georgina looked up at him quizzically, at his frown and the hard set of his jaw. "Why, Alex. Are you *worried* about me?"

"Yes, by Jove, I am!" he cried.

"That is so very dear of you, to worry. I assure you, though, I am an experienced driver. Even though I can be a bit reckless at times, I am not stupid. If something feels not right on the day of the race, I will not drive."

"I know you are not stupid. Far, far from it. It is only . . ." His hand tightened on hers. "If anything were to happen to you, Georgina, when I have only just found you, I think I should run mad."

Chapter Eleven

The day of the race was bright and clear and warm, perfect for the crowds of *ton*nish people who flocked to the old post road in carriages and on horseback. Many had brought picnics, and one enterprising soul was even selling lemonade and sugared almonds.

Lady Kate, on her lead and safely ensconced in the open carriage with Elizabeth and Nicholas, ran from side to side, barking at all the excitement and looking frantically for her mistress.

Georgina, already settled into Nicholas's curricle at the starting point of the race, tried to remain oblivious to all the noise and commotion. She absently smoothed the skirt of her new sapphire blue carriage dress, focusing on the road ahead.

She pretended not to see Lord Pynchon, his balding dome of a head glinting in the sunlight, as he smirked at her from his own equipage. She had greeted him politely when she had first arrived, and she had seen the fear in his eyes, hidden beneath the arrogance.

Alex stood next to her left side, tall and handsome, one hand resting near her knee.

She tried to ignore him, as well. It would never do

to be distracted by the way his hair curled back from his forehead while she was trying to stay on the road!

"I wish you had let me loan you Scylla and Charybdis," he muttered, glaring at Lord Pynchon. "They are the steadiest goers."

Georgina smiled without taking her eyes from the road. "I know they are, Alex, and I vow I would have loved to drive them! But you would not want to cause an *on dit* by loaning me your cattle."

"Do you think people would say I had wicked intentions toward you if you were seen with my horses?"

"Do you have wicked intentions?"

He leered up at her comically. "Of course! Don't *you* have them toward *me*?"

Georgina laughed. "Naughty man! You are trying to distract me. Now, go over and sit with Elizabeth and Nicholas, please."

"Very well." His hand touched hers briefly, warmly, hidden in the folds of her dress. "Georgina," he said solemnly. "Do be very careful."

"Yes. I will. Then we shall all have a lovely champagne supper after, to celebrate my great victory!"

Alex went to the Hollingsworths' carriage, and stepped up to take his seat beside Lady Kate. She clambered up onto his lap, kissing his chin joyously, and he held her paw and waved it in Georgina's direction.

She waved back, then gathered up her reins as Alex's friend Freddie Marlow stepped up to the mark. He fired off the starting shot, and Georgina burst away down the road, neck and neck with Lord Pynchon.

The shouts of the crowd rang in her ears as she urged the horses to ever greater speed. "Come on, my beauties!" she shouted. "You can do it, I know you can!"

The exhilaration of speed sang in her veins, and all she could see was the finishing line just ahead. It was close, so close, and she was so far ahead of Lord Pynchon . . .

Then there was a tremendous jolt off to her right side, a jarring thud as the curricle tilted precariously.

Georgina felt herself falling, an inexorable slide from the curricle's seat. She fell faster and faster, reaching out to grasp something, *anything*, but finding only air beneath her hand.

She landed then, a hard fall on her back. Vaguely, as if from a great distance and through a thick fog, she heard shouts. A dog barking. A woman screaming— Elizabeth screaming.

Alex's face swam into view above her, pale and drawn.

"Georgina!" he cried. "Can you hear me? Are you well?"

"I—believe I am well," she gasped. Indeed, she felt only numb. Shocked. How could it have ended this way?

"Let me help you to rise." He slid one arm gently beneath her, drawing her up.

Georgina screamed at the sharp pain in her shoulder. Then everything faded to darkness, and she felt no more.

The doctor had at last arrived to see Georgina. Alex, from where he lurked in the darkened corridor outside her room, had only a glimpse of her flame-colored hair against a white sheet before the door shut again. Only Elizabeth was allowed in the room with Georgina; Nicholas and several concerned spectators to the ill-fated race were gathered in the White Hart's common room, drinking and waiting.

Alex had refused to leave his place outside that door.

He sat down on the straight-backed chair that had been placed there for him, and buried his face in his hands.

No matter how tightly he shut his eyes, though, he could not blot out the sight of Georgina, so white and still in his arms. Her scream had been horrifying before she fainted, and her arm, before he had bound it up with his waistcoat, had lain at a sharp angle.

Alex had faced battle many times, had had horses shot from beneath him, had seen death at the end of a French bayonet. He had never been so terrified in all his life as he had been to see Georgina's curricle smash, and her lying so still on the ground.

If she was lost to him, after only just finding her . . .

The door to her room opened, interrupting his dark thoughts, and Elizabeth emerged. Her face was reddened from crying, but she seemed composed.

"How is she?" Alex asked her desperately.

"Alex!" cried Elizabeth. "I did not see you. Have you been here in the dark all this time?"

"'Tis of no matter. Tell me what the doctor said."

"He said she will be well. She has a dislocated shoulder, and her arm is bruised. We will have to wait for her to wake to be sure her head is right, but he thinks there is no cause for worry."

"Her arm—her painting," Alex said, his tongue seemingly unable to form complete sentences.

"She will make a full recovery. She must only be careful for a few weeks, which will surely make her wild! Georgina is never happy but when she has a paintbrush in hand."

Alex laughed in utter relief and joy. Georgina would recover! She was not lost.

"Will you not come downstairs with me now?" Elizabeth said gently. "You should have something to eat, or at least some wine."

"No, I want to wait here. Georgina may have need of me."

Elizabeth took his arm, firmly urging him toward the stairs. "She is in good hands now, and she has taken some laudanum. You will be of no use to her when she is awake and *does* need you, if you are ill. Now, come with me. We will have some supper."

Alex went with her reluctantly. "Are you certain *you* are well, Lady Elizabeth? You look rather tired."

"I am, a bit. It has been a very long day, but the babe is quiet now. Earlier she was kicking and rolling fiercely."

"She?"

"Oh, yes. I am sure it must be a girl, and there is only one name for her, with all her energy. Georgina."

"Indeed." Alex smiled. "I would have thought the world full with only one."

"Georgina," a soft voice called. "Georgie dear, can you hear me?"

Georgina's eyelids felt weighted, as if by lead. She could not open them, or even talk through a mouth gone sticky. She opened her hand, and ran her fingers along the soft linen sheet beneath her.

A bed? When had someone brought her home? And what of the race? Had she lost? What had happened?

Then she remembered. The accident; falling from the curricle. Alex coming to her, lifting her. The awful pain from her shoulder.

She slowly lifted her heavy hand to touch that shoulder. She found the gauzy feel of bandages there, holding her immobile.

"She moved!" cried the voice. "I believe she is awake. Georgina?"

Georgina forced her eyes to open, to focus on the woman who sat beside her. "Lizzie?"

"You *are* awake!" Elizabeth said. "Praise be. I was so worried."

"W-water?" Georgina managed to croak.

"Oh, yes, of course!" Elizabeth held a goblet to Georgina's lips, holding her head as she drank thirstily.

Sated, Georgina fell back against the pile of pillows. "How long have I been—asleep?"

"Several hours, dear."

Georgina turned her head toward the one small window, and saw that it was night. Only the lamp beside the bed gave any light. "Hours?"

"Yes. The wheel of the curricle caught in a rut, and you were thrown from it. Remember? You dislocated your shoulder, and the doctor set it while you were unconscious. He gave you some laudanum for the pain. Are you in any pain?"

"Not at all. I am only so very tired."

"Then you must go back to sleep! We will leave you."

"We?"

Elizabeth gestured toward the doorway, and only then did Georgina see the two men hovering there in the shadows. Nicholas and Alex both looked distinctly worse for wear, their hair on end as if they had run their hands through it, their clothes rumpled.

Georgina smiled weakly. "You two look dreadful,"

she said. "A dislocated shoulder hardly calls for a deathbed vigil!"

Nicholas laughed, while Alex shuffled his feet ruefully.

"We did not know if your head was to rights," Elizabeth explained. "You looked so very pale, and your breathing was quite shallow."

"Well, I am fine now. Where are we?"

"The White Hart. And we shall *stay* here until you are completely recovered."

"I will be completely well by morning, I am sure. But you should be in bed, Lizzie. This cannot be good for the baby." Georgina looked to Nicholas. "Take your wife away now, Nick, and make her rest, so that I can get some sleep."

"Happily, Georgie." Nicholas came to help Elizabeth to her feet, and kissed Georgina's cheek gently. "You gave us such a fright today."

"I apologize, my dears. I promise I shall never do it again. Now, good night!"

"I shall look in on you later," Elizabeth warned.

As they left the room, Alex came to take their place, sitting down in Elizabeth's empty chair.

Georgina reached for him with her good hand, and he took it between both of his. His lips were warm as he lowered them to her palm.

"I was so scared, Georgina," he whispered. "When you fainted away in my arms . . ."

"You, Alex? Who led charges into vast regiments of murderous Frenchies? Scared by a woman's faint?"

"Yes," he answered simply.

Despite the sleepy haze she was in, Georgina wanted to cry. She wanted to cry, and laugh, and shout her thanks to God for sending her this dear man.

But she was far too weak to do any such thing. Instead, she just squeezed his hand. "You take such care of me, Alex. I do not deserve you."

"You deserve much better than me."

"Oh, no, my dear. You are a good, kind, brave soul. I am wild and scatty. Everyone says so, and today you had the proof."

"You are far braver than I," he answered. "Fearless, in a way I never have been."

"Alex . . ."

"This is not time for declarations. You are ill. But you must know, Georgina, how greatly I admire you."

"As I admire you. Of course this is a time for declarations!"

Alex pressed one finger against her lips, stilling her words. "I did not want to press you so soon, Georgina. But your accident has shown me that there is not time to waste in this life. Perhaps, when you are recovered, you would consent to go with me to Fair Oak, and meet my mother and sister."

Georgina was almost shocked speechless. No one had ever invited her to meet his *mother* before. That was for sweet young virgins, for intendeds, for brides.

Oh, great heaven. Alex wanted to *marry* her. To make her a respectable woman, a duchess.

Whatever could she do?

"You—you want me to meet your family?" she stammered.

"Yes. There are things, many things, you should know before you commit yourself to—to anything," he said slowly. "Fair Oak is my home, the best place for you to make any decisions. So will you come?"

Georgina's mind raced furiously. Alex's mother was no doubt quite a high stickler, being a dowager duchess. Would Georgina's manners be acceptable to her? Would her clothes? Her past? Her art?

Whatever would she pack to visit a ducal estate? She would have to visit a *modiste*.

"Georgina?" he said, breaking into her dazed and scattered musings. "Will you? Please?"

"Oh, yes," Georgina replied. "I would be honored to meet your family."

Then she swallowed hard, past the knot of trepidation in her throat.

Despite her exhaustion, and the pain that was once again creeping up on her, Georgina lay awake long after Alex left her. Things were moving so very quickly now, her head spun from it. It was as if the moment of her accident, the second that she had thought her life to be over, had changed everything, had propelled them forward.

Alex's intentions *were* honorable. He wanted her to see his home, meet his family. Be very certain before she "committed" herself to anything.

She had thought that perhaps, just perhaps, he had had serious intentions. Maybe she had even hoped it, deep down in her heart. She had known she would never consent to be his, or anyone's, mistress, so if that had been his wish she would have had to break off all contact with him.

She had intended to never marry again, of course. She so loved her life, her work, her independence. She had thought she would never again meet a man who could respect all that—until Alex.

Georgina had watched him on the night of Elizabeth's *salon*, as he looked at her paintings. He had looked at them with appreciation and respect, had listened to her as she spoke of her work. He was never condescending or dismissive, as so many of her so-called "admirers" were.

Alex was a very special man indeed.

Georgina did have some misgivings over his words that there were "things she should know." But surely there was no harm in just *meeting* his family, seeing his home? If his family disapproved of her, or if she felt uncomfortable with them, it would be better to know.

There could be no harm in this. None at all. Surely.

Reassured, Georgina slid down beneath her nest of blankets, and gave in to her sleepiness, warm, comforted, and full of delicious anticipation.

Chapter Twelve

"Are you quite certain you are recovered enough for this journey?" Elizabeth asked worriedly, as she sat on Georgina's bed and watched Georgina and Daisy sorting through gowns and hats. "Does your shoulder not still pain you?"

Georgina laughed. "You make it sound as if I am going to the pyramids of Egypt! It is only a fortnight in the country, and I promise I will not go riding or driving." She held up a lavender-striped muslin gown, with a low, square neckline trimmed in silver lace. "This is not too daring, is it?"

Elizabeth shook her head. "Perfectly respectable. But, Georgie, I still feel this is too sudden. It has only been nine days since your accident. You still need to rest. Could you not put off this trip until next month?"

"If I did that, it would have to wait until after the exhibition at the Royal Academy. Then Alex will have to supervise something or other at his farm, hay I believe, and guests would be a nuisance. And then it will be time for me to go home to Italy." She held up a white straw bonnet trimmed with yellow feathers and streamers. "What about this?"

"Lovely. It will go with your yellow walking dress. But I still think . . ."

"Lizzie." Georgina placed the bonnet back in its box, and went to sit beside Elizabeth. "Is there something you are not telling me? Do you have some sort of—misgivings about Alex?"

"No! I like him. He seems a very good sort of man."

"Yes. I think so, too."

"We had such a nice talk before your race, and I am sure he thinks very highly of you. As he ought!"

"Then, where is the difficulty?"

"It is not a great one, by any means. It is only— well, you know that his brother was very careless, and frittered away a great part of his family's fortune."

Georgina's hands felt suddenly cold. She tucked them into her lap, and somehow managed to ask, "Are you saying, Lizzie, that you think Alex is after my money?"

"No!" Elizabeth cried. "No. You and I have met many men over the years, and have seen many of our friends' romances flourish or wither. I think we could tell when a man is sincere, unless he is a very good actor. Which Lord Wayland is not! I think he is fond of *you*, not your money."

Georgina nodded. "I believe that, as well." Did she not?

"But he did seem quite shocked when I told him of the extent of your legacy from Mr. Beaumont."

"Alex is—a very proud man," Georgina said slowly, thinking aloud.

"Yes. Prouder even than Nick, I fear."

"It would be difficult for him to feel beholden in any way, even though I would never see it that way. I would—if we were married, I would see it as an equal sharing."

"Then, you must make *him* see it that way, as well! There is nothing else for it, if you truly want him."

"Oh, yes. I believe I do." Georgina bit her lip. "It will not be easy."

"No. Not at all."

"Nothing ever worth having was easily come by."

"How true." Elizabeth smiled, obviously recalling her own rocky courtship. "How *very* true. You must promise me one thing, though, Georgie."

"What is that?"

"Well, my determined friend, that when you become a duchess, in the grandest ceremony ever seen in England, *I* shall give the wedding breakfast."

"Shall we see Fair Oak soon?" Georgina asked, straining for a glimpse of whatever might be down the lane.

They were riding in Alex's curricle, with the baggage coach, accompanied by Elizabeth's maid Daisy, behind, since Georgina had declared that traveling in closed carriages made her feel ill. She was very glad of this, too, for the country they had traveled through was exquisite, a rich, verdant green, and their journey had been most pleasant. They had chatted of many things, and had been completely at ease in each other's company.

Lady Kate, too, was at ease, sitting between them, barking at birds overhead and the occasional fox in the hedgerows.

Now, however, they had turned down the winding, tree-lined lane that led to Fair Oak itself, and Georgina was overcome with an uncharacteristic nervousness. She straightened the small net veil of her fashionable hat, and smoothed the skirt of her new lilac carriage dress.

"Georgina!" Alex said. "Never say you are nervous."

"Not at all!" Georgina protested. "Well—perhaps just a bit."

"My mother and sister will not eat you," he laughed. "In fact, I would be willing to wager that they are far more anxious about meeting you than you are about meeting them."

"Surely not! Why would a dowager duchess and her daughter be anxious about meeting a mere missus, an artist?"

"For exactly that reason. You are quite famous, you know. Mother and Emily have lived quietly in the country for many years. Their only news comes from the neighbors who travel into Town, and from less than respectable newspapers, which Mother has a guilty pleasure in. When I wrote to her that you were coming, she wrote back full of excitement."

Georgina was flustered, and oddly pleased. "She did?"

"Oh, yes. She has heard of you, you see, has read of your art and your gowns, and who knows what. She fears Fair Oak will not be grand enough for you."

"What nonsense!"

"I assure you, 'tis true." They turned a corner of the lane, and Alex pointed ahead with his carriage whip. "There is the house now."

Georgina looked to where he pointed, and gasped. Fair Oak might be too much of an architectural mish-mash to be truly *grand*, but it was very impressive. It towered above the drive and the small park, dark and imposing, looking down on the world through mullioned Tudor windows. Stone gargoyles kept watch from the corners of the roof.

It was a bit neglected, to be sure, just as Georgina

had feared. Ivy crept willy-nilly over the half-timbered walls, which in turn needed a fresh coat of paint. The stone front steps were cracked, and the fountain at the center of the drive was dry.

But these were things easily fixed, and the house itself was lovely. It seemed to give off an aura of the many, many years of family life lived within its walls, of all the love, laughter, quarrels, births, marriages, and deaths it had seen.

It seemed to welcome her.

As the carriage drew to a halt, the front door opened and a young woman stepped out. She could only be Alex's sister, for she had a look of him about her oval face, her straight nose, and her blue eyes. Her golden curls were drawn back and tied with a blue ribbon, that matched her rather faded muslin dress.

She smiled at them, clapping her hands in delight when they descended from the carriage and came to greet her.

"Alex, you are home at last!" she cried, throwing her arms about his neck. "Mother has been asking for you every moment since breakfast."

"You are looking well, Em!" he said, lifting her off of her feet until she squealed.

"I *am* well, now that you are come! And this must be Mrs. Beaumont. I know her from the sketches in the newspapers." Emily stepped back from her brother, and held out her hand to Georgina. "How do you do, Mrs. Beaumont."

"How do you do, Lady Emily. I am so happy to meet you at last, after hearing so much about you."

"Not as happy as we are to meet you! And is this your sweet doggie? I will have the maid take her directly to your room. But how ill-mannered I am being, keeping you out here on the doorstep! Mother has

sent for some tea, and she is so eager to meet you."
She leaned forward and whispered, "She has changed
her gown quite five times this morning."

Georgina laughed, feeling much better about the
four times she herself had changed. "Then I will be
sure to compliment her on it."

The interior of Fair Oak was much the same as
its exterior. The foyer was very grand, crowned by a
sweeping staircase and a dome fresco of Grecian
nymphs and cupids cavorting against a blue sky. The
floor was a lovely, intricate parquet. But there was no
rug, no paintings (though there were darker squares
on the blue silk wallpaper where some had once
hung), and the only furniture was a rather battered
mahogany table. The table was itself bare of all orna-
ment except a lovely arrangement of early roses and
wildflowers.

"Mother is waiting in the morning room. I hope that
you do not mind that we don't receive you in the grand
drawing room," said Emily, hurrying across the vast
foyer to open one of the many closed doors. "The
morning room is warmer, and so much *cozier!*"

"Certainly I do not mind," answered Georgina. "I
do so much prefer cozy to grand any day."

Emily gave her a relieved smile. "Wonderful!" Then
she turned and called, "Mother! Here are Alex and
Mrs. Beaumont at last."

Alex held out his arm to Georgina, and she accepted it, looking up at him through her veil. He had
been quiet since they entered the house, and Georgina
had sensed him watching her closely, gauging her reaction to his home.

Or at least she hoped it was her reaction he was
judging, and not her behavior.

She leaned closer, and whispered, "Your house is beautiful."

"Thank you," he whispered back. "You do not think it too vast, or old-fashioned? Or too—empty?"

"It is certainly vast." Georgina glanced around the furniture-less foyer again. "And perhaps a bit empty. But it has such a welcoming warmth to it. I quite like it."

He smiled then, and laid his free hand over hers. "I have often felt the same about Fair Oak."

"Alexander!" a voice called. "You are not going to keep our guest standing about out there all day, are you?"

"No, Mother." Alex led Georgina into the morning room. "Of course not."

"Yes, I thought I had raised you with better manners. The army, though, might have obliterated them. Come closer, now, so that I can see you."

Georgina's hand tightened on Alex's arm as they approached the woman seated by the fire. She felt a small frisson of nerves, an unaccustomed unease.

The Dowager Duchess of Wayland had the look of her children about her. Her hair was a dark gold, somewhere between the light brown of Alex and the guinea gold of Emily, caught up in soft curls beneath a lacy gray cap. She had the same nose and decided jaw, and the hand she held out for her son to kiss was long, slim, and pale.

The eyes that looked up at Georgina were the same piercing, brilliant blue.

"Are you going to introduce me to our lovely guest?" she said.

"Mother," Alex said. "May I present Mrs. Georgina Beaumont? Mrs. Beaumont, my mother, Dorothy, Dowager Duchess of Wayland."

Georgina gave the elegant curtsy she had been per-
fecting before her mirror. "How do you do, Your
Grace."

Dorothy laughed merrily. "Oh, please, none of that
nonsense in my own home! No calling me Your Grace,
if you please. Do be seated, Mrs. Beaumont." She
glanced at her son and daughter, who were hovering
beside her chair. "The two of you sit down, as well.
You have both grown so tall, that I cannot talk to you
without getting a pain in my neck."

Georgina laughed, and sat down in a small satin
upholstered chair opposite the dowager duchess, all
her fears almost forgotten. The duchess was obviously
cut from the same easy cloth as her son and daughter,
and not a high stickler at all.

That was excellent. Georgina had never fared well
with high sticklers.

Emily soon had them all situated with tea and cakes,
and tried to tuck her mother's lap robe closer about
her.

"Are you quite warm enough, Mother?" she said.
"Perhaps I should build up the fire some more."

"I am fine, Em! Do quit fussing, dear." Dorothy
smiled at Georgina over her teacup. "I want to hear
all about our guest. Emily and I have been reading all
the London papers, Mrs. Beaumont, and we understand you are quite famous."

Georgina laughed. "I would not say *famous*. Yet."

"She is being too modest, Mother," said Alex. "Everyone knows who she is, and every family in the *ton*
clamors for a portrait by her. Her latest client was
Lady Harriet Granville."

Emily's eyes were shining. "Oh, you must tell us all
about your life, Mrs. Beaumont! It must be so very

exciting to be in London, and on the Continent. I have never even left the neighborhood."

"Oh, but I think *your* life so fascinating!" Georgina protested. "A lovely home like this, being surrounded by people you have always known—it must be so very comfortable. Much more so than my rackety life!"

Dorothy patted her daughter's hand. "We do truly have a lovely home and fine neighbors, Mrs. Beaumont. Yet I fear Emily longs for operas and balls and bookshops."

"Who would not?" Emily sighed. "You must tell me every detail of Town life, Mrs. Beaumont, I beg you."

"Em!" Dorothy scolded. "I fear, Mrs. Beaumont, you will think my daughter quite pushing."

"Not at all," protested Georgina. "I will gladly tell anything you wish to know, since you have been so kind as to share your home with me for a few days. I could even do a small portrait of you, Lady Emily, if you like."

Emily almost bounced on her seat in excitement. "Oh, would you, Mrs. Beaumont! I will be quite the envy of the whole neighborhood."

"It would be my pleasure. You are such a pretty subject! Though I fear it would be a poor effort compared to the painting you have over there."

Georgina nodded toward the portrait that hung above the fireplace. It was a luminous family scene, of a younger Dorothy, a handsome blond gentleman who must be her husband, two little boys, and an infant in pink ruffles. They were gathered beneath a tree, with Fair Oak in the background.

"Is it a Gainsborough?" she asked.

"Yes," answered Dorothy, turning a fond eye on the

painting. "It *is* lovely. That was quite the happiest time of my life, Mrs. Beaumont, with my dearest William and all our little ones. I insisted that we keep it, despite all the . . ." Her voice trailed away, and her gaze fell from the painting to her lap. "I do apologize, Mrs. Beaumont, for chattering on so, when you must be tired from your journey. Emily can show you to your room."

"Thank you, Lady Wayland," Georgina said quietly. "I am a bit tired."

"Alex's bumpy driving is enough to make anyone so!" Emily said, coming over to take Georgina's arm.

"Ah! You see how I am maligned by my family," Alex protested with good humor. "Tell them what an excellent driver I am, I beg you."

"Well," Georgina said consideringly. "You *are* a better driver than I, but as I am always oversetting myself, that can scarce be in your favor."

"You drive yourself, Mrs. Beaumont?" Emily asked in wonder. "I have a pony cart, but that is not very dashing."

"I do have a curricle," Georgina answered. "But I fear I may not drive for a while, as I have had a mishap."

"A mishap?" said Emily.

"Yes, and she is only just recovered," Alex said sternly. "So see that she rests, Em."

"Oh, I shall!" said Emily, drawing Georgina toward the door. "Just as soon as she tells me everything about it."

Dorothy only had time to call out, "We shall see you at supper, then, Mrs. Beaumont," before the door shut, and Emily had Georgina halfway up the stairs.

"Tell me, then, Mother," Alex said, when Georgina and Emily were gone and things were once again settled in the morning room. "What do you think of Mrs. Beaumont?"

Dorothy took a slow sip of her fresh cup of tea. "She is certainly very beautiful."

"Yes. She is."

"We expected no less of her, after all we had read in the newspapers. No doubt she is also quite talented, as well, if people like Hary-O Granville have her paint their portraits." Dorothy glanced up at the treasured Gainsborough, and went on musingly, while Alex sat silently and listened to her. "She has no title. But then, what did an exalted title ever gain us but trouble?"

She laughed humorlessly.

"Her father was the son of a baronet," Alex said.

"Oh, there is no doubt that her connections are *respectable*, I'm sure, or you would have known better than to pursue her seriously. She is wealthy?"

Alex swallowed. "Yes."

"Hm. We do need the blunt, of course. You see how I have been forced to become practical and cynical since your father died?"

"Mother," Alex murmured. "I am so very sorry . . ."

Dorothy laid her hand over her son's. "My dear, do not apologize again, I beg you! There was nothing at all you could have done. The army needed you. You were far away, and your brother, rest his naughty soul, was the duke. There was nothing anyone could have done. You have always been the best of sons to me, and the best of brothers to Emily."

"I have always tried to be."

"And so, I suspect, you will always go on being. You have brought an interesting lady to Fair Oak. She will make you a fine bride, I think."

"Because she is rich?" Alex asked quietly, his jaw taut.

Dorothy shook her head. "Surely you know me better than that? Because you obviously care for her. As your father cared for me, the daughter of an impoverished, gambling wastrel of a viscount."

"I do care for Georgina. Very much. The money only—complicates matters."

"How so? I think that that is your pride talking, but I will not scruple to say that the money will be useful. Without it we could not give Em a proper London Season, which she so deserves. She has looked after me and this estate, has shouldered burdens no young girl should have to." Dorothy paused thoughtfully. "I will admit I had hopes you would look kindly on one of the neighbors' daughters. But it is obvious that you love this Mrs. Beaumont, and I have always wanted nothing but my childrens' happiness. And I suspect she is just the woman to make you happy."

Alex laughed, a profound relief sweeping through him. "I know that she is. And I pray that I can make her happy, as well."

"Oh, I have no doubt that you can! A handsome man such as yourself. I must say I am quite relieved that you did not bring some giggling miss we do not know! We have always been such an eccentric family, I fear we would have shocked such a creature most terribly. The neighbors are used to us, but I am sure London girls would not be."

"Mother! Surely you must know I would never have chosen such a girl for a wife? Why, all the little debutantes looked at me with abject fear that I might ask them to dance, I am so old and weather-beaten."

"I would wager their mamas would have delighted to have you dance with their darlings, an eligible duke like you," Dorothy said with satisfaction. "I would also wager that your Mrs. Beaumont never shrank in 'abject fear' from anything in her life."

"No, she is quite fearless. She is much like you in that respect, Mother."

Dorothy laughed. "Excellent! She will need much courage to take *us* on. Tell me, Alex, does she ride?"

"I am sure she does, though I have not seen her. She drives like a very demon."

"I do like her more and more. Perhaps she would be interested in joining the local hunt, once you are married and settled."

"Now, Mother," Alex warned. "I have not yet made an offer, and when I do it is by no means certain that she will accept."

"Nonsense! She likes you every bit as much as you like her. And now, as we are speaking of the hunt, help me into my infernal chair. I must be changing my frock for supper."

Alex slid his arms around his mother's shoulders and beneath her frail legs, and lifted her easily from her armchair before the fire into her wheeled bath chair. Dorothy Kenton had lost the use of her legs ten years before, when she had been thrown from her horse during a wild hunt.

"I do hope you will like your room," Emily said, leading the way up the stairs and down a dim corridor. "It is our very nicest guest chamber."

"Then, I'm sure I *shall* like it," Georgina answered. "Your whole house is quite lovely."

"It was once," said Emily, with a flash of bitterness. "And the Queen's Room still is. See?"

She threw open a door, and they stepped into an enchanted room.

Georgina could have imagined herself in the Sleeping Beauty's chamber of one hundred years' sleep. The bed of elaborately carved dark wood was enormous, hung about with deep red velvet curtains embroidered in gold. More red draperies hung at the tall windows, making the room into a rich tent beneath the carved ceiling.

A fire danced in a marble grate, while Lady Kate napped before its warmth. Daisy was already unpacking and hanging gowns in the large wardrobe.

"Oh," Georgina sighed. "It *is* grand, Lady Emily."

"Please! Do call me just Emily." Emily sat down beside Lady Kate, and rubbed the ecstatic dog's tummy. "I hope," she went on shyly, "that we shall be friends."

"I know we shall." Georgina tossed her muff, gloves, and hat onto the high bed, and sat next to Emily and Lady Kate. "And you must call me Georgina. Or Georgie, as all my friends do."

"Georgie," Emily repeated. "What a nice name! I cannot tell you how very, very happy I am that you have come here, Georgie. We have not had visitors in such a long time, not since I was a child really."

"Truly? Did your parents or late brother never have company here?"

Emily snorted inelegantly. "Damian *never* came to the country, if he could possibly help it. My parents used to have parties here all the time, until Mother's accident. Things became very quiet then."

"Her accident?"

"Did you not know? She cannot walk. When I was eight years old, there was a riding accident, and she has been confined to her chair ever since. After Damian's death, I became convinced our family is cursed when it comes to horses."

Georgina was shocked. "I confess I had no idea! She seems so healthy."

"Oh, she is! And her mind is sharper than ever. She simply cannot walk. She would be happy to know that you could not tell it; she so hates pity."

"I certainly do not pity her. Rather, I admire her."

"Excellent! For we certainly admire you, you know."

Georgina laughed, causing Lady Kate to sit up and bark at her. "That is most flattering, but how can you admire me when we have only just met?"

"We have read all about you, as I said. The routs you attend, your paintings, your clothes . . ." Emily stood and went to examine the gowns Daisy had laid out on the bed. She carefully touched the skirt of a cream-and-gold striped satin gown. "Your clothes are truly wondrous. Even Lady Anders, our neighbor, has nothing so fine!"

Georgina rose, and came to hold up the gown, measuring it against Emily's blonde curls and fair complexion. "You will have far finer, I am sure, when you make your bow."

Emily shook her head, turning away to examine a violet silk. "Even if I did go to London, I would have nothing so grand. Mother says white is what a young lady wears." She pulled a face. "I loathe white! I should much prefer a gown like this one."

"I quite agree about white; it can be rather insipid, except on a very few fortunate women. I always looked ridiculous in it! But that gown is too old for you. The blue color you are wearing looks very well on you, and would be quite suitable for your age."

Emily shrugged again, obviously uncomfortable with talk of her own attire and forthcoming debut.

Georgina thought it best to change the subject.

"Tell me, why is this room called the Queen's Room?"

Emily brightened a bit. "Because Queen Elizabeth slept here, hundreds of years ago! It was right after she gifted the first duke with his title. She stayed here for four days, and slept in this very bed."

"Truly?" Georgina cried. She kicked off her shoes and clambered onto the bed, climbing over her gowns to lie down full length against the bolsters. "Queen Elizabeth lay right here, where I am now?"

Emily laughed. "Yes! Well, perhaps not *exactly* there, but very near."

"How very exciting! I have never slept in a queen's bed before."

Emily sat next to her, and Lady Kate leaped up to join in the excitement. "It is said that she haunts Fair Oak. That every year, on the anniversary of her stay here, she walks the corridors again."

"Have you ever seen her?"

Emily shook her head. "Never. Though when I was a child, I used to sneak in here every year on the day, to hide under the bed and wait for her. Alas, she never appeared. My brother Damian tried to scare me with tales that *he* had seen her, as well as her headless mother Queen Anne, but I never believed him. He was usually in his cups, you see, and therefore all his visions were suspect."

"And Alex? Did he ever see her?"

Emily laughed. "Dear, military, proud, rational Alex? He, of course, says it is all a Banbury tale."

"Hm. Well, I think it is all quite bone-chilling, like something in a novel. My own house in Italy dates back to medieval times, but I have never heard a report of a ghost there."

Emily looked down at her lap, suddenly shy. "Will you—will you tell me about Italy sometime, Georgie?"

"I will gladly tell you more than you ever wanted to know!" Georgina answered. "I am always eager to talk about my home. But should we not be dressing for supper?"

Emily glanced over at the small clock on the mantle. "I had not realized it had grown so very late! Yes, I must be going. But . . ." Impulsively, the girl kissed Georgina's cheek. "Oh, Georgie, I *am* happy you have come here with my brother."

"So am I, Emily," Georgina answered quietly. "Very happy indeed."

Chapter Thirteen

"What do you think of Fair Oak now, Georgina?"
Alex asked as he and Georgina strolled about the
overgrown garden after supper.

Georgina turned to look back at the house, serene
in the pale moonlight. The doors to the terrace were
open, spilling out firelight, and Dorothy and Emily
were seated there with their embroidery. It all looked
so comfortable and cozy, and in the darkness there
was no sign of overgrown ivy or peeling paint.

"I think it is lovely," she answered truthfully. "I do
believe it is the first English country house I have ever
visited that feels like a true home. Not just a showcase
for country weekends, or a place to come shooting."

"It is a home," Alex agreed. "My parents came here
soon after they were wed, and seldom lived anyplace
else. They only went to their London house for a few
weeks every Season, then hurried back. My mother
adored the country, where she could be near her
horses and her dogs. And her children, of course,
though we were a distant third!"

Georgina laughed. "Oh, yes!" They had come to a
small summerhouse, and she went inside to sit down

on one of the benches. Some of the roof slats were missing, and moonlight fell in silvery bars across the leaf-strewn floor. "Emily told me there were often parties here when she was a child."

Alex sat down beside her, stretching out his long legs before him. "Yes. Just because my parents preferred the country, that does not mean they were in any way unsociable. They belonged to the local hunt— my mother was the only female member for quite a long time. They would give the hunt breakfasts, and the hunt ball. And there was a grand ball every Christmas, which Damian and I, and later Emily, were expected to attend for an hour."

"Only an hour?"

"Quite long enough to gorge ourselves on sweetmeats and make ourselves very ill! Damian especially was rather greedy."

Georgina laughed merrily. "Oh, Alex! It sounds like you had quite a delightful childhood."

"It was delightful. I fear I did not fully appreciate it until much later. During the most difficult times in Spain, it was memories of my family, of life at Fair Oak, that kept me sane."

"Then, I am very glad you have brought me here, and have chosen to share it with me."

Alex smiled down at her, and reached for her hand. "There is no one I would rather share it with than you. You seem such a part of it all, after only one evening."

Georgina curled her fingers around his, wishing that she had not worn gloves, that she could feel his skin against hers. "I wish that were so. I do so admire your home, Alex, and your mother and sister, as well. They are not at all what I expected!"

"What did you expect?"

"Oh, very grand ladies. A dowager duchess and duke's sister, who were high in the instep, and who insisted on all the proprieties. Exactly how the few other duchesses I have met behaved. I was rather anxious."

"You, Georgina? Anxious about a mere duchess? Now that I cannot believe."

"It is absolutely true, I assure you! I wanted so much for them to like me, but I feared they could not, as our lives are so dissimilar."

"Well, I could certainly have reassured you on *that* point. Mother is very like you; she was always very independent, and quite indifferent to the high sticklers. And Emily looks as if she will turn out exactly the same."

"Yes. They are so very *nice*, all that is welcoming! I am very relieved."

"Excellent!" Alex lifted her hand to his lips, his breath warm and sweet through the thin kid of her glove. "Perhaps we should rejoin them?"

Georgina smiled. "Before your mother recalls her duties as chaperone, and sends Emily out here to fetch us?"

"I doubt Mother would care if we stayed out here for hours!" Alex laughed.

"Truly?" Georgina leaned just a bit closer to him, her hand still in his. "Then, perhaps we should."

"Georgina." He stared down at her, his eyes shining and silvery. Then his arms came about her, warm and safe and sheltering. "Blast it all, Georgie, but I cannot be a gentleman one second longer!"

His lips came down to meet hers. Georgina's eyes widened in surprise, then fluttered closed at the delicious warmth that flooded through her like fine brandy. She looped her arms around his neck, burying her fingers in his soft curls as his mouth slanted on hers.

Oh, it had been so long! So very, very long since she had felt this way. So full of love and longing and hope. Not since Jack. Maybe not even then.

And never had she felt so cherished, so safe, as she did now, with Alex Kenton's arms about her.

"Oh, my dears, there you are!" Dorothy called as Alex and Georgina appeared again in the drawing room. "I feared I would have to send a search party after you."

Georgina laughed nervously. She and Alex had carefully straightened their attire and smoothed their hair, but Georgina feared she might still appear scandalously disheveled. Or perhaps her guilt and delight shone in her eyes?

She peeked up at Alex, and he winked at her.

Georgina laughed. She squeezed his arm gently one more time, then went to take a seat before the fire, where Dorothy was still bent over her sewing. "Oh, no, Lady Wayland! Your son was just showing me your lovely garden."

"Lovely? Pah!" answered Dorothy. "It is quite an overgrown tangle. But once it was very nice." She looked over at Georgina slyly. "My husband and I were especially fond of the old summerhouse."

Georgina could feel herself becoming uncomfortably warm—and it had naught to do with the fire. "Oh! Yes. It is very—pretty."

"I knew you would think so." Dorothy set aside her sewing. "Emily and I were just saying we should have a party for you while you are here."

"Oh, yes!" agreed Emily. "It would be such fun."

"A party?" Alex asked doubtfully as he sat down

next to his sister. "I am not certain that would be a good idea."

"Oh, nothing at all grand," Dorothy said quickly. "No great ball or anything of that sort. A great many of our neighbors are in Town, of course, but there are many left who would enjoy some cards, perhaps a little music, an informal supper. I am sure they would delight in meeting the famous Mrs. Beaumont!"

"Oh, yes, Alex, please!" Emily laid her hand on her brother's arm beseechingly. "We have not had anyone here to dine in such a very long time, excepting the vicar and his wife. And we would not want to bore Georgina to death while she is here. She might never come back!"

Alex's doubtful frown turned to a smile then. "Heaven forfend anyone should be bored at Fair Oak!"

"You could scarce bore me at all, Emily," protested Georgina. "And I vow it would take a very great deal of tedium to bore me to death."

"You *should* meet the neighbors, Georgina," said Emily. "Should she not, Alex?"

"Oh, very well," he agreed, much to Emily's bouncing delight. "But no balls!"

"No!" said Dorothy. "Just supper and cards, as I said. We must invite Reverend and Mrs. Upton, of course. And Lord and Lady Anders are still at Thistle Hill, with their daughters. And dear Mr. Arnum . . ."

"Oh, Georgina, I cannot thank you enough!"

Georgina looked over at Emily, who had lit Georgina's way to her bedroom door. "Thank me? Whatever for?"

"For giving us an excuse for a party, of course. It

will not be what you are used to, I fear, but it will be people in the house for you to talk to."

"Nonsense! I am sure it will be vastly agreeable. You must only let me know if I can be of any help in the arrangements."

"Oh, no! You are here to enjoy yourself. Mother and I will see to everything. But perhaps . . ." Emily hesitated.

"Yes?"

"Perhaps—you would loan me a gown? Everyone here has seen my old evening frocks, and Mrs. Jones in the village could never create anything as lovely as your gowns."

Georgina laughed. "Oh, Emily! I would be more than happy to loan you any gown you choose."

"Truly?"

"Truly."

Emily threw her arms about Georgina impulsively, and kissed her cheek. "I *am* glad you have come to Fair Oak, Georgina! Good night."

"Good night, Emily."

As Georgina sat down at her dressing table to remove her earrings and hairpins, she couldn't help but smile at her own reflection in the mirror.

"Yes," she told herself. "I am quite glad I have come to Fair Oak, too."

Chapter Fourteen

Georgina leaned over her sketchbook, tears of helpless laughter streaming from her eyes as she watched Emily cavorting around the morning room with Lady Kate. The two of them raced from one end of the room to the other, Emily holding Lady Kate's chew ball high above her head while the terrier barked wildly. Finally, Lady Kate gained the advantage, leaping up on Emily's skirts and knocking her back onto a chair.

Lady Kate seized the ball, and pranced about victoriously.

"Oh, you naughty dog!" Emily gasped. "Give me back that ball this instant."

Lady Kate replied by laying down, dropping the ball between her forepaws and grinning up at Emily.

Dorothy was giggling into her handkerchief. "Emily Kenton! Here Georgina will think I have raised a hoyden."

"Certainly not," said Georgina. "Lady Kate is impossible to refuse when she wishes to play."

"Indeed she is," answered Emily. "But I am quite done in now, Lady Kate. You must find another playmate. Perhaps you should have gone off to the farm with Alex."

"She would have enjoyed that," Georgina said. "However, she would have made herself impossibly dirty, and been completely unfit for polite society."

"Never! Lady Kate, you will never be unfit for *my* society," Emily protested.

Lady Kate barked joyously, and jumped up into Emily's lap.

"Good girl, Lady Kate!" Georgina praised. "Now, if you will just stay there as you are, I can finish my sketch."

"Oh, yes! Of course." Emily straightened her skirt, and tugged Lady Kate into the proper pose. "Is this right, Georgina?"

"Perfect." Georgina took up her charcoal again.

"You know, I really ought to have gone to the fields with Alex, to tell him what everything is. I have been watching over them these three years," Emily mused. "But this is ever so much more fun!"

"I should hope so!" Dorothy cried. "I never liked you mucking about the farm, even if there was no one else for it. And you should be helping with the guest list for our supper." She waved about the sheaf of lists she had been bent over on her lap desk.

"Oh, Mother, you are doing an excellent job all on your own," said Emily. "I do think, though . . ."

"Sh!" said Georgina. "I am trying to capture just the right curve of your cheek, Emily. No talking at present, if you please."

"Of course," replied Emily, then snapped her jaw shut.

Lady Kate barked.

"You must be quiet, too, Lady Kate," admonished Georgina.

Lady Kate lowered her muzzle to her paws with a sigh.

Georgina resumed her work, humming a happy little tune as she traced the pretty lines of Emily's face. She had been quite absurdly happy ever since she had woken that morning, and had floated through her toilette and breakfast. She had soared when Alex kissed her hand before he rode out, and she still felt rather light and silly as the morning moved toward luncheon.

And all because a man had kissed her in the moonlight!

But not just any man—Alex. Alex had kissed her!

She had not felt so very giddy over a mere kiss since Jack Reid had slipped her behind the chicken house at Miss Thompson's School, and placed his lips on hers so quickly and furtively.

She had been almost eighteen then. She was thirty now, almost thirty-one. Surely it was quite absurd for a woman of her years to be so giddy over a mere kiss!

Yet it had not been just any kiss. It had been wonderfully thrilling, and sweet, and dear. Surely she deserved this happiness, this moment of soaring delight? Surely she had earned it with all her years of loneliness.

Yes. Of course she had!

"Of course," she murmured aloud.

"Did you say something, Georgina?" Dorothy asked.

Georgina looked up from her sketch, startled. "What? Oh, no. I just have the tendency to talk to myself when I am working. It is of no matter."

"Ah. Well, I think I have finished our guest list at last!" Dorothy straightened her papers with an air of great satisfaction. "I do so want everything to be perfect. This will be our first supper here in a long time."

"Of course it will be perfect, Mother," said Emily, shifting a bit in her chair. "How can it help but be?"

Later that afternoon, when Dorothy and Lady Kate had gone off to take an après-luncheon nap, Georgina and Emily sat out on the sunlit terrace to play a game of Beggar My Neighbor.

As Emily turned over a queen, and Georgina handed over two of her own cards, Emily said, "It must be great fun to be in Town at this time of year."

Georgina shrugged. "I suppose it is, yes. There are certainly a great many balls and routs, and it is very good for my business! But I will tell you truly, Emily, the balls are generally so very crowded one can scarce breathe, let alone move or talk."

"Is there nothing fun about it?"

"To be sure! Gunter's has delicious ices, and there is always someone dressed absurdly at the opera to lend amusement. But I really only go there to see my dear friends, the Hollingsworths."

"Lady Elizabeth Hollingsworth? Who is an artist, too?"

"Yes. We met at school, and have been good friends ever since."

"We often read of her and her husband in the papers. I should so much like to meet her."

"And so you shall! I am sure the two of you would like each other very much."

Emily handed over three cards when Georgina turned over a king, and said slowly, "I suppose you prefer Italy to England."

"In many ways I do. It is warmer there, for one," Georgina laughed.

"Then, you would not care to marry an Englishman?"

Georgina looked up from her cards, surprised. She had not at all seen where this conversation was leading. Was Emily afraid Georgina would not marry Alex? Or was she afraid that Georgina *would*? "I think that I would perhaps feel differently if I had family in England."

Emily nodded, apparently satisfied. "I am sure you have many suitors in London."

"A few," Georgina answered carefully. "Though I would scarce call them *suitors*. Admirers, perhaps. None that I would take seriously."

"How lovely it must be to have so many admirers," Emily said wistfully as she sorted through the cards she had won.

"But you must have every young swain of the neighborhood at your feet. Such a lovely girl as yourself," answered Georgina. "I wager you could have your choice."

Emily shook her head. "We don't often have the chance to go to an assembly or a supper. And when we do, there is a distinct lack of eligible beaux!" She laughed. "There is always Arthur Hoenig, of course. His father would be more than happy to be allied with the Kentons, but unfortunately, poor Arthur has smelly breath and spots!"

Georgina laughed in turn. "Oh, Emily! I know you must have better prospects than that. Is there no young man you find to your liking? No one handsome and charming?"

"Well . . ." Emily hesitated. "Once there was—someone. But that was long ago. I was just a child."

"Really? Will you tell me about it?"

Emily nodded. "When I was just twelve, our neighbor, the Earl of Darlinghurst, returned from India, where he had been for many years."

"And you admired this earl?"

Emily's eyes widened. "The earl? Lud, no! He was fifty if he was a day, and sunburned to a crisp. It was his son. David."

"Ah. I see. You had a *tendre* for this David?"

"Not a *tendre*; I was just a child, of course. He was practically grown up, and scarce noticed me, except to pull my braid and tease me a bit. But he was so very handsome, quite the most handsome man I had ever seen. He had a voice like—like nothing I had ever heard. So rich and sweet, like a cup of chocolate."

"What happened?"

"It was a great scandal. You see, the earl had married an Indian woman. The daughter of a maharaja, so they said. She had died soon after their son was born. So David was half-Indian."

"No!" Georgina gasped, fascinated.

"Yes. I fear it was not quite comfortable for them in the neighborhood. He was an earl, so people felt they *had* to receive them, of course. But they were not exactly friendly to them, especially David. My parents stood as their only true friends. I believe that is why they returned to India, after little more than a year here."

"And you have never forgotten this David?"

Emily shrugged. "We are rather isolated here, and I have few chances to meet such fascinating young men. It was only a schoolgirl crush, really, and I have not seen him since he left. I do not even know where he is now; far away in India, I am sure."

Dorothy, refreshed from her nap, came out onto the terrace, wheeled by her maid. "What are you speaking of so intently, my dears?" she said.

"I was only telling Georgina about the Earl of Darlinghurst, Mother," answered Emily.

"Oh, yes," said Dorothy. "What a charming gentleman he was! And such a handsome young son. William and I were so sad when they left the neighborhood, as I'm sure was Emily. Weren't you, dear?"

"Oh, yes, Mother. Very sad. Quite desolate at not having young David to pull my braids anymore."

"Such a great pity they did not stay to see you grown up." Dorothy opened up her lap desk, and drew out some fresh lists. "Now, my dears, to important business. I have finished the guest list, but we must begin the menus. I do not really think we need forty or fifty removes, as I have read they have at Carlton House, but I do want there to be a choice. And we should have oysters . . ."

"Where shall we find oysters at this time of year, Mother?" interrupted Alex, striding out onto the terrace, still in his riding clothes.

"The fishmonger in the village will have plenty, of course, Alexander," she replied as he bent to kiss her cheek. "We are scarcely living in the middle of nowhere, though it sometimes feels that way. And you are very dusty, dear."

"I apologize, Mother. I was on my way upstairs to wash when I heard you all talking out here. I wanted to see what you are so merry about."

Alex kissed Emily's cheek, and bowed over Georgina's hand. He *was* rather dusty, with mud on his boots and a slightly earthy smell about his coat. But Georgina thought she had never seen anything quite so lovely as his windswept hair and tanned, whisker-roughened jaw.

He smiled down at her warmly.

"We were discussing the supper your mother is to

give," Georgina answered him, with a smile of her own.

"Of what else could we be speaking?" said Emily. "And Georgina has quite beggared me! You see, she has taken all my cards."

Chapter Fifteen

The day of the planned supper began warm and sunny. Emily even rode out to the fields with Alex, and Dorothy sequestered herself in the dining room with her maid, to see to the final arrangements. She shooed Georgina outside to the gardens, insisting that she needed no help.

So Georgina took her sketchbook and went back to the summerhouse, where she had kissed Alex so sweetly. That night it had been dark, and she had not been able to see anything but their immediate surroundings. Today the sun was bright, and she had a full view of the gardens and the back of the house.

It was a pleasing sight, despite the tangles of the flower beds and the spots of peeling paint. It was peaceful and calm, settled.

All the things Georgina was not, and had always longed to be.

Could she, despite her dreamings, really ever be a proper mistress to such a place? A proper duchess? She knew that her money would be useful to the Kentons, to Fair Oak. But could she *herself* be useful to them?

Georgina chewed on her thumbnail, an old nervous habit, as old doubts rose up to plague her. When she was a child, living under her aunt and uncle's cold care, she had often been told that she was unworthy. That she was wild, completely lacking in decorum and natural grace and beauty. That who she was was in no way good enough for polite society.

She had fought down those insecurities with years of self-sufficiency and success in her chosen work. She knew that people admired her, even thought her beautiful. They thought her dashing and sophisticated.

But that did not mean that she had completely fought back that frightened young girl. She still rose up to plague the grown-up Georgina from time to time.

As she did now, when Georgina was contemplating what it would be like to be a duchess.

"Nonsense!" she cried aloud. "I would be a perfect duchess. Top of the trees."

She snapped open her sketchbook, flipped over to the almost completed sketch of Emily, and began to do what she knew she did best. She drew.

"Now. Which gown would you like to wear?" Georgina threw open her wardrobe to Emily's perusal.

Emily's eyes grew wide as she looked at first one gown then another. "I—I hardly know where to begin." She took up the gold-embroidered green velvet that Georgina had worn at the first ball she attended with Alex. "This one?"

Georgina studied it critically. "It doesn't really suit your lovely blonde hair. Perhaps this one?" She showed Emily a gown of pale peach satin, overlaid with soft ivory lace. "I have never worn it. It suits you so much better than me!"

"Oh, yes," Emily sighed happily, clutching the gown to her. "May I, please, Georgina? It is quite the loveliest thing I have ever seen."

"Of course you may!"

"And what will you wear?"

"The blue silk, I think. Do you think it quite appropriate?"

"I think you will be stunning. We will be the envy of all our neighbors, to have such a lovely and famous guest."

Georgina laughed. "You will be the envy of your neighbors because you are so lovely yourself! Sit here, Emily, and I will fix your hair for you. There is a new style I have seen in Town that I think will suit you admirably."

Emily sat down before the dressing table mirror, and watched with sparkling eyes as Georgina brushed out her curls and began twisting them atop her head. "I have a white rose I picked in the garden this afternoon," she said. "Would that look well in my hair? I fear I have so few jewels."

"It would be perfect. Tell me, Emily, how was your afternoon? Did you ride far?"

"Oh, yes! I showed Alex all the fields that are under cultivation, and a few that I hope to have plowed in the fall. Poor man, he does not know a great deal about farming as yet! He is such a military man. But he is learning."

Alex was utterly exhausted.

He and Emily had been out all afternoon. He had seen the fields (few) that Emily had managed to keep under cultivation. He had seen the fields (many) that lay fallow. Emily had talked of possible plans for those fields, of barley and wheat and bringing in more sheep.

They had spoken with the tenants, had heard their concerns and advice.

Alex had learned more about farming in one day than he ever had before in his life, and he felt like an utter babe in the woods. As a younger son, he had been meant for the army since childhood. Thus his father had not thought it important for him to know about the running of the estates. But he intended to know everything about it now, and soon.

He also learned that his sister, only a child when he had left for Spain, had grown into a beautiful young woman. A very smart young woman, who had taught herself about farming when her brothers were nowhere about to see to her welfare. She had kept Fair Oak in good order, and looked after their mother, at the expense of all the normal pleasures of a young lady.

Emily knew so little of parties and suitors; she had few friends of her own age. She was clearly longing for those joys; she spoke so wistfully of London.

It was no wonder she had attached herself so quickly to Georgina's friendship.

Alex owed Emily that friendship, owed her a fine Season, at the very least, for all she had done. His mother would never want to go to London again, so he owed Emily a grand sponsor. He owed her, and himself, to learn all he could about soil cultivation and sheep shearing, so that he could build the Grange into a kingdom any woman would be proud to be duchess of.

Even a woman as glorious as Georgina Beaumont.

Alex grinned at himself in the mirror as he finished off his cravat. Georgina *would* make a splendid duchess. He had known that in London, and seeing her here in his home, seeing how easy and friendly she was with his mother and sister, only proved that.

Yes, he admitted to himself, he quite adored Georgina.

If he could just be worthy of her.

"Reverend Mr. Upton! Mrs. Upton. You must meet our new houseguest, Mrs. Beaumont," called Dorothy from where she sat in the drawing room, greeting the guests before supper. As she smiled and chatted, her cheeks pink beneath the lappets of her lace cap, she looked no older than the woman in the Gainsborough portrait.

"A great pleasure, Mrs. Beaumont," said the vicar, a tall, thin, smiling man. "We saw a portrait you did of a friend of my aunt's, a Lady Treezle. Quite fine, was it not, Mrs. Upton?"

"Oh, quite!" agreed Mrs. Upton, a pretty blonde as short and plump as her husband was the opposite. "It was very like her, Mrs. Beaumont. We were so excited to hear that you were in the neighborhood."

"Thank you, Mrs. Upton," answered Georgina. "I have had such a delightful welcome from everyone."

"You must come to tea at the vicarage before you leave," Mrs. Upton urged.

"I should like that very much, thank you." As the Uptons went on to speak to Dorothy about some new ladies' charitable organization, Georgina stepped away a bit to survey the room.

She had rather feared that her pearl necklace with its sapphire pendant and the sapphire bandeau that held her hair in place would prove too much for a country party. But she saw now that all the ladies wore their finest gowns and their prettiest jewels; Lady Anders even wore a tiara! And quite all the country gentry had flocked to the dowager duchess's supper party, obviously eager to be at Fair Oak again. There was much conversation and laughter, and everyone had greeted her warmly, and even with a touch of deference.

Deference was something Georgina was not accustomed to in the least, and she suspected that was entirely due to Alex's behavior. He had stayed at her side as the first of the guests arrived, introduced her about.

She smiled at him now, where he stood with his sister and a few other people. He smiled at her in return, and nodded. Then he winked.

There was a small fluttering, very low in her stomach. She almost giggled, and clapped her gloved hand to her mouth.

"Georgina, dear," Dorothy said, bringing Georgina back to her side. "I do believe it is time for supper. Will you ask Alexander to come and assist me?"

"Yes, of course," she answered. "Do excuse me, Mr. Upton. Mrs. Upton."

"Of course, Mrs. Beaumont." The vicar gave her a bow.

As she walked away, Georgina heard Dorothy say, "You see how very much livelier we are since Mrs. Beaumont came to visit? Emily has quite blossomed. Such a treasure."

"Yes," said Mr. Upton. "You—and your son—appear to be quite happy in your friends, Your Grace."

Georgina blushed.

"An excellent port, Wayland," Lord Anders commented. "Most excellent indeed."

"Thank you," answered Alex. "I sent it back from Spain."

The ladies had retired to the drawing room, leaving the gentlemen to their port and cigars.

"Shows your excellent taste," Anders said, with a suggestive chuckle. "In port as in other things, eh?"

"Other things?"

"Women, of course, Wayland! La Beaumont. We have only recently come up from Town, you know, and she is all the crack there. A true beauty, and so dashing." Anders laughed, bringing the attention of the others in their direction. "What other woman would challenge old Lord Pynchon to a race, eh!"

There was an answering ripple of laughter. "She *is* a stunner," commented young Baron Patterson. "That hair . . . !"

Alex glared at Anders, just as he had to many an errant subaltern on the Peninsula. It had the same effect on Anders as it had on them—he stammered a bit, turned red, and shifted his gaze away.

All the others turned back to their respective conversations.

"You know, of course," said Alex, "that Mrs. Beaumont was injured in that race. I hardly think she would appreciate that it has now become an object of laughter."

"Oh—yes. I mean, no," murmured Anders. "But—but she does seem quite recovered now."

"She is recovered. Quite. It is still not something to be snickered over, however."

"Oh, no! I was not—snickering. Merely expressing my admiration for her."

"Hm. Yes."

Anders took a long sip of his port, and seemed to recover himself. "I take it, then, Wayland, that your feelings toward La—Mrs. Beaumont are of a rather serious nature?"

Alex was quite taken aback. Surely such bluntness was not quite the thing? It had certainly not been before he left for war; people had at least outwardly minded their own business. But then, he had been gone a long time. And, as he did not wish his feelings for Georgina to be in any way misconstrued, he said, "I brought her here to meet my mother and sister."

"Certainly." Anders drank down the last of his port. "Well, I must say you are a very fortunate man, Wayland. She is beautiful, and, I hear, quite well-to-do." He glanced toward the sideboard, now all but bare of silver where once it had groaned from the weight of salvers and platters. "*Quite* well-to-do."

Alex's hand tightened on his own glass. He only released his grip when he felt the etched design pressing into his palm and the crystal start to give.

Money again. Always the blasted money. Was this what he could look forward to for all his future married life?

"We were all so delighted to hear that you had come to visit, Mrs. Beaumont." Lady Anders, a tall brunette made even taller by the great plumes attached to her ruby tiara, seated herself next to Georgina with a smile. "And now to have the chance to meet you *and* see Fair Oak again! Beyond delight."

Georgina smiled in return, even though there was something in Lady Anders' eyes she was rather wary of. Some sort of—malicious glitter. "I am delighted to be here."

"Though you must find it a bit dull after all your triumphs in Town," Lady Anders whispered confidingly. "I know I find the society rather limited."

"Limited? With a ducal family in residence?"

Lady Anders laughed. "Oh, yes, the Kentons *are*

highly regarded, to be sure. But they have been so quiet since Damian—that is, the late duke—died. The dowager duchess and poor Lady Emily haven't an ounce of his dash!" She sighed. "Not that we ever saw him here in the country. We almost always met in Town."

Georgina carefully studied Lady Anders. Obviously she had been more than acquaintances with the profligate Damian—despite the fact that she was old enough to have two daughters out. "Indeed," Georgina said coolly.

Lady Anders took no note of the frosty tone. "Yes. Fair Oak is so *shabby* without him, quite without style. Though I must say Lady Emily looks in fine form tonight. Is that a new gown even? Quite unusual. She usually takes no interest in fashion at all. Though I have tried to advise her in such things, for her brother's sake, she does not care."

Georgina looked across the room to where Emily, so pretty in her peach satin and ivory lace, was playing whist with her mother and the Uptons. Emily laughed, a sweet sound, like silver bells a bit rusty from disuse. She looked so happy, and so young.

Georgina thought of how many difficulties that young girl had been through, all because her late brother had squandered her fortune. Squandered it with the woman who now sat beside Georgina, sighing about Damian's lost "dash" and Emily's lack of style.

Georgina wanted to flee, but she only nodded and said, "Lady Emily *is* looking well tonight. She is a very lovely young lady. And if Fair Oak is indeed 'shabby,' surely it is only because your Damian took no interest in it."

Lady Anders looked at her, with wide, startled dark

eyes. "Well." Then she looked over to where Alex sat, watching them over his fanned cards. "I see."

Georgina followed her gaze, and saw that Alex was frowning slightly. He seemed uncertain, perhaps even angry.

Why would he be angry?

"Well," Lady Anders continued. "Now I suppose Alexander has returned, he will—take an interest. As, I see, have you, Mrs. Beaumont." Lady Anders looked pointedly at Georgina's sapphires and pearls. "And very fortunate the Kentons are to have your interest. I am sure they must find you quite *useful*. But, if you will excuse me, Mrs. Beaumont, I do believe my husband is calling me."

Georgina nodded briefly. "Of course. So interesting to meet you, Lady Anders."

Georgina watched Lady Anders walk away, her crimson and gold train trailing like a glittering serpent behind her. Lady Anders stopped at her husband's side, whispered in his ear, gestured toward Georgina. He, in turn, nodded, and whispered back to her.

Georgina turned away with a laugh. What a thoroughly irritating wench!

Was she to be plagued with such sordid speculations for all her future married life?

"Mrs. Beaumont."

Georgina turned to see the kindly Mrs. Upton. "Mrs. Upton! Did I not see you playing at cards?"

"Oh, I am terrible at it! I gave the young baron my place."

"I fear I am not a dab hand at cards, myself. Please, won't you sit with me? I find myself in need of some *pleasant* conversation."

"Yes, I saw you were talking with Lady Anders."

"Indeed I was."

Mrs. Upton leaned toward Georgina, her pretty, round face serious, and said quietly, "I know that as a vicar's wife I should show charity to all. But you should not take heed of anything that woman says, my dear. She is a viper, plain and simple."

Georgina could not have agreed more.

Georgina stayed awake that night long after the guests departed and the rest of the household was asleep.

She had been alone for so very long that the new feelings of that evening, feelings of family and neighborhood, felt so strange. She sat beside her bedroom window, looking down at the moonlight-drenched garden, trying to absorb them.

Oh, she had not been strictly *alone* in the many years since Jack died. She had her dear friends, who were like family to her. She had had Mr. Beaumont, who, despite his advanced years, had been a good friend to her. She had her sweet doggie. But she had lived mostly by herself, had gone where she pleased, and had done what she wanted. She had never given the words of vipers like Lady Anders a thought before.

And she liked it. Very much. She did not dwell on things that could not be helped, like Jack's death, or the deep, secret yearning she had felt for a child, a home, and a more secure place in Society.

She had a career, after all. Financial security. She was so fortunate, really.

Georgina sighed. How could she have known, when the handsome Duke of Wayland rescued Lady Kate from drowning, that her life was changing so much from that moment on? That her old yearnings for a home and a family would rise up again? That Alex would show her a world she could so easily live in, one that had once seemed so far beyond her grasp? A world of family and home and lineage. Of complete security and respectability.

Yet so he had. She liked his mother and sister very much. They might be the widow and daughter of a duke, but she sensed in them a kindred spirit to her own. They had, all three of them, been through difficult circumstances, circumstances beyond their control, and had emerged intact. Perhaps even better than before.

She had had fears, before she met them, that they would disapprove of her, perhaps even snub her. That they would have little in common, and this visit would prove a misery. After all, she was hardly the sort a duke would usually consider for a wife.

But those fears had not been realized.

Even the neighbors, who no doubt held the honor of their ducal friends very high, had welcomed her. Perhaps a few had seemed a bit puzzled, but everyone had been civil and charming.

Except the Anders, Georgina amended wryly.

And then there was Alex himself.

Georgina smiled softly. Dear Alex, so handsome, so considerate, so military-proud but so kindhearted. She had wanted him so very much from that first day they met. But she had not wanted him just as an admirer, or even as a lover. She had wanted to talk with him, to sit quietly with him, to dance at balls and drive in the park with him. She wanted to show him all her work, to bask in his approval as she had the night of Elizabeth's *salon*. She wanted to hear of all his experiences in the war; she wanted to know all his hopes for the future.

She wanted to kiss him. Kiss him—and more. Much more.

Yes, now she could bring herself to admit what she had so feared. She wanted to be his wife. She was ready to take a chance on matrimony again.

Perhaps.

Chapter Sixteen

"Oh, Georgina! Such dreadful news." Emily rushed up to Georgina as she entered the breakfast room the morning after the supper party.

Georgina's gaze flew to Alex, where he sat with his plate of kippers and eggs. She noticed that Dorothy was not at her place. "Dreadful news? Is someone ill? Has your mother . . . ?"

Alex shook his head. "Not at all! Really, Emily, you should not be so dramatic. You have convinced poor Georgina that someone has died at the very least. It is not so very *dreadful*." He smiled at Georgina, and came around the table to draw her chair out for her. "Please, both of you, do sit, or your food will grow cold."

Emily sat down, disgruntled. "It is dreadful to me, Alex. We have only had you back for a few days, and now you are leaving us again."

"Leaving?" Georgina cried, aghast that her country idyll, so very perfect only last night, was ending so abruptly. "Where are you going?"

"To Kenton Grange, our estate to the north," Alex answered. "I received a letter from the bailiff only this morning. There is an emergency there that I must go and see to at once." He gestured toward the letter beside his plate. "The Grange is our only other estate besides Fair Oak. Once I have seen it to rights, it can be a dowry for Emily."

"Since I intend to never marry, I shall not need a dowry!" protested Emily. "Therefore you should stay here with us for a few days more."

"I shall not be gone long, Em," Alex answered. "A week, perhaps."

Georgina buttered her toast industriously to cover her disappointment. "I shall be ready to return to London this afternoon, then. I suppose a carriage could be hired in the village?"

"Not you, too!" sighed Emily.

"You must stay, Georgina," Alex said quickly. "I promised you a holiday, which you have scarce had. I would not want to ruin your fun, or that of my sister."

"Oh, yes!" Emily beseeched. "Please do stay, Georgina. I could show you about the farm, and we could call on all the neighbors. And you have not seen the village."

A few more days in the country quiet *did* sound tempting. But would it be quite proper without Alex? "I do not know . . ."

"Georgina! Please," cried Emily.

"I should feel too guilty if I sent you running back to London so quickly, Georgina," Alex said. "I will take you back as soon as I return. Or, if you find your work calls you back to Town before then, you could hire a carriage."

Georgina smiled. "Very well. I will stay for a few days more."

Emily clapped her hands. "Oh, how grand! We *shall* miss you, though, Alex."

"Yes," Georgina agreed. "We certainly shall."

"I will not be gone long enough for you to miss me," Alex protested. "You will be having far too much fun without me. But I know that *I* will miss *you*."

"Are you certain you will be comfortable here while I am gone?" Alex asked Georgina as he prepared to climb aboard his curricle. "If you feel we bullied you into staying, and you really want to return to Town, you mustn't let us hold you."

Georgina laughed. "Not at all! I am glad to have more time to spend here, in your lovely home."

"Good." He laid his hand softly against her cheek. "I am truly sorry to leave you thus. I would never do so if it were not an emergency."

"Of course not! You must safeguard your sister's dowry. I shall do very well here with Emily and your mother."

"I know you will." Alex glanced about at the house, shimmering in the morning sunlight, then down at Georgina. She looked so very *right* there. As if she had been living there for years. As if she belonged.

He leaned forward to kiss her cheek, but longed for so much more.

"I will write to you," he murmured against her soft skin. "As soon as I arrive at the Grange."

"And I will write to you. Have a safe journey, Alex."

He looked into her luminous green eyes, at the slight tremble of her lips as she smiled at him, and he longed to pull her into his arms. To kiss her properly. But he was all too aware of his mother and sister, watching avidly from the window.

He knew they would like it all too well if he were

to make a lascivious cake of himself in their very driveway, but he was not quite prepared to be their morning amusement! So he just took up Georgina's hand, and kissed her ungloved fingers, lingering just an instant longer than was proper.

"Good-bye, Georgie," he said, then swung himself up onto the narrow curricle seat and lifted the reins.

"Farewell, Alex. Drive carefully! More carefully than I!"

Alex laughed. Then he waved once more to his mother and sister, and drove away.

As his day's drive was a long one, and he was alone with no one to converse with, he was left with a great deal of time for thinking. And his thoughts turned mostly to Georgina.

Georgina, so beautiful, so charming. She had certainly wrapped his family and all their neighbors about her pretty finger! He smiled to remember her with his mother and sister, how she had made them laugh with her tales of London and the Continent. She had had the neighbors fascinated, as well, and quite admiring of her—just as she had all of London Society at her feet.

She would truly make a magnificent duchess. He was just fortunate that she seemed to admire him, as well, crusty old military man that he was. Otherwise she would surely spurn his suit! All he had to offer her was a tumbledown estate. And Emily would surely kill him now if he did not present Georgina to her as her sister.

Just look at how she had helped Emily, loaning her a fashionable gown so she would look so grand at their supper . . .

He frowned a bit at the reminder that his sister had

required the loan of a gown at all. He should have been able to provide her with an entire wardrobe!

And that, once again, chafed. Georgina's money.

Alex was a proud man. It was his greatest downfall, and he admitted it. It would perhaps be different if he did not care for Georgina so. If he had met a woman he rather liked, who wanted to be a duchess and who was willing to trade her fortune for it, a woman who wanted only a business arrangement. Then he would not mind so much.

But he loved Georgina. So he wanted everything equal and aboveboard between them. He wanted her life to be as fine with him as it had been without him. He wanted her to never have any regrets that she had chosen him.

Could that be possible, when he had so little to offer her?

Lord Anders's words of the night before came back to haunt him. "She is beautiful, and, I hear, quite well-to-do. *Quite* well-to-do."

Alex saw again in his mind's eye the man's odious sneer.

Anders had been right, though, in his own nasty way. Why would a wealthy woman like Georgina, a beautiful, independent woman, want to take on a family that was so messed up? No woman in her situation would.

But then, Georgina was not just any beautiful, wealthy woman. She was his own unique Georgina. And she seemed to like him. Her kisses were sweet and ardent; she smiled brightly whenever he entered a room. She listened to him, confided in him.

He knew he should let her go, for her own good. He could not, though. He had come to rely on their time together. He was being selfish, he knew that, but he could not give her up.

Despite the difficulties that could lie ahead for them, despite the fact that he was more confused than he had ever been before in his life, he could not bring himself to let her go.

"I am just going out to visit Mrs. Smith, our old nursemaid, who has been ill," Emily said, putting on her bonnet and gloves before the mirror in the morning room. "Would you like to come, too, Georgina?"

Georgina, who had been sketching before the fire and chatting with Dorothy, said, "Oh, I should like to, Emily! Fresh air sounds wonderful. But I should finish this sketch today so that I can finish your portrait before I leave Fair Oak."

"Nonsense," said Dorothy. "There will be plenty of time for finishing portraits later, I am sure." She winked, looking so much like her son that Georgina had to laugh. "Plenty of time. You two should go out into the sunshine, while we still have it. Give my best wishes to Mrs. Smith."

"If you are sure, Dorothy, that you will be quite all right?"

"Oh, yes. I have been intending to finish my book."

Georgina smiled. "Then, I should very much like to go with you, Emily. Let me fetch my bonnet, and we can be off."

Twenty minutes later, they set off in Emily's little pony cart, with Emily competently at the reins, and Lady Kate beside them.

"Most of the fields lie fallow now, of course," Emily said, drawing up the pony cart so Georgina could take a closer look at their surroundings. "A great many of the laborers have had to find other work. We have managed to keep on enough to cultivate those fields over there, though."

Georgina surveyed the recently harvested fields. "What is grown there?"

"Wheat and oats. We used to grow barley, as well. There are some turnips and potatoes just over that hill, and cook keeps an excellent kitchen garden. We are never short of vegetables! And I have kept a few head of cattle, to pull the plows and give us milk and some meat. Only enough for the household, though." Emily's rosebud mouth pursed thoughtfully. "I would like to have some sheep, as well, but they cost dear just now."

"Do you still have many tenants?"

"Oh, yes, some. You will meet some of them today, I am sure. Their rents are very welcome, though I wish we could do more for them. They have been a great help to Mother and me, teaching me about farming and livestock." Emily laughed. "I would not have known a plow from a turnip before last year!"

"What of your bailiff?"

"Mr. Pryor? He left soon after Damian died. When I looked over the books after his hasty departure, I found he had been skimming off the top a bit. So good riddance, I say! I've done better without him. Mr. Montgomery, one of the tenants, helps me a bit."

Georgina was shocked. "Do you mean to say, Emily, that you have been managing this farm all by yourself?"

Emily seemed surprised at Georgina's surprise. "Yes. There was no one else to do it. Mother is not well. Alex, although he left the army as soon as he got my letter about Damian's death, was delayed several times, and did not make it home for many months. And he is a military man, not a farmer; he knew as little as I did. I could not just let us starve."

"So you knew nothing of farming when you started?"

Emily shrugged blithely. "Not a thing! French and needlework were all my governess taught me. But I read everything I could find, and asked all our tenants and neighbors for advice. We have not done too badly, considering."

"I should say not." Georgina looked out at the fields again, in complete awe that this young girl, this duke's daughter, had managed them all on her own. She had been worried about wheat and drainage and soil cultivation, when she should have been enjoying her first Season.

If only there was something Georgina could do to help Emily, to help Alex and his family . . .

"Emily," she said. "I have always lived in cities and towns, and I know nothing of farming. How much would it take to put all your fields under cultivation again, and to bring in a new bailiff, an honest one?"

Emily's forehead creased in thought. When she at last named a sum, Georgina said in surprise, "Truly? I would have thought it a great deal more."

"Oh, we could *use* a great deal more, to be sure. The roof on Fair Oak needs repairing, the garden restoring, and, as I said, I should like to bring in sheep. But to hire a new bailiff, and bring the laborers back in time for hay making in a few weeks and then fall plowing, that should do it."

"Hm." Georgina opened her reticule and drew out the thick wad of banknotes she had been intending to use for some shopping in the village. It was quite embarrassing now, to think of the sums she spent on bonnets and slippers. She tucked them into Emily's market basket. "Take this, then, and use it on the roof, or the plowing, or whatever you see fit. I will write you a draught on the rest when we return to the house."

"What!" Emily cried, staring down at the money in shock. "Georgina, what are you doing? You cannot just give me your money! It—it would not be right." But she reached out one hand, in its mended glove, to touch the notes.

"Emily, please. Please, I want to help. I want to cease being a selfish creature, and help do something truly useful."

"It is so good of you, but—to give me, an almost stranger, your money . . ."

Georgina took Emily's hand, and spoke to her quietly, earnestly. "I will tell you something that mustn't go beyond us just yet."

Emily's eyes widened. "What is it?"

"I love your brother, very much, and I am almost certain he loves me, as well. He has asked me to marry him—or as good as asked. And I will say yes."

"Oh!" Emily cried in delight, throwing her arms about Georgina's neck. "I knew it. I knew it from the way he always looks at you. Oh, I will be the envy of the neighborhood, when they hear I am to have such a dashing sister!"

"So, since I *am* to be your sister, let me help you."

"But . . ."

"Emily. My money shall be yours soon enough. But I am not sure when we will be married, and you need the money now, to bring back the laborers. Please."

Emily bit her lip, clearly torn. Then she nodded. "Yes. Georgina, you are the dearest dear! My brother is so very fortunate to have found you."

"Yes," Georgina agreed. "So he is."

Emily laughed.

The next three days passed most pleasantly. Georgina went driving with Emily, took tea with the vicar's wife, and sat and read with Dorothy in the afternoons. She finished the sketches for Emily's portrait, and began laying it down on canvas in oils. In the evenings, she would play cards with Emily and Dorothy, or listen to Emily play on the pianoforte.

Secretly, Georgina began to make plans for the grand Season she would sponsor for Emily. She had never ushered a young girl through her first Season before, but surely it could not be so difficult for a girl as pretty and wellborn as Emily. There would be a presentation at Court, of course, a coming-out ball, routs and breakfasts and musicales . . .

These plans were occupying her on the third night, as she lay awake in bed, when she heard a noise. A light scratching sound.

Georgina cautiously raised her head from the pillow to look about. There was only the familiar furniture visible in the dying firelight. Her gown draped over a chair, where she had dropped it after supper. The only sound was Lady Kate's light snoring.

Then it came again. A faint scratching in the corridor.

Georgina recalled Emily's tales of Queen Elizabeth, who once a year came back to wander about her bedchamber of more than two hundred years ago.

She sank back down against the pillow, drawing the sheet up to her neck.

"W-who is it?" she called, deliciously chilled. "Do you bring me a message from the other side?"

The door opened, and a blonde head popped into

the room. Very solid, and not at all ghostly. "The other side?" Emily whispered. "The other side of the wall, mayhap, since my room is right next to yours!"

Georgina giggled. "Emily! I thought you were Queen Elizabeth."

"Me? Certainly not. I have no ruff."

"What are you doing wandering about in the middle of the night?"

"I was hungry, so I thought I would go down to the kitchen and see if there was any lemon cake left from tea. Would you like to come with me?"

"I do feel a bit peckish. Contact with the spirit world will do that to a person."

The kitchen was quite deserted when they went down there, and found the lemon cake and some milk. They took their feast back to Georgina's room, and settled down before the fire to eat it. Even Lady Kate got a small portion.

"Do you often make midnight forays into the kitchen?" Georgina asked, scraping up the last of her cake crumbs.

Emily shook her head. "No, but I did when I was a child. Cook would leave little treats out for me, a cake or the last of a meat pie. Sometimes Alex would go with me, though he was quite a bit older and very dignified."

"Did you have a good childhood here, Emily?"

"Oh, yes! The very best." Emily smiled softly at the memory. "My father was sometimes gone, of course, to take his seat in the House of Lords, but when he came back he would bring grand presents, and would take me out riding on my pony every day. He and my mother adored parties, and gave ever so many. Breakfasts, and balls, and suppers. Damian was almost never at home, but I scarcely missed him, he teased me so horridly when he was here. Alex, though, always wrote to me from his school, and was an excellent brother when he was here. It was all such fun." Her face darkened. "Until my mother's accident."

"Did your father stay away then?" Georgina asked gently. Her experience of men had always been that they were seldom about when there was unpleasantness afoot.

"Not at all! My parents *loved* each other. Father never left Fair Oak after that, not even for a day, until he died. But it was much quieter here, and Alex was away at war. He wrote to us every week, but I was terribly worried about him. I felt so very alone."

Georgina reached for Emily's hand. "I am so sorry, Emily. I do know how it feels to be alone."

Emily smiled, and squeezed her hand. "I am not alone anymore, though! Alex is home again, safe. Best of all, he has brought you to us. None of us ever has to be alone again."

"No," Georgina answered slowly. "We never have to be alone again."

Chapter Seventeen

"Georgina, you have a letter!" Emily said as she sorted through the post at the breakfast table. Then she added slyly, "Alas, it is not from my brother."

Georgina laughed, and reached for her letter. "Why ever should it be from your brother, Emily?"

"Oh, I don't know. I just think he should write you again," answered Emily. "That one small note letting us know he arrived at the Grange was so paltry. Has he never sent you any *billets doux*, then, Georgina?"

"Emily!" Dorothy admonished. "That is hardly any of our business."

Emily grinned unrepentantly. "Oh. Sorry."

Dorothy grinned in return. "So," she said. "Has he, Georgina?"

Georgina laughed, choking on her bite of toast. "I am afraid not."

"Hmph," said Dorothy. "Well. That is scarce my fault. I never raised an unromantic child."

"*That* is correct," Emily said. "Who is your letter from, then, Georgina? If it is not too prying to ask."

"Not at all. It is from my friends, the Hollingsworths. Nicholas and Elizabeth."

"The people you were staying with in London?" Emily asked.

"Yes. I have been waiting to hear from them this age!" Georgina broke the seal, and quickly scanned the short missive, written hastily in Elizabeth's sprawling hand. She then read it again, alarm squeezing the very breath from her lungs. The paper trembled in her suddenly chilled fingers. "Oh, no."

"Not bad news?" Emily said quietly.

"I am—not certain. I do hope not." Georgina lowered the letter to the table, and looked up into the other women's concerned faces. "Elizabeth, you see, is in a—delicate condition. It has not been an easy time for her, I fear. And now she writes that she has had some pains, and that her physician has ordered her to bed for a few days. She says all is well now, but her husband has added a postscript, no doubt without her knowledge. Nicholas says she is *not* as well as she wishes everyone to believe!"

"How dreadful," cried Dorothy. "Your friend must be so frightened. To be in danger of losing one's child—that is the very worst."

"Yes. I am sure she is frightened, though Elizabeth would never say so. She is always so very cheerful. She would not want me to worry."

"But you do," said Emily.

Georgina nodded as she folded and unfolded the letter in her shaking hands. "Elizabeth is my very oldest friend. She is—like my own sister. She has always been by my side in my troubles; I must be by hers. I fear, my dears, that I must leave you and return to Town."

"Of course. I shall help you make the arrangements," said Emily, rising to her feet.

"Thank you, Emily, so very much! I only pray that I find all is well when I arrive there."

The town house was very quiet when Georgina at last arrived. There were no chattering voices from the drawing room, as there usually was in the afternoons—no music, no laughter. The curtains were all drawn; the butler spoke almost in a whisper.

Georgina feared for one breathless, dreadful moment that she had entered a house of mourning. That Elizabeth was gone from them.

"Greene, please," she beseeched the dour butler. "Please tell me quickly what has happened. If the worst has happened . . ."

"The worst, Mrs. Beaumont?"

"If Lady Elizabeth has—has . . ."

Before she could choke out the rest of her sentence, there was the soft sound of slippers pattering along the upstairs corridor. Elizabeth appeared at the top of the stairs, looking rather pale in her sky-blue dressing gown, but alive and whole.

Her hand rested atop the growing mound of her stomach.

"Georgie!" she cried, starting carefully down the staircase, her hands on the banister. "You are back."

"Of course I am back! Did you think I could stay away after receiving your letter?" Georgina pushed her gloves and bonnet into the butler's hands, and hurried up the stairs to Elizabeth's side. "Should you be out of bed?"

"I have been up all day," Elizabeth replied, kissing Georgina's cheek in welcome. Her shoulders felt rather thin and frail to Georgina as she hugged her. "I thought I would go insane, laying about up there all alone! I have not seen a soul except Nick all week."

"Here, let me help you down these stairs. We can sit in the drawing room, and you can tell me everything." Georgina slid her arm about Elizabeth, and guided her carefully down the rest of the stairs. "Where is Nick?"

"At Gunter's. I sent him there to fetch some pastries." Elizabeth gave a sigh of relief as she sank down onto the chaise. "I am quite famished."

"Shall I ring for some tea?" asked Georgina. "I could use some myself."

"Oh, yes, please do." Elizabeth smiled up at her. "Oh, Georgie, I am so very happy to see you! But you should not have interrupted your holiday for me. As you see, I am quite well. It was merely a twinge."

"Nicholas said it was *not* a twinge."

"That husband of mine! I told him he must not worry you."

"Of course you should 'worry me'! You are my dearest friend, Lizzie. If you are ill, I want to know about it." Georgina settled into the chair next to her chaise. "And you are not interrupting anything. Alex had to leave Fair Oak; something about an emergency at his other estate."

"He left you all alone?" Elizabeth cried.

"Hardly all alone. I was with his mother and sister, who, by the way, are quite charming. So all was well." Georgina grinned mischievously. "Though I confess, I did rather miss Alex."

Elizabeth laughed. "Of course you did! As I am sure he was desolated to leave you. Tell me more about his family, now. They must not have been such high sticklers as we feared."

"Not at all! They were very welcoming. His sister,

Lady Emily, is a very pretty girl. Just the right age to make her bow."

The tea had arrived, and Elizabeth busied herself with pouring and arranging. "Are you thinking of sponsoring her, then?"

"Perhaps. She is certainly in need of a sponsor. We would have such fun shepherding her about, you and I!" Georgina sipped thoughtfully at her tea. "But then, if she were my sister-in-law, I would be quite obliged to sponsor her, would I not?"

Elizabeth's cup clattered in its saucer. "Sister-in-law? Are you—did Wayland . . . ?"

Georgina laughed. "Oh, no! Nothing of the sort. Not yet. But I have received a few proposals in my time, as you know."

"A few?" Elizabeth snorted. "Only fifty or so."

"And thus I can tell when one is imminent. Usually. I do not think Alex took all the trouble of introducing me to his family, and kissing me in his ancestral garden, if he only meant to offer me *carte blanche*."

"Indeed not! Shall you accept?"

"I think it—very likely I shall. I have not felt at all this way in a very long time," Georgina mused. "Perhaps never. He is so . . . ."

"Handsome? Brave?"

"Oh, yes! And such a divine kisser. It would be such a shame to let those things slip away simply because he is a duke and I should make a most odd duchess."

"Indeed it would be a shame! And you would not make an odd duchess, you would make a fine one. The finest in the realm!"

Georgina smiled, a bit shyly. "Do you really think so?"

"Of course I do! He will be the luckiest man in England to have you," Elizabeth said stoutly. "Oh, I feel I should be bowing and scraping, and calling you 'Your Grace'!"

Georgina giggled. "You should *not!*"

"Should not what?" Nicholas entered the drawing room just then, his arms full of boxes fragrant with cinnamon and sugar.

"Oh, darling!" Elizabeth cried. "Georgina is back, and she is to be a duchess."

"Is she indeed?" Nicholas deposited the boxes in his wife's lap, and grinned at Georgina. "Well, I did say that only the fiery La Beaumont could be a match for old Hotspur Kenton. And I was right, wasn't I?"

Elizabeth bit into a cream cake. "You are always right, darling."

Nicholas looked down at her in surprise. "I thought *you* were always the right one, Lizzie."

"Um, see, there you are. Right again."

Georgina only laughed at them.

Over the next few days, Elizabeth grew stronger and stronger. She was able to come downstairs every day, and even to accept visitors and go for short drives.

One fine, sunny afternoon, Georgina set up her easel near the tall windows of the drawing room to work on Emily's portrait. Elizabeth sat nearby, a book open on her lap. But she was fidgeting and sighing so much that it was obvious she was not reading it.

"What is amiss, Lizzie?" Georgina asked, mixing a bit of golden yellow on her palette. "Are you feeling ill again?"

"Quite the opposite!" answered Elizabeth, closing the book with a snap. "I am feeling very well again.

So well that I want to go shopping, or even to a ball. I have so much work to finish up in the studio, as well."

"You heard what the physician said. No dancing, and no standing at your easel for long periods of time."

"Yes, and Nick is quite fastidious about making certain I follow those orders. As are *you*, Georgie!"

Georgina laughed, and dipped her brush into the paint. "We only want you to be well."

"I am well! So is the baby. I can feel her kicking, as strong as ever. We both want some fun! Do you not think a small party would be all right, Georgie? If I only sat and talked?"

Georgina shrugged. "Perhaps a *small* party. Nothing that would turn into a great crush. Lady Ellersby's card party on Thursday, maybe?"

"I am sure we could persuade Nick that whist is quite unlikely to harm my health!" Elizabeth opened her book again, but she did not look down at it. "Are you not bored, Georgie? We have been so quiet here of late."

"I have not been bored at all. I am enjoying having the time to work."

"Well, it is not much like you to be so sedate! But I am very glad you are here. I should have gone quite out of my mind without your company."

The butler came into the drawing room then, a pair of cards on his silver tray. "You have callers, Lady Elizabeth."

"Oh, delightful!" cried Elizabeth. "Who is it today?"

"Hildebrand Rutherford, Viscount Garrick, and Mr. Frederick Marlow," answered Greene.

"Alex's friends!" Georgina said. She hastily put down her brushes and palette and wiped her hands on a paint-stained rag.

"Do show them in, Greene," said Elizabeth. "And have some refreshments sent in."

Georgina smoothed her hair back, and went to sit beside Elizabeth, smiling in welcome as Hildebrand and Freddie came in. Their arms were full of posies.

"We heard you were ill, Lady Elizabeth," said Hildebrand. "So we brought you these to cheer you."

"And we heard you were back from the country, Mrs. Beaumont," said Freddie. "So we brought these to welcome you."

"How very sweet!" cried Elizabeth, accepting the bouquet of pale yellow roses. "I am quite recovered now, but these are sure to make me feel even better."

Georgina took the mass of white lilies. "And I have never had such a dear welcome back! Won't you sit down, and tell us all the delicious gossip we have been missing?"

"If you will tell us how you enjoyed rusticating, Mrs. Beaumont," said Hildebrand.

"I found it delightful," answered Georgina. "The country air is so *bracing*, you know."

Freddie and Hildebrand looked at each other with matching, gleeful grins. "Oh, yes, we do know," said Freddie. "Did our friend Wayland not return to Town with you? We had not heard he was back."

"Oh, no. He had an emergency to see to at his other estate, so he left Fair Oak a few days before I did."

Freddie looked deeply disappointed. "Do you know when he means to return? Has he written to you, Mrs. Beaumont?"

"Only a note to let his mother, his sister, and me know he had arrived safely at his destination. You seem quite interested in Lord Wayland's doings, Mr. Marlow. And you, too, Lord Garrick." Georgina laughed. "Never fear, though! I am sure he will return to London soon enough."

"Well, that is a relief!" Freddie sighed. "There was that wager, you see, and I owe my tailor . . ."

Georgina's gaze sharpened as she looked at Freddie. "A wager, Mr. Marlow? Of what sort?"

Hildebrand smacked Freddie hard on his shoulder. "Now you have done it, you careless puppy!"

"Ow!" Freddie clutched at his shoulder. "Why did you do that, Hildebrand? I thought she knew of it."

Georgina set her teacup down with a clatter, and stood up, her hands planted on her hips, to loom over them. "Thought I knew about *what*? Tell me. Have I been the object of some sort of sordid speculation?"

"Georgie!" Elizabeth reached out to tug at Georgina's skirt. "My dear, do sit down. He can hardly explain with you looming over him like that."

Georgina reluctantly sat back down. "Well? Do tell, Mr. Marlow."

"It—it was not *sordid*, Mrs. Beaumont," Freddie protested. "I—or maybe it was Hildebrand—merely said that Wayland would—would offer for you before the end of the Season. That is all!" He shrank back in his chair.

Georgina pursed her lips. "I see. And what about you, Viscount Garrick?"

Hildebrand, who had been smirking over his friend's cornering, blanched. "M-me, Mrs. Beaumont?"

"What was your part in the wager?"

"I—or maybe it was Freddie—said it would take him at least a year. Or something of that sort."

"Hm. And did Lord Wayland take any part of this?"

"Oh, no! Never!" Hildebrand and Freddie chorused.

"He said we were fools to make any sort of wager on something as unpredictable as people," said Hildebrand. "And he refused to take any part of it. It was only us, Mrs. Beaumont, and I swear we are heartily sorry for it!"

"Well. At least Wayland showed some sense." Georgina looked at Elizabeth, and grinned.

They both burst into laughter, much to the shock of Hildebrand and Freddie, who stared at them open-mouthed, like landed fish.

"Oh!" gasped Georgina. "You two really are so very funny. It is no wonder that Al—Wayland likes to keep you about!"

"Funny, and dear!" Elizabeth wiped at her eyes. "You have quite brightened our day, I do declare."

Freddie and Hildebrand looked at each other, still bewildered. Then they looked back at the giggling ladies.

"Well," said Hildebrand. "I am only glad I could be of service."

"Oh, you have," said Elizabeth. "We have been quite shut away here, with nothing to amuse us for days."

"In that case, you should come with us to Vauxhall on Friday!" said Freddie.

"To Vauxhall?" said Georgina, with a prickling of interest.

"There is to be a masquerade," Hildebrand said. "Freddie and I have reserved a box, where you would be quite safe. Lady Fitzgerald and her niece are to accompany us. And your husband must come, too, Lady Elizabeth. It will be such a merry evening! You must come!"

"Oh, I should so like to," Elizabeth said wistfully.

"I have not been to a masquerade since last we were in Venice. Would you not like to, Georgina?"

"Yes, of course," said Georgina. "I adore a masquerade! But are you certain you are quite up to it, Lizzie?"

"Of course I am! I will not dance, or wander about. I will only sit in the box, and watch. It will be good for us to get out of this house."

"Wonderful, we accept your kind invitation," Georgina said. Then she added, "As long as there is no more talk of wagers!"

"Oh, no!" cried Freddie.

"Never again, Mrs. Beaumont," said Hildebrand. "We *promise*."

Chapter Eighteen

Alex's heart was filled with excitement—and trepidation—
when he at last turned down the lane that led to
Fair Oak.

He had been gone for several days, trying futilely
to solve the many problems at the Grange, an estate
that was even more ramshackle than Fair Oak. There
had been many problems indeed, and he had been
busy from sunup to sundown every day.

But even all that activity, all those worries, could
not erase thoughts of Georgina. They would come to
him at the oddest times. As he inspected a drain, he
would see her green eyes, sparkling with some mischief. As he repaired a roof, he would see her slim,
pale hands, deftly wielding a piece of charcoal over
an open sketchbook.

As he would drift into sleep at night, he would
imagine they were dancing again, floating across a
ballroom, his arms about her. He would relive their
kiss in the summerhouse, just before he would fall
asleep with a smile on his face.

He wondered often how she was faring with his
mother and Emily. Perhaps they had given another

party, or attended a *soirée* at some neighbor's home. He envisioned her walking in the gardens with Emily, or going to the shops in the village.

He also envisioned her, with a cold pang, examining the house more closely—seeing all the flaws in it, the shabby draperies, the missing artwork and ornaments. Finding it wanting; finding it not at all the sort of place she would want to live in after all.

Alex longed to see her, yet he half feared it, as well. Would she rush out to greet him, to kiss his cheek and say she had missed him? Or would she look at him with reproach, with pity?

Pity was the one thing he could never bear to see in her lovely eyes.

So deeply were his thoughts occupied with Georgina, that he was almost surprised to not see her waiting on the front steps when he turned into view of the house.

What he *did* see surprised him even more.

There were two men on his roof, clambering about with much noise of hammering and sawing. A hearty country housemaid was scrubbing at the windows, while another beat at a dusty rug hung up on a line. A rather gnarled old man was clipping efficiently at the hedges, and a younger man was clearing the brush from the neglected flower beds.

Alex had not seen so much activity about Fair Oak since before he left for Spain.

And in the midst of it all was his sister, flitting from the gardeners to the maids, giving some instructions, pulling up some weeds, pushing aside old roof tiles the workmen had thrown down. She looked like a sunbeam, a dancing sunbeam in a yellow-and-white muslin gown he recognized as one of Georgina's.

She saw him at last as he pulled the horses to a

halt, and waved at him merrily, a broad smile on her face. She hurried across the drive toward him, and he was struck by how pretty his little sister looked. It was not just the fashionable new dress: her cheeks were pink and glowing, her eyes a vivid, sparkling blue. Even her hair shimmered, a halo of shining, sun-yellow curls.

She was no longer the pale, worried young woman he had met upon his return home. She was again the Emily of their old life, who he would seize about the waist and twirl into the air, just to hear her squeals of laughter.

How had such a transformation come about in the days he had been gone?

"Alex!" she cried, only waiting for him to alight from his curricle before she threw her arms around him. "How grand it is to see you! You should have written to us that you were returning. I would have made sure this mess was tidied up!"

Alex kissed her cheek. "There was no time to write. You are looking very pretty, Em!"

"Thank you! It is the dress." Emily spun about, preening just a bit in the primrose muslin. "Is it not pretty? Georgina loaned it to me."

"Loaned?"

"Well, *gave*, I suppose, since I had to let down the hem. There is a matching bonnet, too. Was that not kind of her?"

Alex nodded slowly, a faint misgiving stirring. Georgina was *giving* his sister gowns? "Very kind. Where is Georgina, by the way?"

"Oh, I fear she is not here. She received a letter from her friend, Lady Elizabeth, saying she was not well. So Georgina went back to Town."

"Lady Elizabeth is ill?"

"Yes. But Georgina wrote just yesterday to tell us that all is well now."

"I am very glad to hear it. It seems a great many exciting things have happened in my absence." He gestured toward the activity all around them.

"Yes! Isn't it marvelous?"

"I am not certain. What is *it*?"

Emily bit her lip, obviously beginning to be concerned by his distinct lack of enthusiasm. "Let us go inside, Alex. You must be thirsty after your journey. I can send for some tea, and I will tell you all that has been happening."

"I would like that, Emily."

Even the library did not look the same as he had left it. The furniture had been pushed back so that the rug could be removed and beaten by the maid outside. The scent of polish and beeswax hung heavy in the air, and the tabletops and wooden chairs gleamed. The draperies had obviously been washed, because he could now see their forest-green color clearly, free of dust.

A small oil painting, a view of Fair Oak in a distinctive style he recognized as Georgina's, hung over the carved mantle.

"Things *have* changed while I was gone," he murmured.

"So they have." Emily sat down in an armchair before the now empty and scoured fireplace. Alex sat across from her, just as they had on that bleak afternoon when he had spoken with the lawyer.

"Tell me all that has been happening," he said.

"Well, Mary and Violet came up from the village, to help with some of the heavy cleaning that has been too long neglected. And Violet's brothers took on the roof. It has been leaking terribly, you know; the wallpaper in the gold bedchamber is quite ruined, but now that the roof has been fixed, we can go about repairing it. I have also hired on some laborers to begin the hay making in a few weeks. With that out of the way, we should have a good start on the fall plowing."

Alex listened to all this in silence, his hands opening and closing on the carved arms of his chair. It was excellent that all this had been taken care of, of course; he had been very concerned by how the damp from the leaking roof could be affecting his mother's health. But still . . . "How could you afford to fix the roof, Emily? The money I sent you from the Grange could only have covered the household expenses."

Emily fidgeted, smoothing her skirt, patting her hair. She looked at the floor, at the fireplace, anywhere but at him. "Oh, but it was so good of you to send that money, Alex! You are always such a good brother."

"And you are a good sister. But you are changing the subject. I know you are a fine manager, but how did you stretch that money so far?" He feared, though, that he already knew.

Emily's words only confirmed his fears. "Before Georgina left, she—she loaned me some funds."

"Loaned? Like your frock?"

"*Gave* me, then! But I thought—that is, I was sure, that soon enough she would be my sister, so her gift was quite proper. Was I wrong?"

Alex remained silent. So very many emotions—predominantly an anger whose force startled him, a hurt whose depth startled him even more—swirled through him that he feared to speak. He feared what he would say.

His worries had all come to pass. Georgina had been appalled by his home; appalled at his poor judgment in leaving Damian to manage all and going off to war, at leaving his family to this cruel state. Rather than leave, as he had feared, she had pitied—which he had feared even more.

She tried to fix all his mistakes. She used her money to solve problems that were his alone. *His* responsibility, *his* duty, not hers. He had wanted to take care of her, but instead she was taking care of him.

Emily watched him, her elfin face creased in worry. She had looked so very happy in the garden. He hated himself for killing that joy, for making her look so pinched and worried again. He hated himself for the things that had befallen her and their mother while he was gone.

He hated that he could not solve things for his little sister, as he had always mended her broken dolls and dried her tears when she was a child. Someone else had solved them, and that someone else was a woman he loved. A woman whose admiration he had so longed for.

Alex had been called a hero, had collected medals, and been lauded by so many people. But he had never so wanted to appear heroic in someone's eyes as he wanted to in Georgina Beaumont's.

He wanted her love, her respect, since he so loved and respected her. Instead, she thought him to be pitied and helped.

He was so angry. Whether at her, or himself, or even his dead brother, he did not know. He only knew he must *do* something about it, or he would burst from it.

"Alex?" Emily said quietly.

Alex shook himself out of his dark haze, and looked over at his sister. She had twisted her hands so tightly into her skirt that she wrinkled the fine fabric.

"You *were* wrong, Em," he answered. "You should not have accepted that money, and Mrs. Beaumont was wrong to offer it. She is not to be my wife."

Emily stared at him, her mouth agape. She looked shocked and deeply wounded. More wounded than he had ever seen her. "But—you brought her here! You introduced her to the neighbors. You made her part of us. She was the most exciting person I had ever seen." Emily's lower lip trembled. "I thought she was to be my sister!"

Alex shook his head, feeling even more dismal than ever before. "It was wrong of me. I am sorry. I was mistaken."

Emily leaped to her feet, deeply agitated. "Mistaken? Sorry? It is the money, is it not? This is all my fault."

"Of course it is not your fault."

"It is! It is my fault for taking the money, for misjudging how you would react. I should have known your pride. But it is also your fault!"

"Emily, please."

Emily was beyond hearing. Her voice rose as she cried, "Yes, Alexander, your fault. For making Georgina think you were to marry her; for making me believe she was to be my sister, and that all would be well at last. I would have expected something like this from Damian, but never from you."

"Emily, calm down! Please," Alex beseeched, deeply hurt at being compared to Damian.

"No, I will not calm down! Not this time. Never again!"

With that, she burst into tears and fled the room.

Alex sat there for a long time after she left, still and numb as he listened to the sounds of the roof being repaired, of the new maids singing as they went about their duties. As he stared sightlessly at the new painting over the fireplace.

Then he slowly rose to his feet, and went out to the drive where his curricle still stood.

There was something he must do. In London.

Chapter Nineteen

Vauxhall Gardens was crowded to capacity for the masquerade. Every box was full of brightly clothed revelers, listening to Signora d'Angelo—the new Italian soprano—sing, lots of laughing, talking, getting thoroughly disguised, or making assignations for the Dark Walk.

Georgina watched it all, thoroughly enjoying the spectacle of it, as well as the company in her own box. Nicholas and Elizabeth, dressed as Harlequin and Columbine, fed each other strawberries, while the Fitzgerald ladies, an aunt and niece who could almost have been golden-haired twins, giggled over a naughty story Hildebrand and Freddie were telling. It concerned old Dowager Lady Dalrymple, her poodle, a footman, and a privy.

Even Georgina had to laugh at the story's finale, as she waved her shepherdess's crook at them admonishingly. "You two are really very silly! How Wayland ever puts up with you, I cannot say."

"It is because he is rather a humorless fellow, himself," Hildebrand answered jokingly. "He keeps us about to make him lighthearted! Would you care for some more champagne, Mrs. Beaumont?"

"Yes, please. My glass has been quite empty this age!" said Georgina. "But I have not found Wayland to be humorless. He merely has a—noble bearing. He must have been very dashing in his regimentals."

"I do wish we could have seen him before he sold his commission!" Elizabeth interjected. "He really looks so dignified and elegant, quite Caesar-like."

"You are making me jealous, my dear!" cried Nicholas. "Am I not elegant and dignified?"

"Oh, yes, darling. The most elegant and dignified man I have ever met," cooed Elizabeth.

Georgina sipped at her champagne, and smiled as she watched Elizabeth and Nicholas laughing together. "Lizzie," she said. "I am so happy you were feeling able to accompany us this evening."

"I would not miss a Vauxhall masquerade for anything! It reminds me of the night Nick and I met, in Venice. Do you remember that night, dear?" Elizabeth turned a tender look on her husband, who kissed her hand in return.

"How could I ever forget it?" he said.

Georgina looked away from the romantic scene, feeling a bit wistful. It had been many, many days since she had last seen Alex, and she had not received so much as a note from him. There had been a letter from Emily, but even that had been over a week ago, and she had scarcely mentioned her brother in its contents.

Had Georgina been mistaken, then, in Alex's regard? Had she misinterpreted his attentions?

Even as these doubts flitted through her mind, she dismissed them. Alex's glances, his kisses and em-

braces, had been always full of such sincere tenderness.

Hadn't they?

She *had* been sure of them at the time. But now, with
him so far away and so silent, and with her surrounded
by a noisy crowd so she could scarce think, she was
assailed by misgivings.

Perhaps his feelings had been only of the sort that
soon faded when the object of affection was gone from
sight. She would not have thought Alex's feelings to
be of the fickle kind, but then she had been wrong
before.

Georgina looked off into the crowd, searching for
something, anything, to take her mind away from
these melancholy thoughts. She should not be dwelling
on such things on such a lovely night. What she really
needed was some distraction, some merriment!

Some more champagne.

She poured more of the golden, bubbling liquid into
her glass, and sipped at it as she watched the revelers.
The Italian soprano had finished her song, and dancing
had commenced among the masqueraders. Georgina
giggled as she watched a knight in full armor, obviously quite foxed, wobble and fall over amid great
clanking. Not even his lady fair, with the help of an
Egyptian prince and Henry VIII, could rouse him. The
dancing went on around him.

Then she saw her friend, Lady Lonsdale, clothed as
Aphrodite in flowing white gauze draperies, in a box
across the way.

She seized on the escape.

"There is Harriet Lonsdale!" Georgina said. "I do
believe I will go and say hello to her."

"Shall I escort you?" Freddie offered, though he

looked quite reluctant to leave the side of the younger Fitzgerald lady.

"Oh, no. Her box is just across the way, see? I shall be safe just walking over there. You all must stay here, and enjoy the last of the strawberries."

"Send Harriet my greetings," answered Elizabeth, then she went back to whispering with her husband.

Georgina gathered up her shepherdess's crook and the fluffy blue and white skirts of her costume, and slipped from the box. She skirted the dancers, who were swirling and skipping most vigorously, and dodged a strawberry seller and another shepherdess, who was leading a real sheep on a silk rope.

Unfortunately, the sheep had just done its business, and Georgina was forced to lift her skirts even higher to step over a rather nasty pile.

In order to reach the Lonsdales' box, she had to pass several entrances to quiet, more private walkways. As she walked by one, she heard a voice call her name.

"Georgina."

She paused, wondering if this was something like Emily's Queen Elizabeth again. She *had* had rather a bit too much champagne.

Then she heard it again, louder. "Georgina."

She peered down the walkway. It was very dimly lit, with only a few Chinese lanterns, but she could just make out a shadowy figure standing beneath a tree.

There was something about the figure's height, the set of his shoulders . . .

Could it be? Had her thoughts of him somehow conjured him tonight?

"Alex?" she called tentatively, stepping out of the light and into the walkway.

"Of course it is Alex. Or else were you expecting someone else to be waiting for you on a dark path?"

Georgina laughed in relief and exhilaration. Alex *was* here, at last! "Certainly not, silly man! But I have not heard from you in so long, I feared my ears were deceiving me."

He stepped into a small patch of light then.

Georgina, who had been poised to run to him and throw her arms about him, was stayed by the rather forbidding look on his face. He was all sharp planes and angles in the light and shadow, unsmiling and severe.

Georgina felt rather uncomfortably like a disobedient subaltern, about to be given a severe dressing down.

She advanced more slowly down the path, her grip tight on her crook.

"How did you know we were here at Vauxhall?" she asked.

"I called at Lady Elizabeth's house. Her butler told me you were here."

Georgina glanced at his attire. He wore black and white evening dress, not dusty travel buckskins. "You only arrived in Town today?"

"Yes. I stopped at Fair Oak, only to find that you had departed. Is Lady Elizabeth well?"

"Oh, yes. And your mother and sister?"

"Quite well also, thank you."

Georgina moistened her suddenly dry lips with the tip of her tongue. His stiff formality was quite chilling, after their delightful intimacy at Fair Oak. And puzzling, as well. She could think of nothing she might have done to cause such coldness.

She only knew she could not stand the little politenesses for another moment. She stepped a bit closer to him, close enough to smell the faint spicy scent of his soap.

"Alex," she asked boldly, "are you angry about something?"

Alex looked down at her steadily. Rather coldly, she thought.

"There was a great deal of activity going on at Fair Oak. It was quite lively, really."

"Oh?"

"Yes. My sister had hired new maids to clean the house from attics to scullery, gardeners, and men to repair the roof."

In Georgina's opinion, those refurbishments had been much needed, and not at all something to be angry about. "Did she indeed?"

"She told me that *you* had furnished the funds for those improvements," he said tightly.

If he had suddenly reached out and struck her, Georgina could not have been more shocked. "It is the money you are angry about? The money I gave Emily?"

"Did you think I would not find out about it?"

"It was hardly a secret! We did not mean to conceal it from you. Emily told me of the repairs that were quite urgently needed, and I made her a loan."

"A loan? However did you expect my sister to ever pay you back such a sum!"

"It was not a large sum!" Georgina cried, confused. "It was not so much as a ball gown."

"I suppose it was not much, to a *famous* artist. A wealthy widow." His fists clenched at his sides. "But the Kentons have no need of charity."

"I did not think of it as charity," Georgina said softly. She had thought it a gift to her future sister, an investment in her future home.

Obviously, Alex did not see it that way. In fact, it was obvious that he had never thought of Fair Oak as *her* home at all.

Not as she had dared to.

She looked away from him, to the surrounding trees and shrubberies, which were blurry from the tears swimming in her eyes. She blinked hard against them, determined not to let them fall.

"Please, Alex," she pleaded, "do not be angry . . ."

Alex had stepped back, into the shadows once more. "I am not angry," he said, his voice still a bit distant, but not so inflexible. "I merely wanted things to be made clear. I will pay the money back."

Georgina shook her head. "You do not need to do that."

"I *do* need to. You may expect the first installment within a fortnight. And now, Mrs. Beaumont, I will bid you good night. I wish you every health and happiness."

Then he seemed to melt back into the darkness, and he was gone.

Georgina, when she was certain she was alone, sank down onto the path in the puddle of her skirts. Her crook, which she had been clutching like a lifeline, clattered down beside her.

She felt numb, frozen, shocked, as if she had been left out in a blizzard.

What had just happened? She was utterly bewildered. That man, who had spoken to her so coldly about money, was *not* her Alex. He was not the man who had talked with her of her work with such interest and sensitivity, who had danced with her, walked with her. Kissed her so sweetly.

That Alex had been full of passion, of kindness and dignity.

This Alex she had seen tonight seemed rather a

scared little boy, running from a woman's gift. A woman's love. Hiding behind cold words. Words about money.

Georgina clutched at the pearls she wore at her throat, longing to tear them off and throw them at Alex's stubborn head. Didn't he *know* how fortunate he was to have her? Didn't he know what he was missing?

Georgina pressed her hand to her mouth to still her sobs. How she longed to run after him, to find him, to *make* him tell her what was truly wrong! She knew that her Alex had loved her, that something terrible was keeping him from that love now.

Yet how could she talk to him now, when she was so frozen with hurt? She could not. She would not! She just longed to bash him over the head with her crook, for his bacon-brained behavior!

Georgina took off her frilled bonnet and shook her hair free with a sigh. Love had always been so simple for her. Jack had been as open and sunny as a summer day. He had been easy to understand, since all his emotions could always be read on his handsome face. Their quarrels had always been quick and brief, ended with a sweet romp in the bedchamber.

Paolo, a man she had had a brief flirtation with in Venice, had had flashes of temper that ended as swiftly as a lightning bolt. She had always known what he was thinking, as well, because he always told it to the world. She would just laugh at his tantrums, as he would laugh at hers.

Why must love be difficult *now*, when it was so very important! More important than it had ever been before in her life.

Georgina beat her fists against her knees in frustration.

"Mrs. Beaumont?"

She looked up. Freddie stood beside her; he must have come upon her unseen, while she was wrapped in her misery.

"Are you ill?" he said, his face creased in concern.

"No," she answered, then changed her mind quickly. "Yes. I do feel a bit faint."

And indeed she did. She knew that if she were to stand up, her legs would not support her.

"Do let me help you," Freddie offered, flustered.

Georgina leaned heavily on his arm as he brought her to her feet. "Lady Elizabeth was quite worried when you could not be found."

"Elizabeth!" Georgina cried. "Is she ill? Does she need me?"

"She is well. She was just concerned for you. Here, lean on my arm, and I will see you back to the box."

"Thank you, Mr. Marlow," Georgina said, deeply grateful for his kindness, and for the solid feel of his arm holding her up. "You are a true gentleman."

Freddie blushed a deep crimson.

Elizabeth was pacing the length of the box when they arrived. "Georgie! There you are. Harriet Lonsdale said she had not seen you all evening, and I feared you had become ill." Her quick gaze took in Georgina's pale face, her trembling hands. "Oh, my dear, you *are* ill! We will go home at once."

"Yes," Georgina murmured. "Home. I do want to go home."

Later, curled up before the fire in their dressing gowns, Georgina told Elizabeth all of what had happened in that dark walkway.

"I was such a fool, Lizzie. An utter fool." Georgina

buried her face in a cushion, trying to hide her tear-
swollen face.

Nothing could be hidden from her friend. Elizabeth
laid her hand gently on Georgina's trembling shoulder.
"You, dear? A fool? Never!"

"Yes! A fool to ever think Alex and I could make
a life together, that I could be in love again. That I
could make a proper duchess."

Elizabeth's hand stilled. "Was his family horrid to
you, and you did not tell me the truth? Georgie, you
do not need such rudesbys in your life. You are far
too fine for them . . ."

Georgina shook her head. "His mother and sister
were delightful. Unlike their son and brother."

"What happened, then? I fear I do not understand.
Did you and Alex quarrel?"

"Yes," Georgina wailed.

"About what? You were so very happy when you
left for the country. Lord Wayland adores you, I could
see that!"

"*I* adored *him*. And I confess that I thought he—
admired me."

"So did I, most assuredly. So did Nick. Were we so
deeply mistaken, then?"

Georgina sat up, and accepted the handkerchief that
Elizabeth held out to her. "I fear so. I saw him tonight, you see. He came all the way to Vauxhall just
to break things off with me."

"Well!" Elizabeth huffed. "We shall sue him for
breach of promise."

"Lizzie!"

"We shall. I will summon the solicitor straight
away."

"Oh, Lizzie, we cannot do that. There was never

any promise to breach. He never asked me to marry him."

"He was going to! We all knew *that*. Did he not take you to meet his family? A man would not do that with a woman he wanted only for a mistress."

"Perhaps he was going to make an offer. But he did not. He will not."

"Well. Nick shall just have to call him out, then."

"Lizzie!" Georgina laughed. "No."

"We could draw some unflattering pictures of him, and sell them to the print shops."

"I like *that*."

"I thought you might. Now, will you tell me exactly what happened?"

"You know, of course, that Alex's late brother quite ruined the family's fortunes."

"I had suspected such a thing, yes. But Wayland seemed so very guileless . . ." Elizabeth's lips thinned. "Never say he *was* a fortune hunter. Oh, my dear Georgie."

Georgina laughed bitterly. "He was quite the opposite, I fear."

"What do you mean?"

"He was called away on business while I was at Fair Oak, as I told you, and I was going to stay with his family until he returned. His sister was going out to visit some tenants, so I accompanied her. Oh, Lizzie, you should have heard of the life she has been forced to live! She has been running the farm almost all on her own. I loaned her some funds, just to see her through some very necessary repairs."

"You gave money to Wayland's sister?"

"*Loaned*. Just until—well, until Alex and I were wed, and the farm could be made profitable again."

"I see. Yes. And Wayland was angry?"

Georgina gave an unladylike snort. "To say the least! He was furious when he found out. He—he accused me of trying to *buy* his family. I think he fears it will make him appear weak in front of them."

"What nonsense!" Elizabeth cried.

"Yes. I was only trying to be of some help."

"Of course you were. What did you say to him?"

"Nothing. But I *wanted* to tell him he was being a ridiculous, bacon-brained looby. Among other things. It just all happened so fast that I did not have the opportunity. More is the pity."

Elizabeth giggled. "Georgie!"

"He was not the man I imagined him to be."

"So it is well and truly over?"

"Yes."

"Deep in your heart?"

"Yes!"

"Well, then. What are you going to do now, dear?"

Georgina gave Elizabeth a rather watery smile. "I am going home. To Italy."

Chapter Twenty

Alex was deeply sorry as soon as he opened his eyes the morning after Vauxhall.

And he was not sorry only because he had consumed too much cheap brandy and now his head felt like it was being hammered at from the inside.

He was sorry because he remembered every last horrible thing he had said to Georgina.

Georgina. The woman he loved.

And look at how he had shown her that love! With harsh words, with anger over things as foolish as money and hurt pride.

Well, he had learned more in the never-ending night after he left her at Vauxhall, in the cheap taverns where he had set about becoming thoroughly foxed, than he had in a hundred schoolrooms or a thousand battlefields.

As he had sat in a dark corner with his bottle of brandy, he remembered all the things Georgina had done or said since the day he fished Lady Kate out of the river. He remembered how her green eyes had shone with quiet pride as she showed him her paintings. He remembered how she danced, so light and quick, her waist warm under his hand. He remembered how she would laugh with his sister while they played cards, when Emily had not laughed in so long.

He remembered best of all how very sweet her lips tasted.

He remembered her white, hurt face under the lanterns at Vauxhall.

And he had known, as he stumbled back to his rooms at dawn, that he was a hundred times a fool.

Georgina Beaumont was a talented, beautiful, dashing woman, who every man in London admired. Yet she had loved *him!* Alex Kenton, the crusty colonel. Not the duke. Him. What were pride and money, next to a woman like her? Next to a love like they could share?

Nothing. They were as nothing. Yet he only saw that now, when it was too late. After he had gone charging in like some hell-bent bull, bashing all the beautiful things they had together. He had crushed love, trust, and honor beneath his quick anger.

Alex groaned and buried his face in his pillow. Even that, along with the demons dancing in his skull, could not erase his misery.

He should never have gone to her when he was so exhausted from his journey, and so angry. He should have waited until he could see her again in daylight, clearheaded and rational, when he could speak to her in a calm manner.

Seeing her in the moonlight, so beautiful and radiant, had killed every vestige of a rational thought. And, he was ashamed to admit, the sight of the rich pearls at her neck had only fueled his anger.

Well, his troops had not called him Hotspur for nothing.

Now he saw so clearly what he should have done.

He should have taken her in his arms, ridiculous shepherd's crook and all, and held her so tightly she could never leave.

If she would only listen to him now, give him a chance to redeem himself, he would not care if she wrapped herself from top to toe in pearls! Or if she even papered his house in diamonds.

He did not even care if people speculated that he was a fortune hunter. He only wanted her to accept his love, and give him a chance to win her back.

He knew it would not be easy. Georgina would no doubt blister him with her redheaded temper, challenge him to a duel, run him over with her curricle. He did not care; she could do her worst, for he deserved every bit of it. And more.

But he had to try to get her to forgive him. He *had* to. His very life depended on it.

Slowly, very slowly, Alex rolled out of bed and went to pour some cold water into a basin. He judged from the quality of the light at the window that it was already late afternoon, and he had a very important call to make.

"She is not here, Lord Wayland." Elizabeth Hollingsworth's gaze was cool as she looked at Alex, where he sat across from her in her drawing room.

If Alex needed any reminders of how far and how fast he had fallen from grace, this coolness, after Elizabeth's warm friendship, would have done it neatly. However, he did *not* need any reminders. He needed to see Georgina as quickly as possible, to begin to repair the damage he had so heedlessly done.

"Not here?" he said, stunned. "Has she gone out driving, then? Or perhaps to Hookham's Library? If I could just wait for her . . ."

"I do not think that would be a good idea."

"Oh, please, Lady Elizabeth!" Alex found he was not above begging. Not any more. "I must see her. I must—must tell her how very sorry I am, how wrong I was."

"Yes. Georgina told me of your little—contretemps last night. You were very naughty."

"Then, you know how very desperate it is that I see her, talk to her."

Elizabeth sighed, and he could see her relenting. Some of the frost in her gray eyes melted as she looked at him. "I can see that you are very sorry."

"I am! More than I can say. I should never have said such things. But my blasted temper—oh. Do pardon my language, Lady Elizabeth."

She waved away his apologies. "I myself often say blast, and worse. I fear it is quite appropriate in these circumstances."

Alex felt a chill, as if a cold wind had suddenly blown down the chimney and extinguished the fire. "Has she said she hates me, then? That she will never forgive me?"

"I am sure Georgina does not hate you. But I fear that when I said she was not here, I did not mean that she was at the park or at Gunter's. She has gone back to Italy."

Alex gaped at Elizabeth. "Italy?"

"Yes. She would not be dissuaded from such a rash course, not once I assured her that my health was so improved I could have no need of her until the babe comes. Her ship left on the morning tide, and has surely cleared the Thames by now."

Alex lowered his aching head into his hands. All of the energy that hope had given him, that had kept him upright, had made him hurry to the Hollingsworths' house, suddenly deserted him. He felt as drained and flat as Lunardi's balloon before it was filled. He felt old and weary.

She was gone. She was beyond his apologies, and his love.

Or was she? He looked up, a faint hope starting to bloom.

"I love Georgina as my own sister," Elizabeth was saying. "But I fear she has a fierce temper, and she often does quite rash things. Such as rush off to Italy. I suppose that is the reason she is so very creative, much more fine an artist than I will ever be."

"It is what I love the most about her," Alex murmured. "Her fire."

Elizabeth smiled. "Yes. I was sure you were the man for her, despite your bad behavior last night."

Encouraged by her words, Alex said quickly, "Lady Elizabeth, would you be so kind as to give me Georgina's direction in Italy?"

"Are you going to write to her?"

"I am going to do better than that. I am going after her."

Elizabeth laughed merrily, and clapped her hands. "Oh! How very romantic. She will be so surprised to find you on her very doorstep."

"And pleased, do you think?"

"*Very* pleased, though she will not admit it at first." Elizabeth stood, and went over to her small writing desk, searching through the drawers until she found what she sought. "She is in Venice, and here is her address. No doubt she will rail at you when you first arrive—perhaps even throw things, which she has been known to do in the past. You must take no notice. The storm will soon pass, and she will be very touched that you have come so far after her. A woman cannot help but be flattered that a man would go hundreds of miles, just to apologize and grovel! You do plan to grovel, I hope?"

"Most assuredly." Alex accepted the paper from her, and tucked it away safely in his coat pocket. That slip of paper was more valuable than gold. "I pray that you are right, that she will forgive me and accept me."

"I know that I am." Elizabeth suddenly went up on tiptoe from her petite height, and kissed his cheek. "I wish you *bonne chance*, Alex."

Alex nodded, deeply moved. "Thank you, Elizabeth. I fear I will need all your good wishes and prayers."

Georgina was deeply sorry the moment the English coast disappeared from view.

What had she done? Oh, *what* had she done!

She paced along the ship's deck, her burgundy red pelisse whipping about her in the stiff wind. She wore no hat, and long strands of hair had come loose from their pins and lashed at her eyes and cheeks. But she took no notice of the wind, or of the crew who hurried around her, or of the maid she had hired for the journey, who shivered against a wall.

Lady Kate, sheltered in a coil of rope, watched her mistress with anxious black eyes.

Whatever was she thinking of, to run off to Italy just because she was mad at Alex? Because they had had a quarrel, which had probably been just as much her fault as his?

She should have stayed to see what he would have to say, once he calmed down. *If* he ever had anything to say to her again, after that shocking scene at Vauxhall.

Georgina paused in her pacings, to lean over the

railing and look down at the water below. As if there might be an answer to her dilemma written in the roiling gray waves below.

There wasn't, of course. There did not seem to be any answers anywhere—not even inside herself. She only had the sickening feeling that she had been foolishly impetuous, for the five hundredth time in her life.

Georgina sighed and sank down to sit on the coil of rope next to Lady Kate. She had leaped without looking, as she always did! She saw now, horribly clear, what she should have done. She should have understood what using her money before they were wed would cause Alex to feel—and to do. He was such a proud man.

Just as she was a proud woman. Too much so.

She also should have stayed in London, so they could have talked and come to a right understanding. This craven running away was not at all like her, and she did not know why she had done it. Not even anger should have made her do something so rash.

Oh, yes, you know why you did it, a tiny voice at the back of her mind whispered. *You were afraid.*

I certainly was not! Georgina protested indignantly.

You were, the voice insisted. *And you still are. You are afraid that you love him, and need him. You don't want to need him.*

Of course I do not! Georgina cried silently. After all, if she were to need someone, he could die and leave her all alone, with the entire world shattered about her.

Like her parents. Like Jack. Even like dear old Mr. Beaumont.

Georgina pressed her gloved hand to her mouth. That was it! That was what had driven her to be so alone for so long. Fear.

Beneath all her dash, her bravado, she was scared to death. She had seized on her quarrel with Alex as an excuse to leave him, to scurry back to the safety of Italy. A desperate need to escape her love for him, her fear to lose him.

But she knew now that that was futile. Even if she never saw him again, her love for him would follow her all the rest of her days. It was a love that was stronger than any fear.

She saw that all too clearly now, when it was too late and a sea lay between them. Even if he came to call on her, he would find she had left, and he would think that she no longer cared. Perhaps he would be hurt, but eventually he would marry someone young and pretty and suitably duchess-like. He would take her to the home that should have been Georgina's, to be welcomed by the family that should have been Georgina's.

He would give her the wedding night that should have been Georgina's. He would make love to some milk-and-water miss in Georgina's very bed!

Georgina pounded her heels on the deck in consternation at the melodramatic scenario she had concocted in her mind.

Oh, what had she *done*!

Chapter Twenty-One

Venice was delighted by the return of the oh-so-dashing Signora Beaumont. And Signora Beaumont plunged into the revels of Venice with every bit of her former relish, and then some.

If that relish, that dash, was just a tiny bit forced, well, who could notice? Any hint of melancholy was hidden by exquisite new gowns, a new hairstyle, and plenty of champagne.

Bianca, the loyal Italian maid who had been with Georgina for years, had kept the Venetian house impeccably in her absence—or what passed for impeccable with Bianca, anyway. Georgina was able to move back in as if she had never been away at all.

The society of Venice, both Italian and English, welcomed her back as if she had never been away, as well. From her very first evening home, she was pulled into a whirl of balls, suppers, breakfasts, water parties, and casinos. Her old suitors were most eager to renew her acquaintance, and soon the narrow halls and small, high-ceilinged rooms of her house were filled with the color and scent of masses of flowers.

Georgina had loved this life, had relished the excitement and glitter and noise of it. She threw herself back into it, dancing and laughing as if nothing had ever happened. Every once in a while, in the midst of a merry crowd, she could even feel like nothing *had* happened. That she was the Georgina Beaumont she had been before she left for England.

But something had happened. She was not the same, and she never would be again. She had seen a new life, filled not just with the gaiety of balls, but with family and close friends. Quieter, perhaps, more respectable, certainly. It was not a life she would have thought she would crave, when she was younger and more restless.

Sometimes, in the quiet darkness of her bedchamber at night, she imagined that life. She imagined herself as mistress of Fair Oak, strolling its halls and garden paths with her husband. Lady Kate would run ahead of them, cavorting with Emily and perhaps a few golden-haired children.

She imagined presiding over suppers and balls for all the neighbors, and painting all their portraits.

She imagined long, sweet nights in the grand duke's bedchamber, in her husband's arms.

And then, still alone, she would turn her face into the pillow and cry, with the silvery light of a Venetian moon falling across her bed from the window.

This had to be the house.

Alex looked down at the address Elizabeth had given him, then back up at the house. It was quite pretty, a narrow confection of gray-pink stone, with wrought-iron balconies dotted with pots of vivid red and pink flowers. The shutters were open to the early summer day, and sheer white curtains fluttered in the light breeze.

It *looked* like Georgina's house. Elegant, warm, and artistically lovely.

Alex took a deep breath, and closed his fist tightly about the slip of paper. He had faced French hordes on battlefields, faced death by bullet or bayonet or cannon. But he had never been so terrified as he was now, about to face the woman he loved and had wronged.

He had had many hours to envision this meeting. He had replayed in his mind, over and over, their confrontation on the dark pathway at Vauxhall, until it became worse and worse every time. He berated himself for his ass-like behavior, saw again Georgina's face in the lantern light, pale and stricken and furious.

He had nearly turned and gone back to England, at the thought of what she might unleash upon him when he dared to show his face to her.

But the memory of other times, of happier moments, kept him moving steadfastly forward. If she would only smile at him again, he would gladly *walk* to Venice, and beg on his knees on her doorstep.

If only . . .

The thought of her sun-from-behind-clouds smile sustained him. Alex stepped up to the door and banged the lion head knocker.

For a long time nothing happened. The door did not open; no one appeared at any of the windows. Alex began to fear that Georgina was far from home, that perhaps she had gone instead to her lakeside villa.

Then, so abruptly that he almost fell back off the doorstep, the door was pulled open.

A small, round Italian woman stood there, her dark hair springing loose from her sheer cap. She wore a muslin apron over an extraordinary gown of carmine velvet, and held a bottle of wine in her hand.

"Si?" she said.

"I do beg your pardon, er, signora," Alex said, a bit taken aback. "Is this the home of Signora Beaumont?"

The woman's dark gaze flickered over him, taking in his traveling clothes of buckskins and a deep green greatcoat. He resisted the urge to smooth his wind-tousled hair, and wished he had taken the time to shave.

Apparently what she saw pleased her, though, because she smiled widely. "Oh, *si*, Signora Beaumont lives here. You bring a gift, no?"

Alex thought of the small box in his pocket, that held the ruby ring that had been his grandmother's. He supposed that could qualify as a gift. "No. That is, yes. I bring a gift."

"Va bene. If you give it to me, I will put it with the others."

Others? "I would prefer to present it to the lady myself. If she is at home."

The woman examined him again. "She is at home, but she is working. The Countess d'Onofrio is here for her sitting. I have been with Signora Beaumont many years, and I know better than to bother her while she is working." She winked. "You know how it is?"

Alex smiled. "Of course I would not wish to *bother* her. Perhaps I could just wait in the drawing room until she is finished. I have come a very long way to give her this gift, you see," he said cajolingly.

She glanced over her shoulder, then said, "Very well. But you might have a long wait."

It felt as if it had been an eternity already. "I do not mind."

"Hmph. Then follow me." She opened the door

wider to let him in, then shut it behind him and led him down a narrow, painting-lined corridor. "I am Bianca, by the way."

"How do you do, Bianca. I am Alexander Kenton." Somehow, he did not think it a good idea to throw his title about around here.

"Well, you may wait here, Signor Kenton." Bianca ushered him into a drawing room, and pushed the bottle of wine she held into his hand. "I was to take this to the studio, but you may have it."

Then the odd little maid was gone, closing the door behind her.

Left alone, Alex surveyed his surroundings. It was not a large room, but it was bright and airy from the many tall windows. The chairs and settees were of a light carved wood, upholstered in azure and cream. Small *objets*, boxes and figurines, were scattered on the tables; several paintings in Georgina's bold style hung on the blue-painted walls. He could also see what Bianca had meant when she said *others*. There were flowers piled along one wall, gaily wrapped parcels stacked on the pale blue carpet, letters laying unopened on the desk.

Alex laughed wryly, and turned away from the offerings to where a fire burned in the grate.

Above the fireplace of white marble hung a portrait of Georgina, a lovely work in a somewhat softer style than Georgina's own. The folds of her purple satin gown shimmered as if real; the painted smile was Georgina to the life, mischievous and merry.

Alex moved closer, and saw the "Elizabeth H" signature in the canvas's corner.

There, in that room, he felt closer to Georgina than he had in weeks. Why, he could almost smell the sweetness of her rose perfume.

He closed his eyes and inhaled deeply.

Then he heard soft footsteps in the corridor, a gentle swish of a silk skirt. He opened his eyes.

He forgot to breathe as the door slowly opened.

"Why, Alex!" Georgina cried. "You are turning quite white. Are you about to swoon?"

Georgina had scarce been able to believe her ears when Bianca had told her who was downstairs in the drawing room.

Her hand had begun to tremble, so she carefully placed her brush down on the palette. "Did you say— Kenton, Bianca?"

"*Si*. Alexander Kenton."

"Are you quite sure?"

Bianca snorted in affront. "My hearing is excellent, signora! He said he has brought you a gift, but when I said I would put it with the others, he insisted he give it to you himself."

"Did he?" A gift. Alex had come all the way from England to give her a *gift?*

The mind reeled at the thought of what it could be.

"*Si*. I have put him in the drawing room, signora, because he said he would wait for however long it took for you to finish your work."

Alex, *here!* In her very house. It only just began to sink in. Oh, how she wanted to fly down the stairs to him!

She looked over to the countess, who had been listening to them with the greatest interest.

The countess made a shooing motion with the ostrich feather fan she held. "Go, *cara*, go! I will come back another day."

"Are you certain, Countess?" Georgina said.

"*Amore* is so much more important than any old

portrait!'' she answered, already stepping down from the dais where she posed. "I must be returning to my *caro sposo* now, anyway.''

Georgina laughed. "Then, I will see you again on Wednesday!''

She tugged off her paint-stained smock, and looked quickly in the mirror to smooth her hair back into its ribbon bandeau, and adjust her yellow silk dress. Then she ran off down the stairs.

But as she neared the closed drawing room door, doubts again assailed her. What if he had only come to berate her again? To demand that she cease the correspondence that had been going on between her and Emily? To insist again on paying her back the blasted money?

"Don't be a goose!'' she whispered to herself. "Why would he come all the way to Venice just to quarrel?''

He would not, of course. That would be silly. His presence here could only indicate something positive.

Could it not?

Georgina took a steadying breath, and reached out to push open the door before she could lose her courage.

It was indeed Alex, standing before her fireplace, looking impossibly handsome with his tousled golden brown hair and his beard-roughened jaw.

And also looking as pale as the marble he stood beside.

"Are you about to swoon?'' she cried out.

Alex turned to her, his blue eyes lighting. He started toward her, but then halted abruptly, reaching out a steadying hand to the mantel.

"Certainly not,'' he said, his voice low and rough. "Soldiers *never* swoon, you know.''

"Not even at the sight of blood?" Georgina said inanely, feeling thoroughly giddy.

"Not even then. Though I fear *this* soldier may swoon at the sight of you."

"Why? Because I look that hideous?"

Alex shook his head. "Because you look that lovely. The most beautiful sight I have ever seen."

Georgina gave a half sob, half laugh. Her heart felt so full at that moment, so overflowing with joy. Never had she felt such happiness before; she knew that when she was an old woman, lying on her deathbed, this was what she would remember. The sight of Alex, bathed in golden sunlight, his gaze beseeching and besotted as he looked at her, and the warmth of love wrapped all about them.

She raced across the room to throw her arms about his neck, clinging as if she would never let go, her tears wet on his shoulder. His own arms tightened around her, and she felt the press of his kisses in her hair.

"I thought you would *never* come!" she sobbed. "Emily wrote that you were gone to the Continent on business, and I hoped, hoped against hope, that you were coming here. But you never did!"

"I came as fast as I could, but there was a storm and I was delayed. I went to the Hollingsworths' house the very day after, but you were gone."

"I know, I was so foolish! I was frightened. I ran away." Georgina pulled away to look at him. "I will *not* run away again, I swear to you. I am sorry."

"No!" Alex protested. "I am sorry. I was the one who was such a cabbage-head. Being such an ass about the money. I am surprised that you can even think of forgiving me."

Georgina shook her head, puzzled. "I should not have given Emily that money without your knowledge. You had a right to be upset."

"No. My pride was hurt, true. I, well, I have always been so used to being the one in control. To ordering my regiment about, to having everything that is expected of me, and what I could expect of my men, known," Alex said, struggling to explain something that even he did not fully understand. "Then I came home, and I found that my brother's actions had taken away that control. I knew what was expected of me, as a son and brother and as a duke, but I did not know how to fulfill those expectations. I was so accustomed to quite another life."

Georgina nodded in understanding. "Oh, Alex. Yes, I see."

"And, in the midst of my struggle, you appeared. So beautiful and glorious, like no one I had ever known. I wanted to give you the sun and stars, but I knew I could not."

"Alex," Georgina sniffled. "You *do* give me the sun and stars. Just by being here, by speaking with me so honestly, you give me all the universe."

"I want to give you so much more. I want to give you jewels and carriages and silk carpets."

"I have all those things! I have come to discover that they are all as naught, next to you, next to what we could have together. If we can only quit berating ourselves, and give ourselves a chance."

Alex's grasp tightened on her shoulders. "Yes. That is what I have found myself, when I thought I had lost you forever because I had behaved like a fool. You gave Emily that money out of your generous heart, to help me and my family. And I was cruel to you for it, which I will regret for the rest of my life."

"No, Alex . . ."

"Yes! My ridiculous pride was wounded. But I know that pride was a foolish thing to cling to, when it had lost me you and your love." Alex let go of her shoulders, and went down on one knee before her, reaching into his coat pocket for a small box.

He opened it to reveal an exquisite ring of a deep red ruby surrounded by diamonds.

Georgina clapped her hand to her mouth, her tears flowing down her cheeks.

"I love you, Georgina Beaumont," he said, his own voice thick with tears. "So very much. Please, forgive a foolish old army man his misplaced pride. Please, marry me, and be my duchess."

Georgina removed her hand from her mouth, and choked out, "Yes. I will marry you, Alexander Kenton."

Alex slid the ring onto her finger, above the narrow gold band Mr. Beaumont had given her so long ago. Then he bent over her hand, and placed a gentle kiss there.

It was a tender scene, one Georgina had painted on many a fantastically romantic set for *Romeo and Juliet*, or *Pelleas and Melissande*, but one which she had never thought could happen to her.

It *was* happening, though. Alex's kiss was warm on her skin; the weight of the ring heavy on her finger. It *was* happening, and, for this moment, life was perfection.

Georgina knelt beside Alex, and leaned forward to press her lips against his.

"Oh, Alex," she sighed as their gentle kiss ended and her head sank to his shoulder, "what took you so long?"

He laughed, his breath gently stirring in her hair.

"I do not know. I should have asked you to marry me the very day we met, directly after I fished Lady Kate from the river. How *is* the little imp?"

"Very well, getting fat from all the extra treats Bianca feeds her! She will be delighted to see *you* again."

"As I will to see her. I never liked dogs much, but Lady Kate is quite special."

"Of course she is! She brought us together, did she not?"

They sat together on the carpet, as the shadows lengthened and the fire died, resting in full silence in each other's arms.

Eventually they moved to the settee, where Alex opened the bottle of wine Bianca had given him, and poured out two glasses of the ruby liquid.

"To my bride!" he toasted.

"Oh, no!" Georgina protested. "To *us*."

"Yes, indeed. To *us*."

Georgina sipped at the wine thoughtfully. "There is still one problem, Alex dear."

Alex leaned back against a silk cushion with a contented sigh. "Indeed? I cannot imagine what it is."

"I still have a great deal of money."

Alex laughed. "What, you mean you have not spent it all these last weeks? I promise I will not hold it against you."

"Of course I have not spent it all!" Georgina laughed in return, and nestled her head against his shoulder. She inhaled deeply of his lovely soapy, woolly scent, and smiled in contentment.

"Georgina," Alex said after a moment.

"Yes, dear?"

"I do have one condition on our union."

Georgina sat back up, and looked at him sharply,

startled out of her contented cloud. "Oh? And what might that be?"

"That no matter what the law says, your money is yours alone, to do with as you like."

"Oh." Georgina relaxed, and laughed at her own silliness. She had thought for an instant that he would say she would have to be locked up at Fair Oak for their whole married life, or something of that sort, he had sounded so serious! "Well, that sounds like a tolerable condition, I must say. What if what I like is to buy your mother some new furniture and draperies for Fair Oak? Or give your sister a grand Season?"

Alex laughed, and hugged her close. "I believe that would be acceptable!"

"And what if I like to pay for the laborers needed for the fall plowing?"

At that, he balked. "You mustn't spend your money on the farm, Georgina."

She pressed her finger to his lips. "Ah, now, you said I could spend it however I wished. We are to be a family, which means that we help each other. It is only until the farm begins to show a profit again, which could be with the next harvest. Emily says we have been having exemplary weather and growing conditions. Then I will gladly see you pay for your own equipment and improvements and new roofs."

Alex kissed her warmly and lingeringly. "Georgie! I do love you so very much. No woman ever spoke of new roofs as alluringly as you."

"You cannot possibly love me half as much as I do you," she teased.

"Twice as much, I am sure."

"No. And there is one other thing I intend to spend my money on."

"What is that?"

"The grandest, most glorious, most vulgar wedding ever!" She tilted back her head to smile up at him radiantly. "I never had a proper wedding. And, as this is the last time I intend to marry, I am going to do it right."

Epilogue

The wedding of the Duke of Wayland and Mrs. Georgina Beaumont was indeed the grandest ever seen at St. George's, Hanover Square.

All the grandes dames whose portraits Georgina had painted attended, with their most elaborate jewels at their throats and their noble husbands on their arms. Even the Prince of Wales himself was there, lodging his not inconsiderable girth into a pew next to Lady Hertford.

Lady Emily Kenton was lovely as the bride's attendant, in a gown of pale blue satin, with white rosebuds in her golden curls. She garnered many lingering glances through quizzing glasses, and soulful sighs from young bucks, even though she was not yet officially "out." But stern glances from the dowager duchess, seen in London for the first time in over a decade, quickly put paid to all unruly speculations.

Lady Isabella Everdean scattered rose petals in the bride's path, very prim and proper in her pink muslin dress, but obviously delighted, and a bit smug, to know that *she* had played an instrumental role in the meeting of the bride and bridegroom.

Her parents, the Earl of Clifton and his Spanish countess, beamed in pride as Isabella promenaded up the aisle, scattering her petals more perfectly than any other flower girl ever had before. The newborn Viscount Killingsham slept peacefully on the countess's green-velvet-covered lap.

In the very front pew sat the delighted Hollingsworths. Elizabeth could be seen distinctly wiping away copious tears of joy. Rather less moved were the newly arrived Georgina and Isobel, little angels of perfection asleep in their baskets.

The groom was attended by the Viscount Garrick and Mr. Frederick Marlow, who were still basking in their notoriety after a well-publicized "incident" at Astley's Amphitheater the week before. But they were perfectly dignified in St. George's.

The bride wore jonquil-yellow silk, with a bandeau of topaz and seed pearls in her hair. She carried a bouquet of white roses and lilies. Very striking, all agreed, and most becoming for a fourth-time bride.

The bridegroom was very handsome and most noble—if he could only have ceased *grinning* quite so much.

It was the crowning jewel of a most delightful, and eventful, Season.

Georgina and Alex, after all the ceremony and festivities were concluded, settled into the flower-bedecked carriage with Lady Kate, headed for a Scottish wedding trip.

"Oh, my darling," Georgina sighed happily. "I know that some high sticklers would not approve of weddings with babies and dogs in attendance . . ."

"Like a wedding in a nursery," Alex mimicked in a high-pitched voice, sounding just like old Lady Collins.

"Exactly!" Georgina laughed. "But I think it was the grandest wedding ever."

"My dear Lady Wayland," Alex said, leaning in to kiss his bride. "I could not agree more."

Lady Kate barked out her most hearty agreement.

The Star of India

*To the "Hyde Park set"—Diane Perkins, Julie
Halperson, Deb Bess, Gaelen Foley, and Brenda Hiatt.
I can't believe it's been a whole year since we
trekked through Hyde Park and Mayfair! You were
the best pub mates ever—and we even found St. George's!
And to everyone on the Splendors of the Regency tour—
it was once in a lifetime.*

Author's Note

In the course of researching this book, I came across many fascinating sources that I hope may be of interest to people who would like to read more of India, jewels, or the Elgin marbles (in fact, I had to force myself to stop researching and start writing!). The following were some I found to be useful:

Barr, Pat. *The Memsahibs*. Random House, 1989.

Cook, B.F. *The Elgin Marbles*. British Museum Press, 1997.

Dalrymple, William. *White Mughals*. Viking, 2003. (Highly recommended!)

Durbar, Janet. *Golden Interlude*. Academy Chicago, 1986.

Kincaid, Dennis. *British Social Life in India*. Routledge, 1973.

Rushby, Kevin. *Chasing the Mountain of Light*. Palgrave Macmillan, 2001. (Great book about the gemstone industry, history, and lore of India. The tale David tells Emily about the Star is based on a legend about the Koh-i-noor diamond.)

Tytler, Harriet. *An Englishwoman in India: The Memoirs of Harriet Tytler, 1828–1858*. Oxford University Press, 1986. (Fascinating diary of an officer's wife who lived through the Sepoy Mutiny of 1857.)

I also want to give my deepest thanks to author Meredith Bond, who gave me much advice and help in the course of writing this book, and also to her daughter Anjali, for allowing me to borrow her beautiful name!

From the catalog of the
Mercer Museum, London, 2004

It is said that sapphires are the symbol of love and purity, and the Star of India is a prime example of such a legend. A thirty-carat, flawless oblong Burmese sapphire surrounded by diamonds, it was mined in the seventeenth century and originally placed in a shrine to the god Shiva near Calcutta. In the eighteenth century, it was removed from the temple and gifted by Gayatri, daughter of the Maharajah of Ranpur, to her husband, the English Earl of Darlinghurst. It is not known how the princess obtained the Star from Shiva, but it is said that a curse followed the sapphire and was responsible for Gayatri's early death and the Star's dispersal. The jewel was then owned by the Duke of Wayland, and was sold by his oldest son to Sir Charles and Lady Innis, a wealthy merchant family. Both the duke and his eldest son met early ends, and the duchess spent much of her life wheelchair-bound after a hunting accident. The Mercer Museum obtained the Star from the Innis family during the Regency period. It has resided here ever since, as the centerpiece of the Gemstone Collection and one of the foremost sapphires in the world.

In 1991, a jewel thief was killed by falling through a skylight while attempting to burgle the Star. Has the curse followed the Star here? Well—that remains to be seen.

Prologue

Two Hundred Years Earlier

"*Y*ou can't catch me!" Lady Emily Kenton called gleefully over her shoulder, as she dashed down a hillside into a beckoning green meadow. She might only be eight, but she was fast and she knew it. Racing after two older brothers had made her strong and quick, not to mention impervious to teasing and hair-pulling. Now she ran from her best friend, David Huntington, son of their closest neighbor, the Earl of Darlinghurst.

She heard his answering laugh on the wind. He was thirteen now, older than her and much taller, but she knew he did not *let* her win the race, as her brother Alex often did to humor her. That made the victory all the sweeter.

She neared her favorite tree, a spreading, ancient oak, and reached up to grab a stout, low-hanging branch. She pulled herself up onto it, and then onto the next level. She heard the hem of her muslin skirt tear, and knew that she was in for a scolding from her governess, and probably her mother, too. But that did not matter—her heart was bursting with exhilaration and good fun. Being a girl was sometimes so tedious, with music lessons and stitching. She had to seize her enjoyment where she could, out in the sun and the wind.

She came to a rest on the branch, and leaned against the rough tree trunk to catch her breath. Her pale yellow curls escaped from their confining ribbon and fell into her eyes. She pushed them back, and grinned down at David.

"Do you concede?" she called to him.

He braced one arm against the tree and grinned back at her. The sunlight glinted on his overlong crop of hair, turning it the rich blue-black of a raven's wing. Really, Emily thought, he was the most handsome boy she had ever seen, with his dark eyes and tall figure. Except for her father and brothers, of course.

"I concede, my lady," he said. "You are a veritable Atalanta. Now, will you come down from there?"

Emily slid down to sit on the branch, letting her legs dangle. "Oh, I don't know. It is very comfortable up here. I have a lovely view. Why, I can see your house from here, I vow!"

"Then I will just have to persuade you." He leaped up and caught one of her slippered feet, pretending he would pull her to the ground.

Emily giggled, and kicked out at him. "No, no! I will come down." She leaped to the lower branch and then to the ground, where she collapsed onto the grass. David sat down next to her, stretching his long legs out before him.

"You grow faster all the time," he said, admiration in his voice. "I shall need golden apples to keep up with you."

Emily flushed warmly at his praise, but she shrugged as if it was nothing. "I have to be fast to keep out of the way of Damien and Alex."

"Do your brothers tease you a great deal, then, Em?"

"Damien, yes, when he is around, which isn't often these days. Alex, never. He is teaching me to use a sword, much to my mother's dismay. But it is always useful to be able to outrun them!"

"Swordplay, eh? Then you will be even more fearsome, my little Boudicca!"

Emily laughed in delight at his use of their special nickname—they had been reading Ben Jonson's *The Masque of Queenes* together, and the tale of the fierce Iceni queen was her favorite. How she adored it when he called her Boudicca! It made her feel she *could* be brave and strong, even when her family treated her as a helpless infant who must be sheltered.

Her parents and her brothers (or at least Alex) loved her, she knew that, but to them she was their little baby daughter, to be coddled and protected. Only David spoke to her as if she was an intelligent person, a person who could understand books and art and even swordplay and footraces. He had danced with her at her parents' lavish Christmas ball, went riding with her every week over the countryside. He told her tales of his late mother, the beautiful daughter of an Indian maharajah, and of his early childhood in Calcutta before he came with his father, an earl, to England. He was her truest friend.

"*You* need never fear me, David," she said, leaning against his shoulder. "You are my 'parfit gentil knight.'"

He smiled down at her, but she thought there was something sad and strange in his dark eyes. "Is something amiss?" she asked, sitting up straight.

"No, of course not," he answered. "I *will* always be your knight, Emily, I promise. No matter what. Do you believe me?"

He sounded so very serious, so unlike her merry David. She felt a tiny pang of misgiving in her heart. "Of course I believe you. We are friends—we will *always* be friends."

"Yes. Here, I want to give you something." He reached into a small pouch hung on a leather thong around his neck and pulled out a ring. He placed it on his palm and held it out to her.

It glittered in the spring sunlight, beckoning to her. It was a circlet of nine stones—she recognized emerald, ruby, cat's-eye, topaz, blue sapphire, pearl, coral, moonstone, and diamond.

Emily stared down at it, her lips parted with wonder. She knew it was the height of rudeness to gaze at something with one's jaw agape, but she couldn't seem to help herself. It was so very beautiful—more beautiful even than her mother's diamond tiara, and more grand than anything Emily could hope to own before she was grown up.

"Oh, David," she breathed. "It is so lovely!"

"It is the Navaratna," he said, and pointed to each stone with his dark, slim finger. "The stones are for the nine heavenly bodies which rule our destiny—the sun, the moon, Mercury, Venus, Mars, Saturn, Jupiter. That makes seven. The others are the dragon's head and tail—*rahu* and *ketu*. The empty, black spaces in the heavens."

Emily was mesmerized. "All that in one ring?"

David smiled at her gently, and pressed the ring against her palm. "All that. It belonged to my mother. Before she died, she gave it into my keeping. Now, it is yours."

"Oh, no!" As greatly as Emily wanted to keep the ring—as tightly as her fingers longed to grasp it—she knew she could not. It would not be right. She knew how very much David loved his mother, Gayatri, Countess of Darlinghurst, who had died shortly after David and his family came to England. She knew how he must cherish anything his mother left behind. "You must not give this away, David. I can't take it."

She tried to hand it back, but he refused, shaking his head and reaching out to fold her fingers about the ring.

"You cannot refuse a gift. That would insult the giver. You wouldn't want to insult me, would you, Em?"

Insult David? As if she ever could! "Of course not."

"Then it is yours. It will protect you."

"Protect me?"

"That is what my mother said. The heavens protect and bless us." He took the ring and slid it onto her right index finger. It was too large, and slipped about, so Emily tightened her fist to hold it there. It was far too precious to risk losing. "Not that you will ever need protecting, fierce little Boudicca! You will always be able to take care of yourself."

Emily's gaze shot from the ring to David's dark, lean face. He had been behaving oddly all morning, ever since they met at the stream that divided their families' estates, and just then he sounded so sad . . . "I will *always* need you, David!"

"And I will always be your friend," he answered quietly. "If you ever have need of me, send me the ring and I will be here. From the very ends of the earth, if need be."

"But why should I have to send the ring?" Emily cried in growing panic. She clutched onto his arm, holding close as if it was a lifeline. "You are just over at Combe Lodge!"

"Em, please." He took her hands in his, holding her away. "I vow I will always be there for you, no matter what. That is all I meant. We are friends always, are we not?"

"Yes, of course!"

"Then that is all that matters." He pressed a quick kiss to her brow, and gave her a jaunty smile that was more like the David she knew. "Now, I must go home and help my father with some matters; I am sure your governess will be looking for you."

"Yes," Emily agreed reluctantly. Miss Lynn would indeed be looking for her—it was almost time for their dreaded French lesson. Yet she so hated to leave this bright day, and David's company, for the dusty schoolroom. "But I will see you later?"

He nodded, yet would not meet her gaze. "Later, Em."

She gave him a fierce hug, and leaped up to dash back across the meadow. At the top of the hill, she turned back and waved. David still sat beneath their tree, watching her go.

"Thank you for the ring, David!" she shouted. "I will always treasure it."

"You will not forget what I told you?" he called in return.

"Never!" She gave him a final wave, and spun around to run toward Fair Oak.

She would *never* forget.

"Ah, David. You have said good-bye to young Lady Emily, then?"

David had hoped to slip past his father for the time being, to go up to his chamber and finish his own packing in peace. He had a great deal to think about—a great deal to remember. But apparently that was not to be, as his father caught him walking by the half-open door of the library.

David pushed the door open all the way and stepped into the dark, book-lined room. His mother's black eyes, in the large portrait over the fireplace, watched him closely. "Yes. I told her good-bye."

"Excellent." His father leaned over a crate and carefully placed a stack of books inside, tucking cushioning scraps of muslin about them. Soon, the crate would be added to the dozen others lining the walls. Never mind that the Indian humidity would wilt the pages of the books within weeks.

Surely they would sink the ship with the weight of

their possessions before they could even reach Calcutta, David thought wryly.

"It has been so good of you to befriend the child, David," his father continued. "It must be rather lonely for her, with only older brothers over at Fair Oak."

"It is good of *her* to be *my* friend, as well, Father," David said, feeling strangely defensive at his father's harmless words. Yet how could David explain to him— to anyone—the odd connection he felt to his Boudicca? She was very young, it was true, yet it seemed she held worlds of wisdom in her dark blue eyes. She rode and danced and laughed with great intensity, like no one else he knew, or had ever known. And the way she looked at him made him feel he could be strong and even merry, could laugh, when all he had felt was weakness and sadness for so long. "As you may have noticed, I have precious few friends here in England."

"Eh?" His father glanced up from his task, blinking in the dim light. "Yes, my son, I *have* noticed. That is part of why we are going back to India. I have no family here, and there you can be with your mother's relatives again. There are cousins aplenty at your grandmother's palace."

David opened his mouth to protest, to beg to stay in England. He wanted to remain close to Emily, despite the cold wretchedness of this country and many of its inhabitants. But then he noticed, not for the first time, how pale his father had become, how thin and shrunken. His golden hair was now silver. Once, he had been hearty and robust, turned brown by the Indian sun, full of jokes and laughter. Until his wife died, and they left their home in Calcutta to come here, to their "ancestral home."

England was killing David's father. And David could not add to his troubles with whining and complaints. If his father needed India, needed the sun and the river to feel close to his wife again, then to India they would go.

Even if David had to leave his best friend behind.

"Of course, Father," he said quietly. "It will be good to see my grandmother and cousins again. I will just go finish my packing." As he turned back toward the door, he remembered that he had one confession to make. "Father, I—I did something today you may not approve of."

"And what might that be, David? You have never given me even an instant of trouble before."

"I gave Mother's Navaratna ring to Lady Emily, for her protection."

David closed his eyes against the expected storm of protest. His father held anything that had belonged to Gayatri as sacred. Yet there was no storm, no sound at all. Only silence, and the soft thud of books lowered into the crate.

He glanced back over his shoulder to find his father's head bowed, his clasp tight on the wooden edges of the crate. "Indeed? Well. That *is* fitting, then."

"Fitting?" David asked, puzzled.

"Yes. That we should both leave our treasures in the hands of the Kenton family. They will keep them safe."

Mindful of her torn and muddied hem—and doubly mindful of the scolding she would receive if anyone saw it before she had a chance to change—Emily took off her shoes and crept up the grand staircase of Fair Oak. Thankfully, there was no one to see her except a footman and a maid, who were more interested in flirting with each other than in their employer's wayward daughter. Now, if she could just reach her chamber undetected, and find a fresh frock before Miss Lynn came looking for her . . .

She tiptoed past the open door of her mother's sitting room. It would be the very *worst* if her mother caught her, and gave her a lecture on how a proper duke's daughter should behave! Emily heard her mother's soft tones blended with her father's deep voice, and she quickened her steps past the door. The only thing worse than a lecture from her mother would be one from *both* of her parents!

". . . very sad news about Darlinghurst," Emily heard her mother say. She froze at the mention of David's father, and backed up against the wall so she could hear the rest of the conversation. Miss Lynn said it was very wrong to eavesdrop, but really, how could a girl hope to learn anything if she did *not* eavesdrop? No one told a child anything. The only way Emily knew of her brother Damien's wild ways in London, or her brother Alex's new commission in the Army, was by overhearing.

And now something was amiss with Lord Darlinghurst. Could this be the reason for the sadness she saw in dear David's eyes this morning?

"Yes, quite, my dear," her father answered. "They have been excellent neighbors, and I will miss Darlinghurst greatly at the hunt."

"As will I," his wife said, with a soft sigh. She was quite unusual for a lady in that she relished horses and the hunt—a reason Emily thought it quite unfair that her mother should scold her for lack of ladylike decorum, when her mother herself was out jumping fences! Emily could not dwell on that now, though. She had to find out what was happening with David's family.

"Even if Combe Lodge is leased out, I am sure the new tenants could not be half so agreeable," the duchess continued. "His tales of India are always so entertaining! They could liven up the dullest card parties."

"I fear he was not so well received by others in the neighborhood as he was by us, though."

"Not well received? He is an earl! Surely he is invited everywhere."

"Invited, yes. But not entirely befriended. Not with a

half-Indian heir, and an Indian wife he so obviously still mourns."

There was a long silence from the sitting room, penetrated only by the rustle of the duchess's embroidery cloth, the shuffle of the duke's feet as he paced across the carpet, which was so often his habit.

Emily's mother finally said, "You are right, of course, dearest. Perhaps he will be happier back in India—he does miss it so. Yet I do not understand at all why he would leave such a valuable jewel with you!"

Emily heard a gentle clinking sound, and peeked through the cracked door to see the flash of sunlight on a huge blue sapphire in her father's hand.

She stifled a gasp. The Star of India! It was Lord Darlinghurst's most prized possession. David said it had been a wedding gift from his mother to his father, and was the most valuable sapphire in all of Bengal. She had seen it only once before, locked in a case in the library of Combe Lodge. What was it doing here?

Her father shrugged at her mother's question, and carefully shut the jewel away in a velvet box. "Darlinghurst said there is some dispute with his late wife's family over the true ownership of the sapphire. He does not want to take it back to Calcutta, where it could fall into their hands. He feels it will be safer here with us. And he says you must feel free to wear it, my dear Dorothy! It would look lovely in your hair."

Emily's mother gave a little laugh. "As if I ever *could* wear it! It is too grand for me, and I would be afraid to lose it. But I am happy to keep it safe for him; he has been a good friend to us. Emily will be so sad to lose young David's company, though! They have become such good friends, and I do think she is rather lonely here in the country. Perhaps school would be the answer for her. . . ."

Emily's hands shook, and her stomach ached as if she

would be sick. She did not stay to hear any more. She took off running back down the corridor in a blind panic, uncaring of who might see her.

David was leaving! Going back to India. That was why he gave her the ring, why he seemed so sad and serious today. He was going halfway around the world, and she would never see him again.

She was not thinking clearly at all. No rational images could pierce her mind. She only knew she had to see David, to make him stay here with her.

Emily burst out of the front door past the startled footman and maid, and dashed down the marble steps onto the drive, never slowing. She ran as fast as she could toward the road to Combe Lodge, not noticing the pain in her side, the aches in her leg muscles. She ignored the calls of the farmers she passed.

I must see David, she thought. *I must!*

She swung around the open front gates of the Lodge—only to see a wagon, overloaded with trunks and crates, lumbering its way down the lane. Closely following, coming around to pass the wagon and lead the small procession, was a grand carriage, the Huntington crest painted on its glossy black door.

So it was true. They *were* leaving. David was leaving without saying a proper good-bye.

"David!" she screamed out, afraid he could not possibly hear her. "David, good-bye!"

His dark head leaned out of the window, as the carriage drew farther and farther away from her. He raised his hand in a gesture of farewell, and shouted, "Remember what I told you about the ring, Boudicca!"

Then he was gone. Emily stood there and watched until even the clouds of dust raised by the vehicles had subsided and the road was quiet. She stood there unmoving as a marble statue, as the sun sank lower in the sky and a cool breeze blew up around her.

Her friend was gone. She twisted the ring around on her finger, telling herself that this was all she had left of him. She felt numb now, as if she stood in a snowstorm, but she knew that soon, very soon, the flood of pain would come.

She heard a horse draw to a halt behind her, but she did not turn to see who it was until she felt a gentle touch on her arm. Her brother Alex knelt beside her, his gaze steady and concerned as he watched her. He did not even seem to notice the road dust that marred his new white uniform breeches.

"Are you all right, Buttercup?" he asked softly. "Mother and Miss Lynn are looking for you. It is almost time for tea."

Emily blinked down at him. She felt like she was just beginning to come awake after a very long nightmare. "They have gone away, Alex," she whispered.

"The Huntingtons? Yes, I know. Mother said they were going back to India. I'm sorry, Buttercup—I know David was your friend."

"India is such a very long way away."

"Indeed it is. But I am sure you can write to him once he is settled there. It is not on the moon, you know."

Emily had not thought of that, and it gave her a tiny spot of comfort in her pain. "Do you think I could?"

"Of course. But you must be well when you write to him. He would not want to hear you have caught a chill standing here in the wind. Will you come home with me now, Buttercup, and have some nice, warm tea?"

She nodded slowly, still feeling strangely numb. She let Alex lift her up onto his horse and turn toward home.

I will not forget, David, she thought. *Never.*

Chapter One

Calcutta, Fourteen Years Later

"*I*t is true, then, David *shona*. You are leaving us." The soft, dulcet, yet unmistakably imperious voice of David's grandmother Meena floated to him on the warm breeze from her open windows.

David closed the door behind him and leaned back against it, his arms crossed over his chest. He could not help but grin, despite the seriousness of his errand in the zenana. His grandmother could have made a fortune treading the boards, if she had not married a wealthy rajah at the age of thirteen and lived all her life in splendid, if isolated, luxury. Her voice, full of doom, and her pose of weak prostration against silken bolsters were pure drama.

"I am hardly *abandoning* you, *Didu*," he answered. "You have all my cousins still, and a veritable army of servants at your beck and call at all times. I daresay you will not miss me at all."

"Not miss you! *Ish*." Meena flung out one dark, slender, bejeweled arm, her ruby and emerald bangles clinking like the lightest of music. "You are my eldest grandson, my darling, departed Gayatri's child. You are the father of my prettiest great-granddaughter. I rely on you so, David. And now you propose to leave me. To abandon your home!"

Some of David's amusement faded at this familiar litany. She knew very well why he had to go.

He pushed away from the door and moved into the room. His grandmother's personal sitting room was, as always, the very portrait of luxury and comfort. The tiled floor was covered with a carpet woven in rich, jewel-like tones of red, blue, and gold. Scattered about were low tables inlaid with intricate mosaics of flowers in mother-of-pearl, as well as silk cushions and bolsters in green, red, purple, and sun yellow. Heavy wooden shutters were drawn partially over the windows, letting in a cooling breeze but shutting out the worst of the warm afternoon sun. Servants hovered in the shadows, waiting on their mistress's every whim. One of them worked the punkah that stirred overhead.

David came to a halt next to the cushions where his grandmother reclined. The rich silk of her green and gold sari shimmered around her, and her silver-streaked black hair and unlined skin, the shine of her black, kohl-lined eyes, belied her age. She could easily have passed for David's mother rather than his grandmother, and that included her vibrant good health and energy as well as her beauty. Yet she so enjoyed playing the helpless elderly female, dependent on her grandchildren for everything.

What a hum that was. She ran everyone's life in their family, and she well knew it.

"Didu," David said gently. "This is not my only home, as you well know. My father has been dead for years now, and I have neglected my estate and duties in England for far too long. It is past time I attended to them. I have told you all of this before."

"You have a manager for that wretched English estate! A most competent one, by your own account. Surely that fulfills any duty you have there."

"It would be remiss of me not to take a personal interest, as the earl. Indeed, I *have* been remiss. I would not be the honorable man you and Father raised me to be if I did not go back there."

Meena sighed in resignation, as she always did at the conclusion of these disagreements. She sat up against the bolsters, and arrayed the folds of her sari more attractively about her. "You are too tall, David. Sit down before I get a crick in my neck looking up at you, and have some refreshment." She snapped her beringed fingers, and one of the hovering servants brought forth a tray. As the servant melted back into the shadows, Meena arranged the tea things, the bowls of papaya and guava, the plate of sweet *shandesh*.

"Very well," she said, pouring out fragrant mint tea into paper-thin porcelain cups. "I understand that duty calls you back to the land of your father, and I can even agree that you are doing the correct thing, though I cannot like it. I knew from the moment of your birth that you could not be ours forever. Yet why must you take Anjali as well?"

David sipped at his tea, more to give himself time than for the refreshment. This, too, was an old quarrel, one that had been ongoing ever since he announced his intention to return to England. And it was not a quarrel that was as easy or as clear-cut as his own duty.

"Anjali is my daughter," he answered. "She deserves to know all of her heritage, to decide for herself how she will live in her adult life."

Meena snorted in derision. "Decide for herself! A female cannot decide such things."

"Anjali will be able to, when she is older and clearly aware of her options."

"She is nine years old. We should be thinking of a suitable marriage for her, teaching her more of the female arts such as music and embroidery. You should not be dragging her away to the other side of the world, where she will know little of the customs and manners. The English here in Calcutta are so very barbaric. To think that my own granddaughter will learn their ways!"

David set his teacup down with a sharp click. "I will not argue with you about the manners of the English here. But to learn English ways is precisely why she must come to England with me now. She is just a child—she has time to learn anything she needs to know. Her English is excellent; I will hire an English governess for her as soon as we are settled. She is smart and quick—just as her great-grandmother is. She will be fine wherever she goes. And in a few years, if she wishes it, she can come back here."

Meena slumped back against the bolster, a hint of a pout touching her carmine-red lips. "By then, she will be too old for any suitable Bengali match."

David grinned at her unrepentantly. "Then she will just have to marry an Englishman, won't she?"

"And you, David? Will you marry an English-woman?"

His gaze narrowed as he looked into his grand-mother's oh-so-innocent expression. This *was* a new tack of hers. They had not spoken of marriage for him since his wife, Rupasri's, death two years ago. He should have been expecting it. Marriage and matchmaking were Meena's chief delights in life.

He sat back against his own cushions and shrugged carelessly. "I will probably never marry again."

"Not marry again?" Meena's tone was deeply shocked, as if such a thing was utterly unthinkable. "But, David, you are young! You will want a son, to inherit your wealth and title and say prayers for you when you are dead."

"My father has cousins who can have the title, and

Anjali can have my money when I am gone. And I daresay she can say a prayer for my soul as well as anyone."

"Of course she cannot! She is a female."

"You forget, *Didu*," David said, in a deceptively quiet voice, "that Anjali and I are Christian, not Hindu. Even Rupasri was Christian. God will hear Anjali's prayers as well as He would those of any son."

Meena lapsed into a heavy silence. The point of faith was a sore one with them and always would be. Usually, they just ignored their differences and went on.

Meena was not about to let the issue of marriage go quite so easily, though. "You are a fine match, David. You are handsome, just as your grandfather was, and wealthy. You have a title, which they say the English ladies like."

"Is that what drew my mother to my father? His grand English title?"

"Don't be so impertinent, David! My daughter was a silly, romantic, headstrong girl. Gayatri fell in love with his golden curls and green eyes, and would have no other man. We had begun to arrange a most suitable match for her, but her father foolishly indulged her and let her marry where she would. And now you will be just as indulgent with Anjali."

"It hardly signifies at the moment, *Didu*. Anjali is just a child. Her marriageable years are far in the future."

"But yours are not. You are twenty-eight, David; you have been a widower these two years and more. Anjali needs a mother, and you need a companion. Since you are so determined on your course to leave us and go to England, I suppose it must be an English wife. But even that is better than nothing."

David remembered the chilly reception he and his father had received in England, the whispers about his dark complexion, his "heathen" mother. He shook his head. "I doubt there is any Englishwoman who would have me."

"What? Not one on that entire rainy island? I cannot believe that."

Unbidden, an image flashed in David's mind, a picture of a girl he had known so long ago. Emily Kenton laughed in his memory, the sunlight shimmering on her pale curls, her dark blue eyes full of admiration as she watched him.

I won't forget, she had whispered.

Yes, there *had* been one English girl who stood as his friend. Even after all these years, after everything that had happened—his life in India, marriage to Rupasri, the birth of his daughter—he cherished that memory. With Lady Emily, he had been able to be entirely himself, to forget the bittersweet nature of his life in England, to just laugh and talk like an ordinary boy. She made that time not just bearable, but even—fun. And special.

But that was many years ago. Emily was surely married by now, a grown-up beauty with a family of her own. Perhaps they would even meet when he was back in England, at a ball or a rout or riding across their lands at Combe Lodge and Fair Oak. Yet she would not remember him. Not as he remembered her.

His grandmother watched him with an odd expression on her face, and he realized that his silence had stretched on much too long.

"We shall just have to see once I am settled in England, won't we, *Didu*?" he said lightly.

"Indeed," Meena answered, her tight tone saying she was not entirely convinced by his carelessness. "But there is something else I must speak to you about before you leave, David. Something very important."

She peered up at him with her onyx eyes, and something in their depths killed the flippant remark he had been about to make concerning the relative importance of matrimony. "What is it?"

Meena folded her jeweled hands carefully in her lap. "When your mother married your father, she gave him something—something that was *not* hers to give."

David knew immediately of what she spoke. He had expected her to bring it up as soon as he and his father returned to Calcutta fourteen years ago, yet she never had. She treated his father with the same icy, remote politeness she always had, and she had not even mentioned it when the earl died. Now David knew she had just been biding her time. "The Star of India."

"Yes. The Star." Meena looked more solemn than he had ever seen her, yet her eyes took on a deep glow as she spoke of the Star. "Our family gave the jewel as a sacrifice to the temple of Shiva—it belongs to the god. Gayatri was always a silly girl, and she was overcome by her infatuation with your father. She foolishly took it from the very feet of Shiva and gave it to her husband, in a bid to secure his love to her forever. It was a very great wrong. It brought a curse onto our family—a curse that killed your mother!"

David felt an enormous disquiet at his grandmother's demeanor. She was often full of drama and tears to get what she wanted. Yet now, as she told a very dramatic tale indeed, she was only aglow with quiet intensity, religious fervor.

"Childbirth killed my mother," he told her softly. "She was trying to bring my baby brother into the world."

Meena shook her head decisively. "If she had not stolen the sapphire, your brother would have been safely born and Gayatri might still be with us. It is so written. And then your father left the Star in England, who knows where or with what blasphemous sorts of people! If he had brought it back, we could have returned it to Shiva. Now, the curse—and the duty to erase it—have fallen onto you, my grandson."

So that was it. He was to be the means of erasing a

"curse." David did not believe in such things as curses himself. But he *did* believe in the power of suggestion, and he knew his grandmother sincerely thought she was under a god's curse. A god's displeasure. "What would you have me do?"

Meena took a deep breath. "You must find the Star and return it to the temple. Only then will you and Anjali be safe."

David studied her face carefully, searching for any flicker of deception. "Is this a ploy of yours to entice me to return soon to India?"

She gave an indignant huff, her gold nose ring shimmering. "I might be a foolish old woman, David, but I know when I must be serious! If you are unable to return to India, you must find a safe way to send the Star to me and I will take it to the temple. The most important thing is that you find it. Can you do that for me, David? Please—I beg of you."

He nodded slowly. Begging was not his grandmother's way. This must truly be of deepest importance to her. He did love his grandmother—she had been like a mother to him when his own had died, and he found himself all alone in this strange land. He did not want her mind to be unquiet in any way. "Yes. I will find it for you, *Didu.*"

Meena closed her eyes with a small sigh. Suddenly, she looked all of her years and more. "Thank you, my dearest grandson. *Lokhi mei.*"

David went to her and pressed a kiss to her brow. He did not tell her that he had known all along where the Star was to be found—with Emily Kenton's family.

"Papa, Papa! Here you are at last!" Anjali dashed across the nursery floor to throw her arms around David's waist. "You were gone a very long time."

"I went to see your great-grandmother. She had a great many instructions for our journey." David lifted

Anjali up against his shoulder, even though, at nine years old, she was almost too big for him to do so. She was a tall girl, as her mother had been—tall for a Bengali female, with slender arms and long legs, and a warm, honey-colored complexion. Her hair was the same shining raven black as David's was, as Rupasri's had been, falling to her waist in a shimmering curtain. Yet her eyes were green, as green as emeralds or the English countryside in spring. Those she had gotten from David's own father.

Anjali stepped back from him, a tiny frown puckering her brow at the mention of their voyage. "Yes. My ayah and I have been packing my trunks today, but I don't know what I should bring. What will I need in England, Papa?"

"You may bring anything you like, *shona-moni*," he answered. "Your books and dolls and clothes— everything."

"Ayah says that England is always cold and damp," Anjali said, her tone full of doubt. "I don't think any of my clothes are right. Will you look at what we have packed and tell me? I don't want anyone to laugh at me for not being right."

"No one will laugh at you, sweetest. And of course I will look at your luggage." David took her small hand in his and let her lead him to the trunks arrayed next to the whitewashed wall. They knelt down together on the pink and pale blue carpet, and he watched as she took out and displayed garments and toys for his inspection.

He saw that Anjali was right—few of her clothes would be suitable for an English spring, which was when they would arrive in London. He had always seen to it that she wore English frocks, high-waisted gowns trimmed with ribbons and embroidery, except on very special occasions when she visited her great-grandmother and wore silk saris. But her dresses were all made of light muslins, with tiny puffed sleeves. There were no sturdy wools and tweeds, no cloaks, and only one cashmere shawl. Her shoes were all thin kid and silk. What would protect his girl from the brisk sea breezes they would encounter on the voyage, let alone the winds and rains of England?

He was woefully unprepared to be the sole parent of a little daughter. He realized this as he turned a small slipper over in his hand. Before, his inadequacies had been covered by the advice of his great-grandmother, his female cousins, and Anjali's ayahs. He was a man—he had no idea what wardrobe requirements Anjali might have, what qualities he should look for in hiring an English governess, even what she ate for dinner.

Once they boarded the ship and turned toward Europe, his daughter would be completely dependent on *him*.

"Ayah says I will catch my death of cold in England," Anjali said fearfully.

David felt a deep surge of anger toward Anjali's ayah. This change was hard enough for the girl; how could the woman make it worse by filling her with fears? Anjali was a very sensitive child, and took such things very much to heart. He placed the slipper back in the trunk and turned to give his daughter a reassuring smile. "Ayah is wrong. England is not as cold as all that, though it *is* cooler than Calcutta, to be sure. We will buy you a whole new wardrobe in London, one that is the very height of fashion. You will like that, won't you, my Anjali?"

She gave him a flicker of a smile, and cradled her favorite porcelain doll closer against her shoulder. "May I have a *pink* gown, Papa?"

"You may have as many pink gowns as you like. And a red velvet cloak trimmed with fur, and a bonnet with feathers. Once we are settled at Combe Lodge, we will see about finding you a pony, too, and teaching you to ride. All fine English ladies ride."

"So, I will be a fine English lady? Like Lady Mac-Gregor at Government House?"

David laughed at her doubtful moue, and leaned over to kiss her cheek. "Lady MacGregor is not the *only* English lady in the world, you know! You will be far finer than her. Though you are a very *small* English lady, to be sure."

Anjali laughed, and he reveled in the sweet, sweet sound. Her laughter was too rare since her mother died. "I think I *would* like a pony, Papa."

"I know that this change is not easy, Anjali," he told her. "But England is not such a very frightening place. It has many beauties, and there will be much for you to learn and enjoy there. And you will never be alone. I will always be with you, and you must be sure to tell me if there are things you dislike or do not understand."

"Of course, Papa." She opened her mouth as if to say something else, but then she closed it again, her gaze sliding away from his.

"What is it, Anjali?" he asked her.

"I just—Ayah says that you are going back to England to find me a new mama, because none of the Indian ladies suit you. Is that true?"

Now, where would the woman have heard such a things? David thought wryly. He remembered his grandmother pressing him about marrying again, remembered the lists of eligible ladies his cousins devised. Why would they all think he *must* have a wife? It was maddening!

Then he recalled his utter confusion in the matter of Anjali's clothes. Once they were settled at Combe Lodge, there would surely be other things he knew nothing of, such as housekeeping and meals and hiring

proper servants. As Anjali grew older, there would be
Seasons to plan, gowns needed, suitable suitors found.

Perhaps a wife would have advantages, then. A comfortable home and a properly raised daughter were no
small matters. But—and perhaps this was foolish of
him—he did hope for more. He cared very much for Rupasri; she had been a fine lady, and excellent mother to
Anjali, accomplished in all the arts of a Bengali lady. Yet
their match had been an arranged one, undertaken for the
benefit of their families when they were very young. If
he married again, he wanted it to be from his own desire
only.

But that was a romantic hope, a distant possibility. He
had other, more pressing duties to think of. And his life
would be theirs for a very long time to come.

David drew Anjali close to his side, doll and all, and
said, "We are going to England to see about your grandfather's properties, and so that you can learn more about
that side of your family. We have duties and obligations
there. That is all." And also to retrieve the Star from the
Kenton family. But Anjali did not need to know that. She
had never even heard of the Star of India.

"So, I will not have a new mama waiting there?"

"No, *shona-moni*. No new mama waiting at the dock.
One day I might marry again. But not soon, and only to
a lady who would be a very fine mama indeed. Very
well?"

Anjali nodded. "Very well, Papa. Now, will you look
at these books? May I take them all with me?"

David watched as she pulled a pile of leather-bound
books from one of the trunks, yet he did not truly see
them. For the second time that day, he was lost in the
mists of the past.

Anjali was nine years old now, very nearly the same
age Emily Kenton had been when they parted so long
ago. But the two girls were so very different. Anjali was

quiet and studious, shy and uncertain, where Emily had
been full of vibrant energy and life, always dashing
about, always laughing.

Emily would be twenty-two now. Once again, he
wondered if she was married, if she had grown into the
beautiful, glorious woman she promised to be. A lady
like that would be an exemplary example for Anjali, an
exemplary, passionate wife for any man.

Would they ever come to meet again?

Anjali settled back for her nap after her father left her,
watching the shadows of the punkah move against her
ceiling. She bit her lip as she recalled her papa's answers
when she asked him about a new mama. He was truthful,
she was sure—her papa was always truthful. But she
was unsure, nonetheless.

She remembered all the dark-eyed beauties of the
town, all the pale English ladies with their bonnets and
parasols. Their eyes, whether dark and kohl-rimmed or
lightest blue, were wide with sympathy as they looked
at Anjali, their lips, some carmine and some shell pink,
pursed in coos and murmurs. They patted her head
and gave her sweetmeats, whispering all the while,
"The poor *lokhi mei*. Her mother has been gone so very
long, and she has no lady to teach her proper behavior!"

Several of those ladies, so soft and fluttering in their
silks and muslins, had their eyes on her papa. They
watched him from under their parasols or behind their
ivory screens. They were always trying to gain favor
with Anjali's great-grandmother, or even with Anjali herself. But none of them had ever been right for her papa.

Truth to tell, Anjali had never much missed having a
mama. Her own mother had died when Anjali was only
little, and she remembered her more as a lovely dream
than a real person, a vision of gleaming black hair, a

whiff of jasmine perfume, a soft voice calling her a *gul-poola mei*. For as long as she could truly remember, her papa had been her only parent, and that was fine. Better than fine—it was perfect.

And she never wanted it to change.

Chapter Two

London, Ten Months Later

*H*er mother always admonished Emily not to eavesdrop, always said she would not hear anything to her own advantage.

The dowager duchess was a very sensible woman, Emily knew that and often took her sage advice. But not in this. After all, how else was she to learn anything, advantageous or not? No one told her anything directly. Eavesdropping had often served her well since childhood.

It served her now, as she leaned against the closed breakfast room door, unabashedly listening to the conversation of her brother Alexander and her sister-in-law, Georgina.

Emily *had* been about to open the door and join them in their meal. Then she heard her name, and paused with one hand on the painted porcelain knob.

"I am worried about Emily, my darling," Georgina said.

"Worried about Em?" There was a sharp click of silver on china, as if Alex had abruptly set down his fork. "Why? Is she ill?"

"No, no, nothing like that. At least not that I am aware of."

"Good. I did not think a lady could be ill and still attend two balls, a musicale, and a Venetian breakfast in a twenty-four-hour period."

"Perhaps that is what I am worried about," Georgina murmured.

"Whatever do you mean, Georgie? Do you suspect she is unhappy about something?"

There was a soft rustle of silk; Emily imagined Georgina shrugging her shoulders. "She does not *appear* to be so. She delves into the social whirl of Town with every appearance of enjoyment. But there is something—something not quite right."

"Georgie, my love, we have been married for years now, yet I confess I still do not always rightly understand you. Emily dances and smiles, and appears for all the world to be a happy young lady. Yet you are worried," Alex said, his voice full of fond exasperation.

Georgina gave a little laugh. "Oh, darling, sometimes I do not rightly understand *myself!* But I do worry about Emily. This is nearly the end of her third Season, and she has not yet found someone she can esteem enough to marry."

"Yes. I sometimes worry about that myself, yet truly, I do not think we have cause for concern at present. You and I were not exactly callow youths when we wed. She has time. And I would not want to see her married to someone she cannot truly love, just because he is suitable or it seems like the proper time."

Amen to that, Emily thought fervently. She remembered the parade of suitors over the past three years. Their number had not been insubstantial—her family title was an old one, after all, and she was well-dowered thanks to the fortune Georgina had brought with her to the family. But most of those men were too old or too young, gambling fortune-hunters, merchants seeking a title, widowers wanting a mother for their twelve children.

There had never been one among them with whom she could make a home and family, whom she could truly love. Love as her mother and father had possessed, or as Alex loved Georgina.

Sometimes Emily watched them as they danced together at a ball, or walked in the garden. They had eyes for no one else, and were always holding hands or linking arms, completely uncaring that it was not the done thing for married couples to be *in love*. She watched them as they played with their children, always laughing together. Emily was happy for her brother—truly she was. He deserved his happiness after long years at war, and Georgina had never been anything but the best of sisters to Emily.

Yet sometimes—only sometimes!—her heart would ache with envy at their romance. When would *she* find love like that? Would she ever? Or did it not truly exist, except in books and for a fortunate few? If she did find it, would she be brave enough to embrace it, or would she run?

But she had thought no one noticed these thoughts. She tried so hard to hide those pangs behind the merriment of the Season, filling her time with shopping and soirees. Emily forgot that Georgina was an artist, that her sharp eyes saw even things that were veiled.

"I would not want to see her wed to someone she does not love, either!" Georgina protested. "I love Emily as my own sister, and I want only to see her happy. If the single life suited her, I would be glad for her to live with us at Fair Oak forever. But I cannot be so selfish. Emily has so much love in her heart. And you have seen daily how wonderful she is with the children."

"Yes. I have." Alex's tone grew quiet and serious.

"So, what shall we do, my love? Send out far and wide for every eligible gentleman to come and present their suit for her?"

No! Emily's mind screamed. It was embarrassing enough to be spoken of like a pitiable charity case. She would *never* want her brother to go barreling about in Society *demanding* that someone marry her.

She shuddered at the very thought.

"Of course not," Georgina answered. "Don't be silly, Alex darling. Perhaps she could come to Italy with us this summer? We always meet such interesting and unusual people there. She might encounter someone more to her taste in Venice or Padua."

"You do have a point, Georgie. Emily did not lead the life of a sheltered young miss for many years. She is too intelligent and shrewd for all these London fribbles. Perhaps a change of scene is needed."

Emily gave a silent, humorless laugh. No, she was *not* as all the other misses in white muslin making their bows at Court and Almack's. During the years before her brother Damien's death, while Alex was away fighting in Spain and Damien was gambling away almost every cent of the Kenton fortune, it was Emily who kept Fair Oak going. She scraped together harvests and saw to it that the roof was patched, the fields plowed, the tenants looked after. She took care of her mother, who was confined to a Bath chair after a hunting accident. She had seen things, been responsible for things, that few young ladies of twenty-two ever were.

Those years *had* been difficult. They had hardened her heart and soul in some ways, but she was also proud of them. Proud that she had managed to keep their home together, and upheld the honor of their name when Damien had been doing his damnedest to destroy it. The Kenton name, the title of Duke of Wayland, was one of the proudest in England, and Emily would do it all again to keep it that way.

But it did *not* make the search for a soul mate easy. Men wanted soft, gentle wives, who embroidered and sang and laughed quietly. *Not* wives who could keep farm accounts like a bailiff and scythe hay under the autumn sun. Not wives who rode and walked quickly and spoke their minds.

Emily almost laughed aloud. Those hard days were gone now. Since Alex married Georgina and restored their grand position, Emily had only to enjoy herself. And she *did* enjoy herself. She loved dancing, and shopping without worrying over what she was spending. She loved riding in the park, and playing with her niece and nephew, and buying her mother lovely little gifts. She had a fine life, and she was a great fool to feel even an ounce of self-pity.

But Italy would indeed make a nice change. Perhaps there, under the warm sun, she could breathe again.

Emily pushed open the breakfast room door and breezed in, as if she had not a care in the world. And as if she had definitely *not* been eavesdropping.

"Good morning, Alex, Georgie," she said, kissing them each on the cheek before she sat down in her place and reached for the rack of toast. "I trust you both slept well?"

As she spread marmalade on the triangle of bread, she noticed the two of them exchange a surreptitious glance over the table. She took a large bite to stifle her chuckles.

"Very well, thank you, Emily. And yourself? You danced every dance at the Michaelson rout. you must have been very tired," Georgina said, passing her a platter of eggs.

"Indeed. I slept like the proverbial baby. I also enjoyed the theater last night; didn't you? Mr. Kean was in

fine form. I do not think I have seen a finer Macbeth."
Emily sipped at her tea, and gave Georgina an innocent
smile.

"Quite, my dear," answered Georgina. "Would you
care for kippers?"

"There was an account of the play in this morning's
Times," Alex said, and handed the folded sheaf of newspaper to her. "It says you were wearing a gown of co-
quelicot muslin with white Vandyke trim. And here I
thought you were wearing red with some sort of jagged
ribbons. I am not very à la mode, am I, Em?"

Emily laughed at his teasing, and skimmed over the
account of the play and its spectators. "They liked
Georgina's silk demi-turban, as well. How gratifying.
What do they say about the Hurst ball? I was sorry we
missed it, but I did promise Lady Michaelson first."

"Oh, it was bound to be quite flat," Georgina said,
with a dismissive wave of her teacup. "Mrs. Hurst has
declared she can no longer serve 'intoxicating bever-
ages' since that dreadful Lord Carteret destroyed her
ballroom last year after getting foxed on her husband's
brandy. So there was to be no champagne at all, only tea
and lemonade. As insipid as Almack's, I vow."

"Heaven forfend," Alex said in mock horror.

Emily read over the particulars of the ball. It sounded
quite as insipid as Georgina described. She started to
turn the page, when another headline caught her attention.

SIR CHARLES INNIS TO DONATE THE FABLED STAR OF
INDIA TO THE NEW MERCER MUSEUM.

The shock of those words was like a dash of cold
water to her face. Emily gasped aloud.

"What is it, Emily dear?" Georgina asked solicitously.
"Some unpleasant news?"

"Oh, no," Emily said quickly. "It is just—I swallowed my tea too quickly." She drew the paper up to cover her expression, and read quickly.

It had been many years since the Star passed from their family to Sir Charles Innis and his wife, yet Emily recalled it as if it was only yesterday. There had been a most dreadful scene.

Emily's father was dead for several years by then, yet Lord Darlinghurst had never sent for the jewel. Nor did his family in India, after his passing. It resided in the library safe at Fair Oak, a silent reminder of their old friendship with their departed neighbors. Emily had loved to think of it there, a shimmering blue link to David and a faraway land she would never see. She dreamed of the day she and David would meet again, and she could give the Star safely back into his hands. It took her away from her everyday life of looking after the estate and her mother and drew her into a dreamworld.

Until the afternoon Damien came riding hell-for-leather up to Fair Oak and took the sapphire from the safe.

Damien did not come often to Fair Oak. He detested the country, and much preferred the excitements of Town. All the better to squander every shilling that was not entailed, of course. The country boasted no gaming hells or brothels. Emily had been only sixteen at the time, but she was already fully aware of all these matters. There was no escaping the whispers of the servants and the neighbors, her mother's weeping despair.

So, that morning, Emily was shocked to see him riding down the drive at Fair Oak. She ran out of her chamber and halfway down the grand staircase, just in time to watch him tear into the library. He had once been as handsome as Alex, tall and dark-haired, but by then he was ravaged by his debauchery. He was heavy with excess fat, his eyes red-rimmed and his jaw slack. He was covered with mud from his wild ride.

Emily's mother, confined to her chair, shouted at him from the doorway of the drawing room. "What do you think you are doing, Damien? Get out of your father's library this moment! You have no right to be in there."

"It is *my* library now, Mother," he shouted back. "As is everything in it. I am the duke now, in case you have not noticed. So, I will thank you to be silent."

Emily's mother gasped in outrage at his harshness. Emily, her heart full of her own white-hot anger, dashed into the library to see him take the Star from the safe. For one instant, she saw the rich glow of its blue fire—then it disappeared inside Damien's greatcoat.

"What are you doing?" she cried out. "How dare you? Put that back this very instant!"

He glanced back over his shoulder at her, his eyes full of bitter weariness. "So, you are becoming a harridan, too, Emily. Just like Mother."

Emily ignored the insult, and stalked closer into the room, her hands curled into tight fists at her side. Her nails bit into her palms, yet she scarcely noticed the pain. "That does not belong to you. It is Lord Darlinghurst's."

"He hasn't been back for it in all these years, now has he? That means it is mine, to do with as I like. And I *like* to sell it."

With that, he left the house, the Star in his possession. Emily's screams and shouts as she chased him down the drive had no impact at all. She never saw the sapphire again; the next she and her mother heard, it had been sold to the rich merchant Innis, who was a great collector of exotic items from other lands.

Now he in turn was selling it, all these years later. Or rather, donating it to the Mercer Museum for their gemstone collection. Emily quickly read over the details, then scanned them again. The Star, which had not been seen since Sir Charles Innis purchased it, would be displayed at a grand ball in his London mansion. Then, after being examined by numerous gemological experts to confirm its authenticity, it would make its ceremonious way to the museum.

"This is terrible!" Emily exclaimed aloud, before she could stop it.

"What is terrible, Em?" Alex asked.

Emily lowered the paper to find him and Georgina watching her intently. She had to tell them *something*. Anything but the full truth.

Alex had been in Spain when the drama of the Star played out, and, as far as Emily could recall, he knew nothing of its history. She told him a shortened version of the tale as quickly as she could.

She did *not* tell him of that other scene in the Fair Oak library, the one that took place almost a year after the day Damien snatched the Star away. Indeed, she hardly liked to recall it herself.

Later, when Emily made her excuses to Alex and Georgina and escaped back to her bedchamber, she collapsed onto her chaise. She stared up at the ceiling, which had been whimsically painted by Georgina herself, but she did not see the cavorting gods and cupids against their blue sky. All she could see in her mind, replaying over and over again, was the day she learned the truth about what happened to the Star.

She had not thought about that day, or the sapphire, in a very long time. At first it was too painful to recall how she, in her helplessness, had betrayed her friendship with David. Later, there were so many other things to worry about. The whole ugly story was hidden deep in her heart—a shameful secret. Now it was returned to haunt her.

She rolled onto her side, and reached inside the bodice of her morning gown to pull out her Navaratna ring, suspended on its long gold chain. She always wore it there, hidden from the world but close to her heart, keeping her safe. Holding the circlet tightly in her hand, she closed her eyes, seeing again the day Damien returned to Fair Oak after stealing the jewel. He was in a terrible condition, his skin gray and clammy, his hair long and tangled, his eyes sunk deep in purple circles. He was so drunk he reeked of it from every pore.

He died only a few months later, but she did not know then how truly ill he was. She only knew that she had to hide him from her mother. Dorothy was weak herself, unable to leave her chair. She did not need to see her eldest son in such a pitiful state.

Emily helped him into the library, watched him collapse onto the leather settee. As she pulled off his muddy boots and drew a blanket up over his bloated shoulders, he caught her hand in his.

"Emily," he said raspily, his breath foul on her face. "You have grown into a pretty lady. If you went to London, you could marry a rich man, raise our fortunes again."

Oh, yes, Emily thought sarcastically. She would go to Town in her mended gowns and old bonnets, with her sun-browned face and calloused hands, and snare a rich man so her brother could gamble and whore some more. In the meantime, her mother would be alone and the crops would wither.

But she just gave him a curt nod, and turned to leave him in his disgusting state. He caught her hand again, holding her where she was. His breath rasped in his throat. She tried to pull away, only to freeze when she felt the cold press of coins in her palm.

She stared down at them. It was gold—more money than she had seen in a year. "Where did you get this?" she gasped. "At the gaming tables?"

Damien gave a rough laugh. "Not at all. Lady Fortune has not smiled on me in months."

"Then where did this come from?"

"Does it matter, Emily? Use it to buy yourself some new gowns. God knows you need them."

Her patience, never great when it came to Damien, snapped. "Tell me where you got it!" she shouted.

He fell back on the settee, closing his eyes with a groan. "I did not steal it, if that is what you're implying, sister dearest. And pray do not shout so—my head is splitting. I made it from the sale of that stone you were so damnably fond of."

"The Star?" Emily gasped, appalled. She tossed the coins back on top of him, as if they burned her skin. She did not even question how he had held onto the money for nearly a year since he took the Star away. "I won't take your ill-gotten gains. These *are* stolen."

"Oh, don't be so self-righteous! You're as bad as Mother. Besides, it is not as you think."

"No?"

"No." He opened his eyes, and gave her a sly, bleary grin. "The stone I sold to that vulgar Cit, Innis, was not the real thing. I sold him a paste copy, and gave someone else the real thing. Clever of your old brother, wasn't it? And here you've been looking down your nose at me for years, like you are so much better than me, so much finer. Yet *you* could never have come up with such a scheme, you prim little hypocrite."

"Indeed I could not," was all Emily could say. Then she ran from the library to be sick, appalled that he could do such a horrible thing. He had stolen the Star not once, but twice. Or was it three times? She could not even count.

He left Fair Oak the next day, and Emily never saw him again. A few days later, a new Bath chair arrived for their mother, along with a length of spangled muslin and new cashmere shawls, no doubt paid for with the money she'd thrown back in Damien's face. To her everlasting

shame, she kept them. Her mother needed that chair.
Emily also never told anyone the truth about the Star.
Such a thing would tarnish their honorable name forever,
a name Emily had spent her life protecting.

She remembered the newspaper article, which had
said that experts were coming to examine the Star before
it went to the museum.

There *had* to be something she could do now! Something that would not upset Alex and Georgina, or disrupt
their new, wonderful life. Emily had spent years taking
care of her family alone. She could do so now. She owed
it to them, for all they had done for her.

She could write to Sir Charles Innis and offer to buy
the jewel, of course. And she would. Yet she did not have
very much hard currency of her own, and Sir Charles
was rich as Croesus. He had no need to sell, and indeed
had resisted all offers from many people—even, report-
edly, the prince regent—for many years. She needed a
different plan.

Emily rose from the chaise, and made her way quietly
out of her chamber and up the stairs to the very top of the
house. There were attics there, behind the servants' quar-
ters and above the nursery. Fortunately, it was silent up
there at that time of day; there were no servants about to
wonder why Lady Emily had gone to the attics.

She knew that some of Damien's papers and possessions had been packed into trunks and stored there after
his death, with no one sorting through them beforehand.
With some luck, she could find something there to tell
her where the Star—the *real* Star—had gone.

Chapter Three

"*E*mily, dear, why did you not wear your birthday necklace? It would look perfect with that gown."

Emily heard Georgina's voice, but it seemed to come from a very long distance away, not just from across the carriage. She dragged her distracted attention from the night-dark streets outside the window and blinked at her sister-in-law. "I beg your pardon, Georgie?"

Emily was *not* so distracted that she did not see the worried, speaking glance Georgina shot at Alex. So, they were concerned about her, were they? Was it just that old worry of her lack of a betrothal—or something more? She should watch herself, carefully maintain her façade of cheerfulness. She did not want them to know the truth—not when it was her own problem, her own responsibility.

"I asked why you did not wear the necklace Alex and I gave you for your birthday," Georgina repeated. "It would look lovely with your gown."

Emily pulled her cloak closer about her throat, as if to belatedly conceal the fact that she wore her garnet cross rather than the elaborate web of pearls and diamonds they had given her. It was an exquisite piece, and would indeed have been lovely with her white and silver satin gown. But it , along with the matching pair of earrings, resided now with a jeweler in Gracechurch Street, given in exchange for a genuine sapphire copy of the Star of India.

She touched the tip of her tongue to her dry lips. "I— it is being cleaned."

"Cleaned?" Alex exclaimed. "We just gave it to you last month."

Emily stared blankly at her brother. "One of the stones was loose. I took it to be repaired."

Alex frowned at her. "I thought you said it was being cleaned."

"It will be repaired and then cleaned," Emily said with a little laugh, trying to sound completely unconcerned. She was glad it was dark in the carriage, to cover the hot flush of her cheeks. Alex had always been her favorite brother, her friend and champion. She had never lied to him.

It is for his own good, she reminded herself. *His and Georgina's, and their children's.*

Georgina laid her hand gently on her husband's arm. "It is of no matter, darling. Em has obviously taken care of it all, and there is nothing to worry about. The garnets also look very nice, quite dramatic. Oh, I *do* hope we shall arrive soon, and have no difficulty in getting inside the ballroom! Lady Wilton's balls are always such dreadful crushes, I vow she deliberately invites too many to fit into her house. At least we can be assured of an excellent supper . . ."

Georgina went on chatting about the ball to which they were en route, and Emily turned her attention, with great relief, back to the window. She was tired from the sleepless nights she had endured ever since hearing of the Star, and her head ached with a low, dull throbbing. She did not really look forward to this ball, to all the dancing and the chatter. She had even considered making her excuses and staying home with a book and a tisane, before thinking better of it. When she was alone in her chamber, her thoughts took over, swirling like mad until she wanted to scream with confusion.

At a ball, she would never be alone. She would dance and make polite conversation, and not have to think at all.

Their carriage drew up outside Lord and Lady Wilton's grand London house, signaling the beginning of that mindless evening. There was indeed a great crowd waiting to enter the ballroom, but they moved along briskly, and in seemingly no time Emily found herself in the midst of a knot of revelers.

The ballroom—a long, narrow expanse of red silk wallpaper and glistening gilt trim—was so overrun that the arrangements of hothouse roses and orchids and swaths of greenery could hardly be seen, but she could smell their sweet, cloying fragrance. It mixed with the perfumes of the guests, the warmth of thousands of candles.

Emily felt a bit lightheaded, but she could not have swooned even if she wanted to, she was pressed so closely by her crowd of usual admirers.

"Lady Emily!" Sir Arnold Ellis cried, bowing over her hand. He was one of the most handsome of Emily's suitors, golden-haired with bright blue eyes. Unfortunately, his brains were not as well-developed as his grooming. "May I beg for the next quadrille?"

Before Emily could answer, Lord Pickering slid in and took her hand away from Sir Arnold. Pickering considered himself quite the charmer, and always affected pink waistcoats and jeweled quizzing glasses, along with a multitude of watch fobs. He made Emily laugh, though perhaps not in the way that he hoped to. "I believe Lady Emily promised *me* the quadrille when we met last night at the Hardiman musicale."

Emily recalled no such thing, though Lady Hardiman's daughter's performance at the harp *had* been rather loud and she hadn't heard very much over its strains. But as she opened her mouth to say she did not remember, her hand was seized by Mr. Carrington. He kissed her gloved fingers with his usual puppyish enthusiasm. He was a very sweet gentleman, and not a bad dancer, though she sometimes tired of hearing all about the horses and hounds he kept in the country for his beloved hunting. After what had happened to her mother, Emily *loathed* hunting. "Lady Emily, you will never guess!" he said, in one of his usual non sequiturs.

· Emily smiled at him gently. "No, Mr. Carrington, I will not be able to, er, guess."

"There is a *real* nabob here. Fresh from India!"

Pickering gave a disdainful sniff. "There are a dozen nabobs here, Carrington. Why, I see Lord Montmorent right over there, still sunburned from the Punjab."

Carrington shot Pickering a loathing glance, then turned back to Emily. Behind his back, Pickering and Sir Arnold snickered. "Not that sort of nabob. He is, oh, a what-you-may-call-it. A rajah."

"A native of some sort?" Sir Arnold asked, his tone disbelieving.

"Yes! But a rich one. A native and an earl. An English earl." Carrington frowned, suddenly confused. "Is that possible? Can a man be a native *and* English? With a title?"

Emily stared at him, suddenly frozen to her spot. Her stomach gave a little leap, and the ballroom around her seemed to slow to a blurred crawl.

An English earl who was also Indian? Could it possibly be David? After all these years? Surely not. Yet how many other earls could there be like that? It had to be. Perhaps she could see him again—the friend who had lived in her thoughts for so long!

But it had been so very long. Surely he would not remember her. And he would be so very changed *she* might not remember *him*.

Her heart pounded inside her breast, and she pressed her gloved hand against it. There, beneath the satin of her gown, she felt the outline of her Navaratna ring. It was always there, hidden on its chain around her neck, reminding her of the protection of the universe around her.

Carrington peered at her closely, his high brow wrinkling in concern. "I say, Lady Emily, are you quite well? You look very pale."

"Perhaps she needs some champagne," interjected Sir Arnold. "*I* will fetch it for her."

"No! *I* will," Pickering argued. The two of them dashed off in a ridiculous race for the refreshment table.

It would have made Emily laugh, if she had paid them any mind at all. She stared at Carrington, and swallowed hard past the dry lump in her throat. "I—I am quite well, thank you, Mr. Carrington," she managed to choke out. "Did you mention some sort of rajah? An *English* rajah?"

Carrington's frown cleared, his face brightening at this sign of her interest in his conversation. "Oh, yes, indeed. He is over there with our hostess. Would you care to take a look at him?"

Of course she would! But, then again, if it was David, would she even know it? Part of her heart wanted to turn around and run out of the ballroom, keeping her precious memories exactly as they were. The other part wanted to dash through the crowd, shouting, "Is it you? Is it you?"

She touched her ring once more, and nodded. "Yes, thank you, Mr. Carrington. I find myself—quite curious."

Mr. Carrington offered her his arm, practically leaping about in excitement at having gained her interest over Sir Arnold and Lord Pickering. "Of course, Lady

Emily! It really is most extraordinary. I expected him to be wearing a turban and ropes of pearls."

Emily slid her fingers lightly over his sleeve and followed his escort through the crowd. She smiled and nodded at the greeting of friends and acquaintances, yet did not stop to chat. There was no time for that now!

"And he was not attired thus?" she asked.

"Oh, no, not at all." Mr. Carrington seemed most disappointed. "He wore quite a nice blue coat and ivory waistcoat, surely from Weston. There was one small emerald stickpin in his cravat, but that was it. Oh, and a signet ring, but that's not Indian, is it?"

"I have no idea," Emily murmured. She tried to crane her neck to see through the crowd, but it was futile. She was just too short. And too many ladies of the *ton* favored tall plumes in their headdresses this Season.

"He was quite dark, though," Mr. Carrington continued. "And tall."

Fortunate man, Emily thought, as Lady Birtwhistle, a particularly large matron in bright orange silk, lumbered into her path.

Then, miraculously, the orange-clad lady moved aside, and there was a clear pathway between Emily and Lady Wilton and her group. Only a stretch of polished marble floor separated them.

Lady Wilton wore one of those tall headdresses, this one fashioned of purple and gold silk, with purple plumes and satin roses. She held onto an arm clad in impeccable dark blue superfine. As she laughed up at the man, her plumes waved wildly. The other three people in the cluster, Miss Wilton and Lord and Lady Hapsby, stared in wide-eyed fascination, as if they were observers at a menagerie.

As Emily took a step closer, Lady Wilton turned, and her conversation partner was revealed.

Emily could not breathe. Her skin turned cold—

freezing cold—then burned with a pink flush. Her fingers tightened convulsively on Mr. Carrington's arm.

David. It was David, here, not twenty paces away from her.

He had changed from the boy she knew all those years ago. That boy had been tall and greyhound-lean, with overlong black hair and eyes too large for his oval face. Now he was even taller, but with broad shoulders and powerful arms pulling against the expensive fabric of his coat. There was obviously no padding there, as so many "fashionable" gentlemen affected. His hair, still a shining blue-black, was impeccably cut and brushed into place, and his skin was a clear, dark olive, not burned by the Calcutta sun.

But his eyes—his eyes told her that this was indeed David. They were as dark-bright as a starry sky. Her breath caught, and she could not move.

She almost called his name aloud, but caught it the instant before it escaped. She whispered it in her mind instead. *David. David, you're back.* A ridiculous smile caught at her lips, and that she could not suppress. Her head whirled in sudden, giddy excitement.

"You see?" Mr. Carrington said cheerfully. "A real rajah, eh? Right here in London!"

Emily had a difficult time looking away from David, as if he might disappear if she turned her eyes from him. But she managed to glance up at Mr. Carrington, and gave a little nod. When she looked back to Lady Wilton's little group, her gaze collided with—David's. His lips parted a bit in surprise, and his head tilted, a lock of that hair falling over his brow like a dark question mark.

And then a smile broke across his countenance, one full of recognition and welcome. He knew her, too.

So, you are home at last, Emily thought, and she tugged at Mr. Carrington's arm to urge him forward. A crowded ballroom was not the most auspicious place for a reunion with her old friend, Emily knew that. But she did not care. She only cared that they were together again.

His first London ball. How horrid.

Before leaving England the first time, David had of course been too young for such affairs, and had rarely come to Town anyway, his father much preferring the solitude of the country. David saw now why that was so. A country assembly was much to be preferred over a grand London soiree.

Even an achingly elaborate Calcutta durbar would be preferable!

But David was an earl now. Lord Darlinghurst. He had chosen to come back to England, to take up the old duties, and this ball was the first of them. Lord and Lady Wilton had been friends of David's father, and they were kind to issue the invitation, the first (and thus far only) engraved card to arrive at David's townhouse. It was the least he could do to appear here and pay his respects to them.

He couldn't help but wish himself at home, though, where he could spend an hour with Anjali before her bedtime. They had gotten into the habit of sharing a hot pot of tea against the chill of the spring evening, while Anjali showed him her day's lessons or played him a newly learned tune at the pianoforte. She enjoyed hearing him read, too, from books of fairy tales, or poetry, or especially history. These evenings were cozy and enjoyable, quiet in the grand, if still rather dusty, drawing room.

A more different scene from the one he faced now would be hard to imagine.

David nodded at Lady Wilton's words, and made appropriately polite replies, while surreptitiously studying the ballroom. It was a vast expanse, sparkling with gilt and mirrors, yet it felt small, it was so dense with people. The dance floor was filled with skipping, swirling dancers, while its outskirts thronged with observers who talked and laughed so loudly they almost drowned out the orchestra. Their silks and muslins, their fine jewels and plumes, sparkled in the light of thousands of candles.

It put him in mind of a maharajah's audience day, when petition-seekers gathered, clad in their best garments, their diamonds and sapphires. Those people, too, whispered and watched each other, gauging where they stood in relation to their peers, if their fortunes were waning or on the rise. Were their silks finer than those of that person over there? Were their jewels larger?

David almost laughed aloud at the irony. He had journeyed halfway across the world to find that the old adage was true—the more things changed, the more they stayed the same. He had hoped that here Anjali would find a degree of freedom impossible in India, in his grandmother's world. But London was just like Calcutta in so many ways.

And he was not completely accepted in either.

In Calcutta, his grandmother's grand friends mistrusted him because of his white father, his strange Western habits. They associated him with the strange, pale sahibs. Here, they sought out his title, his English fortune, but they mistrusted his dark skin, his Indian mother. They had never met anyone like him—titled, but foreign—and did not know how to treat him.

He saw this in the sidelong glances, the half-heard whispers dragging out the old scandal of his father's marriage. People acknowledged Lady Wilton's introduction of him; he *was* the Earl of Darlinghurst, after all. But their conversation was stilted, their gazes darted above his head and to his side. He hardly dared to ask any young lady to dance, for fear their mamas would spit in his face!

It all summoned up a long-buried mischief inside of him. What would they do if he suddenly burst into Bengali, sang a song of the medieval poet Kabir, or took off his stylish coat to reveal a striped sash and curved sword? Not that he carried a sword or wore a sash, of course, but still . . . the thought was tempting. Anything to break up this stiffly artificial environment and bring some amusement.

Perhaps next time he would wear a turban. With a diamond set in it. And arrive on an elephant. Where *could* one procure an elephant in London? Or perhaps dancing girls? Yet even as he thought it, even as he was tempted to give it a try, he knew he could not. He was trying to build a new life for Anjali here, a place where she could thrive and find happiness.

But perhaps just a small elephant, in Hyde Park one afternoon. . . .

"And when will you travel to Combe Lodge, Lord Darlinghurst?" Lady Wilton asked, pulling him out of his ridiculous visions.

He smiled down at her, tilting his head to one side to avoid her bobbing purple plumes. "Very soon, I hope, Lady Wilton. I have not seen the estate in many years, and, though Town has been delightful, I am looking forward to the country air."

"Oh, yes, most bracing," said Lady Wilton, with another fervent nod that almost dislodged the plumes entirely from her headdress. "We are going to Ireland ourselves, to visit my poor sister who is forced to live there, but I do not imagine the company will be as congenial as that you'll find in Derbyshire."

"Derbyshire is a beautiful corner of the country," said Lady Hapsby timidly. She had been standing with her husband in their little circle for several moments, but this was the first time David heard her actually speak. Mostly she just clung to her husband's sleeve and stared from wide hazel eyes.

David gave her a gentle smile. "Indeed you are correct, Lady Hapsby. Some of my happiest boyhood memories are of Derbyshire and Combe Lodge. I look forward very much to returning there."

And he looked forward to seeing if the neighbors were as congenial as ever. He wondered, not for the first time, if the Kentons still resided at Fair Oak. It was a pretty place, but not as grand as most ducal seats. He remembered that it did not suit the wild Damien, but he had heard that Damien was long dead and Alex, the military younger son, was now duke. Alex was once a nice young man, who happily took David and Emily fishing and riding, when most young men could not be bothered with their little sisters and their friends. Alex, if he was still the same sort of man, would be easy to approach about selling the Star of India.

And if Emily was still in residence—well, then, the company would surely be most congenial. Unless she had become one of the stiff, formal, timid ladies he observed around him now.

That thought, the image of his pretty and energetic Boudicca turned into a porcelain doll, gave him a strange, sour pang.

"The Duke of Wayland is your neighbor, is he not?" Lord Hapsby asked, almost as if he followed David's own thoughts.

"Yes. At least, I believe the Kenton family is still in residence at Fair Oak. They were friends with my father when I was a boy," David answered. "They are a very fine family."

"Very," Lady Wilton agreed, those blasted plumes bobbing away. "The duke and duchess are meant to attend my little rout this evening, though I have not yet seen them. I am sure they would be happy to find an old friend here!"

"The duchess is so very stylish," her daughter, Miss Louisa Wilton, said wistfully. "Such dash!"

"Indeed she is," agreed a nearby gentleman, and there followed a conversation where David was informed all about the famous, red-headed Duchess of Wayland. She had once been Mrs. Georgina Beaumont, the well-known Society artist, and she still occasionally displayed her work. She drove in the park in her own phaeton, had actually been seen embracing her children in public, and had made dancing with one's own husband almost fashionable!

David could only hope she had not also taken to wearing the Star in her red hair and would thus be loathe to part with it.

The talk turned to fashions in bonnets for the ladies, and the state of hunting in Derbyshire for the gentlemen. David had not much information, or indeed interest, in either of those topics, and his attention drifted back to the dancers. A schottische was finishing, the partners skipping through the circle and swirling about one final time.

Suddenly, the back of his neck tingled sharply, the small hairs standing on end. Someone was watching him, not casually, but quite intently. It felt as if he was back in a Bengali jungle, with a panther staring at him from the cover of trees.

Slowly, David turned away from the dance floor and glanced behind him. His gaze landed on a lady who stood several paces away, her hand on the arm of a plump, red-faced young man. She was certainly lovely—one of the most beautiful ladies in the ballroom. Not very tall, she was slim and delicate-looking, with sunshine gold hair piled up in loose curls and anchored with a white silk fillet. Her gown was Grecian in design, a simple column of white and silver satin that draped into a low décolletage and small cap sleeves. An ornate garnet cross on a gold chain hung about her neck, resting enticingly just above the swell of her ivory-rose bosom.

She would have appeared the veriest wax doll, perfectly pink and white and gold, perfectly still and polite, if not for her eyes. They were dark blue, like an Indian sky right before the onslaught of the monsoons. And they were just as stormy, roiling with a barely leashed intelligence and energy. They stared at him intently, never wavering from his face.

It was those eyes that jolted him, made him stumble back a step. Lady Wilton glanced up at him, startled. David murmured an apology to her, never taking his stare off the golden goddess.

No, not a goddess. A warrior queen. *Boudicca.*

"Emily," he whispered under his breath. It had to be Emily. No other female in the world had eyes like that. His old friend—grown into a beauty beyond all imagination.

He longed to go to her, to take her hands in his, to ask her all about the years they were separated. What had happened to her? What had she seen, done? Lady Wilton's hand on his arm held him where he was.

His hostess followed his gaze, and said, with a little trill of laughter, "Ah, here is one of your neighbors now! How fortuitous. You must remember Lady Emily Kenton." Lady Emily moved closer with her escort, a tentative smile now touching her rosey pink lips. "Lady Emily, may I have the honor of presenting, or rather *re*-presenting, the Earl of Darlinghurst? He is only recently returned from India, and has graced my humble soiree as his first outing. And this is Mr. Carrington, Lord Darlinghurst."

"Of course I remember—Lord Darlinghurst," Emily

said, her voice catching, as if she had run a great distance and was out of breath. It reminded David of the last day they were together, racing across the meadows. "It has been far too long since we met."

She stepped away from her escort, which did not please the young man—Mr. Carrington?—at all. His face grew even redder and he sputtered, but he was impotent to hold her back. She extended her gloved hand to David and he bowed over it. It was a polite salute, yet he was loath to let her go after the obeisance was performed. Her hand seemed not much larger than when he used to grasp it to help her up a tree, but her fingers were light and strong where they curled around his. She smelled of the expensive kid of her glove, of sweet roses, and of her own cinnamon-like Emily fragrance.

"Far too long, Lady Emily. It is—very good to see you again," he told her, slowly letting his hand slide from hers. She gave him a wide, glorious smile, and he was again reminded of the monsoons. She was not like a gentle English rain. Her smile, her scarcely restrained vibrant energy, were like the unspeakable relief of the cleansing, driving rains after unbearable, parching heat.

It was as if they had never been apart—and also as if they were meeting for the first time.

The orchestra tuned their instruments in preparation for a new set of dances. He thought he recognized an old country reel in the strains, a relatively simple dance he could possibly manage.

"Lady Emily, will you do me the honor of dancing the next set with me?" he asked her. He had meant not to dance this evening; his feet were still unused to the English steps, despite practicing them with Anjali for her dance lessons. His ear was unused to the tunes. Yet the chance to hold Emily's hand in his again, to converse with her, even if only in polite niceties, was more than he could resist. He could only hope he would not step on her toes, or knock her over in a turn.

Her smile widened even further, and she nodded over the sputtering, ineffectual protests of Mr. Carrington. "Thank you, Lord Darlinghurst. I would be happy to accept."

Chapter Four

*E*mily slid her hand into the warm crook of David's arm and followed his lead to their place in the dance. *Surely this must be a dream*, she thought. It felt like she was surrounded by a misty haze of unreality; her silk slippers floated above the floor, and she wanted to laugh aloud. She was about to dance with David. *David!*

She knew this was her old friend, she saw it in his eyes, heard it in his voice. Yet also, oddly, he was a stranger. A tall, handsome stranger, who had been away from her, been in a faraway land, for many years.

She wished they did not have to dance. She wanted to go somewhere quiet with him, to pour out all her questions and hear him answer in his rich, dark, musically accented voice. What was his life in India like? Why had he come back to England? Was he—unthinkable!—married? What did he think of her grown-up self?

But they could not do that, of course. They were in a crowded ballroom; everyone was watching them. Emily was accustomed to the *ton*'s eyes on her; speculation was par for the course for a duke's unmarried sister. And, of course, Georgina and Alex drew attention wherever they went in their own rights! Yet this was different. The attention seemed—sharper, somehow. The sister of the Duke of Wayland with the Indian earl? Shocking!

But Emily found she did not care. She had been through too much in her life to care two straws what the pettier members of the *ton* thought of her. As long as her actions were not dishonorable, as Damien's had been, she did mostly what she liked. And right now what she *liked* was to dance with David. There could be nothing improper in her dancing with an earl, her family's neighbor.

As she curtsied to him and took his hand for the first turn in the dance, these thoughts vanished altogether. The crowded ballroom, the other dancers, everything was gone. She saw only him, smiling at her as they came together and swirled apart. She remembered dancing with him at her parents' long-ago Christmas ball, the two of them skipping down the line, laughing as only carefree children could.

He had not been quite so tall then! His hands had not been so strong. But he still smelled of sandalwood soap.

"We were so very sorry to hear of your father's passing," she said. It seemed wrong somehow to begin their reacquaintance with such a sad subject, yet she felt it had to be said. The letter her mother had written to him when the news reached them seemed inadequate. "He was a fine man."

"Thank you, Lady Emily. I was very sorry to hear of your father, as well. And your brother." They linked arms and turned in an allemande.

He was not the best dance partner Emily had ever had; his steps were a bit uncertain, not entirely smooth. Yet he was infinitely gentle with her, not spinning her off into the hinterlands as some gentlemen were wont to do when they grew too enthusiastic. Truly, she would rather dance with David than with any other man on earth.

"Yes. Thank you. It feels such a long time since Damien left us," she answered, watching him closely. "You have been away an age."

His hand tightened on hers for the merest instant. "Much too long, I begin to think," he said.

The dance parted them, and for a while Emily could only watch him across the expanse of the set. It was not a great distance, but it felt a mile. Oh, *blast* the ridiculous rules! She wanted to *talk* to him.

When once again they came together, she asked, "And how do you find England after your years away?"

He laughed—a rich sound that made her want to laugh, too. "Cold, Lady Emily. Very cold."

She *did* laugh then. After he left, she had made it her mission to read everything she could find about India. She had been dazzled by descriptions of heat so heavy it made the very air shimmer, of strange fruits and flowers, of breezes smelling of spices.

To go from that to *this*, gray, damp, rule-bound milieu, must be shocking indeed.

"We are having an unseasonably wet spring, even for England," she said. *Weather?* She was talking of the *weather*, of all things? How ridiculous of her. "But it was quite lovely at Fair Oak the last time we were there, and it does not appear to have harmed the crops in any way. I am eager to go back to the country, as I am sure you must be to see Combe Lodge again."

"I am. I fear I have neglected it shamefully."

Emily saw a dark shutter fall over his gaze, one that spoke of worry and perhaps guilt. She understood those emotions all too well, and she hastened to reassure him. "Not at all. I ride over there often when I am at Fair Oak, and it prospers. It looks very well, the house and the fields, and I am sure you will be content when you see it."

"Thank you, Lady Emily," he said, and she fancied she heard a measure of relief. But she did so wish he could call her just *Emily* again.

"Everyone in the neighborhood will be glad you are

in residence again." She paused an instant before saying the words she was thinking, then let them all go in a rush. "Is your wife looking forward to seeing your family home? It has been many years since Combe Lodge had a mistress."

The corners of his lips twitched—whether in amusement at her presumptuous question or in a flash of pain, Emily could not tell. She did not know which option she preferred less. Why could she not call that question back? *Why?*

"I fear I am a widower," he said.

A widower! Then he was not married, and yet he had once been. What a gulf separated them since they had been apart. She wondered what other experiences he had had that she could not begin to fathom.

"I am sorry," she said simply. Inadequately.

"Thank you. My daughter is looking forward to the country, though she is as yet too young to be a proper chatelaine there. I have promised her a pony, and she talks of nothing else of late."

A daughter. And, of course, she would be beautiful, as no doubt her mother had been.

"The countryside around Combe Lodge is ideal for riding," was all Emily could think to say.

"Yes, I remember. I also remember that you were a bruising rider, who left everyone, including myself, in the dust." He gave her a teasing little smile. "Are you still so fond of riding?"

She couldn't help but smile in return, despite this new fit of self-doubt. Her rage to pepper David with questions had faded into worries that *he* would not be as interested in *her*. How could he be, when he had lived in an Indian palace with a beautiful wife and perfect, almost-pony-riding daughter? All Emily had done was run a farm, turning her hands rough and her mind hard.

"I do enjoy riding, though I do not get the chance as

often as I would like," she said, giving a little leap and a spin. "There is no place for a good gallop in Town. But my sister-in-law is teaching me to drive a phaeton. I hope to have my own very soon!"

He gazed down into her eyes as they turned, and she felt her cheeks grow warm beneath his dark regard. Oh, the curse of her pale skin, that blushes showed so clearly there! Other men looked at her all the time, and she never—ever!—blushed. She was becoming a complete ninny.

"A new chariot, Boudicca?" he asked quietly.

Hearing the old nickname in his new voice made her blush burn out of control, and she had to look away. Over David's shoulder, she saw Georgina and Alex standing at the edge of the dance floor, watching her. Alex frowned in a most fearful way, as he always did when a man he did not know spoke to his sister. But Georgina looked almost—delighted.

"One I hope does not come with blades on the wheels," Emily managed to answer, turning her attention back to her dance partner. "I should hate to frighten dogs and small children in the Park."

David laughed, and the music came to its final crescendo. Could their dance be over already? Surely it had only just begun.

Emily curtsied as David bowed, all that was correct despite the thoughts roiling in her mind. As she straightened and took his proffered arm, he said, "May I escort you to supper later, Lady Emily? If you do not already have a partner."

Did she have a partner for supper? She could scarcely recall. But then, she could scarcely recall her own name at the moment. "Thank you, Lord Darlinghurst. I would enjoy that." She turned to see Alex and Georgina moving toward them, the two of them obviously filled to the brim with filial determination. "You must allow me to present you to my brother, whom of course you already know, and my sister-in-law. They will be most eager to converse with you."

Only after the introductions had been made, and Alex and Georgina engaged David in a lively discourse about Fair Oak and Combe Lodge, did Emily have a most startling thought. Not once during their dance had she thought about the dilemma of the Star. She had been faced with a person most closely concerned with the jewel, and she herself had pondered little else for days. Yet it had completely vanished when David took her hand in his.

How strange. And how worrisome.

The Wilton dining room was almost as long as the ballroom, but it felt a great deal more intimate and less crowded thanks to the arrangements of many small, round tables rather than one long expanse which all the guests had to crowd around. Great silver platters and tureens bearing all manner of delicacies graced each table, surrounded by clusters of hothouse flowers and gold-rimmed crystal goblets of ruby red wine and sparkling champagne.

Emily was ordinarily excessively fond of baked salmon, lobster tarts, white soup, and pineapple (indeed, she knew that if she was not equally fond of exercise, she would soon be quite as large as Lady Birtwhistle in her orange satin). Yet tonight she could do no more than nibble at a few grapes. And that was due entirely to the man who sat beside her.

They were seated at a small corner table with Alex and Georgina, who asked David a myriad of questions about his plans for Combe Lodge. Emily herself managed to articulate a few comments, but mostly she just watched David—this new, fascinating David—and listened to him as he spoke.

It still felt quite unreal—dreamlike, really—that he had suddenly appeared back in her world. His smile still held echoes of the friend she had once known, but it was not as open as it had once been. His laughter held a wry, hard note under its dark music.

Well, it *had* been many years. And no one knew better than Emily the toll that time could take. Nothing stayed the same for even a moment—not even friendship. She was not the same wild, carefree girl she was then. He could not be the same boy who spent patient time with her and was her faithful friend and playmate.

She listened to him speak of his English home, and longed to ask him about other things, things she knew of only from books. Monsoons, ghats and bathing in the sacred Ganges, rajahs atop jeweled elephants, dancing girls in bright silks and belled bracelets. Did the air truly smell of spices and jasmine in India? If she leaned close enough now, could she smell its echoes in his midnight hair?

She even moved toward him, just the merest fraction, when she was brought up short by the sound of her brother speaking her name.

Emily sat up straight, and blinked innocently across the table at Alex. Surely no one looking at her could have even an inkling that she was just about to sniff a gentleman's hair!

"I beg your pardon, Alex? I fear I was examining Mrs. Harcourt's extraordinary turban and did not hear you."

"I was just telling Lord Darlinghurst that you are quite the expert on the most modern farming techniques, and he should ask your advice as well as my own concerning the fields at Combe Lodge," Alex said, with an obviously puzzled frown. Emily was not usually so concerned with such things as turbans, and she had often expressed disdain for the fashion, which of course her brother would remember. She should have conjured up a better excuse for her rude inattention!

Emily gave him another smile, and thought what a very unromantic subject *farming* was compared to jasmine and spangled silks and moonlit nights in Hindu ruins. But she *had* kept up with new farming theories, regularly reading the agricultural reports. As much as she longed to, she could not leave her past work behind her entirely. Whenever she rode over Fair Oak, she thought of planting and crop circulation. And, if all that meant she could converse with David a bit longer, she was glad for it.

"Indeed," she said. "While Alex was so bravely fighting for his country, I did what I could to learn about agriculture. The landscape and soil conditions at Combe Lodge are, of course, very similar to those at Fair Oak. I will be happy to share anything I have discovered."

"Thank you, Lady Emily. You are most obliging," David replied, giving her one of his small, wry smiles. She noticed then the tiny lines that smile etched about his dark eyes—lines carved there by the brilliant Indian sun. "I have much to learn. While I read a great deal on the voyage to England, books are no substitute for experience."

Amen to that, Emily thought. She sometimes felt that all she had ever seen of true life was in the pages of books. First, because books were the only amusement she could afford while she lived alone with her mother in the country. And now—now books were her anchor to a different reality, in the midst of this glittering, artificial world.

"Ah, but I hope you are not going to abandon Town for the country just yet!" declared Georgina, with one of her merry trills of laughter. "The Season may be almost over, yet there are many delights still to be had. The theater, of course, is always amusing, and there is the Mer-

ryvale rout and that ridiculous affair the Innises have devised to display their treasure one last time. And you
must see the Elgin Marbles!"

Emily nodded in fervent agreement, pushing aside the
distressing mention of the forthcoming Innis ball. She
had already seen the Greek Marbles once, in their dark,
cramped display room at the British Museum, and had
been caught up by the *life* of them, the flowing, eternal
beauty. "Oh, yes, you must see at least that before you
leave London, Da—Lord Darlinghurst." She felt her
face warm anew at that near faux pas. Though she could
not *think* of him as anything but David, it would never,
ever do to say it aloud. She turned away to take a cooling sip of wine.

But he appeared not to notice her discomfiture at all.
Or perhaps he was just being polite? "Thank you, Your
Grace, Lady Emily. I would enjoy all of those things, especially the marbles, I am sure, but I do hope to leave
soon for Combe Lodge. I have my nine-year-old daughter with me, and I fear she may grow bored in Town."

"Our children are also here in Town, Lord Darlinghurst, and I know very well the importance of keeping little ones amused and out of mischief!" Georgina
said. "They are probably too young to be company for
Lady . . ." She paused, one dark red brow raised in in-
quiry.

"Lady Anjali," David answered.

Georgina nodded, not even batting an eyelash at the
exotic name. "For Lady Anjali, but perhaps she would
enjoy some of the same amusements they do, such as
Astley's Amphitheatre or some of the museums of cu-
riosities. And the Park is always most pleasant."
Georgina paused again, a speculative glance turned onto
Emily.

Emily held her breath. Whenever her sister-in-law got
that look in her eye, mischief was soon to follow.

Georgina had recently been the orchestrator of her friend Mrs. Rosalind Chase's marriage to the poet Viscount Morley, and the success had put matchmaking into her blood.

"Indeed, Lady Emily knows Hyde Park very well, she is always riding and walking there, often with my children," Georgina continued. "Perhaps she could show you—and your daughter—the best sights."

David glanced at Emily—a quick, unreadable look. She fancied she saw some uncertainty there.

But when he spoke, his voice conveyed no hint of reluctance or sense of being coerced. He smiled at her, and said, "I would be very happy if you would consent to drive with me in the Park, Lady Emily. We have many years to catch up on, after all."

"Thank you, Lord Darlinghurst," Emily answered politely, quietly, as if her stomach was *not* turning over with excitement. And all over a simple invitation to drive in the Park! "We have no engagements tomorrow afternoon."

"Excellent. Tomorrow it is," David said.

Georgina gave a satisfied little smile. "And I hope you and Lady Anjali will take tea with us next week, as well. It is always pleasant to get to know one's neighbors!"

Alex laid his hand over his wife's, and nodded in agreement. "Indeed, Darlinghurst, we will be happy to see you at any time it is convenient. And now that my wife has arranged everyone's social schedules to her liking, shall we find some fresh air on the terrace? It has grown quite close in the dining room."

"A wonderful idea, my dear!" Georgina declared. "We shall all go together."

Emily watched as Georgina and Alex rose from their chairs and ambled happily away, arm in arm, everyone moving out of the way of their ducal path. Then David's gloved hand appeared before her, waiting to help her from her seat.

She gazed up at him, and could not help but grin yet again in abject happiness. Her uncertainties about this new David, her fears about what might happen when he found out the fate of his family's Star, were pushed aside—at least for the moment. For now, for this one evening, she was just glad to see her friend again.

"Shall we join them, Lady Emily?" he asked. "I can send one of the footmen for your shawl."

She slipped her hand into his, reveling in the feel of his fingers closing over hers, holding them safe. "Thank you, Lord Darlinghurst. Some fresh air sounds most— bracing."

David studied Emily carefully in the flickering light of the Chinese lanterns strung along the Wiltons' terrace. She appeared to be everything a young English lady should be—serene, polite, charming, and oh so beautiful in her fashionable gown and jewels. Her gloved fingers were light as a butterfly on his sleeve, and her smile was perfect as she chatted with him about a myriad of inconsequential topics—the weather, the Wiltons' elegant arrangements in their ballroom, his voyage from India and his new London townhouse.

Everything but the things he *really* wanted to ask her. What had she been doing in the years they were apart? She was obviously not engaged, but was there a young swain she favored? Above all, what was it that burned so behind her monsoon eyes, beneath the serene mask of her pretty face?

For there *was* something. He had not imagined the flare of some strange panic in her expression back in the dining room. They had been talking and laughing with her brother and his wife, when suddenly Emily's eyes widened, her breath caught in a sharp gasp, and she withdrew into some secret room deep inside herself. She dwelled in that room still, despite her smiles and polite questions.

He remembered that she would do that sometimes as a child, when she was roundly scolded by her governess or when the wicked Damien broke one of her dolls. What could be affecting her so now? She was obviously a Diamond of Society, admired and lovely. But something plagued her, something that made her go from laughing and open to quietly withdrawn in only a moment.

He would give his newly acquired phaeton to know what it was, to take the burden from her slim shoulders.

"I trust your mother is well now?" he said, trying to fill the silence between them as they turned and made another circuit of the terrace. Several feet ahead of them walked the duke and duchess, arm in arm, laughing together softly, intimately. "I understood she had an accident of some sort."

"Yes," Emily answered quietly. "Many years ago, she was thrown from her horse during a hunt. She has been confined to a Bath chair ever since."

"I am so sorry, Lady Emily," he said, chagrined. "I should not have brought up such a painful subject."

"Not at all! You and your father were always good friends to my parents—it is only natural you would want to know how she fares. And she is very well now. She is at the dower house at Fair Oak now, but she spends part of every year in Bath, taking the waters and enjoying concerts and card parties. She will be happy to hear you are back in England."

"And I am happy to hear she is doing so well." Ahead of them, he saw the duke and duchess stop and speak to another group. Soon, he and Emily would not be alone—or nearly so—any longer. He turned to her, and said quickly, "Lady Emily, shall I call on you at three o'clock to go driving with me in the Park tomorrow? I would so much like to hear more about your life."

She paused for an instant, her eyes wide and uncertain, and he feared he had pushed too much. But then she nodded, and said, "Oh, yes. I would like that very much. Thank you, Lord Darlinghurst."

Chapter Five

"*A*unt Emily, may I go driving in the Park with you, *please*?" Emily's little niece, Elizabeth Anne, caught at Emily's skirt with her chubby fingers and leaned against Emily's chair in her most beguiling manner. "It is such a beautiful day!"

Emily laid down the book she was halfheartedly reading, but before she could answer her niece's entreaties, Georgina broke in.

"No, my darling, not today," she said, barely glancing up from the sketchbook on her lap. Only her tiny, secret smile revealed that she heard all of her cajoling and was vastly amused by it. "Aunt Emily is going on a grown-up outing this afternoon. No little girls allowed. I will stay home, though, and we can have a drawing lesson."

Elizabeth Anne smoothed her palm over the sleeve of Emily's pale yellow silk walking dress. "Is that why you are so dressed up, Aunt Emily? Do you have a *suitor* coming to take you to the Park?"

Emily laughed, and caught up Elizabeth Anne's tiny hand to kiss it. "You are becoming a wild romantic, my cherub! Just like your mama. I have an old friend coming to take me to the Park, someone I knew when I was not much older than you are now."

Elizabeth Anne's brow wrinkled in confusion. *This*

did not fit into her *Cenerentola* view of life as one long
vista of Prince Charmings! "A child is coming to take
you driving?"

Emily could hardly contain her mirth. She pressed her
hand to her mouth, and only when she felt she could
speak without bursting into laughter did she say, "No,
my dove. He was a child many years ago, as I was, but
now he is grown up. He is as old as your mama."

Elizabeth Anne's green eyes widened. "As old as
that?"

Emily could not help it—she let her laughter run free.
"I know, angel. It is difficult to believe."

Georgina tossed a velvet cushion at Emily's head, and
cried out in great indignation, "Oh, thank you *very*
much, sister dear! If I only had my walking stick to hand,
I would hobble my decrepit self over there and beat you
soundly with it. But we elderly folk must content ourselves with our quiet seat, where we may nurse our
gout."

Elizabeth Anne glanced from her mother to her aunt,
obviously now thoroughly confused. "So, an *old* person
is coming to call on you, Aunt Emily? *And* a child?"

"Neither, my darling," said Georgina. "Aunt Emily's
caller is a most handsome gentleman of thoroughly
youthful age."

"Ah." Elizabeth Anne nodded thoughtfully. "Will he
bring flowers, then?"

"If he knows what is good for him. Now, leave your
auntie alone for a time. You will wrinkle her gown and
muss her hair."

Elizabeth Anne immediately removed her hand from
the vicinity of Emily's sleeve. "Oh, no! You must not be
mussed when your suitor comes here." She retreated to
the window seat, where Georgina's white terrier, Lady
Kate, was nursing her new litter of puppies. Next to

clothes and fairy tales, the pups were Elizabeth Anne's first priority in her young life.

Georgina laid aside her sketchbook, and leaned over to be sure baby Sebastian still slept in his basket. "He *is* very handsome, is he not?"

"Sebastian?" Emily said, pretending to be thoroughly ignorant of Georgina's meaning. "Undoubtedly. He looks just like Alex, or shall in fifteen or twenty years."

"Of course not Sebastian! It goes without saying that *he* is handsome. And you know perfectly well who I mean. Your Lord Darlinghurst."

Emily could feel that curse of a flush returning, spreading warmly down into her ruffled white gauze chemisette. She turned away from Georgina's searching gaze, and riffled through the pages of her book. "He is not *my* Lord Darlinghurst, Georgie."

"Hm. Perhaps not yet, but judging from the way he looked at you last night, he very soon will be. Or *could* be, if you wanted him."

"Georgie! I have not seen the man for nigh on four-teen years. How should I know if I *wanted* him? We are merely two childhood friends becoming reacquainted."

"Of course, Em. But perhaps, as you become reac-quainted, you will find you have things in common. Things that might lead you to—become friends again."

Emily could not pretend to herself that she had not contemplated the same sort of thing. Last night, and in the carriage coming home from the ball, and alone in her bedchamber, all she had thought about was David. How he had grown into a very handsome, fascinating man. How strong and warm his arm felt beneath her hand as they strolled along the Wiltons' terrace.

His dark eyes and rich voice, his air of something ex-otic and undefinable, made all her London suitors fade away into pale nothingness. But . . .

"Our lives have been so very different all these years.

Almost as if we lived on two different planets. I am sure that after the Indian ladies he would find me as dull as dishwater." As washed-out as she thought her English callers.

Georgina gave an indignant huff. "How could he possibly find you dull, Em? You have more wit and conversation that any other miss in London! Not to mention a curiosity and intelligence he could not find anyplace else, as well as your quite à la mode prettiness. I have wished all my life to change this red hair of mine into golden curls. You give yourself too little credit. Once he gets to know you again, he will be *yours*."

Emily just laughed. She could think of no reply to make, as was so often the case with Georgina's pronouncements. Emily wished that Georgina's words were true, but doubts plagued her so that she could not quite believe them. Her life *had* been very different from David's. And then there was the matter of the Star.

He would ask about it eventually, she was sure of that. The sapphire rightly belonged to him, to his family, and *her* family had done him a great wrong. She could never make the matter of the jewel right for him, no matter how much she twisted herself into knots about it. She would simply have to confess the ugly truth.

But not yet. Not until he asked. For now, she would be a selfish creature and enjoy having his company again.

"Is this him?" Elizabeth Anne cried, pressing her nose to the window. "It must be; he is stopping here. Oooh, he *is* handsome! But very dark. Do you suppose he stayed too long in the sun, Mama?"

Georgina hurried over to the window beside Elizabeth Anne, pressing her nose against the glass in the exact same manner as her small daughter. "He has been living in India, darling, and sometimes people there *are* dark. Remember the story Aunt Emily has been telling you?"

Elizabeth Anne nodded. "About the blue god with many arms?"

"Exactly. That tale also comes from India, dear."

Emily smiled at Elizabeth Anne's memory. Perhaps it was not strictly proper to read wild tales of "heathen" India to an English duke's daughter, but Elizabeth Anne loved them far above tame Anglo fables. And Emily loved reading them to her—it was good to have someone to share her interest in India with, even if it was just her little niece.

Elizabeth Anne glanced over her shoulder at Emily. "Will he know the blue man, Aunt Emily?"

"No, poppet. The blue man is made-up, remember?" Emily said.

Elizabeth Anne's face fell in comic disappointment. "Oh, yes. I remember now." Then she and her mother returned to spying out the window.

Emily took advantage of their moment of inattention to hurry over to the large gilt-framed mirror hung on the silk-papered wall. Her hair was still confined neatly within its pins, her wild yellow curls turned into a few fashionable ringlets about her face, but she fussed with it nevertheless, pushing some tendrils back, twining some about her finger. The faint, light brown freckles that sprinkled across her nose—a legacy of her seasons out in the farm fields, and now the bane of her life—had only been partially disguised by the rice powder she applied this morning.

But there was nothing to be done about that now. Greene, the butler, was already opening the drawing room door to admit their caller. She gave a final fluff to her skirts, fixed what she hoped was a welcoming and *not* maniacal smile on her face, and turned to greet David.

Georgina, always the most excellent of hostesses, hurried to the door with her elegant hand outstretched.

"Lord Darlinghurst! How very pleasant to see you again. Will you take tea before you and Lady Emily have your drive?"

"Thank you, Your Grace," David answered. "That would be most agreeable." He bowed over Georgina's hand, and tossed Emily a smile over to where she stood half-frozen by the mirror. And—was that a *wink*? Indeed it must have been!

It made Emily want to giggle like a silly schoolgirl. All of this nervous formality did seem a bit absurd. This was *David*, whom she used to race across meadows and with whom she climbed trees. But she did not yet know how she ought to behave with him. They were no longer children, but there was as yet no guide for what they should be to each other as adults.

So, for now, formal politeness it would be.

"Elizabeth Anne, dearest, ring the bell for tea," Georgina instructed her daughter, as she led David to a comfortable grouping of chairs by the fireplace. She gestured for Emily to join them.

Elizabeth Anne rang the tasseled bell pull, her wide gaze never leaving their visitor. She had one finger in the corner of her mouth, a babyish habit of which Georgina had long ago cured her, but which sometimes reappeared in moments of excitement. She came to lean against her mother's knee, and removed her finger to say, "Do you know the blue man with many arms who lives in India?"

"Elizabeth Anne!" Georgina admonished. "What did your aunt and I just tell you about that?"

"That he is a made-up man in stories," answered Elizabeth Anne, completely unabashed.

Emily gave David a sheepish smile. "I am sorry, Lord Darlinghurst. I have been reading her tales of India, and they have rather gone to her head. She was full of anticipation when she heard you had lived there."

David just laughed. "Not at all. My own daughter enjoys tales of Shiva very much. Your daughter is obviously a curious and learned girl, Your Grace."

"Indeed she is," Georgina said fondly, reaching down to smooth her child's wild red curls. She lifted Elizabeth Anne onto the seat beside her, holding her still with a firm arm about her waist. "Sometimes a bit too much so."

The tea arrived then, borne by two liveried footmen and placed carefully on a low table between Emily and Georgina. There were far too many delicacies for four people: trays of sandwiches, cakes, and tarts along with two kinds of tea. It was obvious that Cook knew Elizabeth Anne was in residence. The child had a prodigious taste for cakes second only to Emily's own.

But today Emily found her stomach was too queasy to partake of her favorite cream cakes at all.

"Lady Emily has indeed been reading Elizabeth Anne stories of India," Georgina said, pouring out the steaming tea into her best Wedgwood cups, paper thin and surrounded with pale Grecian figures. Only the most honored guests were permitted to use the Wedgwood. "She knows a great deal about the land."

David shot Emily a curious, questioning glance. "Does she truly?"

"Oh, yes! She is always telling us facts of the flora and fauna of Bengal. As an artist, of course, I have many questions about the landscape and people. Perhaps you could tell me, Lord Darlinghurst, about the grand mausoleum of the Taj Mahal? Is it as wondrous as they say?"

And Georgina went on for the next quarter hour or more, peppering David with questions about India and his life there, thus mercifully saving Emily from having to converse much herself. This gave her the chance to observe David closely as he spoke. He still smiled easily, as he had when they were younger. But there was something different in his eyes—something mysterious and almost sad.

But she could not really talk to him until they left the house in David's new, stylish phaeton and turned into the gates of Hyde Park. Aside from the people riding and walking there, they were quite alone.

It was a bit too early in the afternoon for Rotten Row to be truly crowded—Emily and David were actually able to move forward in the phaeton without stopping every ten paces or progressing at a snail's pace. Riders cantered sedately along, ladies took the air in their open carriages, nannies shepherded their little charges, dogs darted about on leads, barely controlled by footmen assigned to their care. In the distance, Emily thought she glimpsed Lord Pickering and Sir Arnold Ellis, on horseback paused in a small grove of trees. Sir Arnold's emerald green coat stood out like a beacon. She turned her open yellow silk parasol toward them, so they would not see her and come speak to her, as they always did.

She did not want anything to interfere with this moment, this illusion of solitude with David. And she was not sure she could speak lightly and coherently with anyone—not with all the thoughts dashing around in her head.

They had been silent as they drove away from the house, Emily feeling the sharp stares on the back of her neck until they turned the corner. She knew that Georgina and Elizabeth Anne were watching avidly from the window, and it made her want to laugh aloud. Now that they were alone in the sunny afternoon outdoors, she *did* laugh. It was truly ridiculous that her glamorous sister-in-law was so very interested in Emily's own quite dull life!

David glanced over at her, a half-smile quirked the

corner of his lips. She noticed a small dimple, and had the oddest, almost overpowering urge to place her fingertip over it and feel his smooth skin beneath her touch. Was that enticing dimple there when they were younger? How had she failed to see it then?

Ridiculous girl! she chided herself, and tightened her grip on her parasol handle until the carved ivory bit into her palm.

"Something amusing, Lady Emily?" he asked.

Emily started to retreat into her usual reserve, to give some polite, tossed-away answer. She had become quite expert at hiding her true thoughts, her fears and apprehensions and odd sense of humor, behind cool smiles and distant politeness. It was easier that way. It made her feel less apart from those around her and less like a strange creature.

And more lonely.

But this was David, she remembered. Once, she had been able to tell him anything, any fear or joy or silly joke. Just because he was now a tall, handsome, delicious-smelling man with intriguing dimples, that did not mean her friend was not still there under all that splendor. The boy who had been patient and kind with her, who had always been up for a lark or laugh, must still lurk behind his dark rajah's eyes.

She rested her parasol against her shoulder and smiled up at him. She was determined to find her friend there, and to show him that really she was not so very different, either. Surely she could still laugh, *really* laugh, even though she felt one hundred years old so much of the time. "Oh, no. I just—that is, I want to apologize for my sister-in-law's . . . nosiness. That is really the only word for it. She is an artist, you know—quite a famous one—and views every new acquaintance as a potential subject. She meant no harm by asking you so many questions about yourself and your life in India. And she is also a rather informal mother, who gives free rein to her daughter's curiosity. As, I admit, do I."

"Not at all, Lady Emily. There is no need to apologize. The duchess and Lady Elizabeth Anne are quite charming. I can see where it would be impossible *not* to indulge such a child," David said, his voice full of the deep force of his own suppressed laughter. "After so long in India, where everyone is so painfully aware of etiquette that they never say anything in the least bit unexpected, I enjoy true conversation. It is a relief."

"And so do I!" Emily exclaimed in delight. "London is surely no better than India in its formal ways. No one ever says the true, real thing—one must always guess what a person is thinking. The conversation is all weather and fashion and housekeeping and horses."

"I have noticed, in my short time here, that such topics *are* quite common. I spent at least ten minutes with Lady Wilton at her ball speculating on whether or not it would rain the next day. I would have thought the interest in such a question would wane in two minutes at the very most."

Emily laughed. "Ah, but as I recall it did *not* rain this morning. Was that the consensus you and Lady Wilton reached?"

He chuckled, and tugged at the reins to turn the horses for another circuit of the Row. "I fear I cannot recall, Lady Emily. Pray tell me, do you think we will see rain *tomorrow*?"

Emily's laughter grew louder, drawing the surprised glances of a mother and her pastel-clad daughter. Their escort, who looked suspiciously like Mr. Carrington, gave her a hurt stare, but Emily could not care. The nervous knot in her stomach was at last melting, and she began to enjoy herself. "La, Lord Darlinghurst, I could not say! But that cloud in the distance appears quite ominous. I fear it may ruin Lady Egghurst's Venetian breakfast and a planned balloon ascension."

"A Venetian breakfast? This must be a new style of event I have not heard of, Lady Emily. Pray enlighten me as to its function. Or are social events not considered one of the suitable topics for conversation?"

"On the contrary, it is the *most* suitable. Yet I fear a Venetian breakfast is not as exotic as it sounds. My brother and sister-in-law travel to Italy quite often—the duchess owns a house in Venice, and she says there is nothing at all Venetian about such soirees. They are dull affairs."

"Then I should not attend?"

"If you have a choice, no. Alas, I have no choice, as Georgina already promised, in a moment of great weakness, that we would be there. Though, if you do come, we could discuss the weather to our hearts' content."

"I shall be there, then. I cannot resist a good conversation about the rain."

There was a new note in his voice, one Emily had not heard before. It was tinged with a deepness, a seriousness—a flirtatiousness? It was hard for her to tell. Gentlemen were so awed by her brother's status that they seldom flirted with her. Emily peeked at David from beneath the brim of her bonnet, but she could see only his profile, as clear-cut and expressionless as if carved on an ancient Indian coin.

Emily decided she must have been mistaken, and she turned away to nod at a passing acquaintance. "It will be amusing if you are there. At such routs, when I grow bored, I imagine myself taking off my slippers and climbing onto the table to wade in the Roman Punch or some such outlandish deed. It would liven things up immensely, I daresay, but alas, I never have the courage!"

David laughed, and when he spoke again his tone was its usual light politeness. Yes—she had surely imagined any flirtatious admiration. She almost sighed aloud in what felt surprisingly like disappointment.

"So, you have never carried out your imaginings, Lady Emily?"

"I am no Caro Lamb. But the imagining does help to pass the time. I also sometimes make up fairy tales in my head to tell Elizabeth Anne later."

"Tales of blue men with many arms?"

Emily gave an abashed laugh. "I meant no disrespect in telling her that, I promise. But she does so enjoy stories of India, and someone gave my brother a book of Hindu tales. I thought she would like some of them, the more, er, humorous ones." Emily felt that treacherous old blush spreading again as she recalled some stories of the gods' many amorous exploits, stories she would *never* tell her niece, but which she herself quite enjoyed. She strategically turned her parasol so he could not see her red cheeks and guess her thoughts.

"My own daughter enjoys such tales," he replied. "But she also likes old stories of English kings and queens, especially Queen Elizabeth. We read many of them on our long voyage from India."

Emily frowned a bit at this reminder of the family life that had, for David, filled the years they were apart. She wondered again about his wife, his love for her. But she was not quite so willing to let go of the niceties she had just mocked, in order to ask him about those things. "How is your daughter enjoying England, now that she is here?"

He hesitated for an instant before answering. "Quite well, though I fear she has developed a taste for the bloodthirsty. We visited the Tower, and she had no interest in the jewels or the menagerie. She wanted only to see where Anne Boleyn and Catherine Howard are buried. I hope to find a proper governess for her very soon, and hopefully she can turn Anjali's interests toward more suitable avenues."

"If you are having difficulties, I am sure my sister-in-law could assist you. She has only just found a governess for Elizabeth Anne."

"Thank you. I would appreciate any advice very much."

They fell into a comfortable silence as they turned away to drive toward the Serpentine. It was growing more crowded along Rotten Row, but was quiet by the river. David drew the phaeton to a halt under the shade of a tall tree where they could watch the strolling couples and children floating their paper boats.

"You read a great deal about India, then?" David asked quietly.

Emily busied herself closing her parasol, smoothing down the folds of silk. "Yes. When we were children, I was fascinated by the tales you told me. Stories of the people and the land. I always imagined I could see it in my mind: the hot, burning sun, the sweet smell of the flowers, the strange colors. I imagined your mother was like a princess in a book, draped in silks and golden jewelry. And when you left, I wanted to know more. So, I read anything I could find about India. I talked to people who had just returned from there. I—I wanted to be able to imagine what your life was like."

Emily feared she had said too much with that last tentative admission. David was quiet beside her, and she fixed her gaze on a little boy feeding a clutch of ducks. She should never have admitted she thought of him so much when he was gone. Not when she was sure *he* had not thought of *her* in his years of marriage and family.

She felt something light against her hand, like a bird's wing or a butterfly. She stared down, startled, to see his fingers pressed over hers, atop the handle of her parasol.

It looked—*felt*—so right there, so warm and safe and unbearably exciting. She would never have imagined, even in her wildest flights of fancy, that the mere brush of a man's gloved hand could cause such a wild flutter deep in her stomach.

She slowly turned her hand to curl her fingers about his.

"I, too, wanted to know what your life was like here in England," he murmured, his face turned toward her. His cool breath stirred the small curls at her temple. "I wanted to know if you were happy—if you were still at Fair Oak, racing your horses across the fields, or if you were dancing in London. If you were married and had a new family."

"I do not," Emily whispered. "But you do."

"I do—I did. Lady Emily, Rupasri, my wife, was—"

But Emily suddenly did *not* want to hear about his wife, and she cut him off with a gesture. The love he had for his wife, a lady of his own country, a lady Emily herself could never be—how could she hear of it and not be wounded? She could not breathe; she wanted her old, safe façade back.

She slid her hand gently away from his, and gave a light, if slightly forced (even to her own ears) laugh. "La! We have known each other so long it sounds silly for you to call me Lady Emily. You must call me just Emily, and I will call you David, at least when we are alone like this. Agreed?"

He looked very much as if he wanted to say something else, something more. But finally he just nodded, and gave her a gentle, almost understanding smile, as if he could see her fears. Just as he had when they were children. She *hated* that at this moment.

"Agreed, Emily," he answered, her name coming easily from his tongue. "But I would like to tell you—"

"Lady Emily! Good afternoon!" someone called, saving her from whatever David wanted to say.

Feeling like an emotional coward, she turned to that voice in some relief—only to freeze. Sir Charles and Lady Innis were riding toward her on a pair of lovely bays, Lady Innis's stylish dark green habit and veiled hat shimmering under the late sunlight.

The Innises! Who possessed the Star of India. And Emily had *not* yet told David the sad story of the jewel. She didn't want him to hear it from strangers.

She would have to call up every ounce of polite, inane, vivacious chatter she could find to turn them from that topic.

They drew closer and closer, and Emily's mind raced. Weather? Sunny. Fashion? Yes, Lady Innis's lovely habit. Social events? The Innises' upcoming ball. No! Not that! The Star would be displayed there one last time in their house, the centerpiece of the soiree.

"Sir Charles, Lady Innis," she said, as they reined in their horses alongside the phaeton. "A lovely day, is it not?"

Luckily, the erstwhile merchant Sir Charles and his wife were so delighted to be seen conversing with a duke's sister that they happily followed wherever her conversation led. They were glad to meet David, an earl, yet showed no recognition of his name in connection to the Star, or if they did, they did not betray it. Just as they did not, and never had, betrayed the fact that they remembered buying the jewel from her impecunious brother so long ago. They merely chatted lightly about the weather, asked after Emily's family, and rode on.

It had been perhaps ten minutes' conversation, yet Emily felt as exhausted as if she had run a mile. Keeping secrets was a wearying business indeed, and one she could never seem to grow accustomed to, no matter how long she held onto it. Damien's old, shameful deed was like a heavy stone on her soul, and she longed to be rid of it.

But not at the expense of Alex and Georgina, and little Elizabeth Anne and Sebastian.

Her weariness must have shown on her face, for David turned the phaeton again toward the Park gates in the direction of home.

"The Innises are very amiable people," David commented. "Are they great friends of your family?"

"Acquaintances only. Sir Charles used to own a great many warehouses, and made a vast fortune in imports. Now he would like to become a country gentleman. He and my brother meet at Tattersall's quite often, and my sister-in-law and I see Lady Innis at the modiste. She has beautiful taste."

David chuckled. "Ah, arrivistes, then?"

"You could say that, and many people do. They love to entertain, and I am sure that you, a grand earl, will soon receive an invitation to a ball at their home." She glanced at him secretly, to see if he knew the particular ball she spoke of, if she was keeping a secret he already knew.

He did not appear to see that, however. He just gave her a small smile. "Should I accept, do you think? You must be my social adviser, Emily, in this strange new world I find myself in."

His social adviser? If only she could be. She could not even seem to organize her own life to satisfaction. "Oh, yes. I suppose you should accept."

And, she vowed, the next time they met she would tell him why that was. She would tell him everything. But not until then.

David watched Emily disappear behind the grand doors of her house, stopping at the last instant to turn and give him a smile and a farewell wave. Only then did he climb back up into his phaeton and turn toward his own townhouse.

He had been in London for weeks now, but still the streets and squares seemed foreign, unreal. Like an imaginary place in the books he had read to Anjali on their long voyage, trying to ease her transition to this new land. It seemed to have worked for her; she became very excited when she saw landmarks she recognized, and delighted in repeating the historical facts she learned. "Papa, did you know that the Battle of Hastings occurred in 1066? And Henry VIII was married *six* times?"

Her new life here was proving a bit easier than he had feared it would be, though she still pined for her young relatives and constantly asked why the cook could not learn to prepare a proper curry sauce. She loved the English clothes, and the toy shops with their extravagant dolls. But, to David, the houses and the trees, the people and the food and the language all took on a strange gray hue, an odd dreamlike-quality leached of vitality.

What had he been expecting when he came here, driven by duty and restlessness, and a desire for time to himself, far away from his mother's clamoring family? He could not even say. England was a strange land from his boyhood memories. Stranger in some ways than even the shimmering heat and color and music of India. It was a place he did not fully understand, but it was a part of him, just as Calcutta was. Perhaps the ale of England ran in his blood just as *tikka* and *lassi* did. Perhaps he had to be here now—was driven here by fate, to learn where his two halves could meet. Then he could find a sort of peace again.

As he turned his phaeton onto the square where his new townhouse sat, he remembered the strange lift of his heart when he first saw the chalk cliffs of Dover looming in the distance. He had lifted Anjali high, and told

her, "See, *shona-moni*? We are home at last." And, for
one soaring moment, he truly believed that.

He had that same feeling when he glanced up at the
Wilton ball and saw Emily Kenton standing there. A lifting of the heart, the spirit—a feeling of homecoming.
She was *not* the child-friend he left. She was a beautiful
woman, an English rose of ivory and gold, with dark
blue eyes that spoke of some hidden pain, a reserve, a
past he knew nothing of. But he *wanted* to know. By
God, but he wanted that more than he had ever wanted
anything in his life.

Today, when he touched her hand beside the river and
felt her draw in her breath sharply, he only wanted to
pull her into his arms and hold her so close she could
never escape him again. He wanted to inhale the fresh
green-rose perfume that was so much a part of her very
essence, to kiss her hair, her smooth cheek, her mouth, to
bury his face in the curve of her neck. He wanted to tell
her she could leave all her troubles, whatever they were,
in his hands and be free of them forever. That she could
once again be the free soul that ran laughing across
country meadows.

He wanted to break through her wall of reserve and be
as they once were—yet so much more.

It was utterly mad, he knew that—he felt the crazi-
ness of it in the depths of his soul, and thought that this
could not be him. He was a thoughtful person, a man
who always considered the impact his actions would
have on his life, his status, his family. He was not a man
to let passion ruin his existence, like his cousin Nikhil,
who once drew a jeweled dagger on one of the governor-
general's aides and had to be forcibly restrained and reminded of his duty—by David, of course.

That way led to insanity, and David wanted no part in
it. He became the cool head in his family, the one who
held everyone else together and maintained their status

with the Anglo hierarchy in Calcutta. He did not mind; that was who he was, who he had always been. The pragmatic in a family of wild romantics, and that included his own parents.

Now, he did not feel like his steady, stern self at all. He had wanted to kiss Emily in the middle of the Park, to feel her soft lips, parting on a sigh, beneath his—to touch her, hold her.

He wanted that still. His body hummed, as tightly wound as a sitar string. The unreality of London had only increased by a hundredfold, though now the darkening sky was full of some new, strange music. It gleamed like a black pearl.

He drew up the horses in front of his house, and stared up at it as if he had never seen it before. It was identical to its neighbors, a tall expanse of pale stone with a black-painted door and dull, wrought-iron railings. It could have been anyone's house at all—except for the tiny face in one of the upstairs windows. Anjali had pulled back the stiff brocade draperies and watched for him, as she always did when he was gone. She waved merrily as she saw him, and disappeared from behind the wavy glass. She would run down the stairs and be waiting for him in the marble foyer, clamoring to hear about his day.

The sight of his daughter steadied him, made a sense of reality return to the topsy-turvy world around him. He *had* to be steady, for his child's sake. He was all she had here, her anchor in a new society. He could not afford to fly off in a passion, as his cousins did. As his father had once, eloping with a maharajah's daughter to the wailing consternation of all involved. He could not follow in his father's footsteps by grabbing a duke's sister in the middle of a public park.

But he *could* see Emily again. Could dance with her, sit beside her at the theater, maybe. He could talk to her, maybe find a way to win her trust again—to persuade her to tell him of the troubles lurking behind her lovely eyes.

For now, that would be enough.

For now.

Chapter Six

"*E*mily, will you stop that!" Georgina cried, flinging her paintbrush down onto her palette.

"What?" Emily, startled out of her daydream and back into the reality of her sister-in-law's studio, sat up straight and blinked at Georgina. Usually, she enjoyed being a model. It wasn't hard work, aside from muscles that sometimes cramped from staying in one place, and she and Georgina often chatted happily while Georgina painted. Today, though, Emily could not focus on her surroundings. She kept drifting away—back to the Park with David.

Had it been only yesterday afternoon? It felt like a hundred years ago, every minute of it filled with ridiculous yet inescapable thoughts.

Thoughts such as . . . how warm his hand had been on hers. How he smelled of sandalwood soap and clean starch as he leaned close to her. Had he been about to kiss her? Would she have truly let him, if the Innises had not appeared when they had? Was she really that improper at heart?

Oh, who was she fooling? Of course she would have let him! She had not even been aware she was in the Park any longer. They could have been all alone on the moon for all she knew. She only saw *him*, knew *him*.

What a cabbage-head she was. Anyone would have thought she was a sixteen-year-old with her first suitor, not sophisticated, in-her-third-Season Lady Emily Kenton. She had thought of nothing else when she was with David—or even when she was *not* with him, as now. She even forgot all about the Star and her plans. Until the sight of the Innises brought it all back.

"I am sorry, Georgie," she said, turning on her platform toward her sister-in-law and the easel. "What did I do wrong? Did I shift in my pose?"

"Not at all." Georgina dropped her palette onto a nearby table, amidst a jumble of paints and brushes and pots of water. "You have posed for me far too often for that! But you are meant to be Athena, gray-eyed goddess of war. You should be leading your troops forward into battle against the Trojans, resolute and martial. Athena would *not* have such a misty-eyed, daydreamlike expression on her face!"

Emily laughed ruefully, and lowered her bulky shield to the floor. She sat down on the settee, rubbing at her stiff neck as the white muslin folds of her improvised chiton settled around her. "I am truly sorry, Georgie. I suppose I am a bit distracted today. Fighting Trojans is not uppermost in my mind."

"Ah, yes. And may I venture a guess as to what *is* uppermost in your mind, Em?" Georgina gave her a sly smile. "A certain dark-eyed earl, mayhap?"

Emily turned away, letting her loose hair fall forward to shield the wretched blush she felt coming on. But she knew that Georgina would not be put off with a careless comment. Her Minerva Press–loving heart was always attuned to any hints of romance around her. Last year, in Bath, Georgina had even tried to play matchmaker with Emily's chair-bound mother and a retired colonel! "Perhaps I *am* thinking of David, just a bit. We *were* good friends once, after all, and it has been a very long time since we saw each other. It is only natural I would think about him."

"David is it now? You must have been good friends, indeed."

Blast! Emily so hoped Georgina would overlook that little slip, but of course she could not. "Did I call Lord Darlinghurst David? How shocking of me."

"You know you did. And it is not nearly as shocking as I wish you would be!" Georgina removed the paint-splashed smock covering her lavender muslin morning gown and tossed it over the easel before dropping into a chair. "You were gone a long time yesterday afternoon. Much longer than any of your previous drives in the Park, and you go at least three times a week. Now, the only difference I see between *this* drive and all those others is your escort. You must have been enjoying yourself."

There had been no time yesterday evening for Georgina to question Emily about her drive. They had had to dress for their separate outings—Georgina and Alex to the opera and Emily with friends to a musicale—and they had all returned home quite late. Her sister-in-law was obviously intent on making up for that now. Emily had to tell her *something*, or she would not know a moment's peace.

Yet, she could not tell Georgina everything. How could she, when she could not even find the words to explain it to herself? That strange elation at meeting David again, hearing his voice, seeing deep in his eyes that her friend was still there. The surprise and trepidation that she had *new* feelings when she saw him—feelings that made her throat seize shut and her stomach flutter. The gnawing guilt at keeping her secret. There was all that and more.

If there was anyone in the world who would understand, it was Georgina. She was a sophisticated lady, an artist and Society Diamond who was wildly, unfashionably in love with her husband. But she couldn't tell Georgina. She could not tell anyone—even if she knew what it truly was she wanted to tell. What was making her heart burst!

She gave Georgina what she hoped was a reassuring, sunny smile. "I vow to you, Georgie, there is not much to tell. You know how it is in the Park—everyone watching each other, prattling away about nonsensical things. I could scarcely speak two words together with Lord Darlinghurst, and none of it beyond the ordinary." Except when he held her hand ever so briefly. But that did not bear thinking about at the moment. "I do admit I am glad he is in England again, and I look forward to seeing him soon. That is all I can say at the moment."

"Oh, well, if that is *all* you can say at the moment, I suppose I must be content. I must say you are being terribly vexatious, Em!" Georgina's head fell back against the satin upholstery of her chair, as if so *vexed* she could no longer even sit up straight. "It is obvious we will get no work done this afternoon. Shall we go to Gunter's? Elizabeth Anne has been begging for an ice these four days at least, and I cannot put her off much longer."

Emily's interest piqued, and she left off plucking aimlessly at her corded sash. "Oh, yes! An apricot ice is always most welcome. But, please, Georgie, no more questions about Lord Darlinghurst."

"With Elizabeth Anne along? Of course not! It is shocking what big ears my little pitcher has grown. I vow she hears every word that is said in this house, then repeats them at the most inopportune moments."

"Hm," Emily murmured. "I do wonder where she inherited such a trait."

"May we have an outing today, Papa?"

"Eh?" David glanced up from his newspaper to smile at Anjali. "Did you say something, *shona-moni*?"

"I asked if we could have an outing today." Anjali spread copious amounts of marmalade on her toast. David was a bit worried about how fond she had grown of the sweet, sticky treat. "My new governess is to start lessons with me tomorrow? So, I think we should have a treat before that happens." She gave him her sweetest, most persuasive smile.

"And that jar of marmalade is not treat enough, eh?"

Anjali sighed, and rattled the spoon around in the almost-empty pot. "Marmalade is here every day, Papa. Treats are something out of the ordinary."

"Quite right. I think I could use a treat myself. Did you have something particular in mind, Anjali?"

"I would love another ice, Papa, a strawberry one from Gunter's."

"What, just an ice? No diamonds or rubies?"

Anjali giggled. "Just an ice, Papa! I am too young for diamonds and rubies."

"You, my dearest, are quite the easiest female to please whom I have ever met. Gunter's it is, then. This afternoon."

"You are the best papa in the world!" Anjali cried, clapping her sticky hands happily. "And I will play my new song on the pianoforte for you, too. I can play it with *almost* no mistakes."

"I will look forward to it. Now, you should run along and wash up. Molly will help you dress for the day."

"Yes, Papa." Anjali slid out of her chair and hurried over to kiss him on the cheek. "You won't forget—Gunter's this afternoon?"

"I will not forget," he promised.

"You don't have to go driving in the Park again?"

"Not today. Today is just yours."

Anjali nodded, seemingly satisfied, and skipped out of the breakfast room. David watched her go, thoughtfully refolding his newspaper. The pink ribbons tied in her black hair shimmered in the morning light, and she danced lightly on her little slippered toes.

Back in Calcutta, he had feared that bringing her to England might be a great mistake. She was a shy girl, one who was wary of change, and India was all she had ever known. But she seemed to enjoy the cooler environs of London, and did well with her new music lessons. It was true that she still clung closely to her father, and had not made any friends her own age from amongst the girls she met walking in the park with Molly the nursemaid. But surely that would come in time. As she became more assured of her place, she would grow more outgoing.

In the meantime, being away from the smothering attentions of her great-grandmother and female relations seemed to do her good. Not being constantly told that her entire worth to her family as a female was her ability to marry well freed her to think of other things— music, languages, art, history. And ices.

He smiled to think of the glow in her green eyes as she contemplated a trip to Gunter's for a sweet. It made him remember the same glow in another girl's eyes, many years ago.

Emily had once possessed the same sparkle and wonder that Anjali had now, yet something had changed in her. Oh, he knew that years had passed. They had grown up, and things could not stay the same. He himself had gone through such enormous changes.

But somehow he sensed that it was more than that with Emily. David tossed the newspaper onto the breakfast table and leaned back in his chair to remember their drive yesterday. At certain moments, for just an instant, he could have sworn he glimpsed the joyful Emily there. When she laughed at a child chasing a hoop, or watched, mesmerized, as a flock of birds took sudden flight over their heads, he saw the sparkle in her. The sparkle that said she could still race like the wind across the meadows.

But then a veil would drop, and her eyes would become wary and reserved again, her smile stiff, barely touching her lips. It was more than the years between them, the years that had made her a fine lady. She carried some secret burden, and he knew she would not relinquish it easily. Stubbornness was a trait that both the old *and* the new Emily shared.

Well, *he* could be stubborn, too. He was very good at solving other people's problems, and he *always* helped his friends and family. Emily Kenton was one of the best friends he had ever had. So, whether she wished it or no, he would discover what bedeviled her, and set about removing it from her life. Then the mischievous, merry Emily could shine forth again.

David resolutely pushed himself back from the table and stood to leave the breakfast room. He would begin this knight-errant mission with a visit to the florist.

"I beg your pardon, my lady, but these just came for you."

Emily paused in tying her bonnet ribbons to turn to her maid, Becky. Georgina and Elizabeth Anne were waiting downstairs to depart for Gunter's, and Emily was in a great hurry to join them, if only the slippery satin would cease knotting so! She yanked hard at them, drawing the hat from her head.

But her fit of impatience faded when she saw what Becky held.

Flowers—but not just any flowers. Emily received posies almost every day, roses and violets and sometimes lilies. But none like these—great profusions of orchids that were creamiest white at the petals' edges shading into midnight purple in the center. They were arranged in a basket, tied about with purple velvet rib-

bon. They were exotic and enticing, filling the chamber
with rich perfume. Where had they been found, here in
London?

Emily reached out for them, cradling them in her
arms. They seemed almost unreal, as if they had been
blown in from an exotic island, floating on ocean
breezes to land in her room.

Tucked amongst the blooms was a note, yet Emily
knew who they must be from even before she opened it.
None of her usual suitors had the imagination for such
flowers.

*Lady Emily—they reminded me of you. Thank you
for our drive. David*

That was all it said, scrawled in a strong hand across
the rich vellum. But it was enough.

She did not deserve such flowers. Or such a friend.

But she cherished them nonetheless. Her soul seemed
to overflow as she buried her face in the orchids, drawing in all their sweet essence. "Oh, David," she whispered.

"Shall I put them in water for you, my lady?" Becky
asked.

Emily breathed in sharply, and pulled away from the
bouquet. She had quite forgotten she was not alone! She
could not afford to drift so far from reality—not now.

"Thank you, Becky," Emily said, and handed back the
bouquet, her fingers drifting slowly away from the satiny
petals. "Is the duchess still waiting downstairs?"

"Yes, my lady. The carriage has been called."

Emily nodded, and took up her abandoned bonnet before drifting out of the room. In the foyer, Georgina was
putting on her own hat in front of the mirror while Elizabeth Anne fidgeted at the foot of the stairs so that her
nursemaid could hardly button her cloak for her. As soon

as she saw Emily, the child broke away from the frustrated maid and dashed forward to seize her hand.

"Oh, Aunt Emily! Were those flowers for *you?*" she asked breathlessly.

"Indeed they were," Emily answered with a smile, swinging her niece into the air until she squealed with glee. "Are they not beautiful?"

"Bee-yoo-ti-ful!" Elizabeth Anne cried. "Were they from a prince? An Arabian prince?" Elizabeth Anne was reading the *Arabian Nights* with her new governess, and was now full of questions about myrrh and jeweled turbans and flying carpets.

"I would say an *Indian* prince," Georgina said, laughing. "Now, Elizabeth Anne, cease hanging on your auntie like that. You will crease her gown. The carriage is waiting." She tugged her child away, and gave Emily a wink. "I am sure Aunt Emily will tell us all about it later."

Gunter's was crowded at that hour, as it almost always was, with well-dressed hordes in search of fresh ices and delectable pastries. The tables were filled, and customers spilled out into the square to eat their treats on the benches and while strolling the pathways.

As Emily, Georgina, and Elizabeth Anne waited their turn to order, Elizabeth Anne changed her mind at least five times.

No, six. "I want strawberry, Mama. Do they have strawberry today?"

"I thought you wanted apricot, dearest," Georgina said, straightening her progeny's lopsided hair ribbon.

"Perhaps I do. What are you having, Aunt Emily?"

Emily sighed. She loved her niece dearly, truly she did, but sometimes her relentless energy was the tiniest bit wearying. As she turned to answer Elizabeth Anne, she suddenly paused, her attention captured by some

new sweet-seekers just coming in the door. It was a little
girl, not a great deal older than Elizabeth Anne—the
most exquisite child Emily had ever seen. She was tiny,
like a little doll in her white, fur-collared pelisse and
pink frock, a little white fur hat perched atop her head.
Long, glossy waves of black hair framed a small, pale
oval face, and green eyes peeked shyly around the room.
She hung back a bit, as if unsure about being suddenly in
such a crowd.

Emily's heart went out to her. She understood what it
was like to be watched, to be thrust into situations not of
her own making.

The child reached up her hand to catch at a man's
dark-gloved fingers. The gentleman bent down to speak
to her, removing his hat to reveal his own luxuriant black
hair, the same shade as the child's.

And suddenly Emily perfectly understood the girl's
otherworldly beauty. It was *David* she was with. David
who must be her father. This was the little girl he had
spoken of.

Her mother must have been a great beauty, indeed.

Elizabeth Anne turned to see what had captured her
aunt's attention. "Oh!" the child cried out. "That must be
an Arabian princess!"

The other child's green eyes widened at this new attention, and she tensed as if she might flee. David put a
reassuring hand on her shoulder and spoke softly in her
ear.

Emily made her way across the room toward them,
not seeing anyone watching her, not hearing Mr. Carrington calling her name from his table. She only saw
David and that glorious bouquet of orchids before her
eyes, and she had to speak to him.

He glanced up and saw her, and smiled in greeting, a
flash of warmth leaping into his black eyes. That smile

could truly have rivaled the bright afternoon, and it coaxed an answering smile from Emily.

But not from the Arabian princess. A small frown puckered her ivory brow, and she drew back against her father.

David's hand stayed on her shoulder, and that dream-like bubble around Emily burst like an overly full rain-cloud. They were a family, these two, and she was an outsider. Always an outsider.

She did not want to show any discomfiture, though. She kept her smile firmly in place, and said in her most polite voice, "Good afternoon, Lord Darlinghurst. It is nice to see you again."

"And you, Lady Emily," he answered, equally polite. But there was still that smile in his voice. "You are look-ing lovely, as always."

"Thank you, Lord Darlinghurst. I fear not nearly as lovely as this young lady, though. Your daughter, I pre-sume?"

"Indeed. Lady Emily Kenton, may I present Lady An-jali Huntington."

His hand gently urged the girl forward, and she took one small step. Her gaze on the floor, she dropped to give a dainty little curtsy. "How do you do, Lady Emily."

"How do *you* do, Lady Anjali." Emily was not certain what else she could say. The only other little girl she knew anything about was Elizabeth Anne, and her mis-chievous niece was nothing like this porcelain doll. This Arabian princess. But, somehow, Emily desperately wanted this girl to like her. Or at least look at her. "That is a very pretty name—Anjali. So much finer than dull old Emily."

Lady Anjali just stared back at her with wide, doubt-ing eyes. Emily found herself more tongue-tied than she had been when presented to Queen Charlotte. What did one *say* to a silent Arabian princess child?

Fortunately, before she could start babbling about how very much she hated the name Emily, Georgina and Elizabeth Anne appeared at her side, ices in hand.

"Good afternoon, Lord Darlinghurst," Georgina said. "So very good to see you again! And this must be your lovely daughter."

"Do you have a flying carpet?" Elizabeth Anne asked Anjali, her chin already sticky with strawberry ice.

Anjali's startled gaze turned from Emily to the other child. "I—no, I'm sorry, I fear none of my carpets fly."

"Elizabeth Anne! Now, what did I just tell you?" Georgina admonished, taking her daughter's hand in hers. "I am sorry, Lord Darlinghurst. I fear my child has not yet finished learning her manners."

"That is quite all right, Your Grace," David answered, with a smile just for Elizabeth Anne.

"We should take our ices out into the square, if you would care to join us," Georgina said. "Indeed, if Lady Anjali likes, she could wait with us while you order your own treats. It is a fine day, and I promise that Lady Mischief here will hold her tongue."

Emily watched as Lady Anjali's stare darted to her father's face, and her hand tightened on his. David gave it a reassuring squeeze, and nodded to her. Emily had never before seen a man behave so toward his child—not even Alex, who was utterly devoted to Elizabeth Anne and Sebastian. It was almost as if David and his daughter were an insulated world of two, where words were unnecessary for communication.

How could another person ever fit into such a world?

"Thank you, Your Grace," David answered. "I am sure Anjali would enjoy that. She was quite enthralled by a man with a music-playing monkey we saw as we were coming in. And I will be out in only a few moments with our ices. Perhaps Lady Emily will be so good as to advise me on the choice of flavors?"

"Of course, Lord Darlinghurst," Emily answered. She watched as Georgina led the children out the door, Elizabeth Anne still chattering on and Anjali looking like a startled little gazelle. David held his arm out to Emily, and she slid her gloved hand over his soft wool sleeve and walked with him back into the sugar-scented depths of the shop.

His arm was strong and steady beneath her touch, holding her up in this suddenly hazy scene.

"Your daughter is very pretty," she said, pretending to examine the array of pastries displayed before her.

"Thank you," he answered. "I, of course, would never dispute that. She is rather shy, though, and still a bit unsure of her new home."

"Of course she is. Why, I remember the first time I visited London as a child. I thought it wild and a bit frightening, like some strange world in a book. And I was just coming from a country estate, not India! She must be terribly bewildered."

"I think she was, at first, and she missed her relatives. But she is adjusting. She has enjoyed visiting the Tower, and taking a boat ride on the Thames."

"And these activities have inspired her taste for bloodthirsty history? Anne Boleyn and such?"

"Precisely! She is always full of questions about the poor queens of Henry VIII—questions I fear I am ill-equipped to answer. I know precious little about any of those ladies."

Emily laughed. "It is fortunate she met my sister-in-law, then! The duchess is planning a grand painting of the trial of Anne Boleyn, and will be able to answer any questions your daughter may have."

They took their newly made ices—lemon for David and Anjali and apricot for Emily—and carried them out to the sun-washed square. Emily blinked in the sudden rush of light after the dim indoors, and shielded her eyes with her hand to see Georgina sitting on a bench with the two girls. Elizabeth Anne was still chattering away, and Anjali sat with daintily folded hands and ankles, her pretty face carefully expressionless.

They had not seen Emily and David yet, and, for an instant, Emily was tempted to clutch at his arm, to hold him where he was. They could be alone there, in the shadow of Gunter's, for a moment, with no families or painfully polite conversation to catch them.

He must have guessed something of her thoughts, for he turned to stare down at her, his expression shaded by the brim of his hat.

"Is something amiss?" he asked quietly.

"I—no, of course not. Not at all. I just—the light . . ." Emily faltered, not at all sure of what she wanted to say.

But he knew. Just as he had always known. "I want to talk to you, too, Emily," he said, his voice still soft, as if the hurrying masses around them could hear and spoil their moment. "*Truly* talk, not this polite nonsense. Is that what you want, too? If not, just scream at me, slap my face, and I will leave you alone."

Emily had to laugh at the image of her screeching and slapping his face, causing a scene right outside Gunter's. As if she ever could! His face was too handsome to mar with red handprints. In fact, what she really wanted more than anything was to place the tip of her finger right on that enticing dimple . . .

Blast! Emily turned her stare away from him, curling her gloved fingers hard around her container of ice. The chill was a fine reminder of the reality of their situation.

"I *do* want to talk to you," she said. "Very much." But now was hardly the time. Georgina had seen them and was waving. "I am going to the British Museum tomorrow afternoon—alone, because Georgina has a meeting of her artists' salon. If you would somehow—by coinci-

dence, of course—appear in the Elgin Marbles room by
two o'clock. . . ."

He gave her a conspiring smile. "Say no more, Lady
Emily. I will be there."

Emily nodded, and started across the square toward
Georgina and the children. Her attention was caught by
the image of a lady leaving her grand townhouse across
the square—a lady in an elegant mulberry-colored carriage gown and feathered bonnet. She paused to say a
word to a footman, drawing on her gloves.

Lady Innis, going out of the house where they were
meant to attend a ball next week. A ball to view the Star
of India before it was given to the Mercer Museum.

Emily gasped at this cold reminder of reality—a reality that came around to slap her in the face whenever she
dared to enjoy a moment in the sun with David.

A reality that would soon have to be faced, once and
for all.

Chapter Seven

The jeweler's shop was silent and dim as Emily slipped inside the door. At first glance, it would not look terribly promising to shoppers accustomed to the elegance of Bond Street. There were no gleaming chandeliers or enticing window displays, no velvet-upholstered settees or well-dressed attendants offering refreshments. Only if one peered closer, into the slightly dusty glass cases, was its true worth revealed.

Mr. Jervis's shop carried only the most original, the most breathtaking designs. His workers came from Paris and Venice, refugees from the harsh Napoleonic years, and their necklaces and bracelets had a cunning and an elegant lightness many of the wares of the larger shops failed to possess.

Emily had found it when she was helping her brother look for a special anniversary gift for his wife. Georgina loved jewels, but she was not a lady whose tastes ran to the conventional; the emerald and ruby inlaid cuff bracelets Alex found here suited her perfectly. Emily came back whenever she was in need of an unusual item—or when she was in trouble, as now.

Mr. Jervis's prices were very reasonable, and it was not likely that anyone of her Mayfair acquaintance would be here in Gracechurch Street to see her. Mr.

Jervis was also very willing to barter with her, taking her birthday necklace and earrings in exchange for making a perfect—and authentic—copy of the Star of India.

Her opening the door set off a small, tinkling bell, and summoned Mr. Jervis from the back rooms. He blinked at her from behind his spectacles, obviously unable to recognize her in the dim light. Emily pushed the veil of her bonnet back, and a smile broke across his thin face.

"Ah, Lady Emily!" he said. "You are very prompt."

"Your letter *did* say it would be ready today, Mr. Jervis," Emily answered, advancing into the shadowed depths of the shop. Gold and silver, diamonds and porcelain, beckoned to her from the cases, but she did not give in to their siren song.

"Oh, yes, indeed it is! I am sure you will be most happy with it, Lady Emily—it is my very finest work to date, I do declare." He ducked back behind a counter and, after some jangling and crashing noises, emerged with a small black velvet box. "Though I must say it was not easy working only from sketches."

Emily touched the tip of her tongue to her suddenly dry lips. She had not been so very nervous to enter a shop since the days of Damien's debts to every merchant in the village. But this would soon be over. "I do apologize for my poor artistic skills, Mr. Jervis. I am sure you did a superb job, as you always do."

Mr. Jervis nodded agreeably, and pressed the box open. Emily leaned over to see it better—and gave a small gasp.

It was indeed beautiful work, the oblong sapphire surrounded by smaller diamonds. It shimmered like the very sky. Emily herself could not have told it apart from the real Star—except for some elusive *something* the facsimile lacked. When she had held the true Star in her hand all those years ago, it had warmed and tingled on her palm, whispering of far-off lands and doomed love.

This jewel only whispered of cold beauty.

But no one else would ever know that. And the jewel in the Innis mansion was *not* the real Star, after all. It was just paste. The real Star was . . . no one knew where. At least this way the Innises' experts would find a genuine sapphire when they examined it.

"It is exquisite, Mr. Jervis," she said. "You are an absolute artist."

Mr. Jervis beamed. "Thank you, Lady Emily! You do have quite the eye. As you see here, I turned the facets just so, in the Indian manner . . ."

It was the better part of a half-hour before Emily could leave the shop, with Mr. Jervis's assurances he would not say anything to her brother or sister-in-law if he should see them again and the new Star tucked into her reticule. She stepped out into the sunlight, breathing deeply of the fresh air.

Oh, this was all so maddening! She was not cut out for intrigue at all. Her hands were shaking and her mouth was dry, just from traveling to the shop today. At least it was nearly over. Or it would be after the Innis ball, where she would have to find a way to exchange the paste sapphire for the genuine one.

How she would do *that*, she had no idea. Not yet.

"You are a complete widgeon at this, Emily Kenton," she muttered to herself, looping her reticule ribbons securely over her wrist. "You would have made a terrible spy in France!"

She had to return home now, and have a quick luncheon and change her gown before meeting David at the museum. . . .

David! At the thought of him, her hands shook all over again. Meeting him by the Elgin Marbles would be at least as frightening as coming to this shop this morning. Probably much more so. Somehow, every time she saw him, he grew more handsome, his dark eyes more enticing. They watched her as if they could see her soul, all her secrets. They beckoned to her to tell him everything.

But she could not do that. This was *her* burden, hers alone. David would surely hate her if he knew she had allowed her brother to sell the Star and then accepted gifts of the ill-gotten gains. Then the warmth of his gaze would turn to ice.

Emily could never bear that.

She stepped to the pavement to look for the hansom that was meant to be waiting for her—and froze. A dark blue carriage with a familiar crest painted on the door— the Darlinghurst crest—came around the corner and drove slowly past her.

David—*here!* How could that be? It was as if her thoughts of him summoned him in the flesh, right at the worst moment.

She shrank back into the shadows of the building, reaching up to snatch her veil down. But it was too late. From the half-open carriage window floated a sweet, childish voice.

"Papa! Isn't that the yellow-haired lady we met at Gunter's?"

David had thought this morning would be a good time to find gifts to send back to Calcutta for his grandmother and female cousins. Lengths of pale English muslins, with their light colors and dainty prints, would amuse them, and Lady Wilton had suggested this warehouse to him. She had given him the address in a whisper, as if it was a great secret. And, of course, Anjali had insisted on accompanying him.

As he settled her into the carriage, with the window half-open so she would not become ill from the lurching, swaying motion, he told her, "Now, we cannot be long at the shops. I have an appointment I must keep this afternoon." A very important appointment indeed, with Emily at the British Museum. He could feel himself grinning like a fool just thinking about seeing her again.

Anjali leaned forward, and said, in her solemn voice, "Is it an appointment with that lady we met in Gunter's? The one with the yellow curls?"

David stared at his daughter in surprise. He had thought she barely took notice of meeting Emily at Gunter's, she had been so very quiet. Even when they returned home, she retreated into the silence of a book. He certainly had not told her of this planned meeting. Anjali watched him closely with her large green eyes, as he concealed his surprise behind a light smile. He reached out to tweak at her hair ribbon.

"Do you mean Lady Emily, *shona-moni*?" he said carelessly. "I may see her there."

Anjali nodded slowly, her gaze never leaving his face. She looked so much like her great-grandmother when she was in such a mood, stern and all-seeing. At such times, he could hardly fathom that he had fathered such an otherworldly little creature. "Lady Emily is very pretty," she said. "But she is not very much like Mama."

That was certainly very true. Rupasri had been lovely, with her fall of black hair and smooth, honey-colored skin, but she had been quiet, submissive as she had been taught to be. She had no secrets behind her dark eyes, as Emily held in the sky color of hers. Rupasri did not seem to spring as she walked, the way Emily did. Emily seemed almost as if she would break into a dash every time she moved, as if she danced even while standing still. The power of the sun almost burst from her bright hair, from her very fingertips.

But how could he say such things to his daughter? How would she understand how Emily made him feel, when he did not even understand it himself? He only knew that when he saw Emily he felt alive.

"No," he told Anjali. "She is not very much like your mama. But she *is* very pretty, and very nice, too."

"Are you going to marry her, then, Papa?"

Anjali's quiet question conjured a sudden image in his mind—himself and Emily emerging from a church door, wreathed in smiles and rose petals. Emily turned to glance up at him, a lace veil falling back from her face as her mouth lifted for his kiss . . .

And it struck him like a crash of monsoon lightning—that was exactly what he wanted. To have Emily in his life forever, to hold onto all that life and energy and laughter and mystery. It was what he wanted the instant he saw her in that ballroom, standing there in her white gown, his old friend all grown up and beautiful.

But what did *she* want? She seemed happy to see him again; she had even almost kissed him in the park, her lips trembling with a need that echoed his own. Yet there were those secrets she held in her eyes, there was *something* that was not letting her embrace him fully. He would give his fortune to know what it was. Another love—a secret one? A gambling addiction, the same as that which had landed her oldest brother in the soup so often? Was she a jewel thief, a duelist, a French spy? . . .

The list could go on and on, growing ever more absurd. He could not think of it now. Anjali was still watching him, and he had to answer her.

He knew one thing for certain, though—whatever Emily was hiding, it could not be ugly or sinful. His friend had always shone with a pure honesty, and bright souls such as hers did not tarnish.

"Do you remember what I told you in Calcutta, Anjali?" he said. "About when I marry again?"

Anjali nodded. "That you would not marry a lady unless she would be a good mama."

"Exactly. You know I would never bring someone

into our home who would not care for both of us. Do you trust me when I say that?"

"Of course, Papa."

"Then you have no need to worry."

"So, you *are* going to marry her? The Lady Emily from Gunter's?"

David laughed. Yes, Anjali *was* like her great-grandmother—she would never let go of an idea when it was firmly in her head. "*Shona-moni*, Lady Emily and I are old friends who are becoming reacquainted. I do not know what may happen in the future, but I promise you all will be well. Yes?"

Anjali nodded, apparently satisfied—for now. She sat back against the tufted velvet cushions and watched the city scenery change outside the window. As they turned onto the street where the suggested warehouse resided, she suddenly sat straight up, pointing excitedly in direct opposition to all her etiquette lessons.

"Papa!" she cried. "Isn't that the yellow-haired lady we met at Gunter's? Lady Emily?"

"It cannot be," David said, leaning forward to peer out the window himself. His heart gave a small leap of excitement to hear Emily's name, but surely it was not her whom Anjali saw now. Whatever would she be doing in this part of Town? Anjali probably just imagined it, since they had been speaking of Emily only moments before.

Yet it *was* her, standing there on the pavement, staring at their carriage with wide, shocked eyes. She wore a plain, dark blue pelisse and a black bonnet with a veil pushed back, her hand reached up as if to draw it down. Not exactly à la mode, but it was undoubtedly her, with her golden curls blowing loose from under that bonnet, pulled by the breeze.

"By Jove, but you are quite right, Anjali," he said. "It is indeed Lady Emily."

"It is a *sign*," Anjali murmured, clasping her small hands under her chin.

David heard her odd words, yet had no time to question her as he called out to the coachman to halt. He did not wait for the footman, but pushed open the door himself and jumped out.

"Lady Emily," he called, raising his hat to her. "You are the last person I would have expected to see here this morning."

Emily threw a quick glance back over her shoulder, as if seeking some escape. She found only a hansom, and a shop whose faded sign read L. JERVIS, JEWELER. Her gloved hands clutched at her reticule. For one instant, he feared she might dash away from him.

More secrets, then?

But she turned back to him, her shoulders straightening, and gave him a bright, polite smile. She stepped toward him, her hand held out.

"I might say the same about you, Lord Darlinghurst," she answered, as he bowed over her fingers. The tips of her dark gloves were dusty. "I was just here at the jeweler, running an errand for—for my sister-in-law. It is an unfashionable part of Town, I know, but Mr. Jervis has the finest jewels."

"I shall have to remember that, then," he answered, smiling at her as he slowly, very slowly, released her hand. She folded her fingers around the reticule again. "Lady Wilton recommended a warehouse here where I might find excellent gifts to send back to my relations in Calcutta."

"Oh, yes! Of course," Emily replied, still with that too-bright tone in her voice. "Well, you must be in a great hurry to get there. I will just leave you to it, and perhaps we will meet later, at the museum . . ."

David's gaze slid past her to the hansom, where the

driver sat watching them with bored disinterest. "Never say you came here in a hansom, Lady Emily!"

Emily glanced back, as if she had quite forgotten the vehicle was there. "Oh! Well—yes. I did not want to bother with calling for our carriage."

A duke's sister did not want to call for her carriage? Curious. David watched Emily's flushed face with a little frown. Something was quite amiss here, something Emily was trying her hardest to hide. But she was a terrible actress.

And David was good at discovering secrets. He had to be, with his wild-blooded family. Just give him time . . .

"Well, you simply cannot go home in a hansom," he told her. "Please, allow us to take you in our carriage."

"Oh, no, I could not . . ." she began in a rush—then paused, a puzzled frown creasing her brow. "Us, Lord Darlinghurst?"

"Anjali and myself, of course." He smiled down at her. "You did not think I would ask you to come with me unchaperoned, do you?"

As he spoke, Anjali poked her head out the carriage window. Unlike the quiet, solemn girl she had been all morning, she was smiling widely, her green eyes sparkling like spring meadows. She waved merrily, and called out, "Lady Emily! How grand to see you again. We are going shopping for a gift for my great-grandmother. Won't you join us?"

David stared at his daughter, dumbfounded. Was there something in the air in this part of Town that made females as changeable as clouds? This was a great change since only yesterday. What could have caused it?

Emily smiled at Anjali, her frown clearing entirely for the first time since their unexpected meeting. "Good day, Lady Anjali! It is good to see you again, too. I am not certain—"

"Please, do join us, Lady Emily," David said. "Unless

you have another appointment. I confess I am quite hopeless at choosing gifts, and I would very much appreciate your opinion."

Emily looked again to the hansom, the jeweler's window, and David's carriage before saying slowly, "Very well, Lord Darlinghurst. I would be happy to join you and Lady Anjali."

"Excellent, Lady Emily. Thank you," David said, offering his arm to escort her to the carriage.

She securely tucked her reticule against her side before sliding her fingers over his sleeve. Yes, indeed, she was carrying a secret in her heart, if not in that blasted reticule itself.

And David intended to find out what it was.

Chapter Eight

*A*njali peeked out from between two tall displays of bolts of fabric, trying to watch her father and Lady Emily without them seeing her. Not that they were paying a great deal of attention to anything around them—they stood on either side of a table spread with silks and muslins, leaning in to speak together in quiet voices. Lady Emily ran her gloved hand over a length of dark green velvet, a tiny half-smile playing about her lips.

Anjali gave a decisive nod. It was as she thought. Her papa *liked* the bright-haired Lady Emily, in the way that grown-up men sometimes liked grown-up ladies. Anjali might be only nine years old, but she knew these things. Whenever she visited her great-grandmother's zenana, the ladies there would often forget Anjali was listening and would chatter on about romances and new marriages and babies. A girl could learn a lot that way—even a girl with no mother.

Her papa had never paid any attention to the dark-eyed ladies in Calcutta, or to the pale daughters of the English families who invited him to dine or play cards. So Anjali had never really paid heed to the gossip, mostly heard from her great-grandmother's lips, that said he should marry again. Their lives were fine just as they were.

She paid no heed—until she saw that Lady Emily in Gunter's, all white and gold like some ice princess in a storybook. Until she saw the way her father stared at Lady Emily, as if all else had vanished around him. He smiled when he took her hand in a way Anjali had never noticed before.

And she had felt sick to her stomach, as if she had eaten too many sweets. This lady, this—this *English* lady would ruin everything! All their cozy life of Papa taking her for drives, listening to her music lessons, taking breakfast with her—it would all end if he married Lady Emily. English children were banished to the nursery, so she had heard. Cut off from the grown-up life of the house. The thought of it made even the sweet ice taste like dust in her mouth.

It had not helped matters at all that she'd had to spend the afternoon listening to the babblings of that toddler Lady Elizabeth Anne Kenton, either!

So, that night, alone in her bed, Anjali had prayed. She considered these prayers very carefully. At first, she wanted simply to ask for Lady Emily to go away. But she knew that would not be right—God's will had to be done, and not her own. That was what her nursemaid said. If Lady Emily was truly meant to be her new mama, if it was part of the grand design for all things, then so be it.

She asked then for a sign. A sign that all was proceeding as it should, that everything would be well even if Lady Emily came into their lives.

And, surely, finding Lady Emily here, as if waiting for them in this most unlikely spot, was a sign!

And the smile on her papa's face was another. Anjali peeked over the fabrics to see him laugh at something Lady Emily said, his face brighter than the Calcutta sun. Anyone that could make her papa look like that, when he had been so serious and intent for so long, could not be all bad.

"A sign," Anjali whispered. A sign that Lady Emily was *meant* to be her mama, no matter what. Her great-grandmother always said humans must take notice when the gods chose to reveal their courses.

"It was fortuitous to meet you like this, Lady Emily," David said. "I thought fine English ladies did not deign to leave their houses until two o'clock at the earliest!"

Emily laughed. She couldn't help it—despite her trepidation at being here with him, and her panic at being nearly caught at Mr. Jervis's shop, she felt strangely light and giddy. As if she had been imbibing champagne! Even the weight of the stone in her reticule felt lighter.

"Usually I do not," she answered. "It is hard to be an early riser when one has not even returned home until dawn."

"What made today an exception?"

Emily glanced down at the figured muslin she was fingering. She found she just could not meet his open, honest gaze for a second longer. "I—had that errand to perform. I wanted to finish it before I went to the museum this afternoon. Should we find Lady Anjali? I have not seen her for several minutes."

David gave a wry smile, a quirk of his lips that told her he was fully aware of her evasions. He always had been, even when they were children—she could never lie to him. Back then, she had thought it was due to some exotic Eastern mysticism, inborn in the blood of his mother. Later, she laughed at her childhood fancies.

Now she thought she had not been so very wrong in that supposition.

David could tell that she was hiding something. She saw it in the way he watched her.

Just tell him, a little voice in her mind whispered. *He has a right to know.*

No! she argued back. *It has been so many years since we last met. How can I know if I can trust him?*

David at last looked away from her, turning his attention to the bolt of muslin and releasing her from the unbearable tension. Only as her breath escaped in a great exhale did she realize she had been holding it.

"Anjali is fine," he said. "I saw one of the shopgirls bringing her a cup of tea just a moment ago. She will have all the gifts chosen in a very short time, I'm sure. She was so excited about sending our relatives objects from England."

Just a short time. A short time to be alone with David. Emily studied him closely: the strong line of his jaw, the smooth wave of his glossy dark hair over his brow, the elegant gloved hands that lay so near her own atop the fabric.

You can trust him, that insidious voice whispered. *What choice do you have? You must trust someone.*

That was assuredly true. She could not go on all alone with this secret—the weight of it was nigh to crushing her. And David had been her best friend, could still be, if she could just quell the urge to kiss him whenever he drew near!

"David," she said quickly, before her courage could flee. "There is something I must tell you—"

"Papa! Look at what I have found. Would not *Didu* like it?" Anjali's light, childish voice called, drowning out Emily's whisper.

But, as quiet as she had been, David heard her. His hand covered hers briefly, warmly, beneath a fold of the cloth, and he murmured, "Tell me later. At the museum. There is something I must speak to you about, as well, Emily. To do with a certain trinket my father left with your family."

A certain trinket. So, he *did* remember. Emily had begun to wonder. Hope? She nodded, and his hand drew away, leaving her skin strangely chilled. She took a deep, steadying breath, and pasted on a welcoming smile before turning to the child.

Much to her shock, David's Arabian princess daughter walked right up to her and held out a length of silk for her inspection.

Emily could have vowed on their meeting at Gunter's that Lady Anjali did not care for her. She had watched Emily with wide, wary green eyes, silent and observant, as judgmental as an Almack's patroness. All of Emily's attempts at conversation were met with a polite "Yes, Lady Emily," or "No, Lady Emily."

Now, she gave Emily a bright smile. "Your own clothes are so pretty, Lady Emily, that I know you will be able to say whether it is fashionable or not. My great-grandmother will want only the very latest styles."

Emily could not help but smile back at her; the girl's open, pretty face had the attraction of sunlight on a cold, gray day. She obviously possessed her father's easy charm, when she chose to display it.

Emily knelt down beside Anjali to examine the silk. She longed to kiss the child's pretty cheek in absurd gratitude for her sudden show of friendship—and for postponing the inevitable conversation Emily must have with Anjali's father.

"It is very lovely, Lady Anjali," she answered. "This blue is very à la mode this Season. I am sure your great-grandmother could make a fine gown or pelisse from it."

"She would not make a gown or pelisse, Lady Emily. She will make a sari," said Anjali.

"A sari? My, that sounds terribly grand. What does one look like, pray tell?" Emily asked, as if she had never seen so much as a sketch of an Indian lady in her costume before. She had even tried to make one herself, from a length of pink satin, to no avail. The intricate folds were beyond her skills.

But she liked hearing the little girl speak, her tones lilting and sweet. And the solemn expression on Anjali's face as she proceeded to explain the garment was priceless.

Before the horrified gaze of the shopgirl, Anjali unrolled the entire bolt and proceeded to wind the cloth around herself. "First, Lady Emily, you must hold it like this, and turn like this . . ."

Later, when the fabric used for Anjali's sari had been put back on its bolt and the chosen purchases were being wrapped, Emily walked with Anjali among a display for hat trimmings of feathers and flowers. She stopped to examine a basket of silk roses, wondering how a yellow blossom would look on a new white bonnet.

"Lady Emily?" Anjali said softly, leaning against her ever so slightly.

Emily smiled down at her. "Yes, Lady Anjali?"

"You knew my father when you were children?"

"Yes, I did. Many years ago."

The child's pretty green eyes shifted away, as if she was uncertain about something. "Was he—happy here in England? Then?"

Emily thought she understood. After all, she had once been an uncertain child herself. She knelt down beside Anjali, her skirts spreading about her on the wooden floor. "Is there something troubling you about your papa, my dear?"

Anjali shook her head. "It is just that—he seemed unhappy while we were in Calcutta, even though he always laughed and smiled with me. I hoped he would be happy here, maybe like when you were children."

Emily felt such a sharp pang at the thought of David *ever* being unhappy about anything at all, and that it would cause such worry in this child's wide green eyes. "I hope he will be happy here. And you, too. Your papa

tells me you enjoy English history, and seeing all the
sights here."

"I do enjoy that. But it is not as sunny here as it is in
India, and . . ." Her soft voice trailed away.

"But, what?" Emily reached out to clasp Anjali's
small hand in hers. "What is amiss, my dear?"

Anjali stared at her intently, her brow wrinkled. "I see
the way some people look at me when Papa takes me
out, as if I was—strange, odd. My hair is dark, not like
yours. Is something wrong with me? With Papa? Is that
why he is unhappy?"

Emily's stomach cramped with a sudden, fiery bolt of
anger that someone—anyone—could so much as look
sideways at this sweet girl. Unable to stop herself, she
put her arms around Anjali and drew her close. At first,
the child held herself stiff, uncertain. But then she
melted against Emily, her arms going about her neck.
"Lady Anjali, it is true that there are some foolish people
who believe everyone should look and think alike. But
you must pay them no attention at all, for they are mistaken. You should pity them for being so stupid."

Anjali giggled against Emily's shoulder. "Stupid,
Lady Emily?"

"Yes. Stupid. For you are perfectly beautiful just as
you are, and you must always remember that. If anyone
says differently, I will jab them with my parasol."

Anjali laughed again, the sound sweet as springtime
birdsong. Her small hands tightened around Emily—
and Emily felt her own heart laugh in light reply.

Chapter Nine

*T*he British Museum was quiet in the afternoon—so quiet that the soles of Emily's half-boots echoed hollowly on the floor as she moved between the graceful arcs of the pale marble statues, the long stretches of the friezes. That last time she had come here, with Georgina and Alex to see the new rooms for the Elgin Marbles, the crowds had been so thick she could scarcely see without trodding on someone's foot. But at this hour everyone was at the Park, seeing and being seen along Rotten Row. Only a few people, artists with sketchbooks or seekers of beauty and solitude like herself, wandered in the dim spaces like flitting ghosts.

Even with those masses pressing around her on that last visit, Emily had adored these sculptures. The graceful flow of the carvings, as if they were made of silk and muslin—warm flesh, rather than chilled marble. The transcendence of the twisting, reaching figures beckoned to her. When she gazed at them, or even reached out to touch them with the very tips of her fingers, they told her that there *was* beauty in the world. There was truth and grace, and a life to be had beyond the superficial meanderings of London Society.

She saw that same revelation in David Huntington's dark eyes, in the tender way he spoke to his little daughter, the way his laughter echoed with warmth and humor. His life could not have been easy, caught between two worlds, two vastly different cultures and ways of life, yet there seemed no bitterness in him, as she had in herself. The way he looked at Emily, the way he touched her hand, as if she was some priceless, lovely piece of porcelain, coaxed her to be honest with him, to let go of her own anger and move into a future of endless possibility.

She wished, more than anything, that she *could* do that. She was weary of carrying that hard, cold stone in her heart, a stone made out of anger toward her long-dead brother and her own guilt. If she could, she would drop it right now, leave it at the feet of this statue of Hestia, and never look back.

Yet how could she when Damien's actions of so long ago, her own actions, were forcing her now to tell David the difficult truth? Emily's mother always said that the truth will always come out, no matter how hard a person works to conceal it—and a lie would always come back to slap you in the face.

Now Emily had to let the one lie she had ever held onto fly free—and probably slap her in the face.

She found a quiet bench behind the massive Hestia, a dim corner where surely no one could see her in her dark red walking gown and veiled bonnet. Only now, as she prepared herself to be completely and totally honest, did she realize that, in only the few days since she met David again, she had come to depend on his smiles. They had the power to make all else vanish—Georgina's worry over Emily's lack of betrothal, all her unsatisfactory suitors, her mother's chair-bound state in her dower house, her own restlessness at life in London. None of it mattered one jot when she was with David, just driving in the park or eating an ice or dancing. In that shop, laughing together at his daughter's antics and choosing gifts to send to his family, she had forgotten everything but the three of them in a golden circle—she, David, and little Anjali. Even the jewel tucked into her reticule disappeared.

With David, she was no longer restless. No longer bored or angry. She felt only—peace. A sense of some belonging.

She owed him so much, for *that* if for nothing else. She could never repay him for all that his friendship meant to her. But she could at least give him the truth.

Even if that meant he would never speak to her again, and she lost both him and his delightful daughter.

Emily stared up at Hestia, as if she could read some encouragement, some acknowledgment of the rightness of what she did, in the hard curves of marble drapery. But there was nothing. Only cold, still beauty.

She closed her eyes and imagined what it must be like to be imprisoned inside that chilly stone, to struggle to burst forth into the warmth of the sun and be free . . .

Her wild fancies were ended by the sound of footfalls—booted footfalls that ended right next to her secluded bench. Her eyes flew open, and she stared up into David's face.

His expression was veiled by the shadow falling from Hestia; the curves of his dark blue greatcoat almost made him appear to be cloaked in marble drapery himself. A beam of dusty light touched his hair and brow, and a smile whispered over his beautiful lips.

"Is this seat occupied, my lady?" he said, a teasing note lurking in his voice.

Emily laughed, and teased back, "I *was* enjoying my solitary reverie, but I might be persuaded to give it up for *you*, sirrah, if you care to bide with me for a moment."

"I can 'bide with you' happily all afternoon," he said, dropping down to sit beside her. The bench was small and narrow, forcing them into close proximity. Their sleeves brushed, silk catching on wool, and Emily was very aware of his sandalwood scent, the shadowed dark skin of his jaw. "I am quite exhausted after fending off Anjali's entreaties to come along this afternoon. She was more excited than I have ever seen her after our shopping expedition!"

"She is a lovely child," Emily said warmly. She would never have imagined she would say that after their strained hour at Gunter's, but the morning of wrapping saris and being drawn around the shop by Anjali's small hand erased that utterly.

"She is an unruly monkey," David answered, but the proud gleam in his eyes gave the lie to those stern words. "I thought the poor shopgirl would have an apoplexy when Anjali began unrolling that bolt. But Anjali *is* very pretty, I grant you—entirely due to her mother, I am sure. I sometimes think she is a magical elf-child, left in my house by mistake."

Anjali's mother. David's wife. Of course. They had fallen so easily into their old friendship that Emily sometimes forgot that years had separated them. Years which, for David, involved marriage and a new family.

"Were you married very long?" she asked quietly.

David glanced down at where their arms touched, his smile fading away into solemnity. "Almost five years. We were married when we were very young—I was eighteen, Rupasri only fifteen, though that was considered old in her family. She was the granddaughter of a friend of my grandmother; they hoped that stronger ties between the old Bengali families would give us a greater united front against the English."

"So, you did not—love her?" Emily knew she should not ask such things. They were none of her business, and, really, she was not so very sure she wanted to know the answers. But it was already out there, escaped from her own mouth into the cool air of the museum.

And she needed to know.

David glanced at her, his dark gaze opaque. She could read no answers in that at all. "Love her? I never met her before we were married. But I did come to care for her. She had a gentleness and a sweetness about her. I see those same qualities in Anjali, but I also hope that she will grow up with an independence and self-will her mother could never have hoped for. That is the only way she will be strong enough to make her way in this difficult world."

"Does Anjali miss her mother a great deal?" Emily asked gently. She remembered how she had felt when her father died—so scared and confused, so very alone. Her heart ached for the poor child—even if it twinged with jealousy for her "gentle and sweet" mother.

Those were two words no one had ever used to describe Emily.

"I am not sure if she does any longer. Rupasri died when Anjali was very young, still in leading strings. I try to tell her stories about her mother, so that she will not forget. Stories about our life in India."

"What *was* your life like in India, David? I have wondered so often since we parted. I read many books about the land, talked to people who had been there, but it still seems strange to me. Like another world."

"Yes." David turned his head to give her an intent glance, his expression unreadable. "You did tell me you read about India."

"Your stories when we were children always intrigued me. I could never imagine then that there *could* be a world outside Fair Oak, let alone one so full of heat and light and noise."

He nodded, and his gaze turned away from her toward one of the long friezes on the wall. "There is certainly plenty of all three of those in India. And scents! When we first landed in England, Anjali said the air smelled of—nothing. That was before we came into London proper, of course, but there were no spices, no perfumes, no smoke. And our townhouse is not very much like our house in Calcutta, though I tried to make Anjali's rooms as similar as I could."

Emily braced her chin on her hand, watching him with fascination. He seemed a million miles away from her at that moment, his dark eyes seeing something beyond the Marbles, beyond even herself. "Tell me about your house there," she urged.

His voice was quiet and deep as he spoke of that home, pale stucco drowsing behind a garden heavy with red and orange and white flowers, lotus and marigolds and jasmine, rich greenery heavy with the humidity hanging over all. Anjali collected pets there—a gazelle and a squirrel, as well as two little dogs the governor-general's wife gave her—and they gamboled about under the draping pipal trees. In the mornings, servants hurried along the galleries, bearing trays of sweetmeats and tea, hanging out laundry, chasing the pets away from blossoms left on homemade shrines in the garden.

In the hot afternoons, when the light bore down like a bright white-yellow pall and spirits turned heavy, everything slowed down. Carved wooden shutters were closed, canvas shelters lowered over the galleries. Anjali would drowse there with her dogs, lying against the silk cushions while her ayah sang soft songs to her. David would sit close to her with his portable desk and his work, shooing the flying insects away from his documents with the quills of his pens.

In the evenings, the shutters opened again, letting night breezes and starlight sweep through the long, low rooms. Music would drift up over the walls, chanting and the rich strains of sitars. Even when he went out to a party at the home of one of the Anglo gentry, that music would trail after him, sweet and seductive.

Emily closed her eyes as he spoke, seeing all of this

in her mind. The flowers, the heavy air, the music, even the pet gazelle—it all came to vivid, colorful life for her. Only very gradually did she realize that David had ceased speaking, his voice trailing away into the cool marble around them.

She opened her eyes, half-surprised to find herself not in an Indian gallery but in the dim environs of the British Museum. And to find David watching her.

She summoned up a small, strained smile for him. "It sounds—amazing. I imagine I will never see it, though."

"And why is that?"

"A lady—a duke's sister—could never hope to travel so very far alone. Alex and my mother might allow me to go to Brighton or maybe even France or Italy, but hardly Calcutta! Your words took me there, though. It must be just as I imagine it—strange and unearthly beautiful. How glorious your life must have been there! I always thought it must be."

"I thought of you over all those years, too, Emily. Every day, I think." He leaned closer to her, their arms and shoulders pressed together, warm and intimate even through layers of silk and wool and blasted propriety. "I wondered what your life was like, how you were growing up. What you would be like as a lady."

Emily stared at him, mesmerized. She had always thought about him, of course, but she had imagined he forgot about her in that new life of his. She was just the silly, tomboyish girl who followed him all about, and in Calcutta he was surely surrounded by kohl-eyed beauties.

The thought that he had remembered her, speculated on her growing-up, was intoxicating.

"And how did I grow up?" she whispered.

He grinned at her, his dimples flashing enticingly. "Extraordinarily well, I would say. You are beautiful, Emily. And so kind to everyone, especially my daughter.

You have not been hardened by London Society, as so many are. The years have been good to you."

At this reminder of the past, of what she had truly come here to tell him, Emily turned away from the glow in his eyes. She stared at Hestia's draperies, suddenly deeply chilled. She wrapped her arms about herself, and murmured, "They were not always so fine as they are now—the years, I mean."

"What are you talking about, Emily? Your family is obviously happy, and no lady of the *ton* could have a lovelier smile than you do."

"I lost my smile for a long time. Before Alex came back from Spain and met Georgina, many things happened to my family. Things I would want to never think of again."

"Then do not think of them!" David seized her hand in his, his gloved fingers strong around her own. "Emily, the last thing I would want to do is make you unhappy, make you speak of unpleasant matters you would rather forget. I would be a poor friend to bring even a speck of unhappiness into your life."

Emily folded her free hand around their clasped fingers, holding them together. She stared hard at their embrace, unable to look into his eyes, his beautiful face. If she even glimpsed him, she could never tell him this.

"No, David, I must say these things to you. I must tell you the truth; it is why I met you here today. But please, please don't utter a word until I am finished."

"Very well, Emily," he answered softly. "Tell me anything you like. I will listen."

Still clinging to his hand, Emily took a deep breath and launched into her old tale. She told him all about her mother's riding accident soon after David and his father left England—the accident that left her still confined to her chair. She spoke of her father's death, and Damien's disastrous reign as duke. Of how their sudden lack of fortune left her to make ends meet at Fair Oak, to take care of their mother and maintain their good name.

Finally, she came to the day Damien took the Star away. She squeezed her eyes shut as tightly as she could and sped through the story, her voice cracking.

". . . and so you see, David," she finished. "I know that you wanted to ask me about the Star; I am sure you must want it back. It is yours! And my family stole it. I am so very sorry. I can never say that enough. You must hate me now. You must be sorry you ever stood as my friend!"

David said nothing, but neither did he let go of her hand. His clasp tightened around hers convulsively, and she felt the stiffness of his shoulder against hers.

Slowly, very slowly, she opened her eyes and dared to peek up at him. He stared away, over her head, and his handsome features were taut. He was the very portrait of suppressed anger.

Emily tried to pull her hand from his, to move her loathsome presence away so he would not have to look at her and her betrayal. But he refused to release her. Indeed, his other arm came around her shoulders and held her close. His eyes as he stared down at her were burning black.

"How dare he?" David growled, in a voice she had never heard from him before. "A brother is meant to protect his sister, to hold her safe, not throw her into poverty and dishonor. How could Damien have even called himself a man after such disgrace? He had no honor. No strength."

Emily felt a prickling behind her eyes, a harbinger of tears. She could *not* cry now! She had refused to show tears for all this time, refused to be less than perfectly proud. Even when neighbors whispered and snickered about her old gowns, she would not lower her chin an inch. She was a Kenton, and Kentons were *never* ashamed, even when their hearts burned with it.

She blinked hard, and said thickly, "He—he had a sickness for gambling, and for other shameful things as well."

"Drink and whores? That is no excuse, Emily. He was a duke. He owed his family and title a great responsibility. And he did not fulfill it. He left his mother behind to illness, his sister to hard work a lady should never know—and he ended by stealing from my family."

"I should have stopped him!" Emily cried, frantic. "I should have known he would come for the Star and hidden it from him. I should have run after him when he took it—"

"Emily!" David said firmly, seizing her by the shoulders and forcing her to face him, to be still. "None of this is on your head. None of it! You were always honorable. You took care of your mother and your tenants when your brothers could not. You never could have saved the Star from Damien's greed—no one could."

Emily did cry then. Great, salty tears that ran down her cheeks and splashed onto David's wrist. She pressed hard at her lips with her gloved hand, but the tears would not be stopped. She had thought David would hate her when he discovered what happened. Instead, he was angry with *Damien*. He called her honorable, he held her close to him.

For so long, she had felt all alone, even in Alex and Georgina's warm home. Now, suddenly, she was *not* alone. It was too much for all her locked-up emotions to bear.

"I should have tried harder to stop him," she sniffled. "You were my best friend, David, and I disappointed you."

He gave her a wry smile. "Emily, you could never, ever disappoint me." He reached inside his coat for a handkerchief and pressed it into her hand. "Now, here, my brave girl. Dry your eyes before someone notices us and we are ejected from the museum for causing a scene."

Emily gave a watery laugh, and mopped at her eyes and cheeks. Now that a measure of her good sense was returning, she was glad their corner was so ill-lit—her face was surely a mottled mess. "Indeed, you are right. Damien was the one who took the Star, but I am the one left with the consequences. I know you wanted it back, David."

He sat back on the bench, stretching his long legs out before him with a deep sigh. "Yes, I did. Or rather, my grandmother did. Does."

"Your grandmother?"

"Ah, yes. You see, Emily, I have my own tale to tell you."

"A tale?" Emily said warily. "I like tales—usually. Unless they are like my own."

David smiled gently. "You say you enjoy stories of India. And this one is full of curses and spirits and all manner of exciting events. And, according to my grandmother, it is even true."

Emily was intrigued, despite everything there was to worry about at this moment. There was a childlike part of herself, hidden in her heart, that did still revel in fairy tales. "About the Star?"

"Yes. You see, when my grandparents were first married, they were unable to have a child. My grandmother made many sacrifices, visited many shrines. One night, after praying at a temple to the god Shiva, she had a vision."

"A vision?"

"A dream, if you will. She dreamed that Shiva, who is a god of contradictions—the dance and stillness, bounty and wrath, destruction and fertility—told her he would grant her wish if she would bring him the great sky-stone. The most beautiful of all jewels."

Emily was mesmerized by the flow of his deep, rich voice, and the strange story he told. In her mind's eye, she could see his grandmother as a beautiful, dark young woman swathed in bright silks, kneeling at the feet of the many-armed god. "And that was the Star?"

"The Star of India, yes. It belonged to my great-grandfather. He wore it in his turban, and was deeply proud of it. In a land of glorious jewels, the Star was special. But, as much as he treasured the jewel, he treasured the dream of grandsons even more."

"So, he gave her the sapphire."

"He did. And, that very same day, she and my grandfather went back to the temple and laid the Star at Shiva's feet. Nine months later, my uncle was born. Six more children followed, including my mother, who was said the be the most beautiful woman in Bengal."

"The sacrifice worked!"

"It would appear so."

"But then what went wrong?"

"My mother grew up, and met my father, who was in the army in Calcutta. They met in the marketplace and fell instantly in love. She wanted to give him something extraordinary to prove the depth of her devotion. The finest thing she knew of was the Star. She saw it often, for my grandmother liked to take her children back to the temple to make sacrifices in thanks."

"Was your mother not afraid to take the jewel from its sacred spot?" Emily whispered.

A ghost of a smile drifted across David's lips. "My mother was not a superstitious woman. She converted to Christianity when she married my father, and she did not fear Shiva's wrath. Very soon after she gave him the Star, and when I was a small child, my father's older brother died and he was called back to England to take up the earldom. Only after my parents departed Calcutta did my grandmother discover what her daughter had done."

"And then what did she do?" Emily asked.

"I was only a tiny child then, but my grandmother's servants say she wailed and cried, and broke everything in her chambers. She went back to the temple to beg forgiveness, and that night she had another dream."

"Or vision."

"Yes, another vision. Shiva said that her family would be cursed until the Star was returned to him."

"Oh," Emily breathed. In her imagination, the museum around them had disappeared completely. She was in a humid-heavy temple, surrounded by the thick scents of incense and jasmine—feeling the inescapable weight of a curse falling over herself and her family. She could not breathe; her breath caught in her throat, strangling her.

Emily reached up to loosen the ribbons of her bonnet, trying not to reveal the depth of her reaction. She hated for David to think her an even bigger fool than he surely already did. "What happened?"

David shrugged. "It appeared her curse came true. My mother died very young, in childbirth. My father nearly went mad with grief, and he died of yellow fever soon after we returned to India. Rupasri also died young."

Emily's family, too, had been touched by this litany of despair, she realized with a shock. Her mother's accident, her father's early death, Damien's wasted life. Could it all have been the fault of the Star?

Do not be stupid, Emily, she told herself sternly. *This is the nineteenth century, not the Middle Ages. There are no such things as curses.*

Still, a tiny sense of disquiet reverberated in her heart.

"Do—do you believe in this curse, David?" she said slowly.

He stared at her closely. "No. Bad things happen to all

of us in this world. I suppose it *is* a curse, but the curse is called life."

"Yes. Of course."

"However, my grandmother believes entirely in this curse. Before I left India, she charged me with recovering the jewel. I love her, Emily—she was like a true mother to me when my parents died. She is very old now, and I do not want her to live out the rest of her years uneasy because of this."

Emily's heart ached for him. "I am so sorry, David. What a dreadful thing!"

"Are you sure you have no idea where the Star could be now? Where your brother sold it?"

"I . . ." Emily swallowed hard. Her stare dropped to her lap, to the braid trim on her gown. She had been so lost in the tale of the Star in India that she quite forgot her own story was not finished. The hardest part was still to come. "Do you read the London papers, David?"

He gave a rueful laugh. "I do try, but I fear I cannot read too closely when Anjali is at the breakfast table with me."

"But you do remember Sir Charles and Lady Innis? We met them in the park."

One of his dark brows arched quizzically. "Yes, I remember them. I received an invitation to some ball they are giving. What does all of this have to do with the Star?"

"Well, you see, Sir Charles has the Star—or at least the false Star Damien sold him. It is the paste copy which will be on display at this ball, which the experts will then examine. But I have no idea where the real one can be. I have wracked my brain trying to recall every pawnshop Damien frequented, every gaming hell he owed money to, but it is no use! I am sorry, David—so very sorry."

"Emily, I have told you, none of this is your fault.

How could it possibly be? I shall just have to—" Suddenly, David's soothing words broke off. His dark stare veered back to her sharply, and he reached out to clasp her arm. "Did you say experts were coming to examine the paste Star?"

Emily nodded mutely. Her voice seemed to have died in her throat, and she was weary—so very weary. The high tension of the past few days had ground her down, and her very bones were tired. She longed to rest her head against David's strong shoulder and sleep for a month. She wanted to forget all about her family and the jewel, and everything except David.

But that could not be. She had come this far, she could not stop now, not with everything yet undone and the sword of Damocles still hanging over her head. The best she could hope for was that David would help her, be her ally.

She stared deeply into his eyes, but all she saw there were more difficult questions.

"Yes," she answered. "And they will know at once that the stone is false—and Sir Charles will remember that it was my brother who sold it to him all those years ago. But I have a plan, you see. Or at least the beginnings of one. That is why I was at that jeweler's shop in Gracechurch Street this morning."

Still watching him closely, Emily told of her wild idea to switch out the new Star with the paste one at the ball. How she would contrive to do this, she was not entirely certain. She could only hope there would be a moment when no one else was near the case holding the Star. Then she could employ the old lock-picking skills she had perfected as a girl, when breaking into cases was the only way she could obtain needed coins from Damien. The switch could be done in a trice. If only . . .

Her plan was only half-done, she knew that. And that

conclusion was confirmed by the dubious expression on David's face.

"It is ridiculous, is it not?" she said, pulling away from him.

"Not entirely, Emily. The idea of replacing the paste jewel with a genuine sapphire is a very clever one. But you must not get caught in making the switch. You need a better plan for that part of it." He stared past her, at the impervious Hestia. Slowly, resolutely, dubiousness turned to calculation. A smile broke over his face, as the golden sunrise after a very dark night. "You will need assistance. From someone like myself, perhaps."

Emily's heart lightened, as if on new-sprung wings, and she could not stop herself from leaning forward to press a kiss to his cheek. "Oh, David! I was so, so hoping you would say that."

What a fool I am, David thought, as he left Emily with promises to think on her plans and conceive an idea for the night of the Innis ball. What was he doing, contemplating turning jewel thief (well, jewel *switcher,* which was in a way even worse)? He was an earl now, with responsibilities, a daughter to take care of. He was not a wild youth anymore, free to spend all his time running across the country fields with Emily Kenton.

He was a besotted fool. That was the only answer. One look into the sapphire depths of Emily's eyes, and he would do anything to make her smile again. Even turn burglar.

But there was no denying the way his heart seemed to skip a beat when she *did* smile. The way his blood surged and heated when her soft lips touched his skin, even briefly. He wanted to help her, to make her life perfect—now and always.

And there was also no denying the excitement that simmered in his soul at the prospect of intrigue. Life in

England was quiet and staid in comparison with the hot, bright drama of India. Only with Emily did he feel himself come truly alive again, did he hear the distant call of wild birds tempting him onward.

He swung up into his phaeton, turning the horses toward home. Emily's carriage, a proper one this time, with the Kenton crest on the door, had already moved onto the next street, out of his sight.

The thought of the shameful way her brother had treated her made his blood burn hot in his veins. His heart cried out for revenge—yet that could never be. Damien Kenton was dead, forever beyond an earthly reckoning for his dishonorable deeds. He had been dead for many years, and still Emily was cleaning up his messes. Beautiful, sweet Emily, whose young days should have been filled with music and gowns and suitors, not money and farms and family honor.

What was wrong with Alexander and his vivid, clever wife, that they could not see the unbearable pressure their sister was living under?

But that was unfair. Emily had not gone to them for help, insisted they not be "bothered" in anyway by this debacle. He, David, was all she had. He could not disappoint her.

The loss of the Star was a great one, and he felt it keenly. His grandmother had charged him with its recovery, and he never wanted to disappoint her, either. He would give his left arm to release her from her "curse" and ease her old age.

Yet, even more strongly, with a force greater than any he had ever encountered before, he wanted to see Emily laugh again—really laugh, as she had when they were children. Free of all worry and care. He would do anything for that. He would die for it.

Oh-ray-baba. He was a besotted fool, indeed.

Chapter Ten

"*W*ell, well," Georgina murmured, sotto voce, as they left their wraps with the waiting footmen and melded into the throng flowing into the Innis ballroom. "It would seem that even the highest sticklers of the *ton* have allowed curiosity to get the better of them. They have all deigned to enter the house of a 'vulgar Cit.'"

Emily adjusted her kid gloves over her arms and gave her sister-in-law a wry smile. She was trying her hardest to appear cool and amused, as she usually was at such events. She even laughed a bit, but she could see that she had not entirely fooled Georgina, who watched Emily with a tiny frown puckering her forehead.

Before Georgina could say anything, Emily turned away to snatch a glass of champagne from the tray of a passing footman. As she sipped, or rather gulped in a most unladylike fashion at the bracing, bubbling liquid, her gaze scanned the crowd.

It was just as Georgina said—everyone who was anyone in Society was there, despite the fact that many of them declared their intentions of never setting foot in such a "mushroom's" dwelling. Obviously, the burning desire to see the interior arrangements of one of London's largest houses had overcome even snobbery. Emily couldn't help but be a bit glad, despite the anxiety that made her heart pound and her hands tremble. She rather liked Sir Charles and his stylish wife, and if not for the unfortunate circumstance of the Star she would have enjoyed knowing them better. Perhaps in the future—far in the future. . . .

Lady Innis, clad in a very fashionable and stunning gown of a cloth-of-gold tunic over an ivory satin slip, was in radiant form. She greeted and laughed, and gestured with her gold-colored feather fan, trailed by her bemused husband. Lady Innis's diamond necklace and earrings, as well as the large ruby brooch that fastened her gold silk turban, were the grandest Emily had ever seen.

No wonder they can afford to donate the Star, she thought. They obviously wanted the philanthropic prestige of patronizing a new, highbrow museum more than they needed money.

She exchanged her empty glass for a full one and drifted along the edges of the white and silver ballroom, trying to stay out of sight of any of her friends or acquaintances. She saw Mr. Carrington over by the tall windows, but he did not spot her.

The dancing had not yet started, but the orchestra, hidden behind a bank of potted palms, played a soft melody. Mozart, perhaps, or Haydn. Emily could hear it well, because, despite the great size of the gathering, the crowd was strangely hushed. People stood in clusters and knots, whispering and murmuring and staring. She found a quiet corner, half-hidden behind a palm of her own, and scanned the faces carefully.

But the one face she wanted to see above all others was not to be glimpsed. David had obviously not yet arrived.

"Please, do not let him forget," she whispered, half in prayer, half to reassure herself. He would not forget, how could he? Her tale had been one of the oddest he had surely ever heard, and the Star was almost as much his concern as it was hers. But maybe he had decided she was an utter lunatic and he wanted no part in her schemes.

Perhaps he was on his way back to Calcutta even now! And, really, Emily could not blame him if he was. But she needed him. Not just on this evening, but on every evening to come.

The champagne glass almost slipped out of her hand at this revelation, which had come out of the darkness not as a lightning bolt, but as a whisper of music on flower-scented air. The thought of David going back to India did not give her such a sharp pang because she needed his help with the Star—but because she loved him. Not as a child loved her friend, but as a woman loved a man.

Emily took another deep gulp of her champagne, and it helped to clear the sudden misty haze at the edges of her vision. Yes—she did! She *loved* David. In truth, she had never ceased to love him, not over all the years they were parted. But since he had first come back, since she had first seen him at the Wilton ball, her feelings had been so very different. The dark, mysterious depths of his eyes, his elegant hands, so strong when they held hers. The way he laughed at her foibles, the echo of his voice as he told her of the exotic mysteries of India . . .

She wanted to clasp all those things to her and never, ever let them go. When she was with him, she never felt that aching restlessness that had plagued her of late. With him, she was always at peace, even in the midst of all this turmoil over the wretched Star. When he sat beside her and held her hand in his, she knew nothing could go wrong.

When she was alone, as now, her stomach tied itself

into knots, and she was certain her schemes could only go horribly awry.

He surely did not feel the same about her. He had been married, had known the serenity of a beautiful Indian wife—a wife lovely enough to produce the doll-child Anjali. Emily was not a serene woman. She never had been. And the Star was still lost to David's family, no matter what happened here tonight. Her own family had caused that, and even David's understanding could not erase it.

After all this trouble was over, David might try to distance himself and his daughter from her—or he would if he was sensible. But maybe, just maybe, once they were all settled in the country, away from London, she could show him that there was more to her than trouble and wild schemes. She could show him how much she knew about farming, could perhaps advise him on his fields or teach Anjali how to ride.

"One plan at a time, Emily," she whispered.

Oh, horrors! Now she was talking to herself. This would all have to end soon, or she would surely have to be sent to Bedlam.

And her champagne was all gone. She turned her head to see if perhaps there was any more to be had, any tray-laden footmen nearby. As she peered around fruitlessly in search of refreshment, a low, hissing murmur floated through the potted palm to her ears.

"Look, there is the Indian earl!" a voice, which Emily recognized as that of the draconian Lady Linley, said. "How very dark he is. I see nothing at all of his father in him. How handsome that man was in his youth! We could scarce believe he made such a *mésalliance*."

"Perhaps the new earl's father was really the punkah boy!" her companion said, with a nasty little snicker. "One does hear such things about native women . . ."

How dare they! Those shrill old harridans. Emily's

face flamed, and her mouth turned dry and sour. If only she truly was the Boudicca David named her. She would run them over with her chariot. Skewer them with her sword.

But she was not Boudicca. She was simply Lady Emily Kenton. And that title might stand her in better stead here in this ballroom than a spear would. There was only one thing she could do.

She deposited her empty glass at the base of the palm, made certain her hair and gown were tidy, and marched out with her head held high. She swept past the two witches without even glancing at them, her gaze searching the crowd for David. Her Indian earl.

He was speaking with their hostess, too far away to have heard the old gossips' comments—but surely he had heard it before, and worse. It was just such cuts, small but bleeding, that had driven his father back to India.

But they would *not* drive David away. Not if Emily had anything to say about it.

My brother is not a duke for nothing, she thought resolutely. It was high time she used that title to its full advantage.

She marched up to David, laid her hand lightly on his arm, and said, loudly enough for everyone nearby to hear, "Lord Darlinghurst! Such a pleasure to meet with you again. My brother and sister-in-law were just asking about you."

David stared down at her, his gaze startled for an instant. Then he smiled, a slow, secret smile just for her. He crooked his arm so that her hand slid securely into its warm safety, and said, "Lady Emily. How good of your brother to ask after me. I trust that your family is all well this evening?"

"Very well, thank you." Emily turned to nod at Lady Innis, who watched them with great interest. "Our fami-

lies are very old friends, you see, Lady Innis. Our estates
march together."

"Indeed, Lady Emily?" Lady Innis said brightly.
"Fascinating!"

"And I must compliment you on your lovely arrangements, also, Lady Innis," Emily went on. "The colors are
stunning."

"Oh, thank you!" Lady Innis said, her voice even
brighter. "I was not at all sure about the silver . . ."

"It is very stylish." Emily glanced about, but she did
not see Sir Charles. Nor did she see the object of her pur-
suit—the Star. "Is your grand jewel not to be displayed
this evening, Lady Innis? I have been so eager to catch a
glimpse of it again. I have not seen it since I was a tiny
child."

Lady Innis gave a little trill of laughter. "Of course,
Lady Emily! My husband is so immensely proud of his
treasure, I doubt you could escape a glimpse even if you
wished it. He has gone now to be sure all is in readiness.
It will be displayed in the library. I will make certain you
are among the first to see it. But now, you must excuse
me—I have to instruct the musicians to begin playing
for the dancing."

"Of course, Lady Innis. Thank you so much." Emily
watched their hostess hurry away, feeling David watching *her* all the while.

The crowd surged around them toward the dance
floor, but the two of them stayed exactly where they
were, arms linked, as if suddenly turned into the Grecian
statues they viewed only the day before.

"You look beautiful, Lady Emily," David said quietly.
His cool breath stirred the curls at her temple, and she
shivered despite the cloying warmth of the ballroom.
"You could almost be a sapphire yourself."

Emily laughed. She had not chosen her gown, an iri-
descent deep blue silk with silver embroidery on the

small bodice and puffed sleeves, apurpose to imitate the Star, but it appeared as if she had. She reached up to straighten the band of blue silk holding back her hair, and said, "At least I did not wear my sapphire combs! That would have been too much indeed."

"But I see you did wear *this*." David, his gaze suddenly intent, reached out to touch the ring that hung on its chain near the lace edge of her neckline. She had worn it out tonight, for all to see, after all the years of keeping it hidden.

"Yes," she answered softly. "I always wear this ring—next to my heart. Do you remember when you gave it to me?"

"Of course. I remember it very well." The corner of his lips quirked. "It does not appear to have protected you very well."

"Oh, but it has! I always thought that since you gave it to me . . ." But she could not go on. The press of people was too heavy around them, and such things were not meant to be discussed in crowded ballrooms. They were meant for gardens under moonlight, silent and scented with flowers—and dark, so her blushes could not be seen.

He seemed to know what she was thinking, feeling. He gave a short nod, and said, "Would you care to dance with me, Lady Emily?"

"Yes, thank you, Lord Darlinghurst. That would be most—pleasant."

As they moved to take their places in the set, David whispered, "And then perhaps we can catch a glimpse of this little stone that has caused so many difficulties."

The Innises' library was almost as vast as their ballroom, but it was dark and cavernous rather than all airy silver light. Shelves full of books, their rich leather bindings uncracked as if they had never been touched, soared to the gilded ceiling. Heavy furniture, upholstered in forest green velvet and dark red brocade, lurked in the shadows, crouched like jungle creatures ready to pounce on Emily if she made a suspicious move.

The only light in the room came from two tall candelabra fitted with white wax tapers. They were situated on either side of a glass case, casting a sparkling glow on its crystalline edges. A narrow Aubuosson runner in pale shades of blue and cream led to the case.

Emily knew that her feet must be moving along that carpet, because the case was drawing ever closer, but she was not the one controlling them. Now that her goal was literally within her sight, she felt numb, surrounded by a cold mist. Even her lips were chilled.

Only her hand on David's arm held her upright.

"It feels as if we are about to be presented the Holy Grail," she whispered to him, her gaze never leaving the back of Sir Charles's green velvet coat as he led them further and further into the library.

David laughed softly, but his head did not incline to look down at her. When she glanced up at him, she saw that he was taking in the entire room, his dark eyes darting from crevice to corner.

"What are you looking at?" she said, again in a hoarse whisper.

"Sh," he answered. "Later."

Sir Charles halted next to the glistening case, his florid face rapt as he stared into it. "And this, Lady Emily and Lord Darlinghurst, is my treasure. The finest piece in my collection. I am so happy to be able to show it to you tonight." His glance moved from the case to Emily, his brows suddenly raised in seeming astonished remembrance. "Oh, but you must have seen it before, Lady Emily! For indeed it was your late brother who sold it to me, years ago. An act for which I will always be grateful."

Emily forced her frozen lips to stretch into a smile. She hoped it *looked* less like a rictus than it *felt*. "Of course, Sir Charles. But I am sure your great appreciation for the jewel far exceeds any he ever possessed."

"Oh, I *have* appreciated it, I do assure you, Lady Emily! But now I must not be selfish with it any longer. Everyone should be able to see such wondrous beauty, which is why I am donating it to the Mercer Museum."

Emily swallowed hard past her dry throat. "That is very commendable of you, Sir Charles."

"Oh, well—but you must take a proper look! Come closer, Lady Emily. And you, too, Lord Darlinghurst. I know you have spent many years in India, so you will be able to appreciate the fine workmanship."

Emily dropped her hand from David's arm and took a tiny step toward the case, then another, until she was so close that her breath left a small cloud on the glass.

The paste Star looked magnificent, lying there on a bed of luminous white satin. Whoever Damien had hired to make the copy had done an excellent job. If she did not know the truth, she would not have been able to see it. The paste sapphire gleamed a deep sea blue, set off by the ring of false diamonds. It was beautiful, truly, yet it lacked—something. Some ineffable draw that only the true Star, wherever it was, could possess.

Her gaze dropped from the stone to the case itself, to the tiny locked hinge. A thin wire, carefully bent, would take care of it easily enough, if she had space and time to concentrate.

That time was not tonight. Sir Charles watched her avidly, waiting for her to say something.

"It is beautiful, Sir Charles," she murmured. "Obviously, it has prospered under your care."

Sir Charles beamed. "Thank you, Lady Emily! I have loved it very much. My wife has sometimes wished to wear it, but I have insisted that it stay here, safely locked away. The risk of theft is always great if one is known to have such an object."

"You are very wise." Emily stepped back from the case. She could not stand the glaring light any longer, and her fingers itched to snatch open the case right then and there and be done with it.

Patience, she told herself. *You knew this would not be quick or simple.*

Patience, though, had never been Emily's strong point.

"I know that most of your guests are eager for a glimpse of the Star," Emily said. "So, we will not monopolize your time any further, Sir Charles. It was most kind of you to give us the first peek."

"Indeed, Sir Charles," David added. "It is a very fine piece."

"Thank you, thank you," Sir Charles muttered, his attention still focused on his treasure.

David clasped Emily's arm and led her out of the library into the deserted corridor. If possible, it was even darker than the library—a long expanse of blackness broken only by brief intervals where the wall sconces cast out tiny splashes of tawny light. There was one large square of moonlight, spreading from a half-open glass door that led out to a narrow terrace and tiny garden.

David drew her out of the door onto that terrace, where they leaned against the cold marble balustrade.

Emily was grateful for its chill solidity holding her up. She had not realized how tense her muscles had been, how tired she was, until this moment. Oh, why could this whole matter not be over and done with? She was sick of the Star, sick of the whole deceitful thing. She wished she was far from here, riding her horse at Fair Oak, the sun on her face and the smell of green hay in her nostrils.

Then David put his arms around her, drawing her

away from the cold stone, and she thought, *Well, perhaps here is not such a bad place after all.*

In fact, as she laid her hand against his chest and felt the steady thrum of his heartbeat, she knew there was no place in the world she would rather be. She had always hated Damien for the untenable position he had put her in. Now, she was almost grateful. If it was not for what he had done with the Star, she would not be here on this terrace, with David's arms around her.

She inhaled his clean scent of starched linen and sandalwood soap, and thought whimsically, *Thank you, Damien.* She twined her arms around David and drew him even closer.

She felt him rest his cheek against her hair. In this moment, she could forget all about her dilemma, her family—everything but the beauty of this instant, the sweet peace in her heart.

Peace was one thing she had not known in a very long time, and it was like laudanum to her restless heart—she craved it, *needed* it. Just as she needed laughter and contentment and new thoughts and sights.

All of those things David, and David alone, brought to her. Why could this moment not go on and on forever?

She felt David's shoulder shift against her, and she tilted back her head to stare up at him. His face was all sharp planes and angles in the moonlight, the silver glow playing over his high cheekbones and the sensual fullness of his lips.

He was like a god himself, she reflected dreamily. An exotic god of the night and the moon. He needed only to be rid of his fashionably cut coat and brocade waistcoat, though, and draped in pearls and ropes of rubies. A silken turban should be wound about his head, fastened with the Star itself . . .

This reminder of the Star brought her back to earth with a prosaic thud. *That* was truly why they were here, brought to the Innis house by her own crazy schemes. As much as she wanted to lose herself in romantic fantasy, she could not. Not yet. Maybe not ever.

"I am sorry, David," she whispered.

He gave her a lazy smile, one finger catching at her curls and twining them like skeins of silk over his skin. "For what, Boudicca?"

"For bringing you into this hopeless business. You should be at home with Anjali, planning your new life at Combe Lodge, not darting around London with me, trying to figure out how to break and enter . . ."

"Emily, no," he said, shaking his head at her. "For almost the past year, I was on a ship, perishing of boredom and trying to find ways to amuse Anjali so she would not feel the same. I thought that once we were in England the boredom would vanish and I would be far too busy to ever think of it again. But it was not true."

"Was it not?"

"No. You see, I had forgotten how very gray England can be. Gray sky, gray buildings, even gray people. I felt more restless than ever. I did not see color again until you appeared before me at that ball." He leaned down and kissed her brow, the tip of her nose. Tiny, feather-light kisses that warmed her to her very toes.

She leaned into him, trying to grasp that warmth and forget her misgivings about their mission.

But it would not be entirely dismissed. It kept clamoring in her mind, not letting her revel in her new feelings. "But we still have not switched the two Stars . . ."

"Sh!" He caught her face between his hands, holding her still so she must look up at him. His thumbs gently brushed the curls back from her temples. "We will. Just not tonight. I have the beginnings of a plan."

His caress was drugging, turning her blood to a warm rush, lulling her into a glorious haze. "A—plan?" she murmured, going up on tiptoe to kiss his jaw, the skin

like satin beneath her lips. She could not help herself—
something *made* her do it, some imp of mischief in her
mind. "What sort of a plan?"

"I will tell you all about it—later." His strong touch
moved down her throat to her shoulders, holding her
away from him by just a fraction of an inch. A small,
cool breeze flowed between them. "If you will tell me
why you wear my ring." His thumb hooked into the
chain, lifting the ring up to her view. The edge of his nail
rasped against her bare flesh, making her shiver.

Emily stared at her ring, sparkling in the starlight. The
true, simple answer was that she wore the ring because
she loved him. Without knowing it, she had been waiting
for him all these years. That was why she had never accepted any of her suitors.

But she could not tell him that. It would make her
sound too silly, like the girls in the Minerva Press novels
Georgina loved so much.

She covered his hand with hers, pulling the ring back
down, out of sight. "I wear it for protection, which you
promised it would give me."

He tilted his head, watching her closely. "And do you
think it worked?"

"Of course." She gave a little laugh. "I am as healthy
as a country horse, and I always have been. And I have a
very good life." She turned her head to stare up at the
glorious night sky, black velvet spread with glowing
jewels of stars. "Look at this night—the moon, the garden, a moment alone with you, away from that horribly
stuffy ballroom. Who could ever want more?"

Then, to stop him from pressing her to say more—
and because she just really, truly wanted to—she slid her
hands behind his neck and pulled him down to her. Her
lips met his, and all else was forgotten.

*   *   *

David had never tasted anything as sweet as Emily's lips. They were finer than honey or pistachio cream. Her breath was cool where it mingled with his in a great rush, sending purest life through his very veins. He pulled her against him, his hands sliding down the silken back of her gown, their bodies pressed together until he did not know where *he* ended and *she* began. Her rose-petal perfume filled his senses, clouding all else.

The night was cool around them, but his skin was heated as if by a Calcutta summer. He needed Emily—needed her like water, like air.

That sudden realization made him step back from her, holding her by the waist as she swayed. Such need, such *desperation*, had no place in this night, in this situation. Anyone could come along to this terrace and spy their embrace. Gossip about Lady Emily Kenton and the Indian earl would spread like a fire through the Innis ballroom and out into the entire city. While David could certainly think of far worse things than being obliged to offer for Emily, of having her for his wife, he did not want it like that.

And they did still have that dratted Star to think about.

He threw back his head, taking in a deep breath of night air. What he really wanted to do was howl at the sky. He felt Emily slide out from beneath his grasp and turn away, her own shoulders heaving with the effort to breathe.

A tiny sound broke out, and David realized with shock that she was—was *crying*.

"Emily!" he cried hoarsely, catching her by the arm to turn her back to him. One small, crystal tear tracked along her cheek. Her hands shot up to cover her face, and she tried to turn away from him again. But he refused to let her go. "Emily, what is it?"

"I—I am sorry I threw myself at you," she muttered, swiping at her cheeks with her gloved fingertips. "Oh, I

am always saying I'm sorry to you! But I truly don't
know what came over me. The anxiety about the jewels . . ."

"You mean it was not my irresistible self?" he teased.

"Oh, David," Emily moaned, covering her face again.

"Emily, *shona*," he said, taking a handkerchief from
inside his coat and pressing it into her hand. "Please,
throw yourself at me anytime you wish. I vow I do not
mind a jot. Well, you may want to refrain while we are
in a ballroom or in the middle of the Park, but other than
that . . ."

Just as he had hoped, Emily gave a choked laugh, and
then another and another. She mopped at her face with
his handkerchief, and said, "I am still sorry. I am not
usually quite so—so improper. But with everything that
has been happening . . ."

"It is really quite all right, Emily." David took her
hand in his and raised it to his lips. The thin kid tasted
faintly of the salt of her tears, which lingered on his
mouth. "You have been so very brave, shouldering your
family's burden all alone for years. But you are not alone
any longer, Boudicca, I promise you."

Emily smiled at him, a tiny, trusting ray of light that
broke across her tearstained face like the first beam of
hope in a dark, sinful world. She stepped close to him
again, slipping her hands into his. "Oh, David. Whatever
are we going to do about Sir Charles's wretched jewel?"

David was not entirely certain, as he had only the
glimmerings of a plan, but he would not tell Emily that.
Not after having reassured her that she could rely on him
and she was no longer alone. He squeezed her hands and
said, "There is nothing we can do tonight. There will be
guests in and out of that library for the rest of the ball,
gasping and sighing over the Star."

"Indeed."

"When is the stone to be transferred to the museum?"

"Next week, I believe. I am not sure. After those dreadful experts come in to inspect it." Emily's voice was quiet in the night, drained of her usual vitality. His Boudicca had obviously grown weary from fighting her Romans.

David longed to catch her in his arms, to cradle her against him until she slept and found her much-needed rest. But he could not. He did not have that right. The most he could do was tighten his hands on hers and hold her up. "That does not leave us much time. But we will find a way, Em."

"When, David? What can I do?"

"For now, you can come back into the ballroom and dance with me again, before we are missed. You can laugh at my ever so witty jokes and have a glass of champagne, and then we will eat supper with your brother and his wife. How does that sound? Can you do that for me?"

Emily laughed, and tucked his handkerchief away in her reticule. She smoothed back her hair and fluffed out her skirts. "Oh, yes. I think I can manage to do all that."

"Excellent! Then, shall we?" David held out his arm to her and they turned to stroll back inside the house, as if they were just returning from viewing the famous jewel.

And, after they danced and chatted and ate Lady Innis's fine lobster patties, David would go home to his silent house—and devise a scheme to break into Sir Charles's mansion and switch a false stone with a real one.

He was out of his mind, of course, to contemplate such a ridiculous scheme. But somehow he had never felt saner—or happier—in his life.

Chapter Eleven

*I*t was a gray day, with only a pale, watery light escaping from cracks in the low-hanging clouds. It had not rained, but it appeared as if it might at any moment. Emily did not mind the dismal weather, though, for it kept the crowds away from the Park. There were only birds, and a few hearty souls like herself in search of beneficial exercise, to watch her pace the footpath.

She wore her warmest walking dress of yellow wool, with an umbrella in her hands that she only half-remembered the butler giving her as she left the house. But she still shivered.

Where *was* David? He sent her a note this morning asking her to meet him on this very path, yet she did not see him. Every time a brisk stroller or a running child brushed past her, she started—but it was never David.

"Perhaps I am early," she muttered. She knew that she was. She had not been able to sleep at all once they returned home from the Innis ball. All she could do was lie in bed, her wide-open eyes staring up at the embroidered underside of the bed curtains, remembering the events of the night. *All* the events. But especially that kiss.

Oh, what had ever possessed her to grasp at David like that, pulling him to her like a Covent Garden doxy! She had never behaved so before; had never even been tempted. Perhaps it was the moonlight, or the champagne. Or maybe the power of the Star was so great that even a paste copy exuded some of its allure.

Or maybe, if she could only bring herself to admit it, she would know that it was all because she just wanted to kiss David. And that was it.

She would have burned up with shame if not for one thing. The way he reacted to her kiss.

He did not push her away or turn her aside with platitudes about their friendship. Instead, he caught her close to him and returned the kiss with heated ardor. Emily might just be a Society miss still on the Marriage Mart, but she had an outspoken artist for a sister-in-law and she had lived almost all her life on a farm, and she was aware of things other unmarried ladies her age were not. She knew that David had wanted her last night, in a physical way.

Maybe it was only the excitement of their schemes that inflamed their passions. Or the memory of their old friendship. Or maybe it was something entirely new, something terrifying and strange and grand.

She had finally become so confused last night, her mind dashing from one bizarre thought to another, that she finally had to do *something*. She got out of bed and made her way up to the attics to peer into Damien's old trunk and cases one more time. Perhaps there was something in there to tell her more about the Star, something she missed in her first hurried examination.

All she found, of course, was the detritus of a life ill-lived. His traveling trunk was full of old gaming markers and notes, used packs of cards, billets-doux (including some from one of their neighbors at Fair Oak, the married Lady Anders), a few love tokens of lace handkerchiefs and ribbon garters, a case containing dueling pistols, a few velvet coats and silk cravats. The only thing worth saving in there was a small portrait of their parents. There was certainly nothing about the Star of India. It appeared that the receipt she had found before, detailing the making of the paste copy, was all there was. The whereabouts of the genuine Star, it seemed, would always be a mystery.

Yet how could David's curse ever be broken if it was never found!

Don't be silly, Emily, she told herself, shutting the trunk on her brother's dusty remnants. *There are no such things as curses.*

She pushed the trunk back against the wall, where it made a dull, hollow thud. The day was already peeking pale gray above the horizon when she climbed back into her bed. There she fell into an uneasy sleep, to dream of floating jewels grasped at by many-armed gods.

Now, as she paced the footpath, she wished there *were* such things as curses. She would put one on Damien now, wherever he was, for bringing them all to this.

She stabbed at the ground beneath her feet with the tip of her umbrella, nearly catching her hem in the process. As she started to pull the umbrella up, she heard a high, sweet voice call out, "Lady Emily! Good afternoon, Lady Emily!"

She turned to see Anjali hurrying toward her, her pale lilac-colored cloak and bonnet like a bright springtime flower in the dismal day. Close behind her, of course, was her father. David.

He lifted his hat and smiled at her, and Emily's heart lifted like Signor Lunardi's balloon. Curses, jewels—what were they? Nothing, surely, beside such a smile.

She gave them a smile of her own, and went forward to greet them, leaving her umbrella lodged upright in the middle of the pathway.

"Lady Anjali! Lord Darlinghurst! How lovely to see you today." She held her hand out to David and he bowed over it. His lips touched and lingered on her gloved fingers, not just brushing the air above them.

So improper, Emily thought gleefully, and would have giggled if she was not far too old for such things.

But it was not nearly as improper as kissing on terraces at balls. She was practically a scarlet woman.

Anjali tugged at Emily's pelisse, pulling her away from such scandalous and delightful musings. She smiled down at the girl, who said, "My new governess already has a cold, Lady Emily, so I do not have to do any lessons today."

Emily laughed. "You are a very fortunate young lady, indeed, Lady Anjali, to have a whole day free of lessons. But how do you intend to fill such long hours?"

The girl's pink lips pouted. "Papa says the air is too chilly for eating ices, so I do not know."

Emily pretended to consider this carefully. "Yes, it is a bit chilly. But perhaps not too much so for tea and cakes?"

Anjali brightened, her green eyes widening. "Indeed, Lady Emily! Tea and cakes sounds just the thing." She turned a beseeching gaze up to her father.

David's lips twitched, but he crossed his arms sternly and said, "Tea *after* exercise. Why don't you run down to the end of the pathway and back?"

Anjali shook her head doubtfully. "My governess said a lady never runs."

"Well, then, walk as fast as you can. Lady Emily and I will follow."

Apparently, Anjali found walking fast to be acceptable, for she nodded and spun around to take off down the path. David offered his arm to Emily and they strolled in Anjali's wake, following the beacon of her lilac cloak.

"I am sorry, Emily—I had to bring her," David said ruefully. He pulled up her umbrella with his free hand as they passed, tucking it beneath his arm. "She becomes quite restive by teatime if she does not have some sort of activity."

"That is quite all right. I like Anjali." Emily slid him a sly glance from beneath her lashes. "But perhaps you felt the need to bring a chaperone along today, to prevent wild ladies from leaping on you and kissing you."

David laughed, his tone full of humor, though the glance he gave her in return smoldered with quite a different spark. "Shall we hide back behind that tree, and see what trouble we can devise before our little chaperone comes back?"

Emily looked at the tree in question. She knew he was only teasing her, but still there was that kernel of temptation . . .

But, no. She shook her head hard, trying to bring herself back to her senses. Scarlet woman, indeed. "I fear we have trouble of quite another sort to devise first," she said quietly.

David nodded, a somber veil dropping over his teasing gaze. "Quite right, and not much time in which to devise it. Do you happen to know of any social arrangements the Innises might have this week?"

Emily brightened a bit. *Here* was a question she knew the answer to. "Yes. Lady Innis told Georgina they would be attending Mrs. Chamberlain-Woods's musicale tonight. Georgina is friends with the Chamberlain-Woodses—they own two of her paintings. I was planning to attend myself."

"Tonight, eh?" David mused. He stared ahead of them, at where Anjali had paused to inspect some newly planted flowers, but he did not appear to truly see her. His gaze was narrowed, faraway. "That does not leave us much time. But we must make the most of it."

"The most of it?" Despite the chilled day, Emily's fingers warmed with excitement or trepidation. "David, do you have some sort of plan?"

"I may have, Emily."

"Well! What is it? Tell me!"

But he just shook his head. "In India, I have a cousin named Nikhil. In many ways he is very like your brother Damien, always in a scrape of one sort or another. My grandmother quite despairs of him, and he had to go live at our family's home in the mountains last year after a particularly troublesome incident."

Emily frowned at him. Whyever was he telling her tales of his cousin, when they needed to find a way to switch the two false Stars? "Every family has at least one troublesome member, I am sure."

"Indeed they do, and Nikhil is ours. One of ours, anyway." He smiled down at her, his gaze clearing. "Poor Em—you wonder why I am speaking of this cousin now. You see, when we were young, Nikhil devised quite an ingenious way to help his sister retrieve a necklace that she had foolishly lost. You already have the copy, so it should be perfect. We just need the right time."

"Papa!" Anjali was hurrying back toward them. "I walked to the very end. Now may I have tea?"

David leaned close to Emily and whispered, "Can you cry off the musicale tonight? Stay home by yourself?"

"Yes, of course."

"Wonderful. I will send a note later, telling you what we must do."

Before Emily could question these odd instructions, Anjali reached them, bobbing up and down on the toes of her little kid half-boots. Her cheeks were pink from the exercise. "May I have tea now, Papa?"

"Of course, *shona-moni*," David answered, taking her small hand in his while keeping Emily on his other arm. "I would be happy to escort the two loveliest ladies in Town to tea. Where shall we go? Gunter's again?"

"Oh, yes, please, Papa!"

As they turned back in the direction of the carriage path where David's phaeton waited, Emily was struck by the thought that anyone looking at them would think that for all the world they were a family. A couple and their little daughter.

A family of jewel-switchers and crazy relatives, mayhap, but a family nonetheless. Despite everything, that thought made Emily smile.

David watched Emily and Anjali as they sipped at their tea and compared the virtues of almond cakes versus lemon. They laughed, especially Anjali when Emily told her tales about their childhood at Fair Oak and Combe Lodge. He had never seen his shy girl with such a gleam in her eyes before, or her cheeks like rosy little apples as she giggled. He did not know what had affected such a transformation. He had feared, on the day they first met at Gunter's, that Anjali did not care overmuch for Emily and her boisterous family. He knew she was wary of finding herself suddenly with a "new mama," and had been ever since her ayah suggested such a thing in Calcutta. Yet here she was, laughing and smiling, asking Emily avid questions about what life in the English countryside was like.

No, he did not know what had happened. But he was glad that it had—whatever it was. He did not think he had ever been so content as he was at this very moment. The newly emerged sunlight falling from the windows shimmered on Emily's hair, turning it to pure spun gold. Even the curve of her cheek glistened like a gold-veined marble statue, as she leaned forward to whisper a jest in Anjali's ear. His daughter's laughter rang out as notes of music.

This was perfection, indeed, to have the two most beautiful ladies in the world sitting right beside him.

Their conversation was only for the two of them at the moment, but every once in a while Emily would refill David's teacup from the large pot at her elbow and give him a smile, or Anjali would reach out to touch his hand. The afternoon, which had begun in chill, gray confusion, was turned to a treasure just because they were all together.

The nonsense about the false Stars—the curse and the missing real one—receded, leaving only this beautiful, fleeting instant. All those things would have to be faced, and solved, very soon. But not just now.

He had always insisted to his grandmother that he had no desire to marry again, and he had thought that was true. And it *was* true that he wanted no more dutiful unions as he had with Rupasri, the sort of bond that brought no heartache and some contentment, but little joy. The joy he had seen between his own passionately attached parents. Deep down, under all his restlessness, his resolve to live in devotion to his family and daughter, he had wanted such a thing for himself. Longed for it, even, in his darkest heart of hearts. But he knew that it did not exist for people such as him—it belonged only to the chosen few.

Now he saw that he was wrong. Very wrong. Such limitless joy sat right in front of him.

It would probably not last for long. Emily had many suitors, far more eligible than the "Indian earl." And he had his own future to face, with or without the Star. But for now, for this afternoon, he held perfection in his hands.

And it was more beautiful than even the shining blue facets of the Star could hope to be.

Chapter Twelve

"*O*h, Em! You do seem pale." Georgina touched Emily's cheek gently with the back of her hand. Her dark red brows were furrowed in a concerned frown that even her fashionably low emerald bandeau could not hide. "And warm, too. I do hope you have not caught that fever that is going 'round. I knew you should not have gone walking this afternoon!"

Pricked by sharp, tiny needles of guilt over her deception, Emily reached up and caught Georgina's hand in her own. "I am sure I haven't caught a chill, Georgie. It is just a bit of a cold and will surely be gone by tomorrow. I only need a good night's sleep and some of Cook's beef tea."

Georgina seemed unconvinced. "Yes. Of course you must stay home and rest—there is no question of your attending the musicale. Perhaps I should stay here with you."

"No!" Emily cried out. Then, seeing the startled expression on Georgina's face, she carefully lowered her voice back to a hoarse whisper. "No, Georgie, I know how you have been looking forward to seeing Mrs. Chamberlain-Woods again and talking about art with her. Even Alex was saying—"

She was interrupted by a quick tap at her door, and

then her brother stuck his head in. Like Georgina, he was already dressed for the evening. Even the usually unruly waves of his dark hair were smoothed into a stylish Brutus.

"What is this? Did I hear my name?" he said, with a grin.

"Yes, I was just saying that Georgina *must* go to the musicale with you tonight," Emily answered. "Even you said you were looking forward to it, Alex, and you so seldom look forward to any social occasion."

"And I said I should stay home with Emily and keep an eye on her," Georgina said stubbornly. "Colds can be quite dangerous, particularly at this time of year."

"And I have said there is no need," insisted Emily. "I am just going to sleep, and I would feel wretched if I ruined everyone's evening."

"Nonsense, Em," Alex said. "I *do* enjoy some music when it is well played, as it generally is at Mrs. Chamberlain-Woods'. But I have no objection to a quiet evening at home, especially when you are ill, Buttercup. Perhaps we should both stay here with you."

"No, no," Emily protested. She could feel the whole situation sliding out of her grasp, like a wet length of rope, and she grasped at it desperately. If they did *not* leave, if they insisted on staying to play nursemaid to her, she would never be able to slip out of the house and meet David behind the mews. Even if she feigned sleep, they would be peeking in at her every half-hour, quite as if she was little Elizabeth Anne's age.

Relatives, as beloved as they were, could be exasperating at times.

"You two must go," she said, sliding back down her pillows and trying to appear exhausted and in need of solitude. "Mrs. Chamberlain-Woods is expecting you— you are no doubt to be the stars of her soiree. And there will be so many people wanting to speak with you about your paintings, Georgie."

Georgina wavered, glancing back at her husband, who shrugged. It was obvious that she wanted to go out and talk about her art, but she also wanted to stay home. "I am not sure . . ."

"Please," Emily begged. "I would not be able to rest easy if I knew I kept you from the musicale."

Georgina finally nodded. "Very well. We will go, then, but we will be back early. If you are still unwell, I shall send for the physician."

"All right, Georgie," Emily answered. After all, by the time they returned she would be sleeping peacefully. But if they *did* come home early, she and David would have to work quickly. "Go now, and have a fine time."

Georgina kissed Emily's brow, and hurried out in a flurry of emerald green silk. Alex also came in to kiss her. As his lips brushed her cheek, he whispered, "Enjoy your evening of peace and quiet, Em. I will keep her out for as long as I can."

Emily smiled up at him. "I love you, Alex. You are the best of brothers."

"And you are quite satisfactory as a sister."

"Even if I do not do my duty and settle on a suitable betrothal?"

"Em, you would be the best of sisters if you sat on the highest shelf for a hundred years. But I do not think it will come to that, do you? I did hear that you were having a fine afternoon at the British Museum the other day." He winked at her. "I expect a call from Lord Darlinghurst any day now."

Emily felt her face flame as brightly as the fire now crackling in her grate. She sank back under the bedclothes. "Good night, Alex!"

"Good night, Em."

From through the layers of linens, Emily heard the

door close and a brief clamor on the landing as Georgina and Alex put on their wraps and kissed their children good-night. After several minutes, there was the sound of the carriage clattering away down the street.

Alone at last!

Emily tossed back the blankets and sat up to peer at the ormolu clock on the mantel. It was very nearly time for her to meet David—and for them to commence whatever plan he had devised.

Her stomach was in such knots! She had never been as painfully proper as many of the young ladies with whom she made her curtsy to the queen three years ago—young ladies who were now married to painfully proper young men, with proper little babies in their nurseries. She had always thought nothing of talking about farming theories at a ball, or riding faster than was customary down Rotten Row, or even driving her sister-in-law's phaeton.

But she had never thought of sneaking out of the house in the night!

"There is a first time for everything, Emily," she told herself. "Boudicca never would have defeated the Romans if she was too chickenhearted to leave her chamber."

Besides—what would David think of her if she backed out now?

Newly resolved, Emily stood up and threw off her dressing gown. Beneath it, she wore clothes purloined from Damien's trunk—dark trousers and jacket over a soft cambric shirt, clothes he wore before dissipation made him bloated. Unlike Alex, who was tall and solidly muscled, Damien had always been shorter. His garments fit her well enough, and, when wearing her riding boots and with her pale hair concealed beneath a black hat, she could pass for a lad. From a distance. In faint light. Maybe.

Well, at least she could move more freely than in a gown and petticoats. It even felt rather nice, she thought, taking a few experimental strides around the room. She was tempted to jump about, just because she could, but there was no time. She had to meet David. She made a round-shaped log out of pillows beneath her bedclothes—that should fool her maid, if she peeked in on Emily. Becky would never dare to try to wake her. After slipping the new-made Star into her coat pocket and pulling on dark gloves, she slid out of her room and down the staircase, keeping carefully to the shadows.

The house was silent in the wake of the duke and duchess's departure, all the servants gone off to other, quieter duties. The only light was from one candelabrum in the foyer, making it easy—too easy?—for her to ease out of the front door. She crept around to the back garden and down to the mews, where David's note had instructed her to wait for him.

There appeared to be no one about. The area was deserted, silent beneath the moon and stars and the cool evening wind.

Why had she never noticed before how very silent the neighborhood was after dark? Emily shivered a bit, pulling her borrowed coat closer about her. She could almost be the only person in the whole city.

Yet even as she thought this, strong hands grasped her shoulders and spun her about. She opened her lips to scream—only to have the sound caught by a kiss.

A rather familiar-feeling kiss. And a familiar, delicious scent of sandalwood soap surrounded her. Her shriek turned into a soft moan, and she reached up to clasp David around the neck. His skin was hot through the thin leather of her gloves.

She was just beginning to lose herself in that embrace when he pulled away, grinning down at her in the moonlight. "I must say, Lady Emily, you look very fetching in breeches," he whispered in her ear.

His hands clasped her waist loosely as she leaned back to gaze up at him. He did not look like himself this evening—not like the David she had come to know, in his stylish coats and waistcoats, his perfectly tied cravats. Tonight, he wore a strange costume of loose black cotton trousers with a black tunic and long waistcoat. His hair was concealed by the folds of an exotic black turban. The gleam of a dagger could just be seen peering from the folds of his sash.

"You look quite—*fetching* yourself," she murmured. In truth, if he had a gold earring he could pass for a Barbary pirate.

He laughed, his teeth very white against all that black. "I am sure I look like a murderous *thuggee,* but none of my other clothes allow such concealment. Now, come—we have to hurry. The Innises have left for the musicale, but who knows how long they will be gone. We must be well away before they return."

"And before Georgina and Alex get back and insist on checking on my 'fever,'" Emily answered. She took his hand and followed him onto the back street heading away from the mews. "But what will we do once we get to the Innises' house?"

"My dear Boudicca, don't you know? We are going to break in and exchange one false Star for another. Isn't that what you've been secretly planning all along?"

Exchange one Star for the other. It sounded so very simple, Emily thought. It was just too bad that the execution did not prove to be so easy.

Execution. Now, *there* was a word. Surely that was what awaited them if they were caught in this scheme. She and David would be dead or in Australia. Anjali would be parentless and Georgina and Alex would be in despair.

But somehow, even with all that lurking above her, Emily felt alive with excitement. This was what she had been missing in all those ballrooms—missing ever since she and David last dashed across the summer fields at Fair Oak. She had been missing *life*.

If only she could have found it some other way, she mused wryly. In dancing, perhaps, or needlework, rather than breaking and entering. But they would not be caught. They would retrieve the paste Star and be gone from here.

She hoped.

David held her up to the library window at the Innis house, the balls of her feet balanced in his palms as she clung to the cold marble ledge with her gloved fingers. It was pitch black in there, a ray of errant moonlight just catching on the Star's glass case.

"Well?" David asked. "Can you see anything?" He did not even sound breathless from the effort of holding her aloft.

But Emily was not sure how long she could keep her balance. "Not a thing," she said, wobbling against the wall. "There is no one there. I can see the case, but I do not know if it still contains the Star."

"Is the window locked?"

The glass was an old-fashioned casement, unusual for a couple with such modern sensibilities as the Innises. Perhaps they had just not yet gotten around to replacing them, which made Emily's task easier. It was fairly simple to slip her thin wire between the panes and pop up the latch. She pushed open the window and answered, "Not anymore."

"Excellent." David hoisted her up even further, until she could pull herself up into the room. She tumbled to the floor with a deafening (to her ears, anyway) thud.

She lay there on the carpet, breath held as she listened for running feet and warning shouts. Nothing. Only silence.

Her breath left her lungs in a great *whoosh,* and she sat up and turned back toward the window. David's hands, also encased in dark leather gloves, appeared over the ledge and he hoisted himself up and over. Unlike her own ignominious fall, he landed lightly on his feet, like an Indian panther.

He clasped her hands and drew her off the carpet. "All right?" he whispered.

Emily nodded mutely, and turned in the direction of the glass case. As if in a trance, she moved across the library, dodging the dark shapes of chairs and desks and settees, with David close behind her.

This has to be a dream, she thought. Only David's hand in hers was real.

She stopped at the glass case, staring down at it. The Star *was* there, winking and sparkling up at her as if to mock her endeavors. She pressed her fingertips against the lock, suddenly realizing she had lost her wire.

"Looking for this?" David pressed the thin silver length into her palm. "You dropped it on the carpet."

Emily nodded, still silent. She turned the wire over in her hand, staring at the lock.

David's hands landed lightly at her waist, a warm, reassuring pressure. "You can do this, Boudicca."

Could she? It was true that once she had been quite shamefully proficient at picking locks. The blacksmith's apprentice at Fair Oak had taught her, and she had used the skill to break into Damien's strong box on his infrequent visits to Fair Oak. The few coins she took were never enough for him to notice, but they meant extra seed or a leak in the roof patched to Emily.

That was years ago, though. She had not tried it since.

She flexed her fingers and closed her eyes, trying to re-member just the right twist to make the lock open to her.

Steadied by David's nearness, she opened her eyes. Slowly, carefully, she slid the end of the wire into the tiny opening of the lock. She wiggled it around, trying to get it just under the mechanism. She only just felt it, when the library door gave an ominous click behind them. The faint echo of voices, a giggle, came to their ears in the darkness.

"Blast!" Emily cursed under her breath, yanking the wire out of the lock. They were caught!

"Come with me," David muttered. He pulled her across the room, and reached out to draw open the door of a cupboard. It appeared to be a section of a bookcase, tucked into a corner, but Emily saw it was in reality a tiny closet, with banks of crates pushed against the walls. She had only a fleeting glimpse before she threw herself inside, pressing back against the crates.

David slid in beside her, drawing the door shut just as candlelight spilled into the library—across the glass case where they had been standing only an instant before.

David left the closet door open a crack. Emily peered through it, her hand braced against the wall and a prayer of thanksgiving whispering in her mind.

A footman, his powdered wig askew and the jacket of his livery unbuttoned, appeared in the library, a branch of candles in his hand. He was closely followed by a girl in a housemaid's black dress and white apron. Her cap was gone, her light brown hair spilling over her shoulders.

Surely they have not come here to clean, Emily thought.

Her suspicions were quite confirmed when the foot-man placed the light down on the desk and drew the maid into his arms.

"Ooh, Johnny!" the girl squealed. "Yer ever so naughty."

The footman's hand slid down to her backside and squeezed, as he lowered his head to kiss her neck. "I can be even naughtier, Nell, you just watch!"

Nell squealed again, and dissolved into giggles as he proceeded to pull up her black skirts. "We'll be caught! And I'll be sacked for sure. So will you."

"And who's to catch us?" Johnny's voice was muffled in Nell's bosom. "Mr. Hudson and Mrs. Barnes are snoring away, and the master and mistress won't be home for hours. Plenty of time for a bit of fun, eh, Nell?"

Nell went into a paroxysm of laughter as Johnny tipped her back onto a settee. They were mercifully hidden from Emily's view by the furniture's brocade back, but she had to draw the closet door shut when she saw a pair of satin livery breeches and a white petticoat go sailing down to the carpet.

She was quite afraid she was going to have a fit of the giggles herself. She was shaking with the force of her nerves at having her lock-picking interrupted by such, er, lively activity, and hysterical laughter lurked just below the surface.

Fortunately, the cupboard was quite soundproof once closed, and she didn't have to hear any more of Nell's squeals. Unfortunately, all the light was also gone, and the heavy darkness pressed in upon her.

She took a deep breath—and inhaled David's sandalwood scent. Suddenly, the darkness did not seem quite so frightening. His presence was all around her, even though she could not see him, and she had a new fear— that he would touch her, and she would start gasping and giggling just like Nell.

"Are you all right, Em?" he murmured. His voice enfolded her, like a thick velvet coverlet, wrapping about her, drawing her in.

She felt one of the crates at the back of her knees, and sank down onto it, reaching up to pull off her hat and shake her hair free. "Yes. Quite all right." Her voice was hoarse and trembling, but hopefully he would put that down to her shock at being interrupted. Not at the sudden, drugging warmth that flooded her veins and made her weak and slow.

Through the door, a sudden high-pitched scream could be heard. "Ooh, Johnny! Yer ever so big. I don't think as how it'll fit."

Emily choked on a snicker, and pressed her hand to her mouth.

"Well," David drawled, laughter rich in his voice. "I do not suppose we will be free of this hidey-hole any time soon. Not if young Johnny's, er, attributes continue to be as alluring to Nell as they are at present."

Emily moved her hands to cover her whole face, forgetting for an instant that it was completely dark in their closet and he could not see her scarlet cheeks. "Um— no. I daresay you are right. You should sit down, David."

"Where?"

Here, and then I'll sit on your lap and pretend we are Johnny and Nell, Emily thought, then almost slapped herself for such unladylike thoughts. But she could not deny that, for a moment, she had wished she was a housemaid and not a duke's sister.

"There is a crate here beside mine," she said. "They seem quite solid."

She felt the brush of cool air as he moved to sit on the crate behind hers, the caress of muslin cloth on her wrist. She started as his hands found her in the dark, sliding around her waist to draw her close.

For a second, she held herself stiffly, unyielding, scared to let herself give in for fear of what she might do. But the darkness was seductive, urging her to give in to his touch, to let herself be free for just a while. Not as free as Nell, of course, but still . . .

She relaxed against David, letting her head drop back

to rest against his chest. She felt his chin nestle atop her head, his breath stirring her hair. Her hands slid atop his, and they sat there for a few moments, entwined, silent.

Then a long moan broke across the quiet, and Emily knew she had to speak, to cover the noise from Johnny and Nell, or she would go mad.

"David, talk to me," she urged.

"What would you like to talk about?" he said, his voice heavy and rich, like chocolate or sweet brandy.

"Oh—a tale of India. That would be appropriate, I think."

"You probably know more than I do, with all of the reading you have done."

"Of course I do not. You have lived there; you know the sights and scents and feelings. I can only imagine them." And that had been all she had done in her life— imagined. Until now. Here, in this dark little closet, she felt that all the mysteries of life, love, and death could be revealed to her. All in David's voice and touch.

After a long second of silence, he said, "I can tell you a tale of the Star. My grandmother told it to me when I was young."

"Oh, yes! Please tell me, David."

When he began his tale, his cultured London accent fell away, his tones became lilting and musical, touched with the spice and heaviness of his home. "There was once a prince who lived in ancient India. His name was Krishna, and he was an incarnation of the god Vishnu. He founded the city of Dwarka, on the coast of the land of Gujarat before it fell into the sea and disappeared. Some say it was the true Atlantis."

Emily closed her eyes, and she could see it, the shining city by the sea. It made everything—the darkness, the breaking and entering, Nell and Johnny—recede away.

David went on. "In Dwarka lived a man named Sat-

trajit who worshipped Surya—the sun. One day, while
Sattrajit was walking on the shore, Surya appeared before him and rewarded his devotion with a jewel. This
jewel, as brilliant as the sea itself, brought great pros-
perity to the city, and kept away all evil—even thieves
and famine and plague."

"The Star?"

"Perhaps. But Sattrajit feared that Krishna would demand the jewel, so he gave it to his brother Prasena. But,
you see, the jewel would only do good for the good
man—and bad for the bad man."

"And Prasena was bad?"

"Indeed. He went out hunting, and was killed by the
king of bears, who took the jewel to a cave."

Emily was fascinated. "Then what happened?"

"When people found Prasena dead, they said that Krishna killed him for the stone. To prove his innocence,
Krishna found the king of bears in his cave and fought
him for twenty-one days, until the bear gave up the
jewel. When Krishna returned with it, people believed he
was innocent after all. Then he gave it away to a virtuous maiden—and eventually it ended up in a great temple."

His voice stilled. Emily's eyes opened, and she was
half-surprised to find herself still in the dark closet and
not in the cave of the king of bears. "Was that all?"

David gave a low, rumbling laugh. "Of course not.
Such tales go on forever in India. The stone passes from
hand to hand, some worthy, many not. Krishna could not
keep it himself, you see, because he had sixteen thousand wives, and that was hardly virtuous."

Emily laughed. "Sixteen thousand!"

"Yes. One can only hope that they were all as happy
as Nell out there."

Emily laughed even harder, so hard that she was

afraid she could never stop. She muffled the sound behind her hand.

"It is said," David continued, his clasp on her tightening, "that whoever possesses the jewel moves like the sun, wearing a garland of light."

"Then it should be easy to find the Star! We need only look for the person wearing a garland of light."

David's voice, so full of laughter only a moment before, was suddenly very serious. "I would say that was you, Emily. You are the garland of light. My *shona*—my gold."

Emily's own laughter died away. She turned in his arms, staring up at him. She could not see his face—she could only feel him, sense him. "Why did you come back from India after all these years?"

"I thought it was to see my father's home again, to take my daughter away from people scheming to marry her off when she is just a child. And I do want those things. But I think that the truth is—I came back to find you again."

Emily's throat was thick with unshed tears; her eyes itched with them. This was frightening. More frightening than picking that lock. More frightening than being left alone to tend Fair Oak and her mother. More frightening than anything ever. She could feel pieces of the cocoon with which she had surrounded herself for years chipping and falling away, leaving her naked and vulnerable.

But surely David was worth it. She had been waiting for him since she was a child—since before she was born, even. She was meant for him, and he for her.

But how could something that was meant to be be so scary?

Be brave, she urged herself. It was never more important than now. She leaned against him, her lips finding his in the darkness. They met and clung, their breath mingled, and it was perfect—like a garland of light. His hands drew her across his lap, and she gasped in purest pleasure. This was where she belonged.

When they parted, she buried her face against the curve of his throat. "I am glad you came back, whatever the reason," she whispered. "For, if you had not, I would have had to go to India myself to find you."

He held her close, their hearts beating together. "*Ami tomake bhalobashi,*" he said, kissing her hair, her temple, her cheek.

Emily did not ask what that meant—she already knew, in her heart. And her heart whispered back in kind, *I love you.*

It could have been only moments later, or hours, when Emily felt David stir. Only then did she notice that Johnny and Nell were silent, the thin line of light from their candles gone from beneath the door.

Apparently, the amorous pair had concluded their business and gone back to their duties—which meant that Sir Charles and Lady Innis must surely be returning home very soon.

Emily was still sitting with her head resting on David's shoulder. They had not spoken for a long while, just sat together in sweet silence, surrounded by the echoes of their breathing and heartbeats.

She could have stayed like that forever, were it not for the fact that they were illegally in someone else's home, hiding out in a tiny library closet. They had very nearly been caught breaking into the case, and they were not out of danger yet. The jewels still had to be switched, and she had to be home in her bed before Alex and Georgina returned.

But still, despite all of that, this had been a lovely night—one she would not have traded for anything.

She lifted her head from David's shoulder, staring at

the absence of light from beneath the door. "It seems our friends Johnny and Nell have departed," she murmured.

"Indeed it does," David answered. She felt him smooth her hair back from her face, his touch tender. "We should conclude our errand before the owners of the house return. Unless we could take a page from Johnny and Nell's book, and convince them we are just a pair of vagabonds searching for a likely spot for a tryst."

Emily gave a choked giggle. "I somehow doubt that would work! They do know us, you remember, though perhaps not in our current guises."

"Ah, well. No doubt you are right. It might have been amusing to try, though." David gently moved her aside, and she sensed him standing up in the gloom. There was a soft click, and the closet door opened, letting in the glow of moonlight.

"It appears we are alone," he whispered. "Come, my Boudicca, we should complete our errand and depart."

Emily nodded, and reached out to take his hand. His fingers entwined with hers, warm and reassuring even through their gloves. He led her into the library, which suddenly seemed vast after their tiny hiding place, to the waiting glass case.

Amazingly, it looked just the same as it had before they were so rudely interrupted. Somehow, she expected the whole world to have changed, just because her own heart was transformed.

She took out the wire again and fit it back into the lock. It had bent when she stuck it into her pocket, though, and would not easily maneuver into place. Emily bit her lip, twisting at it with her fingertips. In the corner, a tall clock tolled the hour in stentorian tones. She started, the wire slipping through her fingers.

Midnight, she thought, as the last bell echoed away. *The witching hour. How very appropriate.*

"It is just the clock, Em," David said reassuringly. "Everything is fine."

"Yes," she answered. She slid the wire in once again, and this time she felt the tiny locking mechanism pop free. She pulled open the case and reached in to clasp the paste Star, her breath suspended. She half-expected bells and whistles to explode in the room, bringing the entire household at a run. She quickly placed the stone securely inside her coat.

But there was nothing. Only the thick silence of the night. Swiftly, her hands trembling, she took out Mr. Jervis's sapphire and placed it carefully on the satin-swathed platform. It twinkled there in a bar of starlight.

Perfect. She closed up the case and clicked the lock back into place.

"It is done," she whispered.

"Then, let us depart." David clasped her arm and led her toward the half-open window. They were only a few feet away when there was a sudden burst of noise from outside the library.

"I trust your evening was enjoyable, sir," a man said, in a butler's deep, mannered tones. At least it was not young Johnny.

Emily froze, as if by standing very, very still she could disappear.

"It was, until that Miss Freeman insisted on playing the harp, Hudson," Sir Charles Innis replied. "I vow I heard all the dogs on the street howling."

"Oh, my dear, it was not that bad," chided Lady Innis, with the crisp rustle of satin, as if she was shedding her evening cloak. "She had great—enthusiasm for the music."

"Enthusiasm! Is that what they are calling it now?"

"I enjoyed it. Are you going to retire now, my dear?"

"No, no, Alice. You go on. I want to finish some paperwork in the library first."

Lady Innis laughed. "You mean you want to stare at the Star one more time."

David tugged at Emily's arm, pulling her toward the window. She bumped into a chair, and felt the wire fall from her hand onto the carpet. There was no time to retrieve it, though—the knob of the library door was turning.

David shoved open the window, and lifted Emily up to drop her unceremoniously out of it.

"Oof!" she gasped, as she landed in an untidy heap on the grass. She crawled beneath a nearby bush just as David slid out of the casement behind her, as lithe as the jungle cat she had imagined him earlier. He landed silently on the balls of his feet, and ducked down to join her under the bush just as a bellow echoed from the library.

"An open window!" Sir Charles shouted. "How often must I tell those dratted servants how bad the night air is for my artifacts? I won't allow them in my library in the future!"

The window slammed shut. Emily feared she would again burst into hysterical laughter, and lowered her head to the grass to stifle it. "It is a very good thing Sir Charles does not know what else his servants are up to in the library."

"I should say not," David muttered, laughter at the edges of his words. "Come, we need to be away from here."

Clasping hands, they crawled from beneath the sheltering bush and dashed across the small garden. Emily glanced back as David boosted her over the wall. Every window of the library blazed with light now, but there was no alarm raised. The only sound was that of night birds in their trees, and her own labored breathing. It had been years since she ran so freely over the countryside, and this dash through the city streets made her limbs ache. She paused at the edge of her own street to press her hand to her side, trying to calm her pounding heart.

David, she noticed, appeared as if he had only been out for a summer stroll. He stopped beside her, his own breath only slightly quickened.

Emily leaned against a fence rail that sheltered the servants' entrance many feet below. She studied David in the light of the waning moon and stars. He seemed an exotic, nighttime mirage, dark and remote, like the god who coveted the jewel and fought a bear for it. Had he really held her in his arms, and whispered such achingly sweet words? Words she had waited a lifetime to hear?

He reached up and pulled the turban from his head, ruffling his black hair. It fell over his brow like satin commas, and Emily could not help herself—she reached up to sweep them back, the strands catching at her fingers like stray silk.

He grinned down at her. "We did it, Em. It is finished."

She smiled doubtfully. Yes, it was finished. She had what she wanted. Her family was safe. But was his?

The true Star of India was still out there somewhere.

"Yes, we did it!" she said, some of the cold doubt falling away in a sudden rush of exhilaration. "I can scarce believe it." She threw her arms around him, and felt him lift her from her feet. He twirled her around until the night sky tilted tipsily above her, and she laughed, giddy with delight. "I could not have done it without you."

"It was glorious fun, Em," he answered, lowering her slowly to her feet. "I haven't felt like that since we were children."

"Well, we shall just have to find other sources of fun, since I do not think I could survive burgling every night. Not to mention running through the London streets!" She paused, and reached up to gently cradle his cheek in her palm. "I have to admit, though—it *was* glorious. I will always remember it."

David turned his head to press a lingering kiss into her hand. "So will I. But I should be going home now, and you should find your bed before your brother and his wife return."

Alex and Georgina! How could she have ever forgotten them? They would be home at any moment, and expected to find her ill in her chamber. Georgina was daring, but not even she would understand midnight thievery.

"Of course," she said, and went up on tiptoe to kiss his cheek. "Shall we meet again soon? I confess I am quite eager to hear more of your cousin's adventure with that stolen necklace—the one that inspired our little plan tonight."

"Oh, yes. Nikhil's necklace." David smiled at her, and slowly backed away from her embrace. "I would be happy to tell you of it one day. And I am sure we will meet again. Good night, Emily."

With that, he melted into the shadows, leaving Emily alone. She suddenly noticed how chill the evening air had become; it danced over her neck and arms, raising goosebumps. She stood there for a long moment, staring at the spot where David had stood. But she could still sense his gaze, watching her from the darkness.

Only the rattle of carriage wheels broke her strange reverie. She glanced back over her shoulder to see that it was her brother's equipage, returned from the musicale, coming inexorably toward her.

"Blast!" Emily cursed. How could she have gotten through all the other dangers of the evening, only to be caught by her own silly daydreaming? She ducked her head and ran as fast as she could along behind the houses. Praying that she would not run into any more stray servants, she dashed up the back stairs, pulling off her hat and coat as she went.

She scarcely had time to thrust her borrowed clothes beneath the bed, pull on her dressing gown, and dive beneath the bedclothes. She squeezed her eyes shut and struggled to control her breathing. Her door clicked open softly, and she heard Georgina whisper, "She is asleep. Poor Emily! Such a grand party she missed."

Emily smiled secretly into her pillow. A grand party, indeed—if only they knew.

Chapter Thirteen

"*I* am glad you are feeling more the thing this morning, Emily," Georgina said, as she passed a cup of chocolate across the breakfast table to Emily. "It is too bad you missed the musicale last night, but now you can go with me to the mantua-maker this afternoon. There is a new peach-colored muslin there I think you will like."

"I was also sorry to miss the musicale," Emily answered. She took the cup, and reached for the rack of toast, despite the fact that she had already eaten three slices. Somehow, she had an uncommon appetite this morning. "I always thoroughly enjoy seeing Mrs. Chamberlain-Woods."

"Do not be too sorry, Em," Alex said, turning the page of his newspaper. "Miss Freeman was there with her dreaded harp."

Emily laughed. "Oh, yes! I heard that all the dogs on the street commenced howling when she . . ." She broke off, suddenly recalling where exactly she had heard that little snippet. From Sir Charles Innis, while she hid in his library.

Georgina gave her a puzzled glance. "Where did you hear such a thing, Emily? The musicale only occurred last night, surely it is too early for such gossip to be spreading."

"I—must have read it. In one of the papers. They are so quick with tittle-tattle, you know." She tapped at the paper folded up beside her plate.

"Oh, that one!" Georgina said, with a dismissive little wave of her hand. "It is full of nothing but scurrilous gossip. I am sure no dogs howled at all during Miss Freeman's, er, most lovely performance. Don't you agree, Alex darling?"

"Oh, indeed, my dear," Alex said. "I do believe it was a cat that was howling."

"Oh, you!" Georgina cried, laughing as she swatted playfully at her husband's arm. "Very well, so Miss Freeman's performance does not seem to improve no matter how many years she practices or how many music masters her father hires. But the rest of the performances were quite fine—there was even the soprano Madame Cascatti from Drury Lane. Poor Em—how tiresome it must have been to spend the whole night at home feeling miserable!"

"Yes," Emily murmured, concentrating very hard on her plate of eggs and kippers and toast. "Tiresome indeed."

"Here is an article you might find interesting, Em," Alex said. "Gemological scholars are coming today to inspect the Star of India at the home of Sir Charles Innis, and by tomorrow it will be on its way to the Mercer Museum."

Emily's gaze snapped up from her eggs. "Indeed? Today? That is quite—sudden." And quite fortunate that she had taken care of matters last night and not tarried.

"Yes, but of course the museum is very eager to take possession. It should herald many new donations to their coffers." Alex folded the newspaper and tucked it beneath his plate. "It is too bad that Damien lost the stone to Innis so long ago, and that we were unable to fulfill our obligation to Lord Darlinghurst. I did try to purchase it back from Innis, but he was insistent that it go to the museum. And, I suppose, it is truly the best place for it."

Emily stared at her brother, startled and incredulous. "You *knew* the story of the Star's loss, Alex? About how foolish Damien was?"

"Of course. Mother told me, not long after I returned home from Spain. She did not know then who exactly had bought the Star, though, and did not find out until years later. It is a damnable thing, truly." He frowned fiercely down at the paper. "I have tried to set all of Damien's wrongs right, but that one will never be remedied."

"Yes," Emily whispered. "I know exactly what you mean."

"Oh, Em." Alex reached out to squeeze her hand, giving her a rueful smile. "You have been hurt more than anyone by our brother's vices. You must not worry about it any longer. It is in the past."

"It *is* a most unfortunate situation," Georgina said. "But I think Lord Darlinghurst would rather have *another* jewel from our family. One far more valuable than any sapphire could ever be."

Alex grinned. "I think you are absolutely right, darling."

Emily suddenly felt a bit queasy. All of the chocolate, toast, and eggs she had consumed sat uneasily in her stomach with all this talk of jewels and families, and their two stares on her. "I—hm. Excuse me, please, Alex, Georgie."

"Are you quite all right, Emily?" Georgina asked in a concerned tone. "Is your fever returning?"

"No, I am well. I just must— Excuse me." Emily pushed herself back from the table and hurried out of the breakfast room.

"Oh, Alex, you should not have teased her so about

Lord Darlinghurst," she heard Georgina chide her brother.

"I, tease her? What about you, my lady wife? You are constantly asking her about her suitors!"

Emily shook her head, and turned to go up the staircase to her own chamber. As she placed her foot on the first step, she heard the butler call, "Lady Emily. This package just came for you."

"Thank you, Greene," Emily said, accepting the small, flat box wrapped in brightly striped paper.

She turned it over in her hand, puzzled. It did not rattle or rustle, and she was not expecting any deliveries today. She sometimes received flowers from various suitors, of course, but that was all. And this was obviously not flowers.

Emily tucked the box beneath her arm and carried it up to her bedroom where she could open it in private. She climbed up onto the high bed and carefully folded back the paper to find a plain wooden case.

It did not appear dangerous in any way, but she was still a bit jumpy after all the excitement of the night before. With a little laugh at herself, she opened the top—and her laughter faded away.

There, nestled on dark red velvet, were the necklace and earrings she had traded for the new Star at Mr. Jervis's shop. The delicate web of pearls and diamonds that had been Alex and Georgina's gift to her on her last birthday twinkled. It had pained her so to give them up, but she had pushed that down deep under necessity—as she had been doing for years. Seeing them there now, returned to her, she felt a great lump rise in her throat.

Emily took them out of the box, spreading their sparkle across the satin counterpane. As she fastened the earrings to her lobes, she saw the glint of something else in the case. She reached in and pulled out the wire she had dropped the night before. Wrapped about its thin length, tied with a small red ribbon, was a piece of paper.

Grinning helplessly, Emily pulled it off and smoothed it across her lap to read.

My dear Boudicca—I hope you never have need of this little wire again, but just in case (for one never knows what awaits in life) I am returning it to you. I am also returning something else which I believe belongs to you. It took a great deal of time to persuade Mr. Jervis to show me which pieces were yours, but it will be worth it to see them around your neck and in your ears when next we dance at a ball.

Perhaps you would care to join Anjali and myself at Astley's Amphitheatre next week? Or, if elephants and acrobats hold no excitement for you, tea again.

Sincerely, your friend, David Huntington

Emily pressed her hand to her mouth. So, last night had not been some sort of dream. His caresses, his sweet words, were real and true. As real as these jewels that sparkled before her.

If only she had a gift half so fine to give him in return.

There was a quick knock at the door, and Emily hastily thrust the note and wire under a cushion. "Come in," she called.

Georgina stuck her head into the room. "I just wanted to look in on you, Emily dear, to be sure you are not ill again."

Emily smiled at her. "I am well, truly, Georgie."

"Yes, I can see that. You have not smiled so in days." She came into the chamber to perch on the edge of the bed beside Emily. "Oh, I see your birthday jewels are back from being cleaned!"

Cleaned? Oh, yes—now Emily remembered her ear-lier deception about the gems' disappearance. "They just arrived."

"Hm. They do look beautiful, I must say. So sparkling and fresh. Perhaps I should have my emeralds cleaned. But, really, I just wanted to tell you, Emily, that . . ."

Her words were suddenly drowned out by a tumult in the corridor. There was a strange banging noise, and raised voices. Georgina hurried to the door, with Emily close behind.

A procession of footmen were making their way to the staircase, laden with baskets and cases. One of them had just run into the wall with the edge of a trunk, leaving streaks of dust on the silk wallpaper.

Emily recognized that trunk—she had taken clothes out of it just the day before. It was Damien's. But where was it going?

"What is amiss, Greene?" Georgina asked the butler, who was interrupted in the middle of a brisk scold to the young footman.

"I beg your pardon, Your Grace," he said. "We were just taking away the cases, as you instructed, when Timothy lost control of the trunk. I fear the trunk was far too wide for the servants' staircase, or we should never have disturbed you, Your Grace."

"I am ever so sorry, Your Grace," young Timothy stammered. "But this here trunk isn't as heavy as it appears, and I used too much force when I hefted it. It's very light for its size."

"Quite all right," Georgina said reassuringly. "Carry on, please, but carefully."

"What is happening, Georgie?" Emily asked, staring after the vanishing luggage.

"Nothing to worry about, Em. It is just that all this fuss about the Star reminded me of all the things your late brother left in the attics. And Greene complained of some strange noises there, as if mice had gotten in amongst all the clutter. We do not want mice, or Damien's belongings, in our lives any longer, so I instructed Greene to dispose of them."

"Yes," Emily muttered. "Quite right, Georgie. No mice." She was distracted by the way Timothy the footman was able to carry the large trunk on one shoulder. *Isn't as heavy as it appears*—she suddenly remembered the hollow thud the trunk had made as she pushed it back against the wall.

"Wait!" she cried out. "Bring the trunk back. Put it here in my chamber."

"Emily," Georgina protested. "You do not want that dusty thing in your room. It will just bring up old memories."

"Do not worry, Georgie," Emily reassured her. "I just want to go through it, then you may toss it out to your heart's content."

Georgina gave her a worried glance. "Emily," she said quietly. "I do not think it is such a fine idea for you to recall—well, such old occurrences. It is best to let such things go, to look only to the future. Believe me, I know this. There is much in my own past I have had to forget."

"Georgina, I know you only care about me and want to spare me any pain, and I love you for it. But I promise I only want to glance through those things before you send them away. Who knows, there may be something there we would regret throwing out! And I feel no pain over Damien's doings now. I feel only pity for him."

Georgina still did not seem happy about it, but she nodded, and called out, "Bring that trunk back here for Lady Emily to see. She will send for you when she is ready for you to carry it away."

"Thank you, Georgie," Emily whispered. "This will not take me very long."

"I hope not. I am going to the nursery to look in on

Elizabeth Anne and Sebastian. Perhaps then we can go to the mantua-maker?"

"Of course." Emily watched Georgina turn away, then instructed the footman to place the old trunk near the windows. Only when the door closed behind the servants and she was alone again did Emily kneel beside it and raise the lid.

Tiny dust motes rose up, dancing in the sunlight, and she inhaled the old scents of the pine soap Damien used and stale tobacco and brandy. As she stared down at the jumble of clothes and papers, the garments she had rifled and pilfered only yesterday, she realized with a small shock that her words to Georgina were actually true. She felt no pain any longer when she thought of Damien and all the troubles he had caused. She had carried her anger around for years, like a small, hard stone in her heart. It weighed her down, causing such bitterness and confusion that she could not even fully appreciate all the fine things that were in her life.

But last night, in David's arms in the rich darkness, that stone just dropped away, and her heart could take wing again. Just as it had when she was a child and could dance barefoot in the country grass. The lonely years were behind her. Damien was dead, and she could only feel sorry for him. He had never, *could* never, have seen the truly valuable things in life as she did now. Jewels, money, position—they were as nothing. Love and family were all.

She loved David, and she wanted to give him a token of that passion, of all he meant to her. If her suspicions were correct, the perfect "token" might be right before her. It had always been here. She was just too blind to see it.

She had been blind to many things for a very long time. Now, there could only be light and truth.

Emily pulled the clothes out of the trunk, the papers

and old, string-tied bundles of love letters. She piled them up on her carpet, the detritus of a life ill-spent. As she leaned over to peer into the shadowed depths, she saw she had indeed been right—the interior of the trunk was far smaller than the exterior.

The dark blue velvet was old and worn, shredded in several spots. Emily dug her finger beneath one of the holes and pulled it away. Once the cloth was removed, she saw a thin, cheap wooden false bottom.

"Damien," she murmured. "You old cheat." Using a stout letter opener from her escritoire, she wedged up the board—and gave a satisfied sigh.

She *was* right. There, in a narrow compartment at the bottom of the trunk, was a treasure. A small treasure, to be sure, but far more than she would have imagined her reprobate brother could hold onto. A leather purse clinked with gold coins. A little box held loose, snow white pearls. In a velvet case, she found her mother's diamond tiara, a piece that had vanished from Fair Oak many years ago.

Emily smiled, imagining her mother's joy when it was presented back to her.

As she put the tiara aside, her gaze fell on another pouch, tucked in the darkest corner. Holding her breath, feeling her heart pound like thunder in her breast, she grasped the pouch and pulled it out of the trunk.

The Star of India spilled out onto her palm, casting a twilight blue glow over the white fabric of her skirt. *This* was the real Star—she knew it as well as she knew her own name. It was warm on her skin, the facets seeming to whisper and murmur as she turned it over on her palm. It vibrated with a magic all its own.

The Star was rougher cut than the paste copy and Mr. Jervis's excellent sapphire. The whiteness of the surrounding diamonds was muted, and the gold setting was dull. But she had never seen anything lovelier—except for David's dark eyes, and the sheen of his daughter's black hair.

She was not a superstitious person. But still, she had only one thought as she folded her fingers tightly over the true Star. *Safe*. They were all safe now.

The jewel would soon be back in the hands where it belonged, and it could never hurt anyone ever again. Emily slammed the lid of the trunk down, catching the past in its dark, dusty depths.

Chapter Fourteen

*D*avid stared up at the façade of the Kentons' grand townhouse before he reached for the polished brass door knocker. The building was quiet in the late morning light, seeming deserted except for the clatter of coal from the servants' entrance. It was full early for calls— but David had never proposed to a lady before, and found himself impatient to commence. He knew that he could expect a favorable answer from Emily herself. But what about her ducal brother? What would he say to the "Indian earl" paying court to his sister?

He raised the knocker and brought it down with a hollow, purposeful thud. The door handle clicked, and, much to his surprise, he was faced not with a stern butler but with Emily herself. Her smile glowed with a radiance he had never seen; summer sunshine itself poured forth from her pale curls and pink cheeks.

"David!" she gasped, clutching his hands in hers and pulling him into the foyer. As soon as the door shut behind them, she looped her arms about his neck and went up on tiptoe to kiss him. "I have missed you so much."

He laughed, tightening his clasp to hold her against him. "We only parted a few hours ago. You did not have time to miss me, *shona*." Of course, he had missed her, as well, though he would not say it aloud. It seemed ab-

surd to miss someone seen only the night before. But
there it was. Something had happened while they were
locked in the close darkness of that closet. Something
rare and profound. A destiny fulfilled at last.

If there *was* a curse on his family, as his grandmother
believed, surely Emily's kiss had broken it. He felt free,
and as young as the day when he first met Emily Kenton
so very long ago.

"Nevertheless, it has been too long." She kissed his
nose and his chin, giggling like a delighted schoolgirl. "I
do think that you should—"

A discreet cough behind Emily interrupted her. She
swung around, her arms still around David's neck.

"Oh. Hello, Alex dear," she said, her voice just the
slightest bit more subdued.

David untangled her arms and turned toward her
brother, holding her hands in his. The duke's face was utterly unreadable as he observed the scene his sister was
creating in his own foyer. There was no frown, no
smile—just the blank marble of a Roman statue.

"Good morning, Your Grace," David said, with a polite bow. "I hope it is not too early for a—business call."

"Certainly not," was the reply, made in coolly meas-
ured tones. "Depending what that business is. I have been
expecting you, Lord Darlinghurst. Perhaps you would
care to step into the library? If you will excuse us, Emily."

Emily nodded, her curls bobbing. As she stepped back,
she whispered, "After you speak to Alex, David, meet me
in the drawing room. I have something to give you."

David raised her fingers to his lips for a quick kiss.
Something to give him, eh? That sounded promising, indeed.

Emily paced the length of the drawing room, sweeping her fingertips over the tops of the marble and gilt pier
tables as she went. She did not see the garden out of the

tall windows, or the paintings on the walls or the ornaments scattered on the tables. She just turned at the end
of the room and paced back.

David was spending an inordinate amount of time in
the library with Alex. Much longer than it should take.
Was there a problem of some sort? What was happening
in there? She wished she dared go eavesdrop at the door.
She also wished Georgina was here to reassure her, but
her sister-in-law was upstairs dressing to go to the mantua-maker. Even Elizabeth Anne and Sebastian were occupied with lessons and napping. Emily was quite on her
own.

Or perhaps not entirely on her own. She opened the
little pouch she held tucked in her hand and peered down
at the Star's flash of blue fire.

Had it truly been only a few days ago that she was so
overcome with a strange, restless melancholy she could
not explain? When she listened to Georgina express worries about her failure to find a suitable match? That
seemed so far away now—part of another life, another
Emily. Her heart was still now, bathed in the same blue
light of serene happiness and belonging she saw in the
Star. It was David who made that happiness. David who
showed her in so many ways—especially in the way he
so gamely went along with her wild schemes—that they
belonged together. Had always belonged together.

He made her laugh; he made her life seem merry
again, when she thought she had lost the capacity for
such untainted joy long ago. She saw the future now, not
as a vista of the same meaningless balls, routs, and polite conversations and cruel witticisms, but as a series of
endless possibilities. She and David and Anjali—and
whoever might choose to come along later—would be a
true family.

A tiny, nervous flutter ached deep in her belly, and
Emily pressed her hand hard against it. All that would

happen only if Alex gave David his blessing. But why would he not? He and Georgina had been wanting her to wed for the longest time!

Yet they *had* been in the library for an hour at least. Surely more than that—hours and hours! Were she and David going to be forced to make a dash for Gretna Green?

Curling her fingers tightly around the Star's pouch, Emily paused before one of the windows to stare out at the garden. Elizabeth Anne was there now, walking with her nursemaid, the sun turning her long red curls to molten fire. She waved up at her aunt, beaming.

Her niece's smile lifted Emily's spirits again. As she waved back, she heard the drawing room door open behind her, and she spun around to see David there. For an instant, his face seemed so solemn and serious that her heart sank once more. Then, he grinned—and the whole room, the whole world, flooded with light.

Emily dashed into his arms, and he lifted her off her feet, laughing.

"Well?" she demanded impatiently. After all, she had waited for this very moment since she was a little girl.

David just smiled. "Lady Emily Kenton, will you do me the great honor of becoming my wife?"

"Yes!" Emily cried, and kissed him. Once, twice, three times.

David chuckled through their kisses, the sound vibrating warmly through her. "Now, Em, I had an entire speech planned about how I intend to spend the rest of my life making you happy. I was going to go down on one knee and declare my undying devotion. Anjali has assured me, most solemnly, that ladies adore it when a gentleman goes down on one knee to propose."

"I do not need declarations of undying anything," Emily said stoutly. "You more than proved your devotion by hiding in that cupboard with me last night, when any other man would have sent me directly to Bedlam. All I need, David—all I have ever needed—is you."

"Just as I need you." Their lips met again in a kiss of such tenderness that it seemed eternal, made of all the love that had come before them—David's parents, her parents, Alex and Georgina—and all the love that would go on long after they were gone. "I love you, my brave Boudicca."

"And I love you. *Ami tomake bhalobashi.*"

"Ami tomake bhalobashi."

Emily stepped back from his enticing kisses, taking one of his hands between both of hers. "I have something for you, David. An early wedding gift of sorts."

"I thought the bridegroom was meant to give the bride a present, not the other way around."

Emily shook her head. "You gave me back my necklace and earrings, my precious birthday gift. That is all the present I need. And what I have to give you is not so much a gift—it is not really mine to give. It is more of a return. A putting to rights."

David's brow creased in puzzlement. "What do you mean?"

Emily removed the Star of India from its pouch and placed it carefully into his hand. "I believe this belongs to you."

David stared down at the jewel, turning it over so that its facets again flashed. It sparkled even more radiantly than before, as if rejoicing in its freedom after such a long confinement. As if it rejoiced at being home.

But David was silent for several long moments—so silent Emily could almost vow she heard her own heart pounding.

He raised his gaze to hers, the dark depths of his eyes unreadable. "Where did you get this? How long have you had it?" His voice was quiet, but thrummed with a barely leashed power.

"Only since this morning," Emily hurried to explain. "Georgina was tossing out some of Damien's old things, and I realized that there was something not quite right about one of his trunks. It was hidden in a false bottom. He had never sold it at all." Her own gaze dropped to the Star. It was so very lovely, resting there on David's hand. But was there truly a malevolence hidden in its glorious depths? "I vow to you, David, I did not know it was there! I would never have gone to the lengths I did, had I known. I just thought—"

Her words escaped her as she was suddenly caught in a tight embrace, David's arms around her, holding her as if he would never let her go.

"Em," he muttered roughly. "He never deserved such a sister as you. *I* do not deserve such a wife as you. My darling, clever Boudicca."

Emily laughed from sheer relief and utter joy. All was right—she and David *would* marry, and the Star was in its proper place. "So, we shall not be cursed, now that the Star is back? The cows and chickens at Combe Lodge won't wither away, and Anjali won't grow up to hate us for being dreadful parents and elope with her dancing master?"

David threw back his head and laughed. "No, Em. I think any curse was lifted the moment I saw you standing there in that ballroom. We are together again. No ill can come to us. My grandmother always quotes an old proverb which says that a stick floats, as does a swimmer. It is the swimmer that the sea loves to bear, for he has sensed its depths."

"Then I just have one question for you."

"And what might that be?"

Emily smiled at him. "*How soon* can we be married?"

Epilogue

India, Three Years Later

"*I*s it not beautiful, Mama?" Anjali whispered, leaning out of their open carriage as it made its slow progress down a narrow, curving road. Heavy, emerald green trees and thick vines twisted above their heads, casting flickering shadows over her black hair and white muslin dress.

In the valley below them, like an illusion or dream, was the great temple of Shiva, drifting on a fog-shrouded base of tangled blue-black vegetation and moss-encrusted ancient stones. Carved figures covered every inch of the façade, dancing and bathing ladies, warriors on horseback, elephants, and Shiva's bull, Nandi.

Emily put her arm around Anjali, leaning out beside her. "Oh, yes, my dear. It is beautiful indeed."

Beautiful was not adequate. It was—otherwordly. Since their arrival in India, Emily had seen many strange, exquisite sights—things she would never have thought she could observe outside of books. None of them could compare to this, but all were marvelous. Grand dwellings of white stone, their windows shielded from the hot afternoons by elaborately carved shutters; ladies fanning themselves on long terraces as they sipped *lassi* and watched servants building shrines in the overgrown gardens. Deer and gazelles bounding free along the lanes. Bright pink and orange and red flowers, which her maidservants twined in their hair.

She had tasted food unlike any in England: papaya which burst sweet and tart on her tongue, the spices of vegetables and tender meats, leavened by sauces of cooling yogurt. She had danced in moonlit gardens to music of such mystery and a deep, moving spirit.

She made love with her husband beneath a hazy mosquito netting, on mattresses spread with silk and strewn with flower petals. Afterwards, they would lie entwined in the night, the heavy, sweet-scented breeze cool on their heated skin, listening to the far-off music from the water. She thought then of the saying she had seen carved over an ivory screen at the Red Fort in Delhi—"If there is a paradise on earth, It is this, it is this, it is this."

It was an enchanted life—one she never could have imagined. One day, not very far off, they would have to leave it and return to the reality of their lives and responsibilities in England. But she would carry all of this in her heart forever. Along with the family who had brought her such splendors and made her life complete.

She hugged Anjali close to her. How tall her daughter was growing! Soon she would be a young lady in truth.

David's arm came about Emily's waist, holding her safe as the carriage jolted over the rough trail. The rains had not yet come to turn the path to impassable mud and muck, and it was baked to a stonelike hardness. His hand rested protectively over the slight swelling of her belly that was as yet the only outward manifestation of a blessed event still several months in the future.

Emily turned to smile at him, reaching up to cradle his cheek in her palm. He wore his Indian garb today, loose white cotton trousers and tunic, and his raven hair ruf-

fled in the breeze. He grinned at her, looking as young
and free as he had the first day they met, so many years
ago, when his father brought him to tea with their new
neighbors. But the gleam in his dark eyes spoke of a
newer and very grown-up memory, of last night in their
chamber.

"I have never seen anything like it, David," she murmured. "It is wondrous indeed."

"I am glad you approve, *shona*."

"How could I not? It is a fitting home for our treasure."

The carriage rolled to a halt several feet away from
the temple's shadowed entrance, beyond a small pool
that guarded the vast, forbidding portal. Anjali scram-
bled down the steps, pulling up the white straw bonnet
that dangled down her back from its ribbons and tying it
beneath her chin. As she stared up at the temple, wide-
eyed in awe, her merry smile faded and her pretty face
took on a solemn, almost prayerful aspect.

Emily felt that very solemnity deep in her own heart
as she let David help her to the ground. This place held
such mystery, an ineffable spirit that wrapped about her
like incense smoke.

This was not the dwelling place of her own God, to be
sure. But yet something *was* here, something that moved
her, and she felt the presence of the sacred. She felt welcomed and blessed.

The closed carriage which bore David's grandmother,
Meena, and her attendants came to a halt behind their
own vehicle. Emily turned to watch the grand lady step
down, swathed in a sari and veils of deep blue silk embroidered in gold. In her jeweled hands she held the
small, elaborately etched silver box containing the Star
of India.

It was truly home at last.

Meena nodded at David, and even to Emily. When

they first arrived in Calcutta, Emily had received the distinct sense that Meena did not care greatly for her new granddaughter-in-law. But, in recent days, she had thawed a bit—especially when she was given the news that Emily was expecting a happy event.

"Lokhi mei," Meena called to Anjali. "Come, walk in with me. Take my arm."

Anjali hurried forward to slide her hand into her great-grandmother's crooked elbow, giving her support as they slipped off their shoes in front of the tall, carved doors.

"This is a momentous occasion," Meena murmured. "After this, my existence here is complete."

"But not until after you see the new baby, *Didu,*" Anjali answered urgently.

Meena gave her a gentle smile. "No. Not until then." She nodded at David, who stepped forward to knock at the doors.

Emily scarcely dared to breathe as the portals slowly, achingly slowly, swung open, as if pushed by unseen hands. She shivered in spite of the cashmere shawl draped over her shoulders. She had not felt such nervous tremblings since the day she walked down the long aisle at St. George's, Hanover Square, and took David's hand in hers, as she did now. She slipped her fingers into his warm clasp, and together they moved into the temple.

A more different space from St. George's could scarcely be imagined. The room was cavernous, as vast and cold as the stone it was carved from. The walls and ceilings were covered with even more carvings, more dancing figures and embracing couples, arching around them in a living, writhing mass. At the very end, in a high, gilded niche lit by hundreds of candles and with dozens of flowers tossed at its dancing feet and garlanded about its neck, was a statue of Shiva. The god of stillness and dance, bounty and wrath, destruction and fertility—all the contradictions of life. He was gilded and shimmering, with a diamond the size of a pigeon's egg set in his forehead and pearls looped amongst all the flowers.

In the flickering light, he almost seemed truly to dance with joy that he had the Star back in his possession at last.

Meena and Anjali walked up to the jade base of the statue and bowed deeply. Meena chanted some low, keening prayer, her voice echoing to the very ceiling and beyond to the sky.

Emily took this all in, fascinated, but she shrank back in the shadows. This was a part of her—the Star had preoccupied her thoughts for so long, had even, in a way, brought her together with David again. But her part in its history was finished. She had found the Star for David, so he could fulfill his vow to his grandmother. Now it was done. The rest of her life could begin.

"You should go with them," she whispered to her husband.

"Will you be all right?" he asked.

"Oh, yes, darling." She gave him a reassuring smile, and squeezed his arm before letting him go.

She watched as he joined his grandmother and daughter at the feet of the statue. Emily's hands tightened in a prayerful clasp while Meena lifted the lid of the silver case and drew forth the Star. Meena's chanting grew louder, and she raised the jewel high. The glow of the candles reflected the blue depths. What would happen now? Emily thought, aching with suspense. Would the walls crumble? The roof cave in?

Nothing of the sort, of course. This was not one of Georgina's Minerva Press novels. Meena's chant died away, the reverberations of it lingering in the chill air. Then—silence. A silence deeper than any Emily had ever known.

Meena placed the Star into David's hands, and it was he who returned it to the god's golden feet. There it sparkled in an answering dance.

Meena fell to her knees in prayer, but David and Anjali came back to Emily's side. David put his arms around her, holding her close.

"It is done now, my love," he told her.

"*Didu* says that now the curse is lifted. Your son will live a long, happy life and bring you much honor. And I will marry a rich prince." Her small nose wrinkled at this last pronouncement.

Emily laughed gently. "Oh, will you truly, my dear? A prince?"

Anjali shrugged carelessly. "So she says. But I know that is not true."

"How do you know that, *shona-moni*?" David asked her.

"Because I am going to become a famous artist, like Aunt Georgina, and travel the world creating great works of stunning beauty," Anjali declared matter-of-factly. "There will be no time for any silly princes." With that, she turned and made her way back down the long expanse of the great temple, disappearing into the afternoon sunlight.

"I wonder where she got such a notion," David whispered.

Emily tipped her head back to stare up at him innocently. "I am sure I have no idea. At least she has given up the idea of becoming a great circus performer."

"Indeed. We must be grateful for every blessing."

"Yes. We must." Emily lowered her forehead to his chest, feeling the strong, reassuring rhythm of his heart against her skin. Her life was full of blessings, in truth. David, Anjali, the baby. And more. "David, my dearest."

"Yes, Em?"

"Is it really over? Truly?"

She felt his finger slide beneath her chin, lifting her gaze back up to him. "My grandmother's curse—mayhap. Our love—never." And he kissed her, his lips tender and passionate, promising forever in this place of ancient destiny.

It was a promise Emily intended to see was kept.

Read on for an excerpt
from another passionate Regency
romance by Amanda McCabe,
The Golden Feather.
Available in the omnibus edition

IMPROPER LADIES

Coming in September 2010 from Signet Eclipse

It was another busy evening at the Golden Feather.

Caroline stood alone in her small office, peering through her secret peephole at the large gaming room. Every chair was filled, every champagne glass glistened, and every table was piled with coins, notes, and jewels. Laughter and the sweet scent of the many flower arrangements floated through the air to her.

Even though the Season was winding to a close, the more daring of society still flocked to the Golden Feather, just as they had every night for four years now.

She gave a small smile. This was perfect. Perfect for one of her last nights in the gaming club. It would be a grand send-off, and no one in London would ever forget the mysterious Mrs. Archer.

Letting the little peephole cover slide into place, she turned back to her office and went over to the desk. The polished mahogany surface was covered with ledgers and papers, but she ignored them and reached for a small, neatly folded letter. She had read it a dozen times since it had arrived a week ago, but it still never failed to make her smile.

Phoebe was soon to finish her studies at Mrs. Medlock's School for Young Ladies. Her excitement over her girlish plans seemed to spill from the carefully penned words. Caroline couldn't help but feel a bit excited herself. And not just for Phoebe, but for herself as well.

At long last, she was leaving the Golden Feather. The place had served its purpose well. She had a nice, tidy fortune tucked away, and stood to gain even more when she chose a buyer for the Golden Feather. She was a wealthy woman, and she and Phoebe would never have to worry about money again.

And if her soul had shriveled a little more each night as she strolled through the opulent rooms, watching fools lose their money, listening to lechers' suggestive whispers, it was worth it for that security.

Was it not?

Caroline carefully folded the letter and placed it in her locked drawer. Her only escape in these four years had been her annual holidays with Phoebe. Now they could be together all the time, be a true family again. *That* was worth anything, anything at all.

She had already arranged to rent a house for the summer, at the seaside resort of Wycombe-on-Sea, where they had sometimes gone with their parents as little girls. There she could rest at last and wash away the past years in the clean seawater. She and Phoebe could plan how best to introduce Phoebe to some kind of good society. Surely their parents' names still carried weight with someone. . . .

A knock sounded at the inner office door, interrupting these musings.

"Yes?" Caroline called.

"It's Mary, madam."

"Come in, Mary."

Mary was Caroline's maid, and had been ever since she had come to the Golden Feather. Once, in another life, she had been Caroline's nanny. She was the only other person who knew her true identity, and Caroline trusted her implicitly.

Mary bustled into the room, carrying a red wig, a black silk mask, and a small rosewood cosmetics box. "It's almost midnight, madam. They'll be expecting your grand appearance."

The tentative excitement and hope vanished before the prospect of the evening ahead. Caroline sighed. "Yes, of course."

Obviously sensing her melancholy, Mary patted her shoulder comfortingly. "It won't be long now, madam. In two weeks, maybe even less if that buyer comes through, we'll be gone from here."

"You are quite right, Mary. Not long now." Caroline rose from the desk and went around to the small, gilt-framed mirror on the wall. She took the red wig, fashioned into elaborate curls and decorated with ebony and crystal combs, and fitted it carefully over her own short, silvery-blond hair. Over it she tied the ribbons of the black silk mask that covered all her face except her mouth and lower jaw.

"Do you have the lip rouge?" she asked, making sure that no telltale blond strands showed beneath the red.

"Of course, madam." Mary brought the tiny enameled pot of rouge out from the cosmetics box and handed it to her.

Caroline used the little brush to paint her lips crimson, making them appear larger and richer than her usual pale rose bow. Then she slid glittering emerald drops into her earlobes and removed her shawl to reveal a low-cut, deep green satin gown. Long black gloves and high-heeled green satin shoes completed what she thought of as her "costume."

No one who ever encountered her as Mrs. Caroline Aldritch could possibly connect her to Mrs. Archer of the Golden Feather.

"All right, Mary," she said in a voice that seemed even deeper and lower. "I am ready to make my appearance."

Justin stood in the doorway between the dining room and the gaming room of the Golden Feather and looked about in growing boredom.

It was just like all the other gaming establishments he had frequented before he left for India. Fancier than most, perhaps, luxuriously appointed and full of fine flowers and champagne. And the people crowded around the tables were undoubtedly well dressed and well-bred, gentlemen in evening dress and ladies, some masked, in bright silks and jewels. But it was the same.

There was the same look on these people's faces, a mix of desperation and hope. The laughter had the same sharp edge. The same smell of liquor, cigar smoke, and perfume hung in the air.

What had he ever found so appealing in such places? It was appalling, especially after the brutal honesty and the shimmering skies of India. He wanted to run from it all, to breathe in fresh, clean air.

But once he had loved it all with a desperate excitement he saw now on his brother's face.

Harry sat at one of the card tables, avidly studying the hand he had just been dealt. A woman in a blue feathered mask sat beside him. She laid her kid-gloved hand on his arm and whispered something in his ear. Harry nodded and laughed, a sharp, brittle sound.

Justin noted the rather large pile of coins in front of his brother.

He frowned and would have started over to the

table, but someone coming out of the dining room bumped into him. Champagne sloshed from the man's glass onto the marble floor, just missing Justin's shoe.

Justin turned around and came face-to-face with his old friend the Honorable Freddie Reed.

It had been only four years since Justin had seen him, on the morning of that fateful duel, but Freddie looked twenty years older. His eyes were bloodshot, underscored by bags and wrinkles. His skin was a grayish pallor, and his ample belly strained at his yellow brocade waistcoat.

Obviously, Freddie had continued on the pathway to dissipation he and Justin had started on so long ago. It was startling to realize that he himself might very well look like this if he had not gone out to India when he had.

Justin quickly concealed his astonishment behind a polite smile. "Freddie!" he said. "How are you, old man?"

"Eh?" Freddie squinted at him, then cried, "Justin! Dem me if it isn't old Justin Seward. Back from India, are you? Must have been very recently—you're as brown as a nut! Quite the pukka sahib." He laughed uproariously at his own weak witticism.

"Quite," Justin answered. "I only arrived in London today. I just came here to accompany Harry."

"Ah, yes. Young Harry. He's been following in his brother's footsteps, so I hear. I often see him about." Freddie turned to the woman at his side, a petite blonde in pink satin who was boldly unmasked. She was obviously as foxed as Freddie was, swaying unsteadily on her feet. "Meet Justin, m'dear. He used to be the boldest rogue in London. Now he's an old, respectable nabob, just back from India, and an earl to boot."

The woman giggled. "Pleased to meet'cha, I'm sure."

"Run along and wait for me at the faro table, sweet," Freddie told her. "I want to talk to Justin." The woman, sped on her way by a tap on the bottom from Freddie, left in a cloud of more giggles. Then Freddie turned back to Justin. "I am glad to see you again, Justin. Town's not been the same since old Larry Aldritch died and James Burne-Jones left. Not the same at all."

"Oh? Where did James go to?"

"Didn't you know? He left the day after your duel with Holmes, sent off to America by his father. I heard he married a rich widow in Boston." Freddie shook his head mournfully. "No, it hasn't been the same at all. But the Golden Feather is jolly good fun. Don't you think?"

Justin looked back out at the crowded gaming room. Harry was still at the same table with the woman in the feathered mask speaking to him quietly. "Indeed."

"I come here at least twice a week."

"The play is that good, is it?"

"Oh, yes. Champagne's not bad, either. And then there's Mrs. Archer." Freddie gave a blissful sigh.

"The owner?"

"Yes. She's a real beauty. At least I think she must be."

Was Freddie so drunk that he couldn't even see the woman straight, then? Justin laughed. "You mean you're not sure?"

"Well, she always wears a mask. But she has a beautiful voice. And a magnificent bosom. Though she is always so secretive; she will never give any man a second look, so they say. Ah, now see, you'll be able to judge for yourself."

A door at the top of a spiral staircase opened, and

amid a sudden hush, a woman appeared on the landing there.

She was not especially tall, not above middling height, but she commanded the room just by standing still.

She wore a black silk mask that covered all her face except for her full red lips and an alabaster jawline. Her hair, a deep burgundy-red color, was piled atop her head in curls and whorls. The emeralds in her ears winked and dazzled in the light.

Mrs. Archer was very striking. And she did indeed have a magnificent bosom, its whiteness set off by the low bodice of her green satin gown.

Justin very much feared he was gaping, just as everyone else in the room was. But he couldn't seem to help himself; she was such a terribly striking sight.

"You see?" Freddie sighed. "Beautiful."

Then Mrs. Archer came down the stairs, her skirt held up daintily to reveal green heeled slippers and the tiniest amount of white silk stocking, and moved into the crowd.

Justin could see only the very top of her red head as she walked about, stopping to speak to various patrons and accept a glass of champagne from a footman.

He blinked and turned quickly away, feeling as if he were trapped in some bizarre, terribly attractive dream.

Caroline had never seen him before. She was sure of it. If she had, she would have remembered him.

He stood in the doorway between the dining room and the gaming room, surveying the crowd with a look of almost-boredom on his face. He did not look contemptuous or disdainful, only as if he wished he were anywhere else.

And he was handsome. Very handsome indeed. His hair, a sun-streaked light brown, was a little longer than was strictly fashionable and brushed back in neat waves from his face. Unlike most of the men who came to the Golden Feather, he radiated good health and vitality. His skin was dark, as if he spent a good deal of time outdoors, and his tall, lean figure obviously had no need of corsets or of padding in his coats.

Beside all the other men who flocked around the gaming room, he stood out sharply, as a beacon of things that were honest and decent. Things like a fresh morning breeze, a brisk ride down a country lane, or a good laugh.

Things Caroline hadn't enjoyed for years.

She smiled wryly, mocking herself for such fanciful thoughts. A beacon of honesty, indeed! Here she had thought herself far beyond having her head turned by a pretty face. If he was here, he could scarcely be so decent as all that. No doubt he gambled terribly, just as Lawrence had. He was just a new patron, perhaps one who had recently come from the country.

Definitely one she should meet. After all, it was her job to make certain everyone who came to the Golden Feather enjoyed themselves.

Just her job.

Caroline made her way slowly across the room toward him, stopping to talk to people, to sip champagne, to check on the dealers at the various tables. All the while, she kept her eye on the stranger, where he stood talking to Lawrence's old friend Freddie Reed.

As she came closer, she felt a most unusual sensation fluttering in her stomach, tightening her throat. Was it ... could it be nervousness? Nervousness at the thought of talking to a strange man?

Nonsense, she told herself briskly. It was only the champagne.

At last she reached them, and came to a halt to smile up at Freddie. "Good evening, Mr. Reed," she said. "So nice to see you here again."

Freddie blushed at this special attention, and stammered out, "G-good evening, M-Mrs. Archer! You are looking stunning, as always."

"Thank you very much, Mr. Reed." She glanced over at his companion, the handsome stranger, and tilted her head inquiringly.

"Oh!" said Freddie. "Mrs. Archer, I would like you to meet my friend, Lord Lyndon. He is just back from India and has never been to the Golden Feather before."

"How do you do, Mrs. Archer?" Lord Lyndon said, bowing over her outstretched hand. His fingers were warm through her thin glove, his grip steady and sure.

"Welcome to the Golden Feather, Lord Lyndon," she answered. "I do hope you are enjoying your first evening here."

"Of course," he said. "Who could help but enjoy themselves here? You have a lovely establishment, Mrs. Archer." But his eyes, a vivid sky blue in his sun-browned face, still looked bored and perfectly, blandly polite. His gaze slid ever so briefly over her shoulder before focusing on her again.

"Thank you, Lord Lyndon," she murmured, wondering what could possibly be so interesting behind her. Another woman, perhaps?

Her vanity was a bit piqued by this inattention.

Unaccountably, she wanted this man's attention; she wanted his gaze to fill with admiration when he looked at her. Usually she disliked male attention and longed to turn away from their flattery, their long, suggestive glances.

"This may be Lyndon's first visit, but his brother is a regular patron," Freddie said, interrupting her jumbled thoughts.

Caroline turned to him in relief, away from Lord Lyndon's mesmerizing blue eyes. "Oh, yes? And who might that be?"

It was Lyndon who answered, in his deep, brandy-rich voice. "Mr. Harry Seward is my brother." He gestured with his champagne glass toward a table.

Caroline looked back to where he pointed. So that was what had caught his attention. His brother, Mr. Seward, was quite familiar to her. He came to the Golden Feather several times a week, sometimes winning, more often losing. He was a bit of a mischief maker, but she had never had any serious trouble with him. Tonight he sat next to another regular patron, a woman who called herself Mrs. Scott, a bottle of champagne between them.

It was hard to believe that the feckless Mr. Seward was the brother of the serious, solemn man who stood before her.

"We do see Mr. Seward often," she said.

"So I have heard," he answered softly. Caroline had the distinct impression that he did not approve of his brother's pastimes.